Car...
British Columb...
more than thirty years, an ancient, crabby cat, and
several horses. She has three grown children, and
two grandsons.

Susan Meier is the author of over fifty books for
Mills & Boon. *The Tycoon's Secret Daughter* was a
Romance Writers of America RITA® Award finalist,
and *Nanny for the Millionaire's Twins* won the
Book Buyers' Best award and was a finalist in the
National Readers' Choice awards. She is married and
has three children. One of eleven children herself, she
loves to write about the complexity of families and
totally believes in the power of love.

THE WEDDING PLANNER'S CHRISTMAS WISH

CARA COLTER

THE BILLIONAIRE'S ISLAND REUNION

SUSAN MEIER

MILLS & BOON

First Published in Great Britain 2021
by Mills & Boon, an imprint of HarperCollins*Publishers* Ltd,
1 London Bridge Street, London, SE1 9GF

www.harpercollins.co.uk

HarperCollins*Publishers*
1st Floor, Watermarque Building,
Ringsend Road, Dublin 4, Ireland

The Wedding Planner's Christmas Wish © 2021 Harlequin Books S.A.

Special thanks and acknowledgement are given to Cara Colter
for her contribution to the A Wedding in New York miniseries.

The Billionaire's Island Reunion © 2021 Linda Susan Meier

ISBN: 978-0-263-29996-0

10/21

MIX
Paper from
responsible sources
FSC® C007454

This book is produced from independently certified FSC™ paper
to ensure responsible forest management.
For more information visit www.harpercollins.co.uk/green.

Printed and bound in Spain using 100% Renewable Electricity
at CPI Blackprint (Barcelona)

THE WEDDING PLANNER'S CHRISTMAS WISH

CARA COLTER

MILLS & BOON

To Tessa Avon.

With deepest gratitude
for the hope you have brought to so many hearts.

CHAPTER ONE

ALEXANDRA HARRIS HAD an excellent imagination, so if there was one thing she loved—but rarely got to experience—it was when things were actually *better* than she imagined them.

Parker and Parker was just that: better than she'd imagined.

Located at the edge of New York City's Central Park, the soaring Renaissance-style facade of the building made it look like a gorgeous mansion, almost but not quite castle-like.

"Just like a fairy tale," she whispered, not unaware of a feeling of homecoming. Fairy tales, professionally if not personally, were, after all, Alexandra's specialty. There was a reason she and her company, Ever After, were currently New York's most in-demand wedding planners.

She passed through a black wrought-iron gate that was bordered on both sides by a high, well-manicured hedge that was, this first day of October, just beginning to take on the bold colors of autumn. But as glorious as those colors were, Alexandra imagined how it all would look in two and a half months, when the hedge would be leafless but ten times as magical, decorated and lit with a million tiny white lights, not just for Christmas, but for the wedding of the century.

Two and a half months might seem like a long time to most people, but Alexandra was aware how fast that final lead-up time to the wedding would go.

Ivy Jenkins, heiress to the billion-dollar business Jenkins Inc., and Sebastian Davis, CEO of New York's most exciting tech start-up, were tying the knot.

And they'd asked her, Alexandra Harris, to be the wedding planner for their unforgettable Christmas-themed wedding.

Christmas, she told herself, something she was also good at professionally, if not personally. That unshakable feeling of dread...

She ordered herself, firmly, to stop it. She had a wedding that would take one hundred percent of her focus, thank goodness.

Because it had to be perfect. Having the rich and famous fight to hire you came with pressures. These people, with their wealth and influence, could make you with a word. And just as easily break you.

A career always hung on that impossible pursuit of absolute perfection. Alexandra was aware she was always one disaster—or even one tiny bridal disappointment—away from being ruined.

And so in her quest to constantly up her game—and particularly for this wedding—Alexandra had set her sights on Parker and Parker. She'd known instantly it was the only venue that would do. She'd been stunned when Gabe Evans, the head of events for the gorgeous old Jacobean-style castle, built in 1831, had told her they didn't take weddings.

How could they not take weddings when it was so perfect? Parker and Parker was made for weddings!

But no, he'd insisted that the venue in general—and the

owner of the venue in particular, Drew Parker—preferred conferences and events and had made them their specialty.

Conferences? Congregations of boring pediatricians or neuroscientists or whatever other professional group could afford the steep fees? Events? Like stuffy charity balls and mind-numbing auctions for good causes? All right, at least events might be noble. But still, they had nothing on the pure charm of a blissful wedding day!

Alexandra hadn't achieved her success as a dream weaver and fairy-tale provider by taking no for an answer.

Despite time pressures—she had to nail down the venue—she'd kept at Gabe until he'd been persuaded. Now, standing here on the grounds, she knew her persistence had been well worth it. Nothing could be more perfect than this! In an hour or so, Ivy and Sebastian were going to get here and see it for the first time, the extraordinary place that would provide that essential backdrop to build the rest of their day—and the beginning of their life together—around.

Today, she'd meet Gabe in person for the first time, which was a relief. She had the check for the deposit in her purse. Gabe had confirmed for December 14, and the days leading up to it, of course, and they had long since completed the contract using an online signing service.

Even so, Alexandra had experienced a strange sense of him ducking actually meeting her. She wasn't sure why he made her a bit uneasy. On the phone, and in emails and texts, he always seemed gracious and even enthusiastic about the wedding.

And yet, sometimes, he seemed distracted when they spoke. Scheduled emails arrived late. Phone calls were forgotten. Somehow, her dealings with Gabe had an odd feeling of subterfuge. There were even times when she spoke to him that it actually felt as if he was whispering.

But here, on the grounds, with the check in her purse, she dismissed her anxieties. They were as normal for her as they were for the bride—maybe even more so. It was Alexandra's job to worry about everything that could go wrong and fix it before it even surfaced as a problem.

But, finally, she was here, and finally, it felt real. She couldn't wait to explore the property with Gabe, inspect the facilities and kitchens. When Sebastian and Ivy arrived, they could start to narrow down the best locations within the property for the ceremony, the dinner, the dance, the photos.

Later, in the days and weeks ahead, she could collaborate with Gabe on the perfect mix of the venue's traditional Christmas decor with the white-and-silver theme of the Jenkins-Davis wedding.

She eyed the magnificent staircase curving gracefully downward in an ever-widening arc. She could picture the bride and groom right there, the bride's train sweeping down over the stairs, the huge wedding party arranged on the steps around them. There would be thick garlands of pine boughs wrapped around the stone railings, softening them, and banks of white poinsettias flanking the stairs.

Or maybe not poinsettias, as the flowers were not her choice to make, she reminded herself. She was excited that in just three days she would be meeting with Hailey Thomas for the first time. Hailey was just as noted in her specialty of floral design as Alexandra was in hers of wedding planning, and she couldn't wait to work with her.

By December 14, Alexandra, Hailey and their combined teams would have transformed Parker and Parker from what it so obviously was—a slightly exotic rented venue—into a palace worthy of a fairy-tale beginning, and those magnificent oak doors at the top of the stairs would be thrown open to the invited guests of Ivy and Sebastian.

She glanced at her watch. She was a tiny bit early, and so she veered off the wide cobblestone path into the trees that flanked it. It was like entering a forest grotto in the middle of New York. And already, she could imagine silver and white Christmas trees, in the wedding theme colors, threaded into this little wood, turning it into an absolute enchantment.

She was about to turn and find the pathway again when a sound froze her in her tracks.

It was a child's giggle.

It was impossible. The wooded copse was empty. For a moment, Alexandra wondered if her mind had fabricated the giggle, just as how, when she slept, a child sometimes danced through her dreams.

She pulled herself together. Today was just not a good day to indulge the thoughts of a child who had almost been. Invariably, that what-if led to sadness, and Alexandra reminded herself sternly she was in the business of selling happiness.

Alexandra scanned the shrubbery and saw nothing. The giggle came again, breathless, muffled. A heap of raked leaves twitched suspiciously, and then she noticed a tiny black patent-leather shoe sticking out from under it.

She was relieved the bell-like laughter had not been a figment of her imagination, but still, something registered deep within her as being distinctly wrong.

It could be that she was interrupting a game of hide-and-seek, but where were the other players? And where was the adult supervisor?

There was no one else in this shaded area that she could discern. In fact, the silence was deep, given that all of New York hummed only a stone's throw away.

There was another muffled giggle and another tremble from under the pile of leaves.

Alexandra looked at her watch again. She was cutting it close. Still, she didn't feel right about leaving the child to her own devices in the Parker and Parker gardens. Despite the fact it felt like a private estate in the middle of the British countryside, the truth of the matter was they were practically at the center of New York City!

She edged closer to the pile of leaves. She had a wealth of experience with children, because her sister and brother had provided her with a half dozen rambunctious, lovable, energetic nieces and nephews.

That was her family. It was good enough. More than enough! It didn't fill her with longing for what might have been. It didn't!

"I haven't seen a pile of leaves like this in *forever*," Alexandra announced theatrically. "So, even though I am much too old, I'm going to jump in it. Here I go! One. Two—"

Before she counted to three, a small figure erupted from under the pile, squealing.

"No, no! Don't jump! You'll squish me!"

"My goodness!" Alexandra said, pretending to be startled. She took a step back. "A fairy!"

That was, indeed, what the small girl looked like. Leaves clung to a pink angora beret and a white cable-knit sweater, and a pink plaid skirt was stuck to bright pink tights.

But Alexandra realized it did not look like a fairy's face gazing at her—more like an angel's. The child's hair sprang in luxurious black curls out from under the beret. She had thick lashes, emerald-green eyes, plump cheeks and the most adorable bow of a mouth.

Alexandra had not done this for a long time: her baby would have been... She felt a shocking ache of longing, a stage she had thought she was long past. She quickly squashed it.

Not today.

The girl looked no more than four, and there was still no adult in sight.

"I'm not a fairy!" the child declared. "And you're not *that* old. I thought you might be a witch."

"Thanks," Alexandra said dryly. "But if you're not a fairy, who are you? It seems to me only a fairy, not a small girl, would be out in the woods all by herself."

"I'm hiding from my nan," the girl said with mischievous glee. "And I'm good at it, too."

Alexandra tried not to let the alarm show in her face. "But how long have you been hiding? Your grandmother must be very worried about you."

The girl looked puzzled. "I'm not with my grandmother."

"Your nan?"

The child was silent.

"Your mother, then? Honestly, someone must be looking for you?"

The little girl blew out her lower lip and cast her gaze down at her feet. "I don't have a mother," she said sadly. "She died."

"Oh, I'm so sorry!"

The sad tone dissolved, and she lifted her chin to look at Alexandra appraisingly. "Would you like to be my mommy?"

There was a tricky question, loaded with all kinds of potential to cause both hurt and false hope.

"Well," Alexandra offered carefully, "of course, I'd love to be your mother. You look perfectly adorable. But you can't just pick up mothers in the woods on a whim."

"I don't know what a whim is, but I'd like a mother who would jump in leaves," the girl said. "My daddy says I'm not 'dorable. I'm a perfect little monster."

"I'm sure he's teasing when he says that."

"Or maybe it's true," she offered carelessly, then tilted her head and smiled a small, charming smile. "Would you love to be my mommy if I was 'dorable *and* a monster?"

She was unusually articulate for her size. Precocious. It seemed there was going to be no correct answer for that question, so Alexandra felt it might be best to ignore it and address the more urgent matter at hand. Someone was looking for this mite, and probably desperately, too.

Alexandra firmly held out her hand. "Come on, we have to find your nan."

The tiny minx actually looked like she was considering darting the other way, but then, with a sigh of surrender, she took the proffered hand.

There was that *feeling* again, as Alexandra's hand closed around the warmth and sturdiness of the little girl's smaller one. She felt almost dizzy with longing.

This was ridiculous! She spent all kinds of time with her nieces and nephews and didn't feel as if she was being freshly immersed in grief, as she did now.

The child obviously knew her way around this tiny wood very well. She led Alexandra straight out and to the path.

A man's deep voice, edged in desperation, penetrated the silence of the woods. "Genevieve!"

The child giggled.

"That's you, isn't it?" Alexandra asked.

She nodded.

"It's not nice to frighten people," Alexandra said firmly. "It's quite naughty." They stepped out of the shade of the trees and onto the cobblestones.

A man was standing just outside the double oak doors at the top of the sweeping staircase that led into Parker and Parker, his gaze anxiously scanning the grounds. Even from a distance, and even though he was obviously agitated, it was apparent he was an attractive man.

A very attractive man.

He looked to be about midthirties and was dressed with the casual and utter sophistication that those comfortable with wealth were able to pull off: a dark gray sweater over a crisp white shirt and narrow-legged dark denims over boots.

He was tall, probably an inch or two over six feet, and beautifully proportioned, with wide shoulders, a broad chest and the flat stomach of the very fit. His legs, encased in those denims, were long and powerful-looking.

"Who is that?" Alexandra said on a breath. Obviously not *nan*!

"That's my daddy."

Of course. His hair was as black as the child's, and for that matter, Alexandra's own hair. But it lacked his daughter's playful curls and was short and crisp.

The faintest hint of a shadow darkened the hollows of his cheeks, touched the slight cleft of his chin. He was extraordinarily handsome, and Alexandra wasn't sure if the pure potent effect of him was increased or decreased by a sternness in his features that made him seem quite formidable.

Though the little girl didn't seem to think there was anything formidable about the man at all. She let go of Alexandra's hand and skipped away. She turned back to stick out her tongue and then dismissed her and ran toward her father.

"Daddy! Daddy!" she cried. "I was lost."

Instant relief relaxed his features. He came down the stairs with the agility and speed of an athlete. He met the girl as she came up the pathway and swept her into his arms with ease. The look of gratitude on his handsome face was intense, and for a moment he didn't look quite so formidable.

"That lady found me," Genevieve said, pointing at Alexandra.

Alexandra felt grateful, given that stuck-out tongue moments ago, that the little minx had not proclaimed that she was a kidnapping victim, and Alexandra her abductor!

CHAPTER TWO

THEY CAME TOWARD her then, the child riding in the man's strong arms, her own arms wrapped around the gorgeous column of his throat.

Because of her growing success—a recent tabloid had called her Wedding Planner to the Stars—Alexandra increasingly found herself meeting the rich and the famous. She met celebrities, dignitaries, sports stars, entrepreneurs. A prince—Crown Prince Giovanni—was even going to be the best man for the Jenkins-Davis wedding.

She prided herself on the fact she was never intimidated by anyone.

And yet, as this man's shadow fell on her, and his green eyes—so like his daughter's, only minus the innocence—pinned her, she suddenly felt ridiculously tongue-tied, like a high school girl meeting her crush.

There was that renegade *longing* again.

But he was the kind of man who would create those kind of longings—for someone to hold on to, for someone to talk to deep into the night—in every female he encountered. He was one hundred percent confident in his masculinity, utterly breathtaking and stunningly gorgeous! And the ease with which he carried the small girl intensified the nearly magnetic pull of him.

But even as she drank in the tangy scent of him, she was aware of a kind of power radiating off him—a presence.

And there was nothing warm and fuzzy about it, despite the little girl who was so comfortable in his arms.

In fact, the man seemed very intimidating. Cool. Stand-offish. Alexandra's original impression of sternness—of something faintly formidable about him—was underscored by his nearness.

Alexandra glanced at her watch. She was running late now. She was aware of feeling relieved that she had an appointment to get to. She didn't like these longings. She didn't like the fact that things she thought she had long laid to rest—or at least outrun—could be coaxed to the surface in a breath.

She didn't like feeling off balance in her well-ordered world.

"Hello," he said, his voice a gravelly scrape of pure sensuality that felt as if it was touching the back of Alexandra's neck. He freed a hand and extended it. "I'm Drew Parker."

"Of…of Parker and Parker?" she stammered. She *never* acted like a starstruck teenager. Not even when she was a teenager! So why was she suddenly reviewing her outfit—a perfectly professional black blazer, a sweater and slim black Klein trousers—critically? Why was she wishing for higher heels instead of ballet flats? Why was she wishing her hair was down, instead of scraped back into a respectable bun? She had to pull herself together.

Some shadow crossed briefly through the green of his eyes. "Yes," he said, jostling his daughter in his arms. "Here we are. Parker and Parker."

A different partnership was in that shadow that crossed his eyes, and Alexandra remembered the little girl's words.

I don't have a mother. She died.

"It's a pleasure to meet you, Mr. Parker."

"Drew, please."

Alexandra took his extended hand and it closed around hers, his grip hinting at tempered strength, and some terrifying awareness of him shivered through her whole being. She slid her hand back out of his, resisting an urge to look at it to see if it was smoking.

She had been burned by desire before and it had left her life in ashes. To feel it again now was a warning, not an invitation.

"What a beautiful place you own," she said in a rush so that he wouldn't know—or ever guess—what an impact his hand on hers had had on her.

"Ah," he said, turning and casting a rueful glance over the shoulder of the child at the building behind him. "It's much like owning a cat. You don't, really. It owns you. And it will tolerate you, barely, if the pampering is up to its rather exacting criteria."

It was such a delightful way of describing the old beauty behind him. It hinted that he wasn't just attractive, he was intelligent, which made him all the more intriguing. Still, his tone and his eyes remained cool and reminded Alexandra she had a busy, fulfilling life of her own.

That kind of intrigue she could live without, thank you very much.

"I'm Alexandra Harris," she said. Not a flicker of recognition crossed those handsome features. Of course, he owned the place. He probably didn't involve himself in the day-to-day operations of it.

"She said she would *love* to be my mommy," Genevieve announced.

A dark slash of an eyebrow—faintly accusing—was raised at Alexandra. She could feel her cheeks burning crimson.

"That's a bit out of context," she said.

"A contest!" Genevieve said breathlessly. "For a mommy!"

"You don't hold contests for a mommy," Drew said, a trifle wearily. He shot Alexandra a glance that somehow made the quest for mommy her fault.

"But it's a good idea!" Genevieve insisted, taking her father's cheeks between her two hands, and forcing his face toward her, to ensure his full attention. "She needs to jump in leaves. Bake cookies. Tell bedtime stories."

It was exactly the kind of mommy Alexandra had once thought she would be.

"I want an *alive* mommy."

And she had wanted an *alive* baby. Life could be so cruel.

The fact that he was fully aware of that vagaries of life appeared in the expression that crossed those handsome features. It made Alexandra's heart, already in a precarious position, feel as if it could break in two.

He was obviously a man who was successful and in control. A man who would give this small sprite anything she asked for.

Naturally, she had found the one thing that some tragedy had prevented him from giving her.

And if Alexandra was reading his expression correctly, it was the one thing Drew Parker had his heart set against giving his little girl.

An *alive* mommy.

He looked like a man who gave his heart once.

And forever.

Knowing that with a strange certainty filled Alexandra with an acute sense of failure. She had taken those forever vows once. And believed them with all her heart.

And yet, here she was, divorced.

She looked into his stern, closed features and wondered

what he would think of that. And she also wondered what it would be like to be loved by someone so fierce in their commitment to love, to be the one who his face softened for…

Better, Alexandra warned herself, to keep this meeting with Drew Parker all business, as hard as that might be with Genevieve in his arms eyeing her with the avid interest of a child who desperately wanted to interview candidates for a mommy.

"Oh!" Alexandra said, looking at her watch. "I'm afraid I have an appointment. With Gabe Evans. Maybe you would be kind enough to point me in the direction of his office?"

"I'm sorry, Gabe isn't here today."

All those anxieties rushed up her spine. If catastrophe had a smell, Alexandra was pretty sure it was in the air right now.

"Not…not here?" she stammered.

"His mother has taken a turn for the worse. He's had to take a leave of absence."

Gabe hadn't even thought to call her? Still, if his mother had "taken a turn for the worse," that inferred some kind of long illness. It explained so much, really. The feeling she'd had that he was distracted. His near-whispered conversations. Perhaps he'd been working from home? Working around his sick mother?

"Oh, I'm so sorry to hear that." She forced herself to remain calm. She congratulated herself on the even, professional tone of her voice. "Still, there are some things it is imperative I deal with today. Who will be coordinating events in Gabe's absence?"

A shriek interrupted her, and a young woman dressed in a yellow T-shirt, yoga pants and sneakers came around the side of the building, saw them and raced toward them.

"Mr. Parker, you found her. Genevieve, there you are! I nearly had a stroke."

So, this was the *nan* then. A nanny, not a grandmother. She looked like a wholesome young woman, nearly out of her mind with worry.

Which, at the moment, Alexandra could seriously relate to.

"I'm sorry, Mr. Parker," the young nanny said in a rush. "I really am. As I said to you when I reported her missing, I just ducked into the restroom for one second. Honestly. One. Second."

"She was on the phone with her boyfriend," Genevieve announced with grave pleasure.

Drew Parker's face darkened. Alexandra had the cowardly thought she was glad his wrath would not be directed at her.

"Miss Carmichael," he said, his voice icy, "you came highly recommended by the best nanny service in New York."

The young woman's bottom lip began to tremble.

"And you lost your charge? Because you were on your phone?"

"I wasn't *only* on my phone. I was in the restroom. I mean, I can't very well take her in there with me. But it won't happen again, Mr. Parker, I promise."

The young nanny looked so crestfallen, and the child looked just a little too pleased with herself.

Stay out of it, Alexandra warned herself. But, naturally, she couldn't.

"In fairness to Miss Carmichael, Genevieve was not lost. I found her *hiding* from her nan in the trees over there. Under a pile of leaves."

While Miss Carmichael gave her a glance loaded with gratitude, Genevieve gave Alexandra a look that clearly crossed her off the mommy candidate list.

"Did you?" Drew regarded Alexandra with cool thoughtfulness and then asked his daughter gravely, "Did you run away from Miss Carmichael while she was in the restroom?"

"I didn't mean to be bad," Genevieve said.

"No," her father responded, with a sigh that was equal parts affection and exasperation, "it seems to come quite naturally to you."

"Yes, it does," she agreed contritely. She laid her head on her father's shoulder and stuck her thumb in her mouth, suddenly—and deliberately, Alexandra suspected—more baby than articulate little girl.

"How about if you go have some ice cream with Miss Carmichael?" Drew said gently.

Genevieve popped back to life and scrambled out of her father's arms. "I'd like the pink-striped kind," she announced.

Stay out of it, Alexandra warned herself again. But naturally, she could not. "I don't think ice cream is a very appropriate consequence for running away from her nanny."

Genevieve lowered a brow at her. Drew looked at her, stunned. Obviously a man in his position was not used to receiving unsolicited advice from strangers, especially when there was faint reprimand in it.

"And what is your expertise on children, then?" he asked. "You have your own?"

"No," she admitted. "I'm not married."

Now, why had she inserted *that* particular detail?

"I'm divorced," she added, quickly, as if that would put up a much-needed barrier between her and a man who looked as if he would never consider breaking a vow, under any circumstances.

Drew cocked his head at her, but he looked so unimpressed it made her rush on, practically babbling.

"My brother has four kids and my sister has two. I'm

sorry, I realize it doesn't really put me in a position to give advice."

"You're right. It probably doesn't," he said coolly. "Still, tell me, if you must, how your brother or sister might handle a situation like this one."

Alexandra thought this really would be a good time to apologize for offering an opinion on something that was none of her business. On the other hand, even though he was the man least likely to inspire pity, he was going to have a hard go of it if he kept rewarding the little girl for being bad.

Maybe she could offer just a teensy bit of advice before she backed off from it.

"First of all," Alexandra said tentatively, "both my brother and sister would have an expectation that they would be able to make a phone call or use the restroom without having to look for runaway children afterward."

"I see. And if there was an incident of a runaway child?"

"Well, Shaun would not be above raising his voice."

Drew Parker winced at that.

"Because obviously you have to make it quite clear running away, at any time, is not okay, and that running away in the center of New York City is particularly unacceptable. My sister would probably remove a favorite cartoon from the agenda. For a week."

Drew still looked annoyed to be offered advice by a stranger, and he looked unimpressed with the strategies, too. And yet, after looking at Alexandra hard for a moment, he turned and regarded his daughter thoughtfully. "No *Molly Mood Ring*. For a week. Or forever, if you run away from Miss Carmichael again."

Miss Carmichael looked relieved to hear a future mentioned that had her in it. Genevieve was obviously way too accustomed to running the show with charm and guile. Her brows lowered mutinously. And yet, was she ever so faintly relieved to be having some of the responsibility for running that show removed from her? Because, despite that mutinous look, she did not throw herself on the ground and start screaming, as Alexandra's niece Macy, who was quite close to Genevieve's age, might have done.

She tossed her head. And glared at Alexandra. "I don't want you for my mommy anymore."

"I'm very sorry to hear that," Alexandra returned solemnly.

Genevieve took her nanny's hand and marched away, nose in the air.

"Now, Miss Harris—or is it Mrs.? I'm sorry, the etiquette of address after a divorce sometimes evades me."

Was he just aloof naturally, or was he judging her about the divorce?

"I've returned to my maiden name." There was an awful temptation to explain her whole history to him. A hasty college marriage because of an unexpected pregnancy, a union that could not survive tragedy. But she forced herself away from that insane need to excuse her divorce to someone she didn't even know and made herself smile carelessly. "So, yes, Miss, but Alexandra is fine."

"You're not, per chance, in the market for a nanny position?"

She wasn't sure if this was progress: having gone from annoying him to being offered a position.

"No," she said, and glanced down at herself wryly. "When I put this on this morning, I was thinking high-powered executive, not nanny, so I'll be sure and mark that down as a miss. Just to clarify, I'm definitely not someone who'd throw over their whole life for a nanny position, as honorable as I think that work is."

"Just for the record, I don't usually proposition strangers." Her cheeks reddened.

So did his, ever so slightly. "That came out wrong. It wasn't meant as an insult to your professionalism, but you just do seem, um, wholesome…and good with children."

Wholesome? She was going home and dumping this whole outfit right in the trash. Not that there was anything wrong with wholesome, but around a man like this?

He cocked his head at her. "There's something about you that does suggest jumping in leaves, baking cookies, telling bedtime stories. Genevieve spotted it right away."

What kind of betrayal of self was it that Alexandra would have much preferred he find her sexy rather than wholesome?

And what kind of betrayal of self was it that what he described felt just the tiniest bit attractive? To throw away all the stress and pressure in exchange for days jumping in leaves, baking cookies, reading stories?

The life she had once thought she would have…that she had willingly set aside her university education and career plans for.

Though, if she was completely honest with herself, wasn't part of the attraction of the unexpected job offer him? Drew Parker was so obviously in over his head on the single dad thing. It would be rewarding—not to mention fun—to help him navigate that path.

Why was she leaving *complicated* out of that assessment?

"I love my current career very much," she said, the firmness in her tone directed more at herself than at him. "And I think Miss Carmichael looks more than capable."

His look of genuine disappointment could cause the strongest woman to feel weak.

"Ah, well," Drew said, running a hand through the crisp darkness of his hair, and becoming all business once again, "please tell how we, at Parker and Parker, can assist you today. I'm sorry, Gabe didn't tell me you were coming. As I mentioned, his mother is very sick and has been for some time. He's been quite distracted of late."

She'd noticed.

"I'm here about the wedding," Alexandra said.

His mouth dropped open, then quickly snapped shut, tightening marginally, and his eyes narrowed. Any bond that they had just established dealing with his precocious daughter evaporated.

"The wedding?" he said. Was there something faintly dangerous in his tone, and in the spark in his eyes?

"We've confirmed a booking for the entire week leading up to December 14."

His eyes flew to her left hand, looking for an engagement ring. He thought she was getting married!

"I'm a wedding planner," she said hastily. Why did she care what he thought? She wanted this to be completely professional, that's why! "Ever After?"

He looked at her darkly, with absolutely no recognition.

"My client is Ivy Jenkins," she said, a bit desperately, not above throwing some names around. "She's marrying Sebastian Davis."

"I'm afraid there's been some mistake, Miss Harris."

She didn't miss the fact he had returned to formalities.

"We don't do weddings here."

Apparently he was completely unimpressed with her name dropping.

"Not ever. And we are not going to start now."

CHAPTER THREE

DREW WATCHED ALEXANDRA'S mouth fall open. Her eyes—dark, soft, lovely as a doe's—widened in shocked surprise.

To be honest, he was shocked himself. A wedding planner? The unsolicited parenting advice—he hoped she couldn't tell how welcome it had been—coupled with the outfit and the prim hair had made him reach the apparently erroneous conclusion she might be a suitable nanny. But if not that, the no-frills ensemble suggested a lawyer or an accountant.

A wedding planner? Somehow he would have pictured someone a little more flamboyant. Soft pastels and maybe some ruffles.

But, a voice whispered to him, Emily had not been those things, and her vision for Parker and Parker had been all about romance.

Drew gave himself a mental shake. Emily's vision, and how painful it was that it had never reached fruition for her, was the reason he would never hold a wedding here. He had to stand firm on that...despite Alexandra Harris's substantial appeal.

"But...but the invitations are printed," she stammered.

She really was a beautiful young woman, tall and willowy, delicate of feature. That mouth that had fallen open—but was now pressed firmly closed again—was exquisite, wide, plump, sensual. Her hair—thick, black, luxurious—was pinned up in that very prim bun that had led him down the nanny-for-hire road. For some reason, his fingers practically itched to let loose those pins.

Which made Drew feel as shocked as she looked.

It had been a long time since he had noticed... He shook it off. Losing Genevieve, and then finding her, had rattled him. He was well aware he could not withstand another loss. The beating of his heart was just beginning to return to normal. Those moments before she had been found had been a torment of what-ifs.

This woman had found his daughter. And he was deeply grateful, though not grateful enough to have a wedding hosted here. There had been some misunderstanding, obviously. He would figure out what it was and send her on her way.

The quicker the better, because there was a contradiction about Alexandra Harris that was intriguing. She had announced she was divorced with a certain bravery, as if she was revealing her worst failure to him.

Why? Traditional lives were no longer the norm. Many people were divorced, and for many reasons. It was hardly a failure. But if she felt it was, why had she chosen planning people's happily-ever-afters as her profession? Did she want to believe, despite her own disappointment? Or because of it?

Drew recognized he had been lucky to find a love that had felt as if it would last, but even so, his and Emily's relationship had hardly been traditional. They had decided they would get married after Genevieve had been born.

He regretted that now. That Em had died a month before the wedding she had longed for. Here.

It hardened his resolve, even as he tried to soften the blow.

"The invitations are printed but not mailed?" he asked. "That should make a change of venue relatively simple."

It darted across her face that a lie might be helpful here, and he had to admit he admired her for not giving in to that.

"Not sent," she said, "but reprinting isn't really an option. They were designed by Kimura."

He tilted his head at her to show the name meant nothing to him.

"She's a famous Japanese artist. Each invitation has a snowflake on it and is ever so slightly personalized. They were extraordinarily expensive, and they are bound to become collector's items."

"Items that are a mistake quite often end up even more valuable to collectors," he said.

Her face got a tight look on it. "You don't seem to understand. The wedding *has* to be here."

"*You* don't seem to understand. There will never be a wedding here."

"But why?" Alexandra asked, her eyes leaving his and looking at the building behind him with unveiled appreciation. "It's so perfect. It's as if it was made for weddings."

It had been made for weddings, actually. And one wedding in particular. Emily's excitement at the realization of their dream came back to him.

"It's highly personal," he said. "I won't get into it."

Her eyes came back to him. Something in them flashed. Strangely, it made him want to smile. She seemed as if she would be a worthy sparring partner. On the other hand, if they crossed swords, sparks were going to fly.

"I have a contract," she said. Her voice was even and firm, completely professional, and yet there was the slightest bit of panic being betrayed by the tremble of those lips.

"A contract?" he said.

What on earth had Gabe been up to?

"Yes, for the whole week preceding the December 14 wedding date."

"A week?"

"It would be impossible to put together everything for a wedding like this one in one day."

A wedding like this one.

It spoke volumes. It spoke of that one unforgettable day, a dream-come-true kind of day. He wanted to be cynical: a no-expense-spared kind of day.

But instead, a memory that he had locked away for a long time thrust its way forward.

He could see Emily feverishly planning, a notebook in front of her, her tongue caught between her teeth, her hair tucked behind her ear. As she had glanced up at him, she'd been alive with light and laughter, spinning her dreams into reality.

What had triggered that memory? Ah. Hadn't she said those very same words? Teasing him when he'd talked about her time commitment to *the* day?

It would be impossible to put together a wedding like this one in a day.

Drew couldn't do this. He couldn't allow someone else to realize Emily's dream. It felt like it would be the worst kind of betrayal.

"I don't have the contract with me," Alexandra said firmly, "but, of course, I can produce it. It is legally binding, but that's hardly the point. At this late date, I wouldn't be able to find another suitable venue for such a big event."

The week preceding December 14. The very time he and Genevieve were supposed to leave for the many amusements of California, his plan for a perfect Christmas this year, since he felt he had failed his daughter so miserably last year. What did he know about giving a four-year-old a happy Christmas?

He squinted at Alexandra. He'd bet, with her passel of unruly nieces and nephews, she would know. For some reason, it made him resent her.

"I have the deposit check right here in my purse."

"Ah," Drew said, "you haven't paid the deposit yet."

Her face went very white, and he was annoyed to find he felt for her. She had rescued Genevieve, after all, he told himself.

"There's been a mistake, obviously," he said reasonably. "I'll have to speak to Gabe about what happened. I can reimburse you, personally, for having to get the invitations reprinted with a new address on them."

"You don't seem to understand," she said, her voice low and husky in its fury. "It's too late for that. Ivy has her heart set on this venue."

With Ivy Jenkins's kind of money, she could have anything she set her heart on. It would never be too late. Still, he wanted to placate the wedding planner.

"Don't worry. I've got many, many connections," he assured her. "We'll be able to find you another venue."

He was not sure he wanted *we* to be any part of his dealings with her. No, Gabe had somehow gotten them into this, and Gabe could get them out. But could he? His mother had been so sick for so long. Now it looked as if the end was near. Expecting him to look after this—or even explain it—seemed petty.

"There is no other venue quite like this one," she said, "and certainly not on such short notice."

He was right about sparks flying if they crossed swords. There was a light in her eyes that was very passionate.

He did not want to think about Miss Alexandra Har-

ris and passion. At all. Again, his eyes went to her hair.
Again, he could picture pins flying.

"It's not going to work," he said. "I'm sorry."

"I have a contract," she reminded him again.

"But you haven't paid a deposit," he reminded her again.

She sighed, obviously annoyed with going in this circle.

"It's a point of honor, Mr. Parker—" Somehow, that
arrow hit. Being honorable was part of who he was, a value
he wanted to instill in his daughter. "Not legal wrangling,"
she continued firmly. "Your representative signed a contract with me. I trusted that. I counted on that. Now my
reputation is on the line."

Her vulnerability weakened him further. He wasn't
going to be here, anyway. He'd be thousands of miles
away. Did it really make any difference? That's probably
what Gabe had thought. Why make such a big deal of this
at her expense?

"They're coming here," she said. "Ivy and Sebastian."

"Today?"

She nodded.

"Call them and cancel. Until we work this out." He recognized he was already slipping a bit—that this was no
longer the out-and-out no of a few minutes ago.

"It's too late," she whispered. She looked over his shoulder and closed her eyes, tight.

"They're early."

He turned to see whom she was looking at. Of course,
he knew who Ivy Jenkins was. The heiress to CEO Wil-
liam Jenkins's billion-dollar business was walking toward
them. Ivy did not look like the powerhouse she was. At only
a little over five feet, her tininess, coupled with her black
hair being cut so short, gave her the look of a woodland
pixie. Drew had met her socially on a number of occasions.

But he hadn't put two and two together when Alexandra had mentioned Sebastian Davis. He recognized the younger brother of one of his own close acquaintances, Mark Davis.

Sebastian let go of Ivy's hand and came toward him, hand extended.

"Drew, so good to see you."

Drew slid a look to Alexandra. Hope was now fighting with the desperation in her lovely features. She hoped, because he knew Sebastian, he would change his mind.

"I can't thank you enough for allowing Ivy and me to have our wedding here," Sebastian said softly. "I know it must be painful for you. Mark didn't think you'd ever have a wedding here."

Mark—one of the many friends he had lost touch with—had been so right. Out of the corner of his eye, Drew saw Alexandra watching him, her hope for herself being overshadowed by curiosity. And something even more dangerous. Compassion.

Ivy came forward, took both his hands, bussed his cheeks and looked deeply at him. Any question about her prowess in the business world would be laid to rest by the intensity in her eyes.

"Sebastian told me how you and Emily had planned Parker and Parker together and how you thought yours would be the first wedding here. Clearly, I'm beyond honored that you would allow it to be us."

Despite their gratitude, Drew prepared to tell them it had been a mistake and there were going to be no weddings here after all. He hadn't woken up this morning expecting to be confronted with his deepest pain.

But, out of the corner of his eye, he could still see Alexandra watching him. Her new understanding was making her eyes even softer.

He did not want any more sympathy in his life in general, and he particularly did not want the sympathy of such a beautiful woman. Really, the look in her eyes made it more imperative to shut this thing down before it gained speed, like a runaway train.

But instead, he found her sympathy for him, despite his insensitivity to her predicament, touched some place in him that had not been touched for a long time.

Her career probably hung in the balance right now.

A mistake had been made that clearly was not her fault. And even though it was not her fault, the embarrassment it would cause her and the damage to her reputation and her business could be catastrophic.

Something whispered in him, *What would Em want me to do?*

Emily would expect him to be a man of honor.

That whispered inner voice also reminded him that he was a father now, raising a child that he hoped would be good and decent and kind. How could he have those kinds of expectations of Genevieve if he could not overcome his pain to be those things himself?

He pulled in a deep breath.

"Welcome to Parker and Parker," he heard himself say. "Let's have a look around, shall we?"

He dared to look at Alexandra. The light brightening her face felt like just about the most dangerous thing he had ever seen.

CHAPTER FOUR

ALEXANDRA WASN'T AWARE she had stopped breathing until she started again.

It would appear the wedding was on!

And yet her exhilaration at the bullet dodged was tempered by the pain she had seen in Drew Parker's face when Sebastian had revealed the real reason he was reluctant to have weddings here.

She saw the great effort it had caused him to overcome that pain. *For her.* Now he was leading the way into Parker and Parker, guiding a tour of the premises himself.

The building was beyond beautiful. The foyer was huge, with two staircases at the back of it on either side, curving up to the second floor. If she had thought the outside staircase lent itself to photos, this one was even more magnificent.

Ivy, one of the richest women in the world, who had seen everything there was to see, had tears sparkling in her eyes. This was one of the things Alexandra admired most about Ivy. Despite her wealth and all the perks of her upbringing, she was genuine and likable. Ivy consistently used her position of power and wealth to give others—especially small businesses and charities—a helping hand. She probably even would have handled the change of venue with grace.

But given the look on her face, Alexandra was so happy that she didn't have to.

"I couldn't even imagine something this beautiful," Ivy breathed. "I'd love a Christmas tree right here. A huge one. In our colors. Silver and white. What do you think, Sebastian?"

Sebastian obviously thought the sun rose and set by his bride. "I think that would be brilliant," he said.

This was one of the hardest things about coordinating a wedding for Alexandra. When the couples were a perfect match—which Ivy and Sebastian obviously were—something shimmered in the air between them that filled her with a longing that nearly took her breath away.

That longing was uncomfortably intensified today by Drew Parker standing so close to her.

But when she looked at him, his mouth was twisted into a cynical line. He raised an eyebrow at her, letting her know in a glance that he didn't like either the idea of the tree or the colors. But again, he saved her from embarrassment by not saying anything.

Alexandra forced herself into professional mode and slipped her notepad out of her purse.

"I'll take notes as we go. We're meeting in a few days with Hailey Thomas, so we can coordinate the floral design with other decor considerations then. Mr. Parker, you are welcome to join us, of course, as we'll be drawing up the initial plans and you might want some input. Our meeting is on October 4."

"At Hailey's workshop," Ivy said. "I can't wait to see it. She's so amazing!"

Mr. Parker looked like he would rather have toothpicks driven under his fingernails than join them for the floral consult.

Still, he was the model of a gracious host as they toured

the facility together—the sumptuous banquet hall behind the staircase, the huge meeting room that could be converted to a chapel, the lovely suite above it that would be the ideal place for the wedding party to get ready and could provide a sanctuary to retreat to if the day's festivities proved tiring.

"My office," Drew said, waving his hand at a door that was marked with a gold plaque that read Private. "And my daughter's and my living quarters."

She hadn't realized he lived here. She thought it would be an absolutely fabulous place to live. Alexandra was a little perplexed by how much she would have liked a peek behind that Private sign. Only because, she told herself sternly, seeing how and where he lived would give her more understanding of Drew Parker.

And what do you need that for? an inner voice reprimanded her.

She forced herself to focus on the tour. The entire building was the most incredible blend of elegance, opulence and glamour. Despite herself, she wondered if his living quarters would reflect the same style.

In every room, Ivy was full of suggestions to go with the Christmas-themed wedding: she even wondered if they could make it snow in the ballroom!

Alexandra avoided Drew's gaze at that suggestion.

Though Ivy and Sebastian really didn't need to inspect the behind-the-scenes areas, like the huge commercial kitchen, they insisted. Ivy was bringing in her own team of chefs, so that was one less thing for Alexandra to worry about.

Ivy was hugging herself with excitement as they completed the tour at the front door, where it had started. "What would you think about a Christmas-themed merry-go-round on that lawn over there?"

"I'll make note," Alexandra said dutifully, "for our meeting with Hailey." She glanced at Drew. He didn't look very happy.

Finally, Drew and Alexandra said goodbye to the ecstatic couple.

"We'll see you in a few days," Ivy called. "I can't wait to meet Hailey."

"I'm going to have to beg off that meeting," Sebastian told his fiancée, throwing an arm around her shoulder and squeezing her with affectionate regret. "Gio's going to be here."

He sounded genuinely sorry that he was going to miss the flower planning. What a gem he was, Alexandra thought.

Ivy shook Drew's hand once more. "Drew, it was so nice to meet you. I hope to use your venue for many events from here on in. My bridesmaid, and good friend Autumn Jones is involved with a charity called Raise Your Voice. Have you heard of it?"

"I'm afraid not."

"Well, you will. I can see them holding extraordinary events here."

Alexandra turned to Drew once the couple had gone. "See?" she said. "Good things are coming from this already."

He was silent.

"I just love that even today, planning for her wedding, Ivy is still thinking about others."

Again, he was silent.

"Thank you for agreeing to hold the wedding here," Alexandra said quietly. "You saved me, really."

He lifted a shoulder.

"Parker and Parker is incredible," she said, hoping to erase the dark look from his face. "It's far more than I hoped for. I feel as if no detail has been overlooked. It is, of course, the perfect wedding venue."

He looked pained, so she didn't add she felt it was totally wasted on conventions and other totally nonromantic events.

"I'm so sorry for your loss," she said softly. "I didn't know."

She suspected he was a man who was rarely uncomfortable, but he looked uncomfortable now, as he shoved his hands into his pockets and rocked back on his heels.

"I understand perfectly why you didn't want to ever have a wedding here," Alexandra said. "I'm not sure why Gabe didn't just explain it to me when I was so persistent."

Drew's mouth—which was quite lovely—tilted up cynically at the corner. "You? Persistent? I can hardly picture it."

He was being sarcastic, but in light of the fact the wedding was bringing back the pain of his loss, perhaps that was understandable.

"Well, if he had told me," she insisted, "I might have managed to overcome that character defect."

"I doubt it," he said.

He hardly knew her. But since he was insisting on seeing her in such a bad light, now might be the time to come clean on everything.

"I do have a bit of a confession to make," Alexandra said. "It wasn't strictly persistence. There was a small bribe involved."

"A bribe?" he asked, shocked. "Why am I getting this feeling I don't know Gabe at all?"

"Oh! It wasn't a money bribe. It was a funny little thing. After I called the first time, he looked up my company. It's on our website that Ever After had done the wedding for Priscilla Morrison."

He cocked his head at her.

"She's Webber Morrison's daughter."

"The jazz musician?"

"Yes. I promised Gabe an autographed picture."

"That was the bribe?"

She nodded.

"That's strange. It's an odd thing to risk your boss's wrath over, and he knew I wouldn't be happy about this. Plus, in all the years we've worked together, I've never once heard him listen to jazz. If you asked me, I would have said he was a '70s rock kind of guy. I'm beginning to feel like I don't know him at all."

"Anyway, if he had told me your history, I might have backed off."

He didn't look at all convinced. "*Might* being the operative word? Besides, Gabe—or at least the Gabe I thought I knew—would never discuss my personal life with anyone. He knows I'm a very private man."

"Which makes me appreciate what you've just done even more."

"Don't make the mistake of painting me as a knight in shining armor," Drew warned her sternly.

And yet, wasn't that exactly what he'd been when Ivy and Sebastian had arrived? Hadn't he put his own personal feelings aside to ride to her rescue?

But then, as if to prove all that had been a lapse he already regretted, he said, "There isn't going to be any merry-go-round. And no snow in the ballroom. It's all just a little too fluffy. Not to mention it would likely require structural changes to the room."

"Oh, but—"

"I'm not enthusiastic about a forty-foot silver-and-white tree in the front entrance, either. Doesn't that seem over-the-top to you? Grandiose?"

There was a temptation to argue the point, but maybe, given the concession he had already made to allow the wedding, she would save that for a different day.

"Everything is subject to change at this point," she told him soothingly. And really, right up until the wedding day, not that she needed to share that detail with him.

He was not soothed. His tone was very stern. "You're walking a fine line here between a tasteful wedding and a carnival. There aren't going to be any carnivals at Parker and Parker."

Any thoughts she might have had about Drew Parker being her knight evaporated.

"Did someone say a carnival?" Genevieve squealed, coming out the front door of the building. "I love a carnival!"

Thankfully, Miss Carmichael was close on her heels this time.

"It looks like you have your hands full," Alexandra said, still stinging from his insult that she might create a carnival, "so I'll be on my way."

"Are we going to a carnival?" Genevieve demanded. Drew scooped her up with ease.

"No, no carnivals," he said, but he raised a skeptical eyebrow at Alexandra.

"It's my job to make sure everything is extraordinarily tasteful," she said tightly. "Hailey Thomas, the floral designer, is, by my estimation, one of the best in the world."

He looked unconvinced. "Perhaps you could drop by after your meeting with Ivy and the floral designer and we can go over your plan?"

Alexandra wasn't sure if she was pleased or distressed by that. She was going to have to make it clear she, not he, was in charge of this wedding. On the other hand, they were going to have to consult about many of the wedding details, and probably often.

Still, she took out her phone and looked at her calendar. "Would three o'clock work? On the fourth?"

"It would," he said without consulting his own calendar.

"Is that when the carnival is?" Genevieve demanded.

"No," he said. "But it seems to me you have a birthday party that day, don't you?"

Despite his prickliness, Alexandra couldn't help but smile that his parenting skills ran so far as practicing the art of distraction. Even though he was so cranky, she decided to help him out a bit.

"My niece Macy is having her birthday party that day, too. She's going to turn five."

"Does she have a party dress?"

"She's not really a dress kind of girl."

"Oh." Genevieve sighed. "Mine is like a rainbow. I want to show it to you. Daddy, can I show her right now?"

As much as Alexandra was dying to see the inside his private enclave, she decided to show Drew some mercy since he was obviously as uncomfortable with inviting her in as she was eager to be invited.

"I can't wait to see your dress," Alexandra said, "but not today. I'll be here the day of the party, and if you're here, you can show it to me before you leave."

Genevieve beamed at her, carnivals forgotten.

Instead of looking appreciative of her help in the distraction department, Drew was looking at her with mild annoyance, as if she was ingratiating herself into his family unwanted.

Still, she couldn't be ungracious. Drew Parker had done her an enormous favor. His heart wasn't as black as his expression was right now. She was sure of that!

"Thank you again. You saved my life today. I owe you one."

Alexandra put out her hand, and he shifted the child to his other arm and took it.

Something pure, electrical and sensual leaped between

them. Did their touch linger just a little too long? Once again, Alexandra had to stop herself from inspecting her hand to see if smoke was coming off it.

A shiver went up and down her spine. Was he looking at her lips?

Of course he wasn't! Still, feeling wildly awkward, she scrabbled through her purse, found the check and handed it to him hastily.

"Until next time," she said, way too brightly. "Should we meet here on the steps?"

"I think there's a workshop here that day. My office might be best."

The office. The one that was marked private. How silly that she felt eager to see it, as if it would reveal clues about him that his expression did not.

Alexandra, thankfully, had three days to get her composure back. Still, she spent way too much time deciding what to wear. It had to be appropriate to meet with Ivy and Hailey, and it couldn't even have a hint of stodgy nanny for her meeting with Drew after. To add to the challenge, it also had to be appropriate for a child's birthday party, as she was going to her brother's immediately following the afternoon meeting.

She chose a simple but sleek black dress, matching tights and shoes that brought her five foot nine much closer to six feet. Even with the addition of two and a half inches to her height, thanks to the world's sexiest shoes, she'd still be looking up at Drew Parker, and that was a rare thing in her world.

As she regarded herself in the mirror, Alexandra decided her hair pinned up was just too uptight. She let it down and smiled at the effect. She congratulated herself on achieving the perfect look: professional and ever so subtly spicy.

It turned out she was particularly happy for the professional part of that equation, because Sebastian had decided to join them for the meeting with Hailey after all.

And he had stunned them all by bringing his college friend Gio with him. Alexandra knew, of course, that Crown Prince Giovanni of Adria was going to be Sebastian's best man, but she had not made the connection that he was the Gio that Sebastian had referred to the other day.

Once the initial faint discomfort of being in the presence of a prince was put to rest—were they supposed to curtsy?—the meeting was phenomenal, the energy and ideas flying. Hailey, thankfully, was quite good at tempering Ivy's more outrageous ideas. She would say, "I *love* that. But might it work a little better if—"

Together, the five of them—the guys having quite a bit more to add than Alexandra ever would have guessed—had come up with an exquisite rough plan for the wedding decor: rich, stylish, tasteful and utterly, utterly gorgeous.

As always, she made quick rough sketches as the ideas flew, adjusting them as they evolved. When they finally were all in agreement, she put sheets of blueprint paper on one of Hailey's floral tables and, to the delight of the others, did a final sketch for each setting.

"You could have been an artist," Ivy said, studying the drawings with admiration.

Indeed, she could have been. That's what she had gone to college for, after all… But she shoved that broken dream away. Not today. It was not cutting into her elation today.

She wanted to carry this feeling all the way to her meeting with Drew. When a plan came together, it always felt like this: as if she was on fire with excitement. She loved her job!

She headed to Parker and Parker to run the plan by Drew. He *had* to like it.

She found her way to the office and was rewarded for getting her dress just right by the slight darkening of Drew's eyes as she arrived.

The office did not reveal as much about him as she might have hoped. It was, of course, very exclusive, and very much like the rest of the building, with rich furnishings, good paintings, subtle wall colors, aged hardwood floors. But the space was like an exquisitely decorated hotel room and did not reveal anything about Drew Parker's personality.

The office only made her long to look past the next door, the one she assumed led to his private living quarters— she could hear muffled giggles coming from behind it— but that door was firmly closed.

As, she could not help but notice, was his expression. His obviously expensive suit—pale gray, with a dark shirt and a slender aqua-colored necktie—reflected that he was all business today.

"I can't wait to show you what we've come up with for an initial plan," she said.

"Well," he said, his cynical tone like a needle piercing the balloon of her elation, "I hope it's not too much of a carnival."

CHAPTER FIVE

DREW IMMEDIATELY REGRETTED the tone he had taken. There was no need to be rude. On the other hand, a man had to have some defenses!

Alexandra Harris looked absolutely stunning today. She was wearing a simple, sophisticated black dress that she somehow elevated to extraordinarily sexy. The skirt ended midthigh, showing off the incredible length of her legs. She didn't need them—at all—but the shoes gave her added height and made her look willowy and jaw-droppingly gorgeous.

Drew was fairly certain that his assessment that she could have a successful career as a model would be no more welcomed than his suggestion of a career as a nanny.

To add to the subtle sensuality created by the dress and the shoes, her hair was down.

It cascaded past her shoulders in a long, silky waterfall of jet black. If he had to describe it, he would probably use the word *glorious*. It made his mouth go dry.

And speaking of mouths, hers was just about the most luscious he had ever seen. He had embarrassed them both by looking at it a little too long at their last meeting.

She was radiating light, he presumed because she was so excited about the plan for the wedding. He realized it reminded him of Emily's excitement for their wedding, and maybe that was why he had felt compelled to dim her light a little by making that stinging comment.

Alexandra faltered just slightly but then tossed that shining wave of hair over her shoulder and lifted her chin. Her eyes were sparking.

"It's not a carnival," she said firmly, and then added, her tone lighter, "In fact, it's been approved by royalty. Crown Prince Giovanni of Adria, an old college friend of Sebastian's, who will also be his best man, was at the meeting."

Drew had seen many pictures of the prince. He was an extraordinarily handsome man, and notoriously single. Was that why she looked so damned radiant? Because she'd met a prince?

And what was that he was feeling? Good grief! Not jealousy?

That was impossible. He barely knew Alexandra Harris. He certainly did not have any kind of designs on her.

Did the prince? How could he not, when she looked so stunning today?

"Did you enjoy meeting the prince?" he asked, even though he had clearly instructed himself it was none of his business.

"Oh, sure." She said it so dismissively that he wanted to laugh out loud.

With relief.

She opened her satchel—the prince, as far as Drew could determine, completely forgotten—and pulled some papers from it. Sketches?

"I talked to Gabe," he told her. He ordered himself to stay put, but instead he got out of his chair, came around the desk and stood beside her. He told himself it was to see the sketches better. The scent of clean hair and subtle but exotic perfume tickled his nose.

"How's his mom?" She glanced up at him. The softness

in her eyes felt like something that tore away at his carefully constructed barriers.

It told him a great deal about Alexandra that that would be her first question. Not how did this mix-up happen, or why had Gabe defied his boss, but how was his mother?

"He said she was having a good day. But he sounded sad and a bit overwhelmed. Still, I couldn't see *not* asking him how he'd managed to square it in his mind that it was okay to book a wedding without my knowledge."

"What did he say?"

"Genevieve and I are going to California for the latter part of December for Christmas. He actually thought I would never know."

"California?"

"Studios. Amusement parks. The beach. Warmth."

"Just the two of you?" she asked, those eyes still resting on his face, so soft a man could fall into them as if he had been a long way and a long time from comfort, and they were a featherbed.

"The two of us?" He didn't really get her question. "Speaking? Gabe and I?"

She cast him a look that clearly said men were complete idiots. "You and Genevieve. Going to California?"

"Yes, just the two of us."

"For Christmas?"

There was an odd look on her face. "What?"

"It's not really for me to say," she said, but she looked pained.

"No. I'd like to know what you think." Particularly given last year's disaster.

"Maybe it's just me, but Christmas needs snow. Not palm trees."

"The first one would have had palm trees," he said,

and he could hear the defensiveness in his tone. "Besides, snow isn't exactly a recipe for a successful Christmas."

"Well, of course, it's not the whole recipe!"

"What is the whole recipe, then?" He hoped it was that simple. A recipe. And once he had it, he could just follow the instructions carefully and to the letter. He'd bet they would not lead him to Finnish Lapland, where he had taken Genevieve last year.

"I'm not the one to ask for a recipe for Christmas happiness," she said.

He glimpsed something in her eyes. Pain?

"But Christmas, for children especially, is family time," she said and smiled. Had he imagined the pain, then? She continued, "New York is magical at Christmas. The tree lighting at Rockefeller Center, skating at the Conservatory, sledding at Pilgrim Hill, seeing *The Nutcracker* performed onstage."

With every activity she listed, her tone became more wistful...but that underlying thread of pain was still there. As a man familiar with pain, he was certain of this.

Maybe it was the fact he detected some faint common ground of pain, because he found himself sharing something he normally would not have shared.

"Genevieve and I don't have family. Emily and I were both orphans. I think it was part of what made the bond between us so unbreakable. We found each other in a world where we had been alone."

He ordered himself to stop there, but he did not stop.

"When we found out Emily was pregnant, we were over the moon. Not just because of the baby, but because we were finally going to join that exclusive club called family."

Again, he ordered himself to stop. And again, he did not.

"I guess that's not meant to be for some people."

She looked quickly away from him, but not before he glimpsed the genuine concern in her eyes. He should have been furious with himself for telling her things that had earned her pity. And yet, that was not what he felt.

What he felt was not alone. Of course, he had Genevieve, but sometimes being a single dad with a four-year-old made him feel more alone, not less so.

He cleared his throat. He had gotten seriously off topic here.

"Anyway, getting back to Gabe, you were right. It was the bribe that tipped him over the edge."

"He told you that? That he risked your wrath for an autographed picture?" she said, following his lead back to safer ground, thank goodness.

"He didn't have to tell me. I could hear the jazz music playing in the background. I asked who it was. Can you guess?"

"Webber Morrison," she said softly.

"He said his mom loved Webber so much. She had followed his career since she was a young woman. She had all his albums. He said the music was bringing her great comfort. I think he almost mentioned the signed picture and then realized I didn't know about it. I didn't tell him I did."

"He risked your wrath for his sick mom," Alexandra said. How could a tone so tender feel as if it was going to yank your heart right out of your chest?

"That's what I'd like Genevieve to know about family," he said. "All the things I never knew. Family is somebody who has your back. Family is somebody who will risk anything to bring you happiness in your darkest moment."

She actually lifted her hand as if she might touch him. He stepped quickly away from her, and her hand dropped. She looked embarrassed.

He noticed her eyes were fringed with an abundance of

thick, natural lashes, and they were truly amazing. Dark brown, flecked with gold. Richly layered, deeply textured.

"Please don't give up on love," she whispered.

Ah. He needed to remember this. For some reason she could see his soul. He did not like being so transparent.

"How can I?" he asked, his voice stripped of emotion. "I have my daughter. I want her to know love. I want her to feel it from me. The way I feel it from her."

"Why do I hear a *but*?" she asked.

He sucked in his breath. That's what transparency did. Alexandra saw things that were best kept hidden, that made him feel vulnerable. "But I also want to protect her from its pain."

"Oh, Drew," she said, and he heard the impossibility of what he wanted in her tone.

What was it about her that brought this out in him? Really? He was confiding to a near stranger. And he hated it.

"Let's see what you've brought," he said gruffly, needing to move away from the personal, and quickly. "Let's see the grand plans for the wedding."

She opened her folder and laid a large piece of paper on the desk in front of her. She had done a rough colored pencil sketch of the outside of Parker and Parker, transformed for the wedding.

"Your sketch is quite extraordinary."

"Thank you. I took art for a while, before…" Her voice drifted away, and he glanced at her. He realized he did not have a monopoly on suffering.

"Before what?"

"Oh…" She lifted a slender shoulder. "You know. Life."

He did know. Life.

All of it—sharing his vulnerability with her, the quickly shuttered pain in her eyes, the unexpected beauty of the drawing—were evoking feelings in Drew to the point it felt as if his throat was closing. Where was all this coming from today?

He was suddenly acutely aware of the danger of connecting with her, with a person who could pull such deep feeling from him.

Instead, he forced himself to focus on the drawing in front of him. Parker and Parker had been transformed into a vision worthy of a fairy tale. Not just any vision, but a Christmas vision. He did not trust himself to speak. She cast him an anxious look, and he just nodded.

She placed the next drawing in front of him, her shoulder brushing against his when she did so.

Was it partly his awareness of her that made her vision for the front foyer so electrifying? Again, the transformation was complete. The space was always magnificent, and yet the addition of trees and garlands, candles and wreaths, took it beyond beautiful. It was a wonderland of whimsy and wishes. It invited you to do what he least wanted to do right now—to feel something.

To feel the most dangerous thing of all. Hope.

"Did the prince do this?" he asked, and his tone had a deliberate edge to it. "It's all very castle in a fairy tale."

"Of course Gio had input—"

Gio?

"But, no, Hailey, Ivy and I came up with most of this. Do you like it?"

He found he couldn't speak. *Like* did not seem strong enough. It was exquisite. It was also the perfect setting for a wedding, what every single woman would hope for on her special day.

He just nodded. "It's okay," he said gruffly.

One by one, she laid out her drawings, her vision. It was becoming clearer and clearer to him that Alexandra planned weddings all the time. Though she had given the other women credit, he had already seen what Ivy's taste ran to. And Hailey's specialty was flowers.

Which meant Alexandra had largely created the *feeling* that was coming across in each of these sketches.

Hope.

What every wedding, at its core, was about. Hope. A hope that love was real and lasting. A hope that dreams could come true. A hope that, in the face of plenty of evidence to the contrary, love could make life better than it had ever been before.

Alexandra probably created this feeling, wove this magic, into every single wedding she did, even when the backdrop was far less spectacular, even when the budget was less extravagant.

Drew wondered if she had any idea what these drawings said about her.

She believed in something. She hoped for something. *Don't give up on love*, she had whispered to him.

The last drawing showed the main ballroom in two stages: dinner, and then the tables cleared away for dancing.

It was like a magic wand had been waved and the ballroom had become an enchanted forest on a winter's night.

"Are the trees real?" he asked.

"Yes." She glanced at him. He was glad she seemed uncertain how to read him now. "The plans call for thirty of them for the ballroom alone. Forty total. Fraser fir."

"That's a lot of needles to clean up," he said.

"You'll never know they were there," she promised, but he could tell she was hurt by his lack of approval. "Besides, everything is subject to change, right up until the day of the wedding."

"And you're able to create this illusion of a starlit night?"

"I have an excellent team of experts I work with all the

time. What we do is a bit like creating a set. So, yes, it's very doable."

"Is it going to snow?" he asked. "Inside?"

That was hardly his vehement *no to snow* of a few days ago. So clearly, without even trying, she was weaving him into this enchantment of hers. He had to stop it. He had to pull back from it instead of leaning toward it.

She smiled. That smile did not make leaning back from her magic any easier.

"I hope it's going to snow. If you'll allow it. You can actually get fake snow. We thought we'd mix it with silver glitter and release it from hidden compartments in the ceiling during the last dance."

She hugged herself with excitement. "Every single person dusted with the magic of the day before they leave."

He was being dusted with her magic right now.

"Of course, I'll take full responsibility for having it cleaned up, just like with the trees."

He could not trust himself to speak as he stared at her rendering and thought of people being dusted with the magic of love.

She frowned at his silence. "Are the plans okay, then?"

Okay? They were better than okay. He could see that this vision, this wedding being held at Parker and Parker, was so right.

It wasn't, as he had feared for so long, a betrayal of Emily to have a wedding here. It was, in fact, the exact opposite.

It was—particularly the way this was laid out—a way of honoring Em. Her belief in romance. Her belief in dreams. Her belief in love.

It was as if this was the part of his healing that he had been missing. That he hadn't even known he needed.

An *accident* had brought him to this. A mistake in

bookings. This all would have been a secret from him if Gabe had not stepped aside.

He was a man who had lost the love of his life.

A tragedy like that did not lend itself to a belief in a larger plan. And yet, in this moment, he felt oddly illuminated.

And terribly vulnerable.

"Drew?"

He pressed his fingers to his nose and pinched the bridge of it.

"What's wrong?" she asked softly, her eyes on his face filled with concern. Not for her plan, but for *him*.

He pulled himself together. "Nothing's wrong," he said, keeping his voice carefully neutral, stripping all the emotion out of it.

She was still looking into his eyes. It was making him feel weak when he wanted to be strong.

She looked away from him, back at her drawings, something faintly pensive in her look now. He felt as if he started breathing again. She was obviously disappointed by his faint praise.

"So?" she asked, her tone brisk. "You're okay with everything? Not too much of a carnival?"

"I'm not sold on the snow. If you could rethink that…" he forced himself to say. "And it's too many trees. There are probably fire regulations."

"These are just the initial plans, ever changing at this point," she said, her tone clipped with hurt. "The details will come into focus as we go, and I'll need to check with you as they do."

He began to roll up the sheets of paper one by one.

Check with him? Over the details? It made his head ache, thinking of being around her—trying to keep his defenses up like this was exhausting.

"It's an ambitious plan," he said. "Yes, please do check

in with me from time to time. Though hopefully Gabe will be back soon and you can check in with him."

He handed the papers back to her.

"You'll probably be dealing mostly with him," he said.

Her mouth closed. She knew he was dismissing her. Good Lord. She probably had a prince floundering at her feet. Why did she look so distressed that their brief relationship was ending?

For that matter, why did he feel distressed about it?

She was dangerous to him. She was dangerous to his heart. She was opening doors that were better left closed.

"Goodbye, Miss Harris," he said firmly.

CHAPTER SIX

GOODBYE, MISS HARRIS?

Alexandra was stunned. She was really having trouble reading Drew Parker. He didn't seem enthusiastic about any part of her plan. Fire regulations? Rethink the snow, as if that wasn't the best part of the whole plan?

Why did she want his approval so badly? Why did she want his confidence in her ability to pull off the wedding of the century?

"You'll have to be involved," she told him curtly. "Obviously, you've just made it clear I can't just go ahead and plan without consulting you. It's your venue, and I'm not into the surprise of a last-minute veto on your part."

"There's no need to say that as if I'd be unreasonable when I feel I've been very reasonable."

"The snow and trees?" she snapped.

"Oh, that. Why don't you make a few tweaks, and you can text or email me changes and plans as they occur? Please feel free to stay in touch as much as you need to."

She considered the formality of the way he was addressing her. He was definitely trying to put distance between them. It felt as if they had gotten beyond that, somehow, when he had admitted he wanted his daughter both to know love and be protected from it.

It had felt as if a bond had been forged between them

when he had trusted her with his vulnerability, his single dad doubts. She had even considered the possibility that, eventually, she would trust him with hers.

Now, *eventually* was no longer on the table.

Well, what had she thought? That he was going to help her every step of the way? That they were going to meet regularly to go over details of the wedding?

That, as they got to know each other, she was going to rescue him and his adorable daughter from a lonely Christmas?

Really, who was she to give any kind of advice around Christmas—to insist it was a family time—when she had distracted herself with work and had avoided her own family on the days leading up to Christmas for years now?

It wasn't that she didn't love doing the things she had mentioned to him with her nieces and nephews, sledding and skating and going to Rockefeller Center, but doing those things also filled her with a bittersweet longing for what might have been.

And as the days counted down to Christmas, the grief that people insisted time would heal seemed as undiluted as that horrible day a decade ago, when her worst nightmare had unfolded.

Alexandra shook it off. And with it she shook off hope.

Because, hadn't she hoped, in that moment when he had shared about Emily with her, that something powerful had passed between them, that maybe Drew was going to ask her out for dinner?

Hadn't she hoped she might screw up the nerve to ask him out for dinner if he didn't?

She glanced at his face. It was completely closed. His expression was cold. She shoved the rolled plans back into her bag. It was more than evident they would not be going for dinner together.

It was more than evident whatever connection they'd had was over. When Gabe came back, Drew was going to pass on dealing with her to him. And he was clearly hoping Gabe would be back sooner rather than later.

And then he would take Genevieve to California. Chances were he wouldn't even be here for the wedding. How could he not want to see these sketches brought, step by meticulous step, to life? How could he not want to see the flimsy stuff that dreams were made of become the strongly woven fabric of reality?

How silly to feel bereft about that, as if in Drew Parker she had caught a glimpse of a world more enticing than the one she had created on these papers, and the door to that world was being slammed in her face.

She, of all people, should know better than to hope. She turned to go. She did not want to risk shaking hands with him again. She hoped he might say—

"Wait!"

But, of course, it was not him. The door between his living quarters and the office had been flung open. Genevieve catapulted through, wearing the most delightful party dress, fit for a princess with its layers of multicolored ruffles.

"You weren't going to leave without seeing my dress, were you?" she cried, doing a pirouette in front of Alexandra. "I wanted you to see my dress. Do you like it?"

"It's absolutely beautiful."

"Look, my tights glitter."

"Yes, they do," Alexandra said. Her feeling of being bereft deepened as she thought of never seeing Genevieve again. Why such a deep reaction to the loss of such a short acquaintance?

It was better this way. If she could feel so attached— to both this child and her father—after such a short time, what would it be like if she got to know them better and then things didn't work out?

And one thing about being a wedding planner—you had an unfortunate front-row seat to things not working out.

Sometimes the couples didn't even make it to the wedding day.

And other times that couple who had been so in love, who had gazed at each other so adoringly, who had vowed, in front of the world, to stay together until death, didn't make it, either.

Alexandra always felt so sad when she heard of one of *her* couples not making it. She still even felt sad if the bride came to her to plan a second wedding. Once it had even been a third one. Though she tried her hardest, the magic of the first time refused to be recreated.

Of course, her first and only time had not been magic. Ever since she was a teenager, she had longed to have the perfect wedding one day. A surprise pregnancy had changed all that, and she'd had a hurried exchange of vows in front of a justice of the peace.

With a man who cared about her but who did not love her.

And whom she had tried so hard to love, but...

Alexandra shook it off. You would really think she would have the good sense to be cynical by now, to genuinely be glad Drew had dismissed her in the face of that elusive *something* leaping up between them.

"And this is the gift I got Brenna," Genevieve said, not noticing Alexandra inching toward the door. She showed her a very badly wrapped box, and Alexandra cast the nanny, Miss Carmichael, a smile for letting Genevieve wrap it herself. But she frowned at the look on the nanny's face. She looked stricken as she gazed at her small charge.

"It's a Bonnie doll," Genevieve said, unaware of the look her nanny was giving her.

Alexandra stopped inching toward the door and looked again at the nanny, who was obviously screwing up her courage to tell Drew something.

Or was that Mr. Parker now? Since she was Miss Harris to him?

"Do you think she'll like it?"

"Of course she will," Alexandra said, though she was distracted. The only girl child in the universe not enraptured with a Bonnie doll was her own niece, Macy, who was going through a cowboy phase. Her party was Western themed.

Alexandra glanced at her watch. She really needed to go and felt grateful she had a place to go to where she wouldn't or couldn't wallow in her sense of loss.

Goodbye, Miss Harris.

Miss Carmichael was leaning into Drew. "I'm just leaving for the day. Um…"

"Is there a problem?" he asked.

"Well, yes, actually. I didn't want to be the one to tell her," Miss Carmichael said, and then she leaned even closer to him and whispered something in his ear.

He listened carefully and then straightened. He blew out his breath and then rocked back on his heels.

"So, I'll be going then," Miss Carmichael said with loud cheer. She turned and practically bolted out the door. Alexandra wanted to follow her, but there was something about the pained look Drew cast her that made her hesitate.

As she watched, he took a deep breath and crouched down in front of his daughter.

Good grief! What would give him that look, like a soldier about to inform a general of a failed mission?

"I'm afraid I have some bad news."

The child froze and turned slowly to look at her father.

"What?" she whispered, her eyes wide on his face.

He cleared his throat. "The party has been canceled. Brenna is sick."

Genevieve looked at him in silent disbelief. And then her face crumpled. And then the wrapped doll box fell from her hand.

"Noooo!" she wailed. She cast herself on the floor and began to beat it with her small fists and feet.

Drew scooped her up and held her tight. "I'm sorry, pumpkin. She'll have it as soon as she gets better."

That was little consolation to Genevieve. She howled with fresh pain. Her tears ran down Drew's neck.

Drew cast Alexandra a look over Genevieve's head. It was such a look of universal longing: every parent just wanting to make the world right for his child, to take away moments of pain, to smooth over things going wrong.

It made Alexandra feel a foolish longing to do all the same things.

For him.

Or maybe it was really for herself. To delay the goodbye to this man and his child for one more brief period in time, even though logically she knew how unwise it was to do so.

Sometimes, the heart simply would not be overruled. Or maybe, this year, she was looking for a bigger Christmas distraction than ever.

And so, before she could think it through properly, or stop herself, she called loudly, over the heartbreaking wailing of the child, "I know where there's a birthday party."

Genevieve stopped howling with comical abruptness, as if a radio had been shut off. Two identical sets of green eyes fastened on her, Genevieve's hopeful, while her father looked more cautious.

It occurred to Alexandra she really should have taken him aside privately. Now she had really put him in an impossible position if he wanted to say no.

Of course he wanted to say no! That's why he had just said goodbye to her with such finality. He didn't want to spend more time with her.

Still, she had jumped in now. Alexandra tried to tell herself it was strictly for Genevieve's sake, and not to draw out her relationship with her father.

So, she went on bravely, "It's my niece Macy's birthday today. I was just on my way there. You are welcome to join me."

Drew, to her everlasting relief, did not look at all as if he felt she had backed him into a corner. Despite the fact he wanted to distance himself from her—hand her off to Gabe as soon as possible—he looked at her now like he was a drowning man and she had thrown him the life preserver. He looked at her with the heartfelt relief of a man who loved his child unconditionally.

"Are you sure?" he asked. "You don't need to check that it's okay to bring extras?"

He was certainly a different person when his daughter's happiness was at stake! It made her heart melt.

She actually laughed. "Last I heard the entire preschool class was going, her cousins, her sister and her two brothers. And probably whoever they want to bring." She couldn't resist teasing him a tiny bit. "It *will* be a regular carnival."

"Oh!" Genevieve said. "Daddy! I told you I love carnivals!" And then she scrambled down out of his arms and turned a joyous circle, laughing merrily.

Then he laughed, too.

Alexandra had not seen Drew laugh yet. In fact, she had barely seen him crack a smile. She was sadly aware of what a rare event it must be when Genevieve stopped midcircle and looked at her father with astounded delight.

His laughter chased some shadow from his eyes and

lifted some weight from his shoulders. It also made him—in a flash of brilliant white teeth—possibly the most attractive man Alexandra had ever laid eyes on.

"Let's go then," he said, and Genevieve squealed her delight. "Shall I call a car?"

"I was just going to take the subway," Alexandra said. "We're going to the Flushing neighborhood in Queens."

"The subway!" Genevieve said. "Can we go on the subway, Daddy, please?"

"I hate to say it," Alexandra said, because of course riding in any car he called would probably be a luxury, "but at this time of day, the subway might be faster."

And so they ended up walking to the subway station with Genevieve skipping between them, holding both their hands.

Alexandra could not help but notice that in New York, the city where people made a point of not noticing each other, the little girl, her party dress peeking out from under her parka, attracted indulgent smiles.

And so did she and Drew. Of course, people would be assuming Alexandra and Drew—Drew holding the badly wrapped birthday present—were mommy and daddy, and that they were a perfect little family unit. It was a fantasy that was very hard not to enjoy.

Riding the subway was such a simple thing. Alexandra had probably done it hundreds—if not thousands—of times, and yet, today, experiencing it with Genevieve's wonder made her so aware of every little thing, not the least of which was Drew's shoulder pressed against hers as he held his daughter on his lap.

Her brother lived in a middle-class section of New York, not the kind of neighborhood or house Manhattan people like Drew Parker or Ivy Jenkins would be familiar with, and as they got off the subway, Alexandra had a moment's doubt.

What was she doing?

This wasn't Drew Parker's world. This was working-class New York. What if Genevieve—children being children—blurted out something about where her brother lived that hurt everyone's feelings?

They came to her brother's block. It looked a touch shabby to Alexandra now, even though she had grown up in this neighborhood and still lived in an apartment around the corner from here. Despite the breathtaking expense of the real estate, this was still where the plumbers and electricians and secretaries and shop clerks lived. For the most part, this was not where the moguls and millionaires were.

She was aware that the yard was a shambles of toys and bicycles, the paint was peeling, and the front porch was leaning as if it might fall off. The Christmas lights from last year had not been taken down, and one string of them hung drunkenly off the peak of the roof.

And she was suddenly aware of Drew's suit, the dark knee-length cashmere coat he'd thrown over it, the expense of the plaid wool scarf knotted so casually at his neck.

What had she been thinking, bringing a millionaire here?

Genevieve stopped and looked at the house for a long time. And then she turned to Drew. Alexandra held her breath. Maybe they would decide not to even go in.

"Daddy," Genevieve said, her tone reverent and excited. "Look. It's a *real* house."

"It is," Drew said, and he shot Alexandra a smile so loaded with gratitude she thought she might melt.

She had the awful thought that maybe it was she who had become the snob!

Party noises were already spilling from the house, and the laughter called to them like a lighthouse that would beckon sailors who had been lost at sea.

"Give me the present," Genevieve said excitedly, as if it were her entry pass to the festivities.

It was utter chaos inside. Alexandra cast a worried look at Genevieve. She was an only child. How was she going to handle this? But Genevieve was not shrinking behind her father's leg, at all. She looked enchanted.

"Auntie!"

Alexandra bent over to give her niece Ashley a hug. "These are my friends, Genevieve and her father, Mr. Parker."

"Drew is fine," he said.

"Genevieve, I love your dress," Ashley said. "And your tights are the best. Sparkly!"

Genevieve preened at the approval of someone just enough older than herself to really count.

"Is that a present for Macy? Let's go put it in the present pile." Ashley held out her hand, and without so much as a backward glance at her daddy, Genevieve went with her.

Alexandra's sister-in-law, Shelley, made her way through the crowd of rambunctious children.

As a mother of four, she looked slightly frayed, as always, but so at home in all this happy chaos that Alexandra felt that familiar stab of longing.

Alexandra introduced her to Drew. Her eyes went back and forth between Alexandra and Drew with such embarrassing hope that she *finally* had a boyfriend that Alexandra felt compelled to speak up.

"Drew and I are working on a wedding together."

"But you aren't even engaged yet!" Shelley said. She was so pleased with how hilarious she found herself that she didn't appear to notice the sudden awkwardness between Alexandra and Drew.

CHAPTER SEVEN

ALEXANDRA FELT DREW shift his weight uncomfortably beside her. She gave her sister-in-law a warning look.

"We're business associates," she said sternly, trying to stop any further shenanigans from Shelley.

But Shelly did not look chastised in the least. Instead, she cocked her head at Drew and studied him with avid interest.

"Somehow," she decided, "you don't look like someone involved in the wedding business."

Alexandra slid him a glance and couldn't help but notice he looked insultingly pleased by that assessment.

"I'm not involved in the wedding business. Genevieve, unfortunately, had a party canceled this afternoon," Drew said. "At the point when she was on the floor screaming like someone being murdered, Alexandra obviously saw I was in over my head and took pity on me. She rescued me, so thank you for having us on such short notice."

"I thought it would be a shame to let such a beautiful party dress go to waste," Alexandra said, trying to head Shelley off. It didn't work.

"But how did you happen to be together?" Shelley asked, with way too much interest.

"I own a venue Alexandra is using for an upcoming wedding."

"Oh? Which venue?"

"Parker and Parker," he said.

"Oh! I love that building. So enchanting!" Shelley shot Alexandra a look. She might as well have had a blinking neon banner running across her forehead that said *keeper*.

"Thank you," Drew said with genuine pleasure.

"It looks just like a mansion. Have you ever considered having a Halloween event there?"

"I haven't," he said.

Shelley rolled her eyes. "As Genevieve gets older, you will see Halloween is *the* second most important event on the junior calendar."

"And the first?" he asked.

Shelley looked at him closely. "Are you a single dad?"

Alexandra realized that she might not have thought through this part of inviting Genevieve to her niece's party—the inevitable interrogation of showing up at a family event with a man.

He nodded.

"A single dad," Shelley said with a sigh, as though this status made Drew more irresistible than the crown prince of Adria. She shot another look at Alexandra. The blinking *keeper* banner was stronger now.

"What made it obvious?" he asked.

"Oh, first that *you* were dealing with a child screaming on the floor. That's usually pretty solidly in the mommy department. And also that you had to ask what the first important event on the junior calendar is. So, for future reference, this is what you need to know. Any child divides up their year by events, and how importantly they rate them. Christmas is number one."

Alexandra noticed he frowned at that.

"Followed by Halloween. Then their birthday—not their brothers' or sisters' birthdays—theirs."

"Genevieve is an only child."

"Oh, dear," her sister-in-law murmured.

"Oh, dear?" he prodded her for her meaning.

"Well, it's just that that comes with its own set of problems, along with the—" Shelley finally caught the fact Alexandra was glaring at her, and didn't, thank goodness, finish her sentence where she was going to give poor Drew a complex about the set of problems that his child was going to endure as a result of being raised by a single dad.

"Anyway," Shelley finished a bit lamely, "*the* list in order of importance—Christmas, Halloween, birthday, summer vacation, Easter, spring break."

Alexandra was not unaware her sister-in-law shot her an accusing look when she mentioned the importance of Christmas to her children. She wasn't going to be made to feel guilty. She did lots of things with her nieces and nephews around Christmas. It's just as it came nearer, she withdrew.

"Should I take notes?" Drew asked. His brief frown at the mention of Christmas again—at the head of the list— had disappeared, and his voice held only smooth good humor.

He was being very good-natured about the whole thing, which Shelley would probably take as an invitation to keep questioning him.

Thankfully, Alexandra was spotted by four more of her nieces and nephews, and they were swarmed. She had to comment on each one's party finery, and she received sticky kisses and long hugs.

She finally pulled herself from the heap of children.

"This is my friend Drew," Alexandra said. She placed her hands affectionately on the head of each child as they were introduced, Shelley's remaining children, Colin and Michael, and her sister Heather's girls, Adelle and Catherine.

She had always felt you could tell a great deal about a

person from how they were around children. She loved how solemnly Drew greeted each child, and said their name, and how he offered his hand, and didn't even try and wipe it surreptitiously on his pants after he got a sticky handshake.

"I want to show you my new skates," Michael said.

"And I built a fort," Colin said. "It's in my room. Can you—"

"Not now," Shelley said firmly. "Off with all of you. I think we're about to begin decorating cupcakes in the kitchen."

The children stampeded off at the mention of cupcakes.

"Is Heather here?" Alexandra asked. If she had thought Shelley's interrogation of Drew was invasive enough, it would be nothing compared to what her sister, Heather, was capable of.

Obviously, she really had not thought this through. And what would happen when her brother, Shaun, showed up? He'd be grilling Drew mercilessly, and then the whole gang of them would be getting ready to post banns at the church.

"Heather had the good sense to drop off the kids and leave," Shelley said. "It's going to be chaos here and we're bursting at the seams. If you're okay leaving Genevieve, and unless you're wild about decorating cupcakes, why don't you two go grab a nice quiet drink somewhere and come back in a while?"

Alexandra was aghast at how obvious Shelley was being.

Shelley turned away as if it was already decided.

"Maybe I should just tell Genevieve," Drew said uncertainly.

"Never mind that, it'll be an hour before she notices you're gone," Shelley said with the ease of someone who dealt with children all the time. "I'll tell her when I see her. I can always text Alexandra if there's any problems."

The noise and chaos seemed to fade away. Alexandra was aware of Drew watching her, faint amusement upturning his mouth.

He pushed open the door behind him.

"Shall we?" he said.

Alexandra was distressed to find she felt as tongue-tied as a teenager on her first date as she stepped back out the door into the crisp fall air.

Drew took in a deep breath of the fall-scented air, trying to center himself.

He had known when he saw Alexandra's drawings today that she hoped for *something*. He had tried, almost desperately, to distance himself from that. And yet, here he was.

Seeing her, so much a part of that family, those children swarming her adoringly, the light that had come on in her face as she bestowed kisses and dispensed hugs, had solidified exactly what it was she hoped for.

And deserved.

A family.

Of course, he was the man least likely to give that to anyone. He didn't even know what it was. He and Emily had had that in common.

And still, they had hoped.

He could not have such a hope crush him again. But what about Genevieve? It was what he wanted for her, wasn't it?

For her to be part of something? To belong? To have hope?

"Do you know where to go?" In light of his thoughts, what was he really asking? Did Alexandra have the road map for life?

"This is my neighborhood."

This was *her* neighborhood. Children. Family.

"There's a cute, quiet place around the corner."

They were talking about places to go for a drink, nothing more. Except she seemed to sense something more.

"You seem pensive," Alexandra said, a reminder it would be very hard to have secrets from a woman like her.

"Do I?" he hedged. "I guess I'm just thinking of all the things I don't know about raising a child. I don't even know how to give her a good Christmas, and apparently, that's the most important one of all."

"Here it is."

It was a small brick building with a sign over the door. He read it out loud. "Tequila Rockingbird?" Despite himself, he laughed. "It's clever. What's a Rockingbird?"

"Their specialty drink," she said in a whisper. "Created, I think, to make the name work. Don't try it."

He opened the door for her. Such a simple thing, holding open the door for a woman.

But when she brushed by him, it filled him with a longing he had not allowed himself to feel for quite some time.

A longing to not be quite so alone with it all.

That was a longing that had been exacerbated by the visit to that delightfully chaotic party. By her sister-in-law, knowing, with such ease, all the rules for raising children, how it all went, how it all was supposed to go.

The pub was tiny, nearly empty and cozy with its rabbit warren of cubbyholes and eclectic furniture. Alexandra knew her way around it, because she led him to a little enclave at the back. They sat at coffee table by a stone fireplace. She took a love seat, and he took the deeply distressed leather chair across from her.

"We have a special," the waitress told them when she arrived. "Our very own Rockingbird cocktail."

Alexandra cast him a look and ordered a glass of the

house white. He liked that. There was something very unpretentious about it.

He would have normally ordered a scotch, even though he didn't really like scotch, not even the much-touted Glenfiddich he would usually ask for. Now that choice seemed pretentious, even though not liking it would keep him sipping slowly, or barely touching it. One thing about being around a woman like this one? You did not want to drink too much.

You did not want to let your guard down at all.

So, what devil inside him made him order the Rockingbird?

He looked at her. She raised an amused eyebrow as if to say, *I tried to warn you.*

Everything about her seemed like a warning. The light from that flickering fire illuminated her, and though she had looked radiant when he'd first seen her today, when she was brimming over with plans and excitement, now that radiance had deepened, as if she had pulled all that love from her nieces and nephews inside her, and she was lit from within.

He realized his guard was already down. Her scent, already familiar to him, wrapped around him. Her foot accidentally brushed his under the table, and it felt as if an electric shock went up and down his leg. She felt something, too, because she withdrew her foot rapidly.

"Sorry," she said, her cheeks coloring, and making her look even more beautiful in the warm glow of the fire.

Though he felt like he had seen her true beauty as those children swarmed her.

The drinks arrived. She took a satisfied sip of her wine. He took a taste of the Rockingbird.

"Well?" she asked.

"It's shockingly good."

"Uh-huh. That's tequila. It's the Samson and Delilah of drinks. Careful, it's hiding a pair of scissors in its pretty dress."

That was also love, he thought. And it was a good reminder to be wary of the charms of this beautiful woman.

"You seem pensive again."

He had hoped for small talk. He had assumed Alexandra would be good at small talk. He supposed she met all kinds of people—including, he reminded himself a little sourly, princes. He had hoped she would guide the conversation easily and they would talk about safe things like music and movies, maybe the weather. Perhaps they would touch lightly on politics.

But, oh, no, here he was contemplating love's daggers, not that he intended to let her know that, charms of the Rockingbird notwithstanding.

"Just mulling over all the things your sister-in-law made me so aware I don't know," he admitted. "I'm dreading Christmas."

It felt like a confession, not really much better than love's daggers as a nice, light conversation.

She cocked her head at him.

"I made a mess of it last year."

"In what way?"

"I took Genevieve to Finland."

"What?"

"Obviously, when she was two, Christmas was no problem. She was hardly aware of what Christmas was. But last year was different. I wanted it to be spectacular. Memorable."

Being around people like Shelley made him aware of what he had really wanted. To not feel so alone with it all. To somehow capture the *feeling* of it. In this he had failed miserably.

"So, I took her to a real, live Christmas village."

"There's such a place?"

"Finnish Lapland."

"It sounds perfectly lovely," she said dubiously. "What was wrong?"

"Besides everything? We had jet lag. There was a sauna in our cottage. It burped a little steam at her and she decided monsters lived there. The Northern Lights confirmed her suspicion we were in a deeply strange place. Then, Santa didn't *look* right. Or sound right. The reindeer smelled, and there was no Rudolph. You cannot even imagine how cold it was as we took our sleigh ride across the Arctic Circle. To add to that, she told Santa what gift she wanted, but it was a secret from me, so guess what?"

"Wrong toy," Alexandra said. Her eyes were so warm, so full of tenderness and sympathy.

"So wrong."

What had happened to his drink? He hadn't had the whole thing, had he? That was impossible. Still, there seemed to be a fresh one there. He put it to his lips. It felt like he was drinking a spell. No, a curse that was making him talk too much, reveal too much.

"And this year, California," she said, that same annoying, dubious tone in her voice.

"The amusement parks have Christmas themes," he said defensively. "They're famous for them!"

"Ah."

Alexandra didn't ask him why he wasn't going to stay here. There was no reason to tell her. None.

"Emily loved Christmas," he heard himself tell her, and took another deep drink from his Rockingbird.

CHAPTER EIGHT

"I THINK," DREW CONTINUED, despite ordering himself to stop—both talking and drinking the drink, "Christmas may have been the only thing Emily loved better than a wedding."

"Ivy said yours was supposed to be the first wedding at Parker and Parker."

"It was," he said. His words didn't seem slurred. Not at all. It felt as if they were rising from some place deep inside him. Trying to stop them was like trying to stop bubbles rising in champagne. Impossible.

"The whole thing—Parker and Parker—was her idea, start to finish. She was in love with love. She radiated love. And she wanted to create this perfect, magical place for couples to begin, for them to dedicate their lives to each other."

"She succeeded," Alexandra said quietly.

"We actually bought it and started the renovations before she got pregnant. That was an incredible surprise, because she'd been told she couldn't have children. I wanted to get married before the baby was born, but she was desperate to have the wedding there—the first one in Parker and Parker—and she wanted it to be perfect. The renovations went longer than she'd anticipated, so she insisted we reschedule the date."

He heard his voice crack ever so slightly and took another drink. Just to lubricate his throat.

"She died when Genevieve was two months old, one month before our wedding."

"I'm so sorry."

"Part of the reason we bought Parker and Parker," he said, "was she wanted Christmas there. Our first Christmas there—our only one, as it turned out—we had just taken possession. We'd spent all our money. We didn't have any furniture or any decorations. She was pregnant, and we lay in front of the fire on a stone floor wrapped in a blanket and she dreamed out loud. Of decorating the building for next year. Of December brides. Of hosting Christmas parties for homeless kids."

Enough! He looked at the drink accusingly. Well, it wasn't as if Alexandra hadn't warned him.

"She dreamed," he said, and heard his voice crack again, despite his efforts to lubricate it, "of our first Christmas with our baby. That's why I can't be there. I just can't."

"I understand," she said, and he looked at her and knew that she did.

"That's why, as much as possible, I haven't been involved in the hands-on running of Parker and Parker. Thankfully, I still have my career, just for those moments that being a single dad doesn't keep me fully occupied."

As he said it, Drew was deeply aware how he had filled every moment trying to outrun pain, trying to protect his daughter from pain.

Alexandra cocked her head at him, an invitation to talk more, though he knew he had talked quite enough.

"I'm an architectural engineer, which is every bit as dull as it sounds. When we found the building, it had been abandoned for some time. It needed a lot of work. Recreating it as a venue was the perfect melding of our different strengths, but after the refurbishment, I considered my job done. I could never take over the making-dreams-come-true part."

Was he babbling? If there was one person who was not a babbler, it was him. Not that anyone would know it at the moment. He ordered himself to be silent. And then kept talking.

"And what kind of dad can I be to Genevieve when I can't be the making-dreams-come-true type? Last Christmas being a case in point."

There it was. His deepest insecurity laid out shamelessly before Alexandra.

"You're doing a great job with Genevieve," Alexandra said, and there was something so firm in her voice, he wanted to believe her.

"Really?" He heard the cynicism in his tone.

"Of course!"

She was just trying to make him feel good.

"What about the Christmas fiasco?"

"Life is full of fiascos. Your job isn't to give Genevieve a perfect life, it's to give her the tools to cope when life is not perfect."

"Your first meeting with her," he reminded Alexandra, "she was running away from her nanny. Who was, by the way, the seventh or eighth one I've had. That's hardly an A-plus on the parenting report card."

"There are no A-pluses on the parenting report card. Ask Shelley. Or my sister, Heather. You've raised a very confident little girl. Given the number of nannies, it really speaks to you that Genevieve feels so safe and secure in an ever-changing world."

He regarded her thoughtfully. It occurred to him she was being genuine.

Still, it was hard to accept the compliment. "Maybe

if she was a little less confident—some might call it naughty—we'd be able to keep a nanny."

"I doubt that," Alexandra said. "I doubt it's Genevieve at all. Look at the nanny you have now. She's at that age— marriage, college, travel. Life calls."

He had never once seen a nanny leaving as anything but his own fault for having such a headstrong daughter, and he was surprised by how grateful he felt to see it in this new light. "Thank you," he said. It shouldn't have meant quite so much to him, but it did.

As they talked, it became very apparent to Drew that Alexandra was smart, sophisticated and successful. And utterly gorgeous. And also deep, sensitive, compassionate, talented, with a dash of wise added to the whole picture.

And yet...single. And for some reason, that didn't seem right to him. He was shocked by how badly he wanted to know her at a different level, at a deeper level, and shocked by how the Rockingbird seemed to have erased his own boundaries and made him ready to push against hers.

"Why aren't you an artist, covered from head to toe in paint and surrounded by a million children of your own?" he blurted.

She raised an eyebrow at him. "What makes you think the life I have isn't perfectly satisfying?"

"I think it is perfectly satisfying. But not wildly exuberant."

"Who has a wildly exuberant life?" she asked him, a bit defensively.

This was going wrong. He was being too personal. He needed to leave it alone. It was certainly too soon in their relationship for this.

Their relationship? They did not have a relationship!

And so, he was shocked when he could not leave it alone. "What is in this drink?"

"About three ounces of tequila," she said.

"And a little black magic," he muttered.

"Possibly," she said, and that beautiful mouth quirked upward.

He wondered what her mouth would taste like. Tasting it might be the perfect thing to shut him up.

But since he couldn't very well just lean across the table and kiss her, he just kept on talking.

"When I saw your sketches today, and then saw you with all those children, it felt as if I was seeing what your dreams are made of.

"I'm sorry," he said when she looked stunned by his way-too-personal observation.

"The life you have is not always the one you dreamed of," she said.

So she didn't have a wildly exuberant life? Or she didn't have the one she had dreamed of?

She blushed, as if she had revealed way too much about herself, which maybe she had.

"And now I'm sorry," Alexandra said. "I don't really have to tell you that."

"I want to know about the life you dreamed of," he said softly.

She hesitated. And then she took a sip of her wine and looked at him appraisingly.

Drew was aware he was holding his breath. She was trying to decide whether to trust him with something deeper of herself, something that she was acknowledging he had already guessed.

To be honest, he did not know if he was worthy, and at the same time felt as if he would be crushed if she found him unworthy.

"I was going to be an artist," she said. "Or at least have a world that had something to do with art. Ever since I was small, I was that dreamy kid with the sketch pad. Drawing was as natural to me as breathing. A few pencil lines could become a butterfly, or the cat sleeping in the flower box. I didn't have to labor over it. I could do a sketch in minutes.

"When I was a teenager, I was obsessed with castles and princesses, but by the time I was going to college, I had put that aside—publicly, at least—and considered myself quite the serious artist."

"And what were you drawing privately?" he asked her.

She took a sip of her drink and looked at him, again, deciding.

"Brides, weddings, flower arrangements. I was hiding my secret romantic self from the very serious world I was entering."

Warning, his mind screamed, *she has a secret romantic self. Run!* But he didn't run.

"And then what happened?" Drew heard himself encouraging her softly.

Alexandra had not expected this conversation to take a turn like this or for him to ask her to be so transparent. Nor had she expected to *want* to tell Drew her secrets. But he had told her some of his, and there was an intensity building between them that demanded honesty. That demanded, somehow, she leave the polite conventions behind and bring her complete self to him.

"What happened?" she said. "I met a boy. Isn't that always what happens? I was at college, living away from home for the first time. I was learning exciting new things and trying on exciting new ideas, and I felt so grown-up and independent. I was basically bedazzled by life.

"He was in my art class, and we were both just brimming over with fresh ideas and discovery, and the discovery extended to each other.

"Only once. But guess what? Once was enough." Her voice cracked. She had never really told this story, start to finish, to anyone. Why start with him?

Because his extraordinary green eyes had darkened to moss. Because he was watching her so intently. Because he was a man a woman wanted to give everything of herself to. Her successes. Her failures.

Her deepest secrets.

"I was pregnant. And terrified. But he was excited. He knew what to do—said we'd give that baby a mommy and a daddy. We'd make a family. He'd get a job. I'd get a job up until the baby was born. We could return to school later. We didn't have any money, but in this kind of blur of fast decisions, I found myself quitting college and getting a job. I found myself at city hall saying *I do* to an almost complete stranger."

"How was your family with all this?"

"It was a shock, at first, of course. My brother, Shaun, wanted to kill Brian, as if he'd made that baby all by himself. But pretty soon everyone saw how eager he was to do the right thing by me and the baby, and they welcomed him in. You've seen my family. Controlled chaos. There is always room for one more. Everybody in my whole family believes a baby is always a blessing. They celebrate life, no matter what it throws at them."

"That's pretty amazing," he said. "What everyone wants in a family. A great backdrop for happily-ever-after. So, what happened?"

"We lost the baby."

"I'm so sorry," he said, and his voice was pure gravel. "I should have known that. When I first met you, I asked about children. I'm glad you have your family."

But that was where the love of her family got complicated. They didn't really understand, after the loss, her need to hold that grief to herself. They couldn't understand how everything they had—the babies, the homes, the laughter, the chaos—made her so acutely aware of a baby with perfect fingers. And perfect toes. And one shock of golden hair. Who had never drawn a single breath.

She realized she had started to tremble. He realized it, too. He came around the table, unhesitatingly, and sat on the love seat beside her. His hand covered hers. His scent—clean, masculine, spicy—was reassuring in a way she couldn't quite understand.

"It was a stillbirth," she told Drew. She hadn't expected to cry. Not after all this time, but she did.

As if it was the most natural thing in the world, he put his arms around her, drew her into his chest. His hand found her hair and stroked it. It felt as if it were a homecoming. It felt as if he was pulling more words out of her. They spilled out of her mouth and onto his chest, right above his heart.

"Brian and I didn't have anything in common beyond that baby," she choked out. "And art. It wasn't enough. Our shared grief held us together for a bit, but then his brush with captivity made him long for freedom, and so when that door opened, he leaped through it. We were divorced before we'd even been married a year."

She didn't tell him they still talked once a year. On an anniversary of sorts, and not their wedding anniversary, a day that was completely forgettable. No, they talked on that sad day that they had lost the baby. No matter where he was on the planet, when the clock struck midnight on that mid-December day, as the rest of the world was entering, in earnest, the happiest season of all, her phone rang.

She pulled away from Drew's chest and found a beautiful, pristine white square of linen pressed into her hand. She dabbed at her eyes and gave him a watery smile.

See? I'm pulling myself together.

"When I quit college, I went to work for a company that catered events. I couldn't go back to school. I was too changed. Over the years, the business evolved into a full planning service that did weddings. When my boss decided to retire, she split off the wedding planning part of the company and sold it to me. And so here I am, giving the beautiful wedding—and the happily-ever-after—I never had to everyone else."

CHAPTER NINE

ALEXANDRA WONDERED IF she had ever said that out loud before. It felt as if she had just blurted out her deepest secret.

She looked into the deep green of Drew's eyes and realized the danger of starting to believe in those kinds of dreams ever again.

Those kinds of dreams just ended in disillusionment and brokenness if you allowed them to see the light of day. But he already knew the price of believing in dreams. Their shared pain leaped between them, a bond.

She had gotten the tears under control, but she was still trembling.

But she realized the trembling wasn't from her memories now. It was from an awareness of how close he was, an awareness that a perilous electricity was shimmering in the air between them.

She put her hand on his chest, not to push him away, but to feel the beat of his heart beneath her fingertips, and then to guide herself in closer. She leaned toward him.

He did not seem surprised.

No, it was as if he had been waiting for this. As if this moment was inevitable between them. She lifted her chin and touched his lips with her own.

That destructive force that she had been trying so hard

to hold at bay—hope—crashed in around her like the sea waves exploding over rocks.

His lips carried the sharp tang of tequila. They were soft and the furthest thing from soft at the same time.

Alexandra was sure she had only had half a glass of wine, and yet the taste of his lips made her feel utterly intoxicated, as if she was swan-diving into a star-studded black night and had no idea where she would land when she finished dropping through the darkness.

She felt weak in a way that made her welcome weakness, even though she knew that the world required her to be strong.

His hands tangled in her hair, and he claimed her mouth completely. And she let him. She welcomed him.

And as their encounter deepened, she was so aware this was not the clumsy, driven passion of youth. As much as it was spontaneous, it was also a conscious choice between two adults.

The kiss was mature, like spirits aged in an oak cask, rich and deep with a hint of darkness. It was exhilarating, and she rose to it, her every nerve end singing.

It penetrated her awareness that her phone was announcing an incoming call. She didn't care. It could wait.

Except, annoyingly, the sound penetrated the deliciously altered state she was in, like an alarm bell stridently announcing danger. Didn't that distinctive *boing, boing, boing* belong to someone?

Someone important?

She drew herself away from his kiss.

"Shelley," she announced out loud, and saw the instant fear of a man who had lost everything once already cross his face.

Alexandra wrenched herself completely away from Drew and pawed through her bag for the phone.

She put it on speaker. "Shelley? Is everything okay?"

"There's just a little problem at the party."

"Is Genevieve all right?" Drew asked, despite Shelley's relaxed tone. He went from seductive kisser to protective daddy in the blink of an eye, and there was something extraordinarily compelling about that transformation.

"Oh, yeah, nothing urgent. No blood, hysterics, tears or bruises. But Genevieve has retreated to the upstairs linen closet. She would like her daddy to come get her now." Shelley's tone was amused rather than concerned.

"What brought that on?" Alexandra asked, worried.

"Apparently Macy told her she doesn't like Bonnie dolls. A catastrophe in a four-year-old's world."

"Tell her Daddy is on the way," Drew said.

He got up, dropped some bills on the table and reached for her jacket and helped her slip it on before he put on his own. That gesture made her aware there was no point in offering to pay her share.

His smile was self-deprecating. "So much for the confident little girl who feels safe and secure in the world," he said.

"You're way too hard on yourself about this parenting gig."

"Easy for you to say. It's not your kid crying in the closet." He started humming. "It's my party and I'll cry if I want to..."

She smiled at him, and they went out into the crisp night. Somehow everything seemed more vibrant than it had before they had gone into the pub. Before he had kissed her.

She felt like a princess, awaking from a long sleep. The autumn night seemed alive. The air tingled in her nose and throat and lungs. Leaves, enchantingly outlined in gold under the streetlights, shivered on their branches.

"She's four," Alexandra said, "and I assume she's not used to being around a ton of people. She wants her daddy. You're what makes her world safe and secure."

He looked at her, and she saw she had managed to validate him in an area where he felt insecure. He looked like the kind of man—confident, successful, in charge—who was probably very unaccustomed to insecurity in his world. Being a daddy had humbled him.

His hand closed around hers, and the feeling of the night being alive intensified as they walked through it hand in hand.

Also intensified was Alexandra's awareness that a man like this could set back the recovery of a wounded heart.

Could she enjoy this moment and not ask for others? Maybe she should enjoy this moment all the more for knowing she would have to let go of this man after tonight.

Of course, they would still have to discuss some details about Ivy and Sebastian's wedding. Of course, she would still have to confer with him.

But the dreams that had been let loose with that kiss— all her wild need, and her desire so long bottled up, so long seen for what it was, disruptive and dangerous—needed to be put back in their vessel.

Before it was too late. Before they passed the point of no return.

She slipped her hand from his as they approached the house. There was no need to add to the complexity of this with family conjecture, since she had already decided it must end before it started.

Really, it was akin to stamping out a little tiny spark before it was allowed to become something else.

A single spark of passion had ruined Alexandra's whole life once already, burned it to the ground. She, of all people, should know the danger of playing with fire. And there was no denying it was fire she had felt when she had invited Drew's lips to her own.

By the time they arrived at the house, Genevieve had emerged from the closet. In fact, she danced to the door, her face alight as Drew walked in.

"Look, Daddy, I have a Bonnie doll."

Genevieve looked like a different child to the one who had been dropped off. Her sparkly tights had a rip in them, and her dress was crumpled and had a cake stain on it. Her hair was also a mess under a princess party hat.

Though her cheeks had tear streaks on them, she looked all better now. Still, in retrospect, Alexandra thought, she might not have been quite ready for this rambunctious crew.

Not that that was her call to make! She had better be very careful before playing mommy without an invitation.

Did she want that invitation?

"So I see," Drew said, his lips twitching, thankfully with amusement and not horror. "How did you happen to get a Bonnie doll?"

"I gave it to her."

"This is my niece Macy," Alexandra said, scooping her cowboy outfit–clad niece up into her arms and kissing her plump cheek. "Macy, this is Drew. He's Genevieve's daddy."

"She was in the closet," Macy reported. "So I went and got her. I told her she could have the doll if she came out."

"That was very nice," Drew told her.

"Not really. I don't like dolls."

Macy was apparently impervious to the fact that her rejecting the gift might have driven poor Genevieve into the closet in the first place. For someone who had been contemplating the role of mommy just moments ago, this was one of those times where it was a relief to be an auntie. Shelley could deal with the etiquette of rejected gifts.

Or maybe she had—maybe that was why the peace offering in the closet had been made. And it had worked, too.

"Macy's my best friend now," Genevieve announced solemnly. "We're coming here for trick or treat, aren't we, Macy?"

Macy scrambled down out of her aunt's arms. "Yup," she cried.

Shelley came across the living room. She looked nearly as disheveled as Genevieve.

"Yes, please come," she said. "It's a block party. So much fun. Everybody dresses up. Adults and kids. I think they've booked some kind of spooky bouncy tent."

"A spooky bouncy tent," Genevieve breathed excitedly. "Daddy, we'll come, won't we?"

He hesitated. His eyes found Alexandra's. In them, she saw the same struggle she was experiencing.

Did they let this spark find the life it was looking for, or did they squash it out, firmly, before it took hold?

But there were larger questions.

To be open to life, or not?

Looking into the depth of his eyes, other questions rushed at her. To be open to the unexpected? To be fully alive, instead of just going through the motions?

She had lost that baby such a long time ago. How long was she going to protect herself from pain? How long was she going to live in fear of making a mistake? How long was she going to be controlled by the past?

Maybe it had been too long already.

"It might be nice to come to a party I didn't plan," she said tentatively.

"Are we going to come, Daddy?"

Drew didn't look at Genevieve. He looked at her. Long

and hard, his gaze opening a world of possibility that had been completely closed to her.

"We would love to come," he said.

Suddenly, Alexandra felt frightened. What was she doing? She was so rarely impulsive, and she reminded herself that she almost always regretted it when she was.

On the other hand, she had weeks to think about this. To back out. There was no reason he and Genevieve couldn't come without her.

Though she knew they wouldn't.

When had she become this person? So eager to protect her heart, she would keep a little girl—one who had lost her mother—from knowing the joy of community? Of family?

"I would love to come too," Alexandra said.

But if it was about Genevieve, if she was being as altruistic as she wanted to be, why was she already thinking of her costume?

She already knew it wasn't going to be Little Bo Peep or Little Red Riding Hood or any of the things anyone would expect of her.

Drew sat in the deep, luxurious leather rear seat of the car he had called. The company knew him, and so they had sent a car with a child seat. Genevieve, new doll clutched against her, had fallen asleep almost as soon as she had been strapped in.

Her hair was matted and stuck to her forehead and her cheek. Her dress was wrinkled and stained. The little stocking had a rip in it. A funny little smile played across her slack, chocolate-stained mouth.

He remembered her declaration that the house they were visiting was a *real* house.

And that's what she looked like right now. A *real* little girl. The observation stung.

He turned his thoughts away from his failings as a parent, to the woman who had said he was too hard on himself. He'd offered to drop Alexandra somewhere, but she had said no, she lived just around the corner.

It must have shown in his face that he didn't want her walking home alone, because she had laughed and said she would stay at the party until her brother got home, and then he would insist on walking her to her place.

One kiss.

And Drew was feeling protective of her.

One kiss.

And he felt restless.

One kiss.

And he felt hungry for more.

One kiss.

And he felt helpless to say no to that party invitation. But was it really the party invitation—and his daughter's excitement about it—that he'd been helpless to say no to?

Or was it the chance to see Alexandra again?

He would put it all from his mind. His biggest responsibility, of course, was Genevieve. His business kept him occupied. Last time they had spoken, Gabe had said that Drew should begin to think about replacing him. It looked as if it was going to be a long haul with his mother, but now Drew realized he welcomed the extra duties to fill up his days. He told himself, firmly, that putting that kiss from his mind was going to be the easiest thing he had ever done.

The car pulled up in front of Parker and Parker. Drew carefully undid the harness of the car seat and hefted his sleeping daughter in his arms.

She nestled against him, a puddle of warmth, boneless. She barely shifted as he made his way, carrying her inside. Genevieve was trusting him completely. To put her needs first. Always.

And what did that mean in terms of that kiss with Alexandra?

Drew realized, irritated, he had managed to put that kiss—the one that was going to be the easiest thing ever for him to forget about—from his mind for all of thirty seconds.

CHAPTER TEN

ON THE DAY of the Halloween block party, Drew stared at himself in the mirror, aghast. He was aware it was possible for a man to push a kiss to the back of his mind, just as he had vowed to do. And yet, still, here he was, being confronted with how that kiss had changed him, regardless of how successful he had been at not thinking about it.

Maybe it shouldn't be as surprising as it was that the—white-hot—meeting of lips had altered him. Heat melted things, after all. But what it seemed to be melting was some barrier around his heart.

He'd sensed it when he started calling Gabe every day, not just to discuss business, but to find out how he was doing. How his mom was doing. He'd sent dinner over for them, twice. He'd also found a rare Webber Morrison session online and sent Gabe the link.

But now the proof of some new and uncomfortable softness confronted him in the mirror.

Naturally, Genevieve had told Miss Carmichael about her new best friend, the *real* house and the invitation to the party.

Miss Carmichael had come to him and offered, shyly, to take care of their costumes, as she helped with costumes for an amateur theater group. She said she could borrow some things and make others.

This was one of the changes to his heart: he saw her differently. In a gentler light than he had before. As a whole person, with a life outside his household. He noticed how young she was. He noticed she'd been crying. It didn't take much prodding of Genevieve to find out there had been a breakup with the boyfriend.

And still, she wanted to make them costumes.

Before the kiss, he wouldn't have noticed a kind of bravery in that. And to be honest, it had been a relief to hand over the whole costume question to someone else, so it was helpful to both of them.

Genevieve was totally enraptured with the whole idea of Halloween. She was no longer a baby, content, as she had been last year, to be stuffed into a coat with bunny ears and taken around to the apartments of a few friends.

No, this year Halloween was taking on a production-like ambience. Genevieve and Miss Carmichael had decided on a Bobo Robbins theme. This was a surprise, as Drew had thought Genevieve would lean more toward princesses. However, Bobo was a cowboy cartoon character—Macy's favorite, apparently—who had a faithful dog, Chance, and a talking owl, Cowly, who rode on his shoulder.

Drew, thankfully, hadn't had to give costume selection another thought. He'd been grateful for the giggles coming from the playroom, paint coming off his daughter at her bath at night. He'd been grateful that there had been no more escape attempts. In fact, Miss Carmichael and Genevieve appeared to be completely bonded over the Halloween project.

Now, his daughter—make that Chance—was dressed in a delightful costume, head to toe fluffy brown curls, a hood with ears, her brows thickened, her nose red and whiskers on her cheeks—and was running around him, barking excitedly.

He was wearing a plaid shirt and an oversize cowboy hat. The plaid shirt had been padded, as it would act as a jacket on a night that had turned quite cold. It made him look quite rotund.

But being fat was nothing on the final piece of the costume. It was a large cardboard box that had been transformed into a horse, the box its body, a cardboard cutout of a neck with a thick wool mane attached. At the end of the neck was a hand-painted horse's head, wild eyes and flaring nostrils, and a surprisingly good facsimile of reins and a bridle.

According to Miss Carmichael's instructions, Drew stepped inside a hole in the top of the horse box and pulled it up. It was held in place around his waist with straps over his shoulders. False human legs, denim-clad and fat as sausages, ended in cowboy boots and stirrups. They had been attached to the outside of the box horse. Two false horse legs dragged along behind the box, and Drew's real legs were the horse's front legs.

It was really an ingenious contraption. And hilarious. A tubby guy in a too-large hat on a comical horse.

It was also completely without sex appeal. He had, without evidence, reached the incorrect conclusion that Genevieve was going to be Bobo Robbins, not him.

Not that he had thought about it, but if he had, he would have cast himself differently. A prince, maybe. Or a pirate.

A dashing and romantic hero who would have made Alexandra's mouth fall open and her eyes darken with lust.

Lust.

Maybe it wasn't too late to pick up a different costume somewhere on their way to the Halloween party. It wasn't that this one wasn't brilliant, it's just that Drew was not sure he was comfortable in a role so without dignity. Plus, this costume was going to attract attention. It would be so much easier to fade into the background as a Count Dracula or King Arthur.

On the other hand, this getup should protect him from anything even remotely lustful. He wouldn't be getting within three feet of another person with his box horse surrounding him like a suit of armor. Sneaking kisses would be out of the question.

He turned to look at Genevieve and Miss Carmichael. As he moved, the crazy legs attached to the horse flopped about madly in their stirrups. The girls were in absolute hysterics.

The new Drew—the one he had not been at the beginning of October—cast dignity aside in favor of that squealing laughter.

He rocked the box up and down as if the horse was bucking, and he held on to his hat as if he was in danger of being thrown off. He was rewarded with more laughter. He was aware Genevieve was looking at him with total delight and surprise.

Had he really become so dull? The dad who was absolutely no fun to be around? Maybe that's why Christmas in Lapland had been such a bust.

"Let's go, Chance," he said to Genevieve.

It was then he noticed that Miss Carmichael was dressed as the third member of the trio, the owl, Cowly.

He was aware, again, that the man he had been at the beginning of this month might not have noticed the intricacies of a costume she must have worked on for hours. He might not have noticed her eagerness, that she was just barely more than a child herself, still excited about Halloween.

"What are your plans for tonight?" he asked.

"Oh, I don't have any. Not really. I just made the costume for me because it was fun. It made Genevieve happy."

He thought of the giggles that had been coming from the playroom, a tired, contented little girl in the tub at night, the water turning blue and pink as the paint sluiced off her. It had, indeed.

That's what thawed hearts did. They made other people happy.

"Would you like to join us, Miss Carmichael?" he asked.

Her face lit up as if he had showered her with stardust and diamonds. That's what thawed hearts did. They felt the radiant warmth of moments when they gave other people joy. The feeling was addictive.

"It's Lila," she said shyly.

When they went outside, it was damp and foggy. Miserable.

"Perfect for Halloween," Lila told Genevieve, and his daughter beamed.

The car was waiting, and he removed his horse and it was placed carefully in the trunk. He got in beside the girls and gazed out at the New York skyline, just beginning to be smudged with the late-fall darkness.

What would having a heart this open mean around Alexandra? It was all her fault that he was a different man than he had been a month ago, and to be honest, he did not know if he was resentful or grateful.

He did not know if accepting it was bravery or cowardice.

A two-block area had been closed to vehicular traffic, and the car dropped them at the corner.

"Can we go find Macy?" Genevieve asked, getting out of the car and hopping from foot to foot.

"Of course."

There were a lot of people here. He wanted to tell Miss Carmichael—Lila—to keep a close eye on Genevieve, but when he saw her hand close firmly around her small charge's, he knew it wasn't necessary.

They took off into the crowd and were soon lost in the fog.

He sighed, and his breath made a cloud in front of his mouth. He was glad that Genevieve's outfit looked warm and was thankful his own plaid shirt was padded against the cold. No, he didn't have to worry about Genevieve with Miss Carmichael. She had thought of everything.

The driver came around and opened the trunk and took out the horse. Drew carefully climbed in it, put the straps over his shoulders and gathered the reins.

"I must say, sir, best costume ever."

"I have to agree," he said.

"Never mind," the driver said hoarsely. "I've changed my mind."

Drew turned in the direction the driver was looking. His mouth fell open. The damp mist parted a bit, and he saw a vision in a hooded cloak was standing a few feet away and appeared to be watching them. She stood, frozen like a deer in headlights, as if at one move, she would turn and run.

Instead, she reached up and pulled the hood down. It took him a very long thirty seconds before he realized it was Alexandra.

And he was not sure he had any defenses against *that*.

Nor was he sure he wanted any.

He lifted a hand in greeting, and she came toward him. Alexandra was dressed as the sexy seductress from the hugely popular movie *Kiss of Death*. She was wearing a heavy black cape, fur lining the hood. As she came toward him, the cape swung open and revealed the blood-red dress underneath it. The dress clung to her like a film and had a plunging neckline. It was very short and revealed a stunning length of legs, clad in black fishnet stockings.

Her makeup, in keeping with the character, was exaggerated, but it made her eyes look as dark and as sensuous as a spell, and her lips look as tempting and juicy as a poison apple. Her hair had been braided into a single thick plait that fell over her right shoulder and made his fingers itch to unweave it.

People who believed in such things said that each good turn you did for another returned to you, a karmic gift.

He had not expected any kind of return when he'd invited Lila to come, but now he saw how that spontaneous invitation to the young nanny was returning something extraordinary to him.

He was free of all the normal Halloween responsibilities any dad might feel. Free to see where an evening with Shanna, the Sorceress, would lead.

The word *lust* appeared inside his head, bright as a sign made of neon tubing.

He was momentarily taken aback by it. He hadn't known her long, but certainly long enough to know she wasn't that kind of a woman. She had been consistently professional. He had seen how wholesome her family was. She had revealed to him she held a reservoir of pain at least as large as his own.

Except then they had shared that kiss.

That had changed everything.

And maybe Alexandra Harris was not the same woman she had been a month ago, either. Because Drew was pretty sure *that* woman would have never worn a dress—even if it was a costume—like the one she had on tonight.

If Drew hadn't spotted her, Alexandra might have, at the last moment, changed directions to run home to find a different costume. How had he managed to find a costume that was so lighthearted and *fun*? She had managed the exact opposite.

Though "managed" was a bit of an exaggeration. It had

been a super-busy week. She'd had another meeting with Ivy, and she had also met with Hailey and seen samples of the first flowers for the wedding. Added to that, she'd put together the final details of a Halloween wedding, which had, thankfully, gone off without a hitch an hour ago.

With everything going on, however, she hadn't had time to plan a costume, and so she'd had to run into a store and grab the first costume she saw. Well, not exactly the *first* one, which had been Little Red Riding Hood. Instead, she'd looked right past that one and had gravitated to a rack of rather sexy items, no doubt spurred on by a kiss that she hadn't quite been able to put out of her mind for weeks, not matter how hard she worked, no matter how deeply she immersed herself in her world of creating perfect days and dreams come true for others.

She had almost lost her nerve when she'd first seen herself in this outfit, but then she'd talked herself into it. She didn't have time to change it. Now, she wished she'd slapped together something out of her own closet.

She had jeans and an old cowboy hat. Wouldn't that have looked cute with what he had on?

It would have been perfect. Safe, but perfect. On the other hand, something flashed through his eyes, white-hot, as he took in her costume. She was pretty sure a pair of jeans wouldn't have done that.

"That is the best costume ever," Alexandra told him.

"I disagree," he said, his voice gruff. "Yours is the best costume ever."

"Definitely yours, miss," the driver said, then ducked his head and slid into the car.

"You look like someone else completely," Drew said.

That's what she had told herself when she had looked in the mirror and seen the look was a little more over-the-top sexy than she had guessed it would be when she grabbed it off the rack.

Don't be chicken, Alexandra had told her reflection sternly. Wasn't that what wearing a costume was about? Giving yourself permission to be someone else?

Now, she wondered if a chicken might not have been better.

"Well," she said, "You don't exactly look like yourself, either. A perfect Bobo Robbins."

"You're familiar with my character," he said with a roll of his eyes.

"With the number of nieces and nephews I have? Of course. Who made it? It's brilliant."

She debated leaning in and giving him a kiss—just a little hello buss on the cheek—but she had chosen a crazy shade of red lipstick, and it would leave a mark on his cheek.

The thought of marking him—look, he's *mine*—had an odd appeal. Until she reminded herself she was related to half the people in this throng, and they would be making deliriously hopeful note of such things. They were going to make note of her outfit, too. She definitely should have thought this through more carefully.

And yet, after that kiss they had shared the last time they'd met, she wasn't feeling like she wanted to be careful. Was she feeling a little deliriously hopeful herself? For a repeat of last time?

Ridiculous.

"It turns out Miss Carmichael—Lila—helps make costumes for a theater group."

"Oh! I saw her and Genevieve race by me. Genevieve barely acknowledged me, though. She was rushing off to find Macy."

"Ah, Macy. I think there is a little case of hero worship

unfolding there. I have her to thank, in a roundabout way, for the costume."

"You don't seem that enthused about your costume," she said. "And it's perfectly adorable."

"Do I look like a man who wants to be perfectly adorable?"

Her eyes drifted to his lips. "No," she admitted.

"I had pictured something a little more dashing. Or even sinister. Can you picture me as a villain?" He twirled an imaginary mustache and lowered his brow at her.

She could, indeed, picture him as a villain, the bad boy—the gunslinger, the pirate, the jewel thief—who created unwanted stirrings of longing in the pure, sweet hearts of every single good girl he ever met.

CHAPTER ELEVEN

"I DON'T CARE for villains," Alexandra told Drew primly, though in truth she had never considered whether she liked them or not. In the context of *him*, it was an absolute lie.

"Oh. Villains are out, then."

As if her opinion really mattered to him. Why would that create such an unexpected feeling of warmth in the region of her heart?

"Superman," he suggested. "A sheikh. A prince. How could that girl miss my potential so completely?"

As he said it, she could picture him in each of those roles *completely*. Unfortunately.

"She did what would make Genevieve happy," Alexandra said. "You have yourself a gem of a nanny there."

"Thanks to your intervention. So, no more complaining or conjecturing. I promise I will appreciate my costume completely." He pretended the horse was rearing up and swept off his hat to her.

Alexandra laughed, even as she made note of how dashing he was even in the silly costume. In fact, Alexandra thought it was probably a very good thing for both of them that his costume did not show off his full masculine charm.

They were going to put that kiss behind them. Become friends. Enjoy a really fun night with no strings and no complications. She couldn't even remember the last time she'd just given herself over to having lighthearted fun. She was pretty sure he couldn't, either.

Kisses, she reminded herself, were complications of the worst variety.

He pretended the horse was getting away from him, sidling sideways. She laughed more, and so did he, and it boded well for the evening.

They explored the block party. And it *was* fun. There was almost a giddiness to them, as if they were two children let loose at a country fair. Every house looked as if it had tried to outdo its neighbors with decorations. There were gravestones in front yards and skeletons hanging from roof peaks. There were inflatable werewolves and witches. The mistiness of the night was a perfect backdrop for all the spookiness.

They stopped at a bonfire, where there were vats of hot chocolate, hot dogs and freshly made candy and caramel apples. They admired costumes and were admired. Hordes of screaming, costumed children ran by them with loot bags filled with candy. Occasionally they would catch sight of Genevieve and Macy, still with Lila Carmichael.

They watched people bob for apples and each took a few blindfolded swipes at a huge pumpkin piñata. There were a couple of game booths raising money for charity, and despite how difficult it was for him to get his costume close to the counters, they played whack-a-witch, beanbag toss and spin-the-wheel.

Drew won Alexandra the homeliest stuffed toy she had ever seen, a plush warty toad. Winning it probably cost him the equivalent to a month's rent for her, but it wasn't the expense that made her aware she was going to treasure it forever. It was his tongue caught between his teeth in concentration—it was the fact that he wanted it so badly *for her.*

They ran into her sister, Heather, and her brother, Shaun, shepherding kids with pillowcases already filled with candy from house to house. Thankfully, introductions were brief. It looked as if Shaun desperately wanted to interrogate Drew, but there was too much chaos going on around them to encourage conversation.

Finally, just as the mist was turning to rain, they found themselves at the promised bouncy tent. It was filled with shrieking pint-size superheroes and ghosts, princesses and space creatures.

Shelley and Lila were outside it, and Macy and Genevieve were inside, holding hands, jumping facing each other.

"I'm going to take them home after this," Shelley told Drew and Alexandra. "They're just at that turning point—happiness to hysteria."

"*All* kids reach that turning point?" Drew asked.

"You poor man," Shelley said. "Of course they do. Usually once a day."

"Oh."

"It's not a failure on your part, believe me. Anyway, I'll grab them and put on a movie at home. I think they'll probably both be sleeping in minutes. Drew, you can come get her when you're ready to go." She looked from him to Alexandra. She looked at how Alexandra was dressed, and how she was clutching the toad. "Or you can leave her with me for the night."

Alexandra felt a Shanna the Sorceress desire to make her sister-in-law, who was being embarrassingly obvious about her hopes, disappear in a puff of smoke.

"I shouldn't impose on you. I should take her home—"

"No. Go enjoy."

He honestly looked like he did not know how. But after a moment, he said to Shelley, "Let me leave you my number, in case Genevieve wants to say good night."

After he had given out the phone number, he turned to his nanny. "Miss Carmichael—Cowly—can I arrange a car for you?"

She waved her hand. "No. I'm great. I'll figure it out, but thanks, Mr. Parker."

"Well," he said, looking at Alexandra as they moved off. "This is unexpected. For the first time in four years, I find myself one hundred percent responsibility-free. Have you any ideas?"

It was starting to pour rain and it was putting an obvious damper on the party, not to mention his poor cardboard horse.

Alexandra was shocked to find herself leaning close to him. She whispered in his ear, "Well, yes, I do."

He raised an eyebrow at her.

"Would you like to come to my place?" Alexandra blushed. Did it sound as if she was propositioning him? Along with her rather outrageous outfit, who could blame him if he reached that conclusion? She could feel her cheeks turning red. Maybe she had on enough makeup that he wouldn't notice.

"I always watch a spooky movie on Halloween," she said hastily. Her tone was almost defensive.

He cocked his head at her. Okay, it was probably more than obvious that she—the artistic type and wedding planner—did not lean to this kind of movie.

"Just…just on Halloween," she stammered. "And I live close to here. In case Genevieve needs you."

He was smiling slightly, as if he was enjoying her embarrassment.

"I just meant," she stumbled on, "it's starting to rain quite hard. It's going to ruin your costume."

"We can only hope!"

"But that's all Lila's hard work!"

"You are intent on showing me how to be a better man, aren't you?"

"Not really," she said. And then realized that could be interpreted incorrectly, too. Nice girl inviting bad boy back to her place. On Halloween. To watch scary movies. Which could lead to clutching at his arm and hiding her head against his chest.

Her eyes skittered to his chest. At least, for someone less disciplined than herself, of course.

"And yet I seem to be becoming a better man, despite myself." He said that almost to himself, then shook it off.

"I'll make popcorn," she said hastily, as if that somehow legitimized the whole invitation.

"Good idea," Drew said. "To get out of the rain. And to still be relatively close to Genevieve."

No, it wasn't. It was a bad idea. And like most bad ideas, it was nearly irresistible. He fell into step beside her, the horse's poor head drooping in the rain. The Halloween celebration was winding down quickly now that it was past the bedtimes of most of the little ones and the rain was starting in earnest. Teenagers were trying to set off fireworks, but the weather was not cooperating and their efforts fizzled weakly.

By the time they got to her place, a turn-of-the-century brownstone, they were both soaked. He carefully took off the somewhat wilted horse and set it in her narrow front hallway to dry. She took off the cloak.

The dress had been clingy before. Now it was damp and downright sinful. He suddenly didn't look like he thought this was such a good idea after all. She reached into her coat cupboard and pulled out a ratty old sweater, which she threw over the damp dress.

"Do you…do you want something?" she stammered.

His eyes went to her lips and then skittered away. They

both wanted something. Oh, this had been such a bad idea. Why did she feel on fire?

"To put on?" she clarified hastily. "Your shirt is soaked. Not that I have any men's clothes—"

She was blushing again.

"Sure, if you've got something that might fit me, that would be great."

He stood in the hallway, dripping on the floor, while she went and looked. She found an extra-large T-shirt that she sometimes used as summer pajamas.

The hallway seemed very cramped as she handed him the shirt. Was that steam rising off him? Or was it rising off her?

"What can I get you?" she asked, her tone strangled, backing out of the entrance cubicle as he began to undo the buttons of his soggy shirt. "Coffee? Wine? Soda? A Rockingbird?"

He laughed. He had laughed a lot tonight, and she loved the sound of it. She suspected his laugh—and the way he looked when he laughed—had a lot to do with that feeling of fire burning inside her. With all that heat, no wonder her tiny front entryway was getting steamy.

"I've sworn off Rockingbirds. For life. Whatever you think goes with popcorn will be great."

What a wise choice, she thought, given how much she loved the sound of his laughter. No alcohol. No lowering of inhibitions.

"Soda it is." She left the front vestibule quickly. She ordered herself not to look back. And yet, she did. She caught a glimpse of the absolute male perfection of his naked back as he turned away from her and stripped off that wet shirt.

He was not perfectly adorable anymore. Just perfect.

His shoulders were wide, and his back was broad and sculpted. She loved the composition of it, the slight jut of back ribs, how his back narrowed where it disappeared into his pants. His chilled skin was marbled with goose bumps.

The artist in her appreciated him and wanted to draw him, just like that. Standing there, shirtless, light spilling over his shoulders, unaware his masculine beauty was being watched.

No, it was more than wanting to draw him. She wanted to touch him. To explore his skin with her fingertips, to *know* the surface of him completely. Her awareness was so sharp it felt like hunger, and it rippled through her.

As if he could feel her energy vibrating through the air, he glanced over his shoulder and caught her staring at him.

She waited to turn into a pillar of salt, the way that women did when they were caught looking at things they weren't supposed to look back at.

She felt like a lot of things, but a pillar of salt was not one of them! She scurried into the bathroom and washed most of the Shanna the Sorceress makeup off her face. Then she went to her tiny kitchen and busied herself making popcorn. Her hands were trembling as she poured kernels into hot oil, and it wasn't all because she had gotten too cold on the walk home.

"Nice place," he called to her.

She knew it was a nice place. Why did it matter so much what he thought of it? And yet, it did matter what he thought of it, and she liked that when she came back in with the tray of popcorn and drinks, instead of sitting down, he wandered around looking at the art on her walls.

"You can tell an artist lives here."

"I'm a wedding planner, not an artist."

"Humph," he said. Why did it feel as if he was seeing who she really was?

"I like the way everything is put together. There's a

sense of *you* in this space. Of home. I don't think I've ever quite achieved that."

He looked as if he thought he'd revealed too much about himself, and maybe he had, because it didn't really matter how much success a person had achieved—it didn't matter if they lived in New York's answer to a royal palace—if they didn't have a place that felt like home.

"Did you do these?" Drew paused in front of a series of paintings that she'd done at the family summer place when she was young.

"Yes."

The T-shirt was too small for him. It pulled tight over his shoulders, his biceps, the depth of his chest. Her awareness of him felt as if it would shatter her.

"They're really good," he said, sinking down on one end of the sofa. "I like the one of the dog on the dock, snoozing."

"Thank you." Her voice was normal, as if she wasn't vibrating with tension. She should have taken the chair across from him. She didn't. It was practical. She wouldn't be able to see the movie from the chair.

She set down the tray and took the other end of the sofa. "We had a cottage when I was growing up. We'd take out the canoe, and the dog would wait for us to get back."

The couch was extra tiny, because of the space.

A love seat, really. Who named these things?

"Let's put on the movie!" she said.

They perused a number of titles and picked one that sounded the worst: *Hatchets for Halloween*.

Alexandra promised herself she would not be scared. She would just see the silliness of it. She vowed off any bicep clutching or head burrowing.

At first, it was funny. They laughed at the poor acting and the terrible premise. They pointed out the outrageous choices and improbable setups.

But then, despite all the flaws, it was scary and she yelped with fright in spite of herself. Somehow, the popcorn bowl was moved, and Drew was right beside her, his arm over her shoulder. Somehow, she was burrowing under his arm and hiding her eyes.

"You know," he said, an hour later, when the movie had deteriorated into a bloodbath of not-very-good special effects, "I'm not married to it, if you want to shut it off. I'm afraid you're going to have bad dreams."

She shut off the movie very quickly. The silence after all the shrieking on-screen was a relief. She waited for him to move his arm off her shoulder, but he didn't.

It felt so good to be cuddled under his arm that she didn't move, either. She savored the sense of being cared about, being protected in some delightful way.

He leaned his head on the back of her sofa and closed his eyes. "Thank you for tonight. I feel like it was my first real Halloween."

She let her eyes wander the column of his throat, rest on the hump of his Adam's apple, move on to the tantalizing texture of whiskers thickening on his face. Very villain-like, those whiskers. Though not anything like the villain in the movie, thank goodness.

"Your first true Halloween as a daddy?" she asked, trying to clarify what he had just said. "It was probably the first year of real trick or treating for Genevieve, wasn't it?"

CHAPTER TWELVE

LET HER BELIEVE THAT, Drew ordered himself. But he'd noticed, around Alexandra, his customary self-discipline fled him. "I meant for me."

There it was, Drew thought. Even though Alexandra had covered up the sorceress dress, he felt as if he was under a spell. When he'd pulled on that shirt in her front hallway and turned and seen her looking at him, it had felt as if the bottom was falling out of his world.

The whole evening had been so laughter-filled, carefree. There had been a feeling in the air, a community celebrating. Families being together. Loving being together.

Her house intensified that feeling. *Home.* That series of paintings called to something in him. The ramshackle cottage with a hammock on the porch. A clothesline, strung tree to tree, with colorful, worn towels hanging on it. An old, loyal dog who waited for the family.

Of course Alexandra had grown up like this. She had grown up in a neighborhood that held Halloween parties. And knew what to do to make Christmas magic. They probably had Easter egg hunts, too.

An awareness crystallized in Drew. All his life, he had longed for *this*. It felt like the weakness, left unguarded, would destroy him. It seemed to him it was a defect, that he could bring nothing to her world. She needed to know *all* of him if they were going to follow that look that had passed between them when he had stripped off his wet shirt in her hallway.

If they were going to follow what he felt with her trembling, and letting out little yelps of fear, and hiding under his arm from that dreadful movie.

She made him feel like a man in a way he had not for a long, long time.

"What do you mean?" she asked uncertainly. "Didn't you have Halloween at the orphanage?"

"I said I was an orphan," he told her. "I never said I grew up in an orphanage."

"Oh. No, you didn't. For some reason, I just assumed."

"I dreamed of an orphanage when I was a kid. I thought it would be full of other children. Rambunctious activity. Hijinks. Friends. Coconspirators in escape attempts. Maybe we'd even all be conscripted into a band of thieves by a Fagin-like character."

Did he sound self-pitying? He did not want to say these things. Why was he saying these things? Her nearness was drawing a long-ago whimsy from him. Her space— so cozy, though maybe a touch too warm—was drawing secrets from him.

You had to be careful around a woman like her. He knew that. And yet he could not summon caution.

"My parents died in a car accident when I was seven. What I remember the most was how they were with each other. Always laughing. Touching. Exchanging looks. It was the kind of love that excluded everything—and everybody—else.

"My dad had a sister who took me. My aunt Sarah. She was older than him. A college professor in a small town. She didn't believe in *nonsense*. Which included Christmas, Halloween and Easter."

He smiled and could feel the faint bitterness in it as he imitated her voice. "'Bunnies and bearded men. What are we teaching children?' She had her own ideas about what children should learn. I didn't really have friends my own age. I had her friends. I was included in adult discussions. It had its good points, but—"

"But it's horrible being treated like an adult when you're a kid," she said firmly.

"Emily's childhood was even worse than mine. She *was* raised in an orphanage. In Eastern Europe. Together, we thought we'd find our way. We wanted to give Genevieve the childhood neither of us ever had. We thought we could fix it somehow for the next generation."

"You can," she whispered.

He opened his eyes. She had crept very close to him. He could feel her warmth. He felt like a sailor who had been lost at sea and finally spotted a lighthouse.

"I can't," he said. "I realize that now. I realized it tonight. I don't know the first thing about it. I don't even know how to have fun. There's something else my aunt believed."

Don't say it. He begged himself not to say it.

"She believed love caused the worst kind of pain. I think she adored my father. I think she felt excluded from that love he had for my mom. As if she had lost him. And, in some way, I think she felt their love was responsible for their deaths. My dad, her younger brother, was the only light in her small, dark little world.

"But, still, when I met Emily, I thought my aunt was wrong. So wrong. She would look at us together, and instead of being happy for us, she'd give a warning—*people can love too much.* She died, of old age and crankiness, before Emily did. Before," he said softly, "she ever found out how right she was."

"She wasn't right," Alexandra said.

He opened his eyes, expecting to feel ashamed of all he had just said, like someone who blurts out their life story to a stranger on a bus.

But when he looked at her, it didn't feel as though she was a stranger. It felt as if he knew her. It felt as if some burden that he had carried alone was suddenly lighter. Was that fair to Alexandra? To lighten his burden at her expense?

But there was something fierce in her as she gazed steadily back at him. Something compelling. Something a man could lean toward, grab, hang on to.

At some point, he wasn't sure when, she had washed all that makeup off. Incredibly, she was more a sorceress without it.

"She wasn't right about anything," Alexandra said, not the same woman who had been hiding under his arm a little while ago. She was strong now, like a warrior, sure of herself. "Not about loving too much. Not about everything fun being nonsense."

Her fierceness was like a warm light flickering on a cold night. He still had his arm around her shoulder. He was suddenly so aware of how she fit against him, how *right* it felt where their bodies were pressed together, side by side.

He relished the warmth of her like a man who had lost his way on a bitter night, when the cold was killing, and who had been so close to giving up hope.

When her lips touched his, there was nothing fun about it. Nothing at all. He felt everything that had been frozen in him shatter. The layers of protection around him had felt so strong, so impenetrable. Now he saw that what he had considered to be a fortress had really only been the thinnest layer of ice. It fell away from him in fragile, broken shards.

His hands found the thick plait in her hair, and he did what he had wanted, at some primal level, to do all night. He removed the band from the end of it and then inserted his fingers deep into the plaits and tugged softly as he ran his hands down the length of her hair. The plait dissolved. Her hair was wavy from it, and it fell, freed, in a magnificent wave to the luscious swell of her breast.

He accepted the invitation of her lips with all the desperation, all the urgency of a man saved from a cold and lonely death.

In exploring the softness of her lips, the moist, warm cavern of her mouth, a new awareness exploded within him.

Drew didn't just want to live. He didn't just want to go through the motions, of breathing in and out, of getting up each day, of trying to be a great dad, of trying to figure out what was best for his little girl.

He wanted to be alive.

He tangled with her: his hands in her hair, his tongue with her tongue, his body up against hers. He reveled in how, even as they fit so perfectly together, there were magnificent contrasts between them. Soft. Hard. Smooth. Jagged. Gentle. Rough.

For one brief moment in time, he was just a man. Primitive. Wanting what she offered. No, more. Needing.

His world became only sensation. Only him. And only her. The rest of the world at bay, outside this white-hot circle they had created.

She took his hand and gently guided it to the end of that cascading wave of hair, to her breast beneath it. The white-hot heat intensified. An inferno that could consume them both.

He could feel the beat of her heart and the whisper of her breath. He looked into the soft suede brown of her eyes and saw the tender, fierce invitation there.

But then, something penetrated it all. A whisper. A reminder he did not have the luxury—not anymore—of living solely for himself.

He did not have the luxury of wildly pursuing pleasure.

There was a responsibility that outweighed all other considerations. What was best for his little girl?

What did being a daddy require of him? Decency. Honor.

He moved back from Alexandra. He broke the contact between them. It felt like just about the hardest thing he had ever done, especially when she looked at him, her expression dazed, confused, hurt.

This raw passion, this need, felt so right, but it was wrong. It was wrong for her, this woman who had grown up with cottages and Christmas trees, and it was wrong for Genevieve.

This was not what he wanted to teach his daughter about life.

This was not what he wanted her to accept from a man one day. Passion without commitment.

He pulled completely away from Alexandra. He could see he had wounded her. He could see she read it as rejection.

"We can't," he said. "Not like this. Alexandra, we barely know each other."

That felt, weirdly, like a lie. He felt as if he knew Alexandra to the core. As if he knew her heart and her soul. He didn't feel as if he had met her weeks ago, but a lifetime ago. Or maybe even several lifetimes ago, if a person believed in that sort of thing.

She ran a hand through the gorgeous mess of her hair. Her lips were swollen. Her eyes were wide, and if he wasn't mistaken, a tiny diamond of a tear was forming in the corner of one of them.

She looked utterly crushed. This was the danger of not closing doors completely. It could crush her more to follow these threads of desire. It could crush them both.

"We have to slow it down," he said. His voice was ragged with thwarted desire.

But he could not close the door, not completely. He wanted what he had felt when he kissed her. He wanted to feel alive. She did, too. Both of them had been damped down by the burdens they carried for way too long.

Of course there was risk. He knew there was risk. She knew there was risk. You could not get through life without risk.

He threw her the lifeline, the very same way she had thrown it to him.

"You're right, of course," she said, looking deeply embarrassed. "I don't know what I was thinking. As you said, we barely know each other."

"But we can change that," he said softly. It felt like the biggest chance he had ever taken, the most dangerous risk. And the most glorious. "Let's get to know each other."

Her eyes flew to his face, searching.

"Yes, of course," she said, and she moved away from him, shoved her hair out of her face, made a move like she was going to get up.

He wanted to do the honorable thing. But he couldn't quite let go of her, either. He caught her hand and pulled her back to him. He guided her head back onto his chest.

His hand went to the back of her head, as if he could pull her in even closer to his heart. He felt her hair, stroked it, and a finely held tension dissolved slowly in her as her muscles relaxed against him. Her breath grew deep and formed a pool of warmth on his chest.

He knew if he went to sleep like this, he was going to wake up with a sore neck in the morning.

Somehow, it didn't matter. He could not bring himself to move out from under the sweet weight of her.

His eyes closed and he slept the deep, untroubled sleep of a man who knew he might be flawed, and he might make mistakes as a dad every single day, but in the end he had the most important quality of all. He could be trusted to do the right thing.

Alexandra startled awake to a vibration right in her ear. She had been fast asleep on Drew's chest and realized it must be a phone going off in his shirt pocket. And if she was not mistaken, that was a little pool of drool next to said shirt pocket.

As if she didn't have enough to be embarrassed about! She'd lost control last night. Completely. Had she actually taken his hand and… She went crimson just thinking about it.

He's the one who had stopped it. With some variation of *We should just be friends*. Really, it was too embarrassing for words. She should just creep off and lock herself in the bathroom until he was gone.

On the other hand, he was still here. Did that mean something?

He was stirring, and it was too late to make her escape, so she sat up, and with all the dignity she could manage she ran her hand through her hair and acted as if everything was completely fine. It would have been easier if the motion didn't make her think of his hands in it, unweaving the braid.

Out of the corner of her eye, she watched him come to life, disoriented, slapping at his shirt as if the buzzing was coming from a bothersome bee.

His hair, always so tidy, was sticking straight up. His whiskers had darkened around his face.

She wanted to touch both. Which wasn't, apparently, within the parameters of *We have to slow down* and *Let's get to know each other*, which, in the watery light of a new day, she read to mean Drew Parker wanted a platonic relationship, even if he had stayed the night.

With her slobbering away on his chest.

He'd found the phone and scowled at it. "I don't know this number. Damnably early for telemarketers."

Alexandra glanced at his phone. "It's Shelley."

He answered quickly.

"Daddy?" Alexandra could hear Genevieve's voice, excited and happy, no worse the wear for her night away from her dad.

"Good morning, sweetheart."

Did he have to say it like that? As if a light had come on in his world? Alexandra was trying to maintain some of her composure, keep her distance from him. It was much harder to do when witnessing that tenderness for his daughter in his tone.

He laughed. "No, it's not Christmas, it's the day after Halloween."

This was followed by a stream of chatter that Alexandra couldn't make out. Drew shot her a look and put the phone against his chest. "It seems I'm getting an early start on Christmas fails this year."

He put the phone back up to his ear. "Okay, okay," he finally said, exasperated. "It's Christmas. What do you mean, go look?"

He lifted a shoulder at Alexandra. "She says we have to go look out the window. That it's Christmas."

She loved that he was indulging Genevieve. She loved the little girl's insistent belief. She loved that they both got up and went to the window, where the shades were still drawn tight.

"Are you ready?" Alexandra said, fingers on the cord of the blind. Such was the power of Genevieve's belief that Alexandra half expected to see a sleigh and reindeer outside her window.

As she rolled up the shade, her mouth fell open. At some point, last night's rain had turned to snow. The world had turned into a magical place, sparkling, clean, brand-new. She felt Drew looking at her.

She was aware her hair was wavy from the braid and terribly tangled. Her sweater was lumpy. There was a slobber spot on his shirt, and no doubt the pattern of that shirt was imprinted on her cheek. So the look on his face—the look of wonder—had to be because of the snow.

Not because he had woken up beside a woman he wanted to slow things down with.

"It's snowman weather," Alexandra said to keep herself from blurting that he was the most handsome man she had ever woken up beside. Of course, that would be an exclusive club of two, one of those being her ex-husband.

Drew was still holding the phone, and Genevieve heard her. She didn't ask why her daddy was with Alexandra, or even seem surprised by it. Her sigh came over the phone.

"That's *exactly* what I thought," his daughter said dreamily. "Can we build a snowman today?"

"Of course," he said. "I'll be over to get you soon." He disconnected, and his gaze settled on Alexandra. "You'll come, won't you? You probably know a lot more about snowmen than I do."

"It's hardly rocket science," she said, a touch grouchily. She'd only been invited to join them because she might be an expert on something as nonthreatening as building a snowman. It was the type of activity you invited the person you'd relegated as your platonic friend to do with you.

She suddenly felt ashamed of herself as a light bulb went on inside her. The reason for his rejection was obvious to her—Drew Parker still loved his wife.

CHAPTER THIRTEEN

DREW PARKER STILL loved his wife, and he wasn't ready to move on. Alexandra told herself that wasn't something to take personally. If anything, his ability to love so deeply was admirable.

When had she become *this* person, who could look at a single dad, in hopelessly over his head—he already thought he was failing at Christmas—and his adorable little daughter, and say, *If there's nothing in it for me, if you can't love me the way I can love you, forget it*?

Love?

Where had that thought come from? She didn't love him. He was absolutely right. They hadn't known each other long enough for that.

So, she lusted after him.

There it was. The truth—as ugly as a bad Christmas sweater—that he had managed, ever so sensibly, to head off at the pass last night.

If anyone should know what a bad road lust was to follow, it should be her. She needed to be a better person than she had ever been before. She vowed to be. She sucked in her breath. She drew back her shoulders.

She looked at the green of his eyes, and the muss of his hair, and the stubble on his chin. She remembered his breath stirring her hair and his lips laying claim to her.

"I've got a very busy day," she said. What had happened to her vow to be a better person? Life had a way of testing vows.

And then it tested them yet further.

He lifted a shoulder, letting her know whatever worked for her was okay. "Do you mind if I use your shower?"

"No, of course not."

But then when she went into the shower, still steamy from him, it was as if wisps of him were in there with her. His scent, his masculinity—his nudity in this very space just moments ago—floating around her, teasing her, taunting her, tormenting her.

There was no sense trying to look gorgeous for a man who just wanted a platonic relationship, but still, she put on makeup. She blow-dried and curled her hair. She was way too careful in her selection of a creamy angora sweater, flattering narrow-legged pants.

It was good that he'd set a limit, Alexandra thought as she looked at herself in the mirror, her dark hair spilling over her shoulder in sweet contrast to the lightness of the sweater. She recognized that now. But she wouldn't be human if she didn't want Drew Parker to regret it.

A few minutes later, Alexandra took a deep breath as she went up Shaun and Shelley's front step. Drew's hair was still wet from the shower, and he was wearing the same padded plaid jacket he'd been wearing last night.

Her brother and sister-in-law were going to draw inevitable conclusions.

She knocked at the door and went in without waiting for someone to answer it, as was their custom at each other's houses.

Genevieve, in a pair of borrowed pajamas, rocketed across the room, and Drew scooped her up.

"I had the best time *ever*," she squealed.

Alexandra did not miss the slightly pained look on Drew's face at that announcement. He was a man who had, quite literally, gone to the ends of the earth to give his daughter the best time ever. And somehow, she'd had it without him.

Shaun padded out of the kitchen, munching on a piece of toast. He was eyeing Drew with way too avid interest.

"It's not what you think," Alexandra whispered at him in an undertone.

He raised an eyebrow at her and made absolutely no attempt to follow her lead and keep a confidential tone of voice.

"I'll always be your big brother, but honestly, Alex, you're thirty-one years old."

She glanced at Drew and blushed. Good grief. Her brother *wanted* her to have an affair. He'd probably be as disappointed as she was if he knew about the very platonic nature of her evening.

But then she realized, that's not what Shaun wanted. Not at all.

He wanted her happiness.

He wanted it in the same way, she realized, she wanted it for Genevieve and Drew. And for the first time in a long time, for herself, too.

Could her happiness be intertwined with theirs? Even if she had the hots for Drew and he did not seem to return the sentiment? What if, for once in her life, she just took a chance?

She did something she hadn't done, not even once, since she had started her business. She fished her cell phone out of her bag and called the office.

"I won't be in today," she said. She waited for the protests, the questions, the *need*, and felt irritated when it didn't come.

"Did you just take the day off work?" Drew asked, smiling. In that smile, already it felt as if her gamble with happiness was paying off.

"Yes," she said.

"To build a snowman?"

"Yes. This kind of snow has a way of disappearing fast." There. That should show him. It was about the *snow*.

"Then why are you glaring at your phone like that?" Drew asked.

"Quite insultingly, no one seems to think the world of weddings is going to fall apart if I take the day off."

"I guess Miss Carmichael can have the day off, too," Drew said, and then he laughed. "And me."

Happiness gathered in the air and fell toward them, like fairy dust.

An hour later, after going back to her house to retrieve snow clothes, Alexandra stood inside the door of Drew's private quarters, trying not to gawk like a peasant granted entrance to the palace.

He had been right last night when he had confided in her that he had never quite achieved the ambience of home in his space.

It was beautiful, no question, with its gorgeous interiors: soaring ceilings and huge arched windows that looked toward the park. The decor echoed what she had seen in the public spaces of Parker and Parker. It was opulent, with knotted silk rugs, expensive paintings and exquisite furniture. But, even with the odd toy on the floor, it seemed more like a movie set—where the script read, *extremely wealthy person's house*—than a real home, where people laughed and played and spilled juice on the couch.

"Come help me with my snowsuit," Genevieve insisted, tugging on her hand.

"Yes," Drew said, "you go help her. I'll see what I can dig up for snowman accessories."

Genevieve's room was truly lovely: a princess room with a canopied bed and hand-painted bunnies on the walls.

Alexandra remembered Drew saying his aunt had disapproved of *nonsense* in general, and bunnies in particular, and so she loved it that he had given his little girl a room filled with whimsy.

The snowsuit was tucked into a large closet, and Alexandra helped stuff Genevieve into it. She had helped with snowsuits dozens of times with her nieces and nephews, but she was not sure she had ever quite felt like this before.

She had a tenderness for the motherless little girl that made her heart feel as if it was swelling unreasonably.

They met Drew in the hallway. He had found mittens and hats and scarves, both for the snowman and him and Genevieve.

He looked utterly dashing, with a woolen hat pulled on and a scarf wrapped around his throat, like the star of a Christmas movie, or the model for the front cover of a romance novel.

Alexandra didn't think she looked quite as appealing in her padded jacket and bulky snow pants she'd pulled over the pants she had selected so carefully this morning. She might as well not have bothered finding an attractive outfit. Unlike Drew—poster boy for winter fun—she looked ungainly.

"I look like the fat little baker on bread bags," she said.

Genevieve and Drew both eyed her appraisingly. "More like the tire man," Genevieve decided, and Drew's laughter was almost worth sacrificing a sexy look for.

"You have the best front yard in all of New York," Alexandra told Drew once they were in the snow-covered park. Parker and Parker soared behind them, regal, as picturesque as a winter-bound castle in a fairy tale.

"I want a big snowman, Daddy."

"Here," he said, "let me show you how to start it. You make a little ball like this, and then you set it on the ground and roll it."

Just as Alexandra had suspected this morning, the snow was perfect for building snowmen, sticky and wet. Genevieve was soon totally engrossed in the pure magic of creating the snowball. It quickly gained size, leaving a trail of bare ground behind it.

Alexandra and Drew both started their own, but soon the balls were too heavy for one person to move and they had to be on the same team. They joined Genevieve. She had given up and was resting her back against her snowball, eating snow off her mitten.

With Genevieve between Alexandra and Drew, at first they were able to roll it with their hands, but it got even larger and they put their shoulders to it. They grunted. Laughed. Slipped. Fell. And then pushed some more.

Finally, they were all satisfied with the first ball of the snowman. They joined together on the ball Alexandra had started and pushed it.

When it finally rested against the base of the snowman, Alexandra realized the second ball was nearly as big as the first.

The three of them stood there gazing at it.

"I think it might be a little too ambitious," Alexandra offered.

"What does that mean?" Genevieve asked.

"It's too heavy to lift up."

"My daddy's really strong," Genevieve told Alexandra

seriously. "He's probably the strongest man in the world. He can do it."

"Yeah," Drew said, throwing Alexandra a look. He crouched in front of the ball. He put his arms on either side of it, he deepened his squat and then he straightened his legs.

Some of the snow shaved away, but the ball did not move.

Alexandra giggled. She put on her Olympic announcer voice and said solemnly, "And it looks like Parker's first attempt at this weight has failed."

Drew sent her a dark look and squatted again.

In her announcer voice, Alexandra said, "Ignoring the possibility of personal injury, Parker is going to make a second attempt at the lift. Quiet from the audience, please. Intense concentration will be required."

He shot her another dirty look and got himself ready. With a shout worthy of that fictional Olympic weight lifter, he pulled up with all his strength. The ball actually wobbled and lifted a full inch off the ground, but then he lost his grip on it, and staggered backward, falling on his backside. The snowball broke in two. One half crumbled completely.

"Daddy, you broke it," Genevieve said accusingly.

"It looks like a clear disqualification for Parker," Alexandra announced solemnly.

He glared at both of them as he scrambled to his feet and brushed off his rather delectable derriere. For a man who wanted to go slow, he shouldn't be drawing that kind of attention to himself. He twirled what she assumed was an imaginary mustache and gave a villainous and menacing chortle.

Drew leaned back over and scooped up some of the crumbled snow. His eyes fixed on Alexandra, he rotated the snow in his gloved hands, taking his time, shaping it.

Alexandra read his intent. "It's not my fault you were disqualified."

She could clearly see they were past the point of reasoning, so she took off running. The snowball splatted in the middle of her back. Laughing, she turned back to him and made her own menacing face. She scooped up a handful of snow and compacted it into a ball that was satisfyingly hard and should fly like a missile. She ran toward him and let it loose, right at his face. He ducked, and it missed.

She ducked behind Genevieve, using her as a shield but keeping the little girl supplied with snowballs.

Chortling madly, Genevieve threw them at Drew.

"Get him, Gen!" Alexandra called, crouched behind her, peeking out from behind the snowsuit.

How sweet was it that, over and over again, he would come close enough to let Genevieve's snowballs hit him. He put on such a great show of being grievously wounded that soon both Genevieve and Alexandra were helpless with laughter.

He took advantage of their distraction, filling both his arms with snow and coming and dumping the whole load over their heads. They got up and went after him. The snowballs, the yelled threats and the shouts of laughter were flying through the air. They ran through the heavy snow until they were breathless, until Alexandra could run no more.

"I surrender," she gasped, going down on her knees. She held out a snowball in her hands. "Take my sword."

Genevieve swooped in and grabbed it and threw it at her dad. And then, giggling, she came and lay beside her. Drew came and lay on the other side of Genevieve.

"I don't know which I like best," Genevieve said with a sigh. "Halloween or Christmas."

Their breath formed clouds above them, and happiness

shimmered in the air around them. But they were soaked, and lying in the snow wasn't helping. Genevieve shivered.

"Come on," Drew said. "Let's finish the snowman and go for hot chocolate." He got to his feet.

Alexandra closed her eyes before he did the brushing part. When she opened them, he was standing above her. He offered his hand. And she took it.

He pulled her to her feet with just a little more force than was strictly necessary, and she found herself thrust against the full length of him.

She looked up at him. His gaze, despite the playfulness of what they had just been through, was smoldering. He let her go.

"We can't finish him," Genevieve said, inspecting the snowman. "We made him too big."

"Ha!" Drew said, "Your dad may not have brawn, but he has brains."

"What's brawn?" Genevieve asked.

Alexandra thought of the ease with which he had just pulled her to him. She thought of how his naked chest had looked in her front hallway last night. That was brawn, not that she felt inclined to explain it to the child.

Drew went and inspected the snowman. He salvaged the broken ball, pasting it back together with more snow. And then, engineer that he was, he started building a ramp to roll the ball up. Soon, Alexandra and Genevieve had joined him in the engineering project.

But as it turned out, it was completely unnecessary. Three teenage boys came along and, without being asked, picked up the second ball and plopped it easily on top of the first one.

"Utterly humiliating," Drew told her with a self-deprecating grin, watching the boys saunter away. "This is really no way to impress a lady."

He'd had his chance to impress her last night and had taken a miss. But she found she couldn't sacrifice the utter magic of this moment by dwelling on that one. Besides, was there really anything more impressive than watching a man delight his daughter?

CHAPTER FOURTEEN

GENEVIEVE WASN'T TALL enough to help put the head on the snowman, but Drew and Alexandra managed to get it placed and snow-glued it firmly to the second ball. And then Drew put Genevieve on his shoulders and handed her the bag he had brought. She put on the finishing touches: a red licorice cord mouth, a carrot nose, two Oreo cookies for eyes and more for buttons over the round snowman belly.

Drew took off his own hat and scarf and put them on the snowman.

"Those are too good for a snowman," Alexandra protested.

He shrugged. "If they're still here after the snowman melts, I'll come retrieve them. If not, I hope somebody who needs them gets them."

With great foresight, he had brought extra cookies. They stood back munching and admiring the snowman, and then Alexandra took out her cell phone and took pictures of Drew and Genevieve posing proudly with their creation. And then, laughing, they took some selfies before Genevieve insisted on taking one of Drew and Alexandra.

Alexandra stood on one side, turned sideways, lifted one foot and kissed the snowman's cheek.

"Daddy, you do that, too."

And so they both kissed the snowman's cheek. And

then, unexpectedly, with a whoop of pure joy, Drew came and picked Alexandra up and twirled her around, and then kissed her cheek when he set her back down.

It was all very platonic. Not at all worthy of the shiver of awareness that went through her like a bolt of fire.

"Time for hot chocolate?" he asked.

"Yes!" Genevieve said.

"I think I'm too wet," Alexandra said. She was soaked through in the bulky snow pants and jacket, right to her skin, and had already started to shiver.

But was that from being wet, or was it from the light shimmering inside her from the simple joy of being here, together, with Drew and Genevieve, like a small family?

It made her achingly aware that they wanted different things. It was time for her to break away from this before she wanted too much.

"We can go to my place," he said. "I have some dry things you can throw on."

So, there she would be again. Intimate. Sharing his space. His clothes. Watching his lips. Wanting to touch his whiskers. She had to go home. Maybe she'd go home, have a nice hot bath and then drop into the office, after all. She had two weddings coming up this weekend. She also wanted to touch base with Hailey.

"Please, come," Genevieve said.

The plea in her voice was hard to resist. Plus, it was a reminder, that no, they didn't want all different things. They wanted some of the same things. His little girl's happiness, for one.

And so she was just going to have to suck it up to achieve that.

But as they trudged through the wet snow back to his place, Genevieve between them holding their hands and swinging, she was aware she didn't exactly feel the dull weight of a person doing their best to suck it up.

No, she felt the guilty exhilaration of someone who knew it was wrong but still couldn't stop playing with fire.

Genevieve got tired partway back to his place and held out her arms. Drew picked her up easily, and she fell asleep almost instantly.

"I think it's just too much," he told Alexandra. "Christmas falling so closely to Halloween. There's a reason these events have a break between them."

They both laughed.

"I'm going to go take her wet clothes off and put her in something dry. I have a feeling—even though she's way too old for naps—she may be out for the count. Do you still want to come in?"

There was no excuse to say yes. The little girl, whose happiness was in question, was fast asleep. There were weddings to look after, meetings to hold, clients to reassure and coddle.

Alexandra realized she was already in way over her head when she found she could not say no.

He carried Genevieve up the stairs and indicated with a tilt of his chin that Alexandra should follow him.

"You'll find dry clothes in there," he said. "Closet, top drawer, far cabinet."

She went through the door and realized it was his bedroom. It was very grand and very tidy. The bed was huge, masculine, the bedding, in subtle shades of gray, sumptuous.

Trying not to be too much a voyeur, she went through to his closet. It was about the same size as her entire living room. It was a dressing room, really, with built-in cabinets, suits hanging neatly, color-coordinated shirts on top rungs, knife-pressed pants on the bottom ones. There was a huge island in the middle of the room, a stainless-steel washer and dryer tucked under it. She slid open one of the drawers to see rows of silk ties.

It was the space, she realized, of a man with no secrets. No one who had anything to hide would ever send someone into their bedroom. Or their closet. For some reason the fact he was so open endeared him to her.

As if she needed to like him any more.

She went to the far cabinet and slid open the drawer. It felt strangely intimate to shed her wet clothes. She was wet right through to her underwear, and so she took that off, too, and tossed it in the dryer. She put on one of his T-shirts and a pair of flannel pajama bottoms over naked skin. Both items were way too large, but it also felt good to be dry. And to have her skin surrounded by *him*, his scent clinging, ever so subtly, to the clothing.

She padded down the hall and found him just tucking his deeply sleeping daughter into her bed. He picked up her stuffy—a bunny—and popped it in beside her.

"I see you found what you needed," he said.

She was aware she did not look sexy. At all. And yet the look in his eyes made her feel sexy, which was irritating and confusing, because it was not the look of a man who just wanted to be friends.

"How about if you go rummage around my kitchen while I find something dry?" He nodded in the direction Alexandra should go.

His kitchen, like the rest of his house, was like something out of a photo shoot. But unlike the open concept that was so popular these days, it was tucked in behind the living room, a spacious bright room that looked as if it was rarely used.

Still, it was well stocked, and Alexandra found all the

things to make hot chocolate. He came in just in time to pick up the tray and carry it out to the living room.

She took a seat on the couch. He went over to the fireplace and began to ball up paper and add kindling.

It was a good thing he'd made it clear this wasn't going anywhere, because otherwise a woman could make the mistake of thinking it was all very romantic.

Then Alexandra noticed the photo in the frame on the rough-hewn mantel. It was of a very beautiful woman, masses of dark curls falling around an exquisite face. She was very like Genevieve, and Alexandra knew instantly who it was.

Had she allowed herself to think—because he had stayed the night, because he didn't seem to want the day to end any more than she did—that maybe this was going somewhere after all?

The fire crackled to life.

Drew turned and looked at Alexandra, came and took the chair opposite her.

She didn't meet his eyes. "You must love her very much," she said, her tone strangled.

At first Drew looked puzzled by the statement. "Do you mean Genevieve? Isn't that quite obvious?"

Her eyes went to the silver-framed photo of Emily on the mantel. "I meant her," she said.

His eyes went there, too, and his face softened. "I did," he said, simply. "I loved her very much."

She noticed he used the past tense.

"I think of her every day—Genevieve reminds me of her every day."

For a moment they were both quiet, sipping their hot chocolate. Then he spoke again.

"You know, I never wanted weddings here because I felt as if it would be a betrayal of Emily. That was her dream.

Our dream together. And yet, now that it's happening, I feel completely differently about it. It's not a betrayal of her. It's a way of honoring what mattered to her. I know that Ivy and Sebastian's wedding here is going to be everything she ever hoped a wedding at Parker and Parker could ever be."

No pressure there, Alexandra thought.

"And now," Drew said softly, "I feel the same way about you as I felt about the weddings."

She was so surprised she burned her mouth on the rim of the mug. She set it down hastily.

"It's not a betrayal of Emily," he continued, "to see another woman. To start living again. For the longest time, just like with the weddings, I felt it would be. But now I see saying yes to life is a way of honoring her. It's honoring everything she stood for. She believed in love more than any other thing."

"Love?" Alexandra squeaked.

He looked slightly abashed. "I don't know if it's going to go there, Alexandra. That's why I wanted to take our time."

Our time, she thought, as in her and him together. As if somehow, suddenly, time belonged to both of them. She felt almost dizzy from the shock of what he was saying.

"That's why I wanted to slow everything down," he continued, his voice so soft, so serious.

So sexy.

"That's why I said I wanted to get to know you first."

"First?"

"Passion confuses everything."

You don't say, she thought, her heart racing.

"Not that the passion isn't there. I mean, it's more than obvious, isn't it?"

She nodded, unable to speak. The scent of him on the

clothing she was wearing seemed to intensify. She was way too aware that the cloth on her skin had touched his skin not so long ago. In combination with his words, it was a strangely intense intimacy.

"But I want to be the man Emily would have expected me to be. I want to be the kind of man I would hope for for my daughter."

"Oh," she said. Her voice came out a strangled croak.

"I know it's old-fashioned, maybe hopelessly so, but I want us both to be sure what's happening between us is as strong and as real as it seems in this moment."

Alexandra started to laugh.

His brows lowered. "I'm sorry. I'm kind of making a declaration here. I don't see what's so funny."

The laughter was hard to bite back. It was as if there was a well of joy inside her, and it was bubbling over.

"Drew, when you told me you wanted to slow down and get to know each other, I thought it was a variation of *I really like you, but let's just be friends.*"

The tiniest smile played across the beautiful line of his mouth.

"I thought," she continued, "it was like, *Let's have a platonic relationship.*"

"Forever?" he said, so obviously appalled at the idea that she laughed again.

"That's what I thought."

"Huh," he said. "Clearly I suck at wooing a woman in the same way I suck at making Christmas for a little girl."

"Wooing a woman?"

"I'm being old-fashioned again. That was a stupid choice of phrase. Sheesh. It's not like I keep a stack of old gothic novels under my bed."

The fact that he—the man who had everything, the

man who was so successful and so sophisticated—was so awkward and so uncomfortable totally enchanted her.

"So, just for clarity," Alexandra said, still feeling laughter gurgling inside her, "you're proposing to romance me?"

"Exactly," he said, looking deeply relieved that she had gotten it. "And just for the record, I think having a platonic relationship with you *forever* would be impossible."

"Oh," she said, suddenly serious, that gurgling laughter dying abruptly. She swallowed.

"So, as far as dates go, the first two probably sucked."

"We've had two dates?" she said.

"See? I told you I sucked. You didn't even know. Well, who can blame you? For the first one, last night, I was a horse's ass—"

"Not just the ass," she clarified, and there was the laughter again, a well that would not be capped.

"And for the second one, the building of snowmen, I failed to impress with a feat of strength."

"I think, actually, it might be *three* dates," she said, getting into this lovely spirit of teasing. "If we count the Rockingbird cocktail night."

"See? I'm in hopelessly over my head."

"Well, we did kiss," she reminded him. "So I think it qualifies."

His eyes moved to her lips, his expression smoky with remembrance.

CHAPTER FIFTEEN

"I'M COUNTING ON you to be the expert on romance," Drew told Alexandra. Was he still looking at her lips?

She had a feeling of wanting to pinch herself. Drew Parker wanted to have a romance. With her.

"Me?" she said. "The expert?"

"Wedding planner?"

"Oh, that." She blushed. "It's not really what people think. It's a lot of hard work and basic business. It's having an eye for detail—being a perfectionist, really—and having superb organizational skills."

"I see," he said. "Kind of like being the librarian of the wedding world."

She was making herself sound dull! Or as if she was reciting her résumé.

"Well, not quite like that."

"Oh," he said, as if he was disappointed. Good grief. Did every man have a librarian fantasy? She thought of his fingers pulling that braid from her hair last night, and shivered more than she had when she had gotten snow soaked.

"Not that there isn't an artistic side to it. Not that I don't use imagination, and often…" Now she was chattering.

"I've seen your website."

"You have?"

He looked a little embarrassed. "I had a little peek after

we first met. It looked pretty romantic to me. From a male perspective, frighteningly so."

"Oh. I mean, being able to infuse a single day with a sense of romantic bliss is not really the same as conducting a romance, uh…day to day. Personally. I think you're probably far more an expert than me."

"Me? The expert?" He looked terrified. It was adorable.

"Well," Alexandra told him, "you've actually had a successful relationship. You must have been romantic with Emily. It sounds as if she loved romance. Look at this place. Look at the dream she had for it."

He considered that, and then in a low tone, like a man giving a confession, he said, "I'm afraid Em's love of romance made me quite lazy in that department. She came up with ideas, I went along. Happily. But I'll confess to never having an original romantic idea in my life."

"Well, you didn't get so lucky this time. Except for the fact I plan weddings, I really haven't gotten out much." The way he was looking at her lips was making her think, *Romance equals kisses. Lots and lots of kisses.*

He smiled at her. "Alexandra Harris?"

"Yes?"

"Would you like to conduct a romance with me?"

He was annoyed with himself. How had he managed to make that sound like a science experiment? And yet, the look Alexandra gave him, Drew realized, could only be described as radiant.

She was in his house, on his couch, in his clothes, looking radiant. He hadn't really seen this coming when she had rescued his daughter just about a month ago. He thought he had protected himself from unexpected turns in the road of life.

"Yes," she said softly, tentatively, almost shyly. "Yes, I would. I'd like to conduct a romance with you."

Her sweet tone made him quite glad that somehow she had sneaked by all his defenses. But then it struck him that all that radiance was a huge responsibility. What if he let her down? But wasn't that the whole point of going slow? Building in safeguards. Against broken expectations. And broken hearts. Revealing to her slowly how flawed he was.

What if he broke her heart? What if she broke his?

It was a little late for doubt. He'd already asked her if she wanted to conduct a romance. She'd already said yes.

He felt a little thrill, even though it was apparent neither of them knew the first thing about it.

"So," he said, feeling his way, "maybe we should go on a date. Luckily, we've gotten the first two—possibly three— dates out of the way. They can be notoriously awkward."

"Notoriously," she agreed with a smile. Was she looking at his lips? It was going to be hard to keep this on the straight and narrow if she kept looking at him like that.

"What would you like to do for our next date?" he said.

There was that look again, smoldering. Her eyes said, *I know exactly what I want to do.* Out loud, she said, "I don't know."

"Tell me what your perfect fourth date would be," he insisted, "Hopefully, something better than the first three."

"I thought the first three were just fine," she said.

"Hardly romantic."

"But definitely fun. And I don't know, Rockingbird night was a bit romantic. And you did end up at my place last night. Undressed. And I'm here today. Also undressed."

She laughed, and in her laughter he heard that nothing was ever going to quite go as planned with her. For a guy with control issues, that should have been terrifying. Instead if felt exhilarating.

"But let's step up our game," he suggested. "What would be the perfect romantic date for you?"

"You tell me first."

The silence stretched between them.

"I have an idea," Drew finally said. "Let's both write down three ideas for a perfect date and we'll pull them out of a hat, one at a time, until we've done them all."

And he was thinking, *at the end of six dates, we'll know.* Which felt faintly ridiculous, because watching her, her bare feet tucked under her, in his pajamas and his T-shirt, her hair cascading over her shoulder and absorbing the light of the fire as if it had flame sewn into the strands, it felt as if he already knew.

Slow, he warned himself. He reached into a drawer on a side table and pulled out a paper pad. He ripped off a piece and kept it for himself, then handed her the pad and a pen.

"You're getting the hang of this," she said, taking the pad of paper from him, "because *that's* romantic. Three ideas each for the perfect date."

Honestly, the look she gave him was as if he had written her a love sonnet.

"Let's make the ideas just about us," he said. "No Genevieve."

He wanted to tell himself it was to protect his daughter, just in case there was a heartache hidden in there somewhere.

But the truth was he wanted the intensity of alone time. Just the grown-ups.

"But I wanted to make cookies with her! Christmas cookies."

"It's a bit early for that. Christmas, that is, not cookie making."

"According to Genevieve, it's Christmas right now."

"Well, until the snow melts. Don't get me wrong, I'm

all for cookie making, Christmas or otherwise, but for a *romantic* date? No."

She looked down at her paper, her tongue caught between her teeth in the most delectable way. She chewed on the top of the pen.

He looked down at his own paper. He had a vision of looking at her through steam, across a bathtub filled with hot water, candles surrounding it and rose petals floating on top. Would renting a place with an outdoor hot tub be too risqué?

Way too risqué. And risky, given his honorable intentions. He wouldn't look at her.

He wrote down *Candlelit dinner*. He was quite pleased with himself. He had managed to include candles in a non-X-rated way. He glanced at her. Now she was smiling slightly as she looked down at her paper. Her pen moved across it.

He wrote *movie*. Then he crossed it out. He checked his phone to see what was popular on Broadway right now. He wrote that down. He frowned. Would that be two dates? One, out for dinner, and two, live theater? Wouldn't it be more romantic if it was one?

Way more romantic if it was one. Should he name a restaurant? It should be exclusive and expensive. A special-occasion kind of restaurant.

This seemed to be getting complicated, but he wrote down the name of a restaurant he had enjoyed with a business acquaintance and the name of a play that was popular.

But that meant he still had to come up with two more dates. He was beginning to think this had been quite a dumb idea.

He wrote down *National Hockey League game at Madison Square Garden*. He glared at it. Obviously, that would be perfect for *him*.

Dating a woman like Alexandra Harris required him to be a better man. He needed to think about what she would like. He glanced at her. He scratched out the hockey idea and wrote, *Carriage ride in Central Park.*

Central Park! Skating. It was a little early for that, though. Despite today's unexpected snowfall, the Conservatory Water wasn't frozen yet. And actually, the rinks didn't seem as if they would be any more romantic than bringing her to a hockey game.

Was he sweating?

He glanced over at her. She looked as if she was having fun!

He looked down at his paper. *Think.*

He saw a vision of them, sitting on this couch, a fire in the hearth, covered in a blanket, a bowl of popcorn between them, a movie on the flat screen that was revealed when he pushed a button and the picture covering it rolled away.

But they'd already done that. At her place. He wanted to be original. And spectacular.

She was done. She had been for some time. And she was watching him with amusement. He felt faintly panicky. In a rush of desperation, he wrote down *Lunch and wine in a hot air balloon.*

He didn't even know if such things happened in the wintertime. It would probably be cold. And uncomfortable.

"Done?" she asked.

"Sure," he said. He could work out the logistics later. They could go to California. Hot air balloons probably ran there year-round, if they didn't run here. She could come with him and Genevieve.

Though, the truth was, California was feeling less attractive by the minute. Things were not getting any better for Gabe, so it was possible they wouldn't be going to

California and maybe the hot air balloon would have to be postponed…

He was making it too complicated. He left the hot air balloon suggestion. He tore his piece of paper into three, and with no hat in sight, dumped them in a bowl beside him. He crossed over to her and held out the bowl. She put her scraps of paper in.

"Be careful with that," she said. "I think it's Ming."

"It's okay. Pick one."

"You pick one," she said.

"Okay." He closed his eyes, reached into the bowl and shuffled through the papers with his fingertips. He drew one out.

He stared at it. *Hot tub under the stars.* He frowned. Hadn't he written that down and then scratched it out? He realized it wasn't his handwriting.

"Uh…" he said, crumpling the paper in his hand, and shoving it deep in his pocket. "Hockey game at Madison Square Garden."

The exercise had been to select an activity that was romantic, he reminded himself. A hockey game was something he and Gabe might do. He'd already eliminated it, so why had he blurted that out?

Obviously pure panic had set in. He had needed to escape from an evening in a hot tub. With her. That was a test he just wasn't ready for. Would she be a one-piece gal? Or two-piece? Or maybe—

How did a man keep his decency about him in the face of all this temptation? Yes, hockey was a good choice. A safe choice. A surrounded-by-a-zillion-people choice. A something-to-focus-on-other-than-her-lips choice.

Still, had he disappointed her?

She didn't look disappointed. "I've never been to a live hockey game before. I think it will be fun."

He squinted at her to see if she was being sincere. He had the feeling she didn't know how to be anything else.

Unlike him, who was willing to fudge the results of a simple draw. For the best of reasons, though. To protect them *both*.

"Even though I've never been to a live game, I do love the Rangers," she said.

He figured it was pretty much hopeless to protect himself from a woman who loved the Rangers. And she wasn't just saying that, either, because she knew Madison Square Garden meant the Rangers, not the Islanders or the Devils.

"My brother is going to be so jealous," she said gleefully.

He needed to remember that. It should keep him on the straight and honorable path. She had a brother, who, if he was not mistaken, while telling Alexandra that she was thirty-one and it was none of his business what she did, had shot Drew a not-very-subtle warning look this morning.

Don't hurt my sister.

Drew looked up the game schedule on his phone. "Are you free next Thursday?"

"Thursday is perfect. Most of my weddings are on Saturdays, so Saturday is out for me, right up until Christmas."

Christmas, he thought. If he didn't manage to blow this, they would still be together at Christmas. She seemed to have an expectation they would still be dating at Christmas.

Which meant two people would have expectations of him. What did you get someone you were dating for Christmas?

"Friday is always a crazy day," she said. Apparently the mere mention of Christmas had not sent her into a cold sweat. "Last-minute details. Who are they playing?"

Who was who playing? Oh, the Rangers. There was

no sense getting ahead of himself. He could just take this one date at a time.

"Um," he looked back to his phone. "Boston."

He was going away for Christmas.

But just like that, he knew wasn't. Gabe wasn't going to be back at work by then, though that had the feeling of an excuse. Drew remembered Alexandra had mentioned baking Christmas cookies. California and all its manufactured cheer suddenly seemed to dull in the light of making Christmas cookies.

Of getting ready for Christmas with her.

He felt something in him relax. With her, he didn't think it would be about meeting her expectations: the perfect gift, the great tree, the right feeling.

With her it would be about sharing both the stresses and joys of the season.

The last thing he had expected when he'd suggested they try conducting a romance was this. It had been a long, long time since he had felt this way.

Not alone.

CHAPTER SIXTEEN

THE ARENA ERUPTED in a cheer that deepened to a deafening roar as the New York Rangers scored the winning goal in the second minute of overtime.

Alexandra leaped to her feet and screamed until she was hoarse, just like everybody else. She became aware Drew was looking at her, smiling.

He looked so wonderful, his face alight with the excitement of the game, casual in a sports jacket, a button-down shirt, jeans. He was wearing a plaid scarf tucked loosely under the lapels of the jacket. It wasn't the one he had put on the snowman, because she had returned to get that one, and it was now wrapped around the neck of the stuffed frog he had won for her on Halloween.

So few men wore scarves well. He was definitely one of them. They had on the matching ball caps Drew had bought for them from a vendor in the lobby. She had put hers on and then turned it backward.

"I like it," he'd said, regarding her with laughter-filled eyes. "The sexy tomboy look."

She had told her brother where she was going and borrowed his treasured Rangers jersey for the occasion.

He wouldn't surrender it until she texted Drew and asked him where the seats were.

Then he had handed it over willingly, with a little whistle under his breath.

"A Rangers game," Shaun said. "At the blue line, second level, first row. So much better than ice level. This guy knows what he's doing. He's a keeper—you know that, right?"

The jersey wasn't really sexy—it was way too big—but when she saw how Drew's eyes lit up when she'd met him outside the Garden, she knew there were things more important than being sexy.

He had kissed her on the cheek in greeting, and she had known her brother was right on all counts. Drew knew what he was doing. He was a keeper.

They both had to work in the morning—she had an extra-challenging wedding coming up over the weekend— so they reluctantly parted ways after the game. He touched his lips to hers, a mere brush, but long after he had put her in a car, the excitement of the evening shimmered inside her. It felt as if her tummy was full of butterflies.

It felt exactly the way it was supposed to feel.

And had never felt before.

It felt—terrifyingly and exhilaratingly—as if she was falling off a cliff, waiting to see if she would crash or if she would fly.

Her phone buzzed with his ringtone.

"Hey," she said.

"I'm at home."

"I'm not quite, yet."

"I've got the bowl in front of me. Should I pick the next one?"

"You have to pick it blind."

"I know the rules!"

She closed her eyes as she heard him rustling through the papers. She knew which one she wanted.

The dangerous one. A night in a hot tub under the stars.

"Huh," he said. "This is one of yours."

She could feel herself crossing her fingers...and her toes. Like a gambler begging for the perfect numbers, please, please, please...

"A dance lesson?" he said. "Alexandra, have mercy."

"It will be fun," she said. Not as much fun as a hot tub, but still—

"I'm a terrible dancer."

"Me, too!"

"Then why torture us?"

"It's important to stretch," she said.

"Let's switch it out for a yoga class then!"

Why had she chosen a dance class? First of all, she'd been trying to think fast. But secondly, more and more weddings featured a dance sequence the bride and groom worked on for weeks—sometimes months—before the wedding. She could see a difference in couples after even the first lesson: a subtle deepening of the connection and laughter between them.

She often had couples tell her that turned out to be their favorite memory of the day.

"As tempting as it is to see you in downward-facing dog, I don't think we should start changing the rules." Because what would that mean when the hot tub came up?

He sighed dramatically. "I take it you'll line this up?"

"I have contacts," she said. "I'll be in touch."

"Soon?" he whispered. Even with his reluctance to take a dance class, he was eager to see her again, soon.

"Soon," she whispered. As she disconnected, that feeling of leaping off the cliff intensified.

The next day at work, her assistant kept giving her sideways looks.

"What is going on with you?" she finally asked. "New vitamins? An exercise program? You look so—"

"What?" Alexandra squeaked.

Her assistant regarded her thoughtfully and then smiled. "You look like one of our new brides, just flushed with love. Alexandra! Are you in love?"

"Don't be silly," she said hastily, even as she felt the shock of that question. She realized why the sensation of falling was so strong. She was falling, all right—she was falling in love.

Even though she knew it took some of her couples many sessions to learn a dance sequence for their weddings, Alexandra soon realized her expectations of the one-hour dance date had been unrealistic.

As it turned out, along with her own lack of skill, Drew had two left feet. And a personality conflict with the teacher, Claudia, who had all the charm of a drill instructor. In a whisper, Drew dubbed the instructor Clattila the Bun because of her attitude and the way her hair was so severely pulled back.

"Man hater," he whispered in Alexandra's ear, as he was finally allowed to take her hand after they had practiced a box step by themselves, mirroring the instructor, for a painfully long time.

Clattila the Bun shouted out the cadence.

"One, two, three…no, no, no, Mr. Parker. Hips, hips. Argh! Let me show you *again*. You—" she pointed at Alexandra "—stand over there."

She shoved Alexandra out of the way and took Drew's hand. Over the instructor's shoulder, Drew shuffled along with deliberate clumsiness and made faces at Alexandra that dissolved her into giggles.

When they moved close to her, he muttered to Alexandra, "I thought nobody put Baby in the corner?"

Then he took charge. He put his cheek to the instructor's, executed an about turn, shot their arms out like arrows from their shoulders and practically dragged her in the opposite direction, across the room.

"You are not taking this seriously, Mr. Parker!"

He glanced over his shoulder and lifted a fiendishly uncooperative eyebrow at Alexandra. He let go of the instructor, ran across the highly polished floor, fell to his knees and slid to Alexandra, his arms spread wide.

Unfortunately, Drew's pants weren't quite up to the strain put on them by the move. They tore open with a loud ripping sound.

Alexandra laughed so hard she doubled over from it. If she wasn't such a good customer, she was fairly certain they might have been kicked out of class, but to the obvious relief of the instructor, Drew, with a comically regretful look at the damage to his pants, voluntarily withdrew.

With his jacket tied around his waist, standing outside the studio, they called a car.

"Thanks for trying to rescue that," Alexandra said, the laughter still trying to bubble to the surface. "I did hope it would be a little more like an '80s musical. You would have made an awesome Catskills summer resort dance instructor, by the way. A born rebel."

As he held open the car door for her, he grinned that wicked bad-boy smile that sent her stomach spinning down to her toes. She slid past him and sank into a luxurious leather seat.

"To be honest," he said, getting in beside her, "when you said dance class, I had hoped for a little more maraca shaking myself. Clattila suspected. That's why she hated me. And yet still?"

He wagged mischievous eyebrows at Alexandra. His eyes looked as green as a cool pond on a hot summer afternoon. Awareness of him tickled along her spine in the way she had hoped it would when she had suggested a dance class as a date idea.

"Still, I'm having the time of my life." And then he hummed a few bars of a familiar song. He took her hand. After a moment, she hummed, too.

He started to sing. And then she sang along. She'd always thought it was dumb when people burst into song in musicals, but it didn't feel dumb at all. It felt joyous and connected and funny and lovely.

It was true. Here they were sitting in a car, all the life and bustle of New York unfolding outside the windows, as they enjoyed their own private world and sang the same song. She *was* having the time of her life.

The car pulled up at Parker and Parker.

"Should I ask the driver to take you home or are you coming in? I don't think it made the list of romantic dates, but I heard you can have a mean game of Candy Land here."

Alexandra considered the invitation. She had so much work to do. And yet, it was irresistible. Genevieve and Lila greeted them both with such enthusiasm, especially when Candy Land was mentioned. They eagerly hauled out the game while Drew went and changed his pants. They set up at a table in the playroom that was much too small for everyone but Genevieve.

"I just remembered why I hate this game," Drew said later. "No skill, no choice. Just follow the directions. And mine say I have to go back three squares."

Genevieve chortled. "You're going to lose, Daddy."

He made a face, and all of them dissolved into giggles. After that he had them howling as he tried on different facial expressions to express dismay and glee over the game.

"As tempting as it is to while away my life playing Candy Land," Alexandra finally said, noticing the room had gotten quite dark, "I'd better go."

Drew got to his feet and winced from being in such a cramped position so long.

"Before you go, let's pick our next great date out of the bowl."

They went downstairs, and he held it out for her. She peered at it, hoping she might see a little ink bleed-through that would let her know which one was the hot tub one.

He noticed and held the bowl over his head.

She stood on her tippy-toes and reached into it. She held her breath. She opened the folded paper. "Cook a new recipe together," she read and felt the stab of disappointment. Really? She was ready for something steamier, figuratively and literally!

"That must be your idea. I don't cook. I hope it doesn't involve lessons."

She laughed. "Of course it doesn't involve lessons. I thought we could do it at my place. Even though the kitchen is tiny, I know where everything is."

Or was it because that tiny kitchen gave them much more opportunity to bump into each other than his rather large one?

"We just have to pick a recipe neither of us has made before," she told him.

"Well, that's easy for me."

She thought of her schedule. She wished she had picked something else out of their dating bowl. Because she had been thinking about what they could make together ever since she had written down the idea and put it in that bowl. The recipes she had narrowed it down to—beef Wellington, baked Alaska—required quite a big commitment in time, and so it meant she wouldn't see him for a week.

"How about next Sunday, my place?" she asked.

"I don't want to wait that long," he growled. She shivered. They were more and more on the same wavelength.

"But when I wrote it down," she said, stubbornly, "I was thinking about a meal that was complex."

"Like a great book," he said. "Like a good wine."

"Exactly," she said. "Layers of discovery."

"Every time you open it, you notice something new. A texture, a nuance, a secret that wasn't apparent at first. Like you."

He was being a flirt. And she loved it.

"I did want the cooking challenge to be difficult," Alexandra told him, trying to stay on track. "Not a workaday meal. Something that requires a stretch."

"Stretching again! I'm sure, subconsciously, what you really want is to see me in yoga class. You probably want to see my pants rip again."

She did want to see his pants ripped again. Off. By her. Alexandra was shocked by the thought. She made herself talk about their next date.

"What I hoped for was a sense of a mission completed together."

Heads bent over the cookbook. Hands accidentally touching. Bumping into him on the way to the fridge. Lips tasting off the same spoon.

"A recipe that's hard," she went on. "That requires teamwork. That requires us to see how we work with one another."

"If we cooked a dish that was a little simpler, I could ask Lila to stay late Tuesday night," he said.

"Hot dogs it is," she said. "See you Tuesday. My place."

He grinned at her. "See? We've just demonstrated how well we work together."

And then he kissed her goodbye and demonstrated that things did not need to be any more complex between them than they already were.

CHAPTER SEVENTEEN

THE FIRST TEXT arrived from Drew at 9:00 a.m. Tuesday morning while Alexandra was working with her assistant on Ivy and Sebastian's wedding. Her first thought, when she saw it was him, was that he was going to cancel.

And so, when she read the text, her heart stood still.

I have a confession to make.

A thousand possibilities raced through her mind.
There's someone else.
I can't get over my wife after all.

Oh?

I said we worked well together, but I wasn't being totally honest.

Damn. Damn. Damn.

Oh?

I don't really like hot dogs.

She laughed out loud, mostly relieved, partly delighted at his teasing. Her assistant shot her a look.

Smokies?

What's a smoky?

A kind of sausage. There's different flavors. The cheese-stuffed ones are good.

I do like a girl who knows her sausages. Do you prefer big or little sausages?

She chortled. She blushed.

Her assistant muttered, "I knew it."

After that little exchange, Alexandra thought she should shut off her phone, and yet somehow the more they went back and forth, the more her creativity was fed and the better her ideas for Sebastian and Ivy's wedding became. It seemed as if she was infusing it with an element of fun—and even sexiness—that she had never had quite like this in a wedding before.

They ended up deciding on homemade pizza.

Had a grocery store ever felt quite so dazzling as it did when she was selecting ingredients, and just the right wine, to share with Drew?

There was no awkwardness when he arrived. There was just a sense—she hoped in both of them—of this being where they belonged.

Together.

Her kitchen was so small that there was lots of bumping into each other. Plenty of hand touching. Much tasting of ingredients off the same spoon. There was laughter threaded through with a lovely tension, a sizzling awareness of each other, as the conversation flowed freely.

He made her laugh with a story about Genevieve. But

then, when he updated her about Gabe and his mom, it was just as easy to be serious with him as it was to laugh.

She told him about the bridezilla of last weekend's wedding and gave him the latest changes to Ivy and Sebastian's wedding details that she had made that day.

An unspoken anticipation was building as they headed toward the inevitable. They were both aware that yet another layer of this relationship was calling to them, crooning to them, begging for their discovery.

And yet, Alexandra was aware of wanting to not rush this part, either. Because once they let the other out—once they opened the door on all the passion that shimmered and sparked in the air between them—it would become everything. It would be all encompassing. It would swallow up everything else.

No, it would be wise to wait, to hold that change at bay. Then, if it did go somewhere else—and she felt no doubt that it would, once the hot tub date came up—they would know each other completely on so many other levels first.

The pizza was dreadful: the crust burned on the edges and doughy in the middle. Neither of them noticed.

"Of all the dates so far," Drew said, lying on the couch, his head propped up in her lap, eating ice cream from a bowl, "this is my favorite."

"Even though there was no beef Wellington?"

"We'll save that for a different time," he said.

A different time. A future beyond the dwindling date ideas they had both put in that bowl.

They had known each other just about six weeks. And already it was becoming difficult to picture a life without him in it.

He stayed too late for a work night. She had no regrets and found that when he was at the door, bundling up against a very cold November night, she didn't want him to go.

"I took the liberty of picking our next item out of the bowl. I didn't look, though. A surprise for both of us."

He handed her the slip of paper. Again, she felt herself wishing. Even though she knew this wasn't wise, she was aware of feeling *ready* for what came next.

Maybe even beginning to need what came next.

She unfolded the paper and read it and tried not to look too crestfallen. It was delightful, after all. Dinner and live theater. He'd even picked the restaurant and the play. Both had been on her list of *want to* for some time.

And after this, there would be only two more things. They were drawing ever closer to investigating the sensuality that was in the background of everything they did. Maybe, she thought whimsically, a force greater than her was saving the best for last.

"Do you want to do it tomorrow?" he asked.

She laughed. "Won't it be hard to get reservations and tickets on such short notice?"

"Where there's a will, there's a way."

It made her tingle that he felt exactly the same way as her. As if they could not get enough of each other.

Not ever.

And so the next night, drunk on each other's company, Alexandra and Drew had the most perfect New York City evening. They had an exquisite dinner. They saw a play that was funny and well done.

As they walked, hand in hand, through the park, back to his place, breathing in the clouds of each other's breath, Alexandra realized she had joined a club that she had always felt excluded from.

She was part of a couple.

When they arrived at his place, Lila had not been successful in getting Genevieve to bed, and she looked exhausted.

"I'll take care of it," Alexandra said, and she felt the most heart-warming sense of homecoming as Genevieve took her hand and they went up to her room.

Soon, the little girl was in bed, a favorite storybook out. Drew saw Lila home and then came and joined them. Alexandra scooted over, all three of them in the bed.

She had felt like part of a couple earlier, but the magic deepened as Drew took the book from her and read it, his voice deep and soothing.

She felt like part of a family. Genevieve sagged against her, fast asleep in seconds. Alexandra and Drew tiptoed from the room.

"Let's pull from the bowl before you go," he said.

Again, she felt exhilarated, the anticipation building. And again, she felt disappointed as she read the paper.

That was crazy! Who could possibly feel disappointed that the man she was falling in love with had come up with such an incredibly romantic idea?

"A hot air balloon ride," she read. "With wine. And lunch. Um... Drew, it's November. Do they go in November?"

"I wondered the same thing. So I checked."

Just like she had been checking. She had spent way too much time dreamily looking up where one went to spend an evening in a hot tub under the stars in New York. And how fitting was it that that would be the final occasion they pulled from the bowl?

"And yes, hot air balloons go all year round. Over the Hudson Valley."

"It sounds slightly terrifying," she said.

"I know," he agreed. "That's the best part, isn't it?"

She looked at him. She was aware his face had become

so familiar to her. Drew Parker did not even seem like the same man she had first laid eyes on weeks ago.

He didn't seem formidable at all. The darkness seemed to have been chased from him; his eyes danced with light. His smile was playful.

She couldn't help it.

She stood on her tiptoes and put her hand on his neck and drew Drew's lips down to her own.

"Wow," he said, pulling away from her after a long time. "If terrifying is the best part, I don't think we have to go on a balloon ride."

But they did go on a hot air balloon ride. It wasn't terrifying. Not even a little bit. It was absolutely exhilarating, and surprisingly warm, as they caught the morning updraft. Drifting with the wind gave the illusion of there being no wind at all. And the balloon, after all, was fueled by a propane heater that allowed them to feel toasty warm even as it provided lift.

The morning had been frosty, and as Alexandra looked down at the world from the great height of the balloon, everything was gilded in silver. The fields, the trees, the doll-like barns and houses, were all sparkling.

And Drew stood behind her, his arms wrapped around her waist, and she leaned into the now familiar strength of him.

Alexandra allowed herself to relax against him, to feel the magic of the moment deeply. What a wonderful world it was that an ordinary woman like her could have an extraordinary moment like this.

He gently turned her away from the view so that she faced him. She looked at him with complete wonder. How had this happened? Her ordinary life transformed into an absolute fairy tale. And this man: so funny, so smart, so handsome, her perfect prince.

Indeed, she felt like a princess, as if she had been asleep for a long, long time.

She knew what would wake her up. And so did he. With their hearts soaring as high as that hot air balloon, their lips touched, held, tangled.

And just like the princess in every fairy tale, Alexandra was awoken by a kiss.

The sensation of soaring lasted in Drew long after the balloon had landed. It had nothing to do with the champagne they had sipped and everything to do with her lips.

Not just her lips. *Her.* Her hand in his. Her eyes on his face. Her sense of wonder. The way she saw the world. Her laughter. The way she made him laugh. The ease of being together. The tension that sizzled tantalizingly between them.

He had told himself he would *know* at the end of six dates, but he knew now.

"I know what the last date is," she told him softly when the balloon had landed. "I wrote it."

"I know what it is, too."

"What? You cheated? You looked?"

"Confession time. I picked it first."

She stared at him. If he'd expected annoyance or anger, he was surprised. She laughed, delighted.

Alexandra, he realized, would be a constant surprise to him. Even if they were together thirty years from now. Forty. Fifty. Even when Genevieve was all grown-up and they were bouncing their grandchildren on their knees.

He felt something go very still in him.

"But there were six pieces of paper in there," she said.

"I made up the hockey game on the spot and put the hot tub suggestion in my pocket. The one left is a carriage ride in Central Park."

"A carriage ride?" Her breath was frosty in the air. "I've always wanted to do that. Funny how you can live in a place like New York City your whole life and not avail yourself to what it offers."

As she spoke, he *knew*. It was the sound of her voice and the light in her eyes; it was the puffiness of her just-kissed lips and her willingness to explore the whole world with him, to make even the familiar seem new and shiny.

He knew he wanted to spend the rest of his life with her.

"Drew?" She reached up and touched his face. Her hands were encased in angora mittens. Her touch, even through the mittens, felt as if it could melt him.

He wanted to blurt it out, right here, right now.

I love you. Marry me.

But it was a bit like making Christmas for a child. It was an occasion he wanted to be memorable. He wanted to be the better man. He didn't want his marriage proposal to be about meeting some need in him, but about making wishes—that she might not even know she still held deep in her heart—come true.

He wanted romance. He wanted fireworks.

He wanted Alexandra to think back on that moment for the rest of her life with joy and remembered bliss.

"I looked it up," she admitted, her shyness endearing. "There's a lovely inn in the Catskills that has a hot tub. A pool, really. It's like a secret grotto."

She was blushing.

"You've given this some thought," he teased her.

Her blush deepened. A lifetime of making her blush…

But then Drew had the horrible thought that at the inn in the Catskills, as lovely as it might be, not everything would be in his control. What if it wasn't completely private? What if someone else was using it at the same time? What if they were interrupted? What if the pool and the rooms didn't look as good—as was so often the case—as the pictures showed?

"Not that I have time to go to the Catskills right now," she said, suddenly uneasy. She was reading his silence as reluctance. "December is always such a frantically busy month. Ivy and Sebastian's wedding is around the corner. And all the nieces and nephews have Christmas concerts."

How could you not love a person who gave their nieces' and nephews' Christmas concerts the same priority as the wedding of the century?

"How about if we plan our last date—" *and the first day of the rest of our lives* "—for the day after Ivy and Sebastian's wedding?" he said. "And how about if I look after all the details?"

She looked at him, her eyes huge, her lower lip trembling. He was aware he was holding his breath, waiting for her answer.

It was the next stage unfolding. And it was momentous. She knew it. And he knew it.

"Yes," Alexandra said.

CHAPTER EIGHTEEN

ALEXANDRA HAD BEEN RIGHT, Drew thought. December was a frantically busy month. He had just come out from the banquet hall of Parker and Parker—almost ready for the big day—and been led by laughter, and the smell of baking, to the kitchen in his house.

Genevieve and Alexandra were giggling over cookies, laid out, individually, on one side of the long kitchen island. It looked as if there were, easily, a hundred cookies there. They were golden around the edges and shaped like stars and trees and Christmas ornaments.

At the other end of the enormous island were stacks of brand-new backpacks, the tags still on them.

He wandered in. "What is all this?"

The kitchen was a disaster of open cupboard doors, leaning bags of ingredients, used bowls and spilled flour. Sprinkles crunched under his feet. The space had never seemed more welcoming.

Genevieve was standing on a chair. Her hair was pulled back in a ponytail, and she had on a pinafore apron. She had confectioners' sugar on the tip of her nose, and she had found a place on the dress not protected by the apron and managed to get a green food coloring stain on it. She had a piping bag in her hand and, if he was not mistaken, there were sprinkles in her hair. Her lips were the same color as the icing in the piping bag.

"We're making cookies for Mr. Evans and his mom."

"That's a lot of cookies for Gabe and his mom." Drew sidled over. "I guess I can have one?"

He reached, and Alexandra smacked his hand lightly with a wooden spoon. He yelped loudly, put his knuckles to his mouth, and while she went wide-eyed, wondering if she had hit him too hard, he snaked out his other hand, grabbed a cookie and stuffed the whole thing in his mouth.

"Delicious," he proclaimed.

"Daddy, we need them all!" Genevieve nodded toward the backpacks. "For those. We're putting other things in, too. Socks and toothbrushes. And what else, Alex?"

"Um… Books. Scarves. Soap. Toothpaste."

His house had become this: chaos, laughter, energy.

His life had become this place: going to see the tree lit up at Rockefeller Center, Christmas concerts, sledding on Pilgrim Hill, skating on the now-frozen Conservatory Water.

His work had become this: helping get Parker and Parker ready for Ivy and Sebastian's wedding.

Though his input, as far as the wedding went, was completely unnecessary.

He'd seen that right away. That Alexandra had an extraordinarily talented and skilled team. She was a magic maker and an enchantress.

And yet when she was over there working, so close to him, Drew found he could not *not* be there. Seeing her at work and in her element revealed yet another facet of her, as sparkling and deep as the facets on a diamond.

And then, once he'd been there, he'd made a suggestion. And then another one. And then he'd been part of that team, fully engrossed in working toward someone else's perfect day.

But it wasn't just a day. He could see that in the way Alexandra worked on it. For her it was keeping a promise.

She had promised this couple a wondrous beginning. Magical. Beautiful beyond their wildest imaginings.

And Drew was shocked by how much he loved being part of her vision for Ivy and Sebastian.

He was delighted by how well they worked together. Reading each other's thoughts, on the same wavelength, sharing similar tastes. They were such an extraordinary team.

It solidified the commitment he was going to make to her the day after that wedding. In a setting as romantic as he could make it—at least as romantic as these settings she created, which set the bar high—he was going to ask her to share the rest of his life with him.

To be a mother to his daughter. And maybe, someday, other babies, too. He could see now, as he had seen dozens of times over the last weeks, with Alexandra's head bent over what seemed to be hundreds of cookies, exactly what a good mother she was going to be.

Wife.

He felt a shiver of pure anticipation for all the things that word meant. Of course, she still had to say yes.

"How come you're filling these backpacks?" he asked. "Who are they for?"

"They're for homeless people," Genevieve said, her face lit as she bent over her task. She deposited quite a large blob of red icing on one of the cookies. She regarded it for a moment, picked up her shaker of green sprinkles and doused it.

"I think you missed a spot," he teased her.

She regarded her cookie. "I didn't. Did I, Alexandra?"

She moved closer to the little girl, rested her hand lightly on her shoulder, regarded the cookie in question solemnly. "I think it's perfect."

Genevieve beamed. "We're buying toys, too. For the kids at the shelter. Daddy, did you know there are kids that don't get presents? What about Santa? Doesn't he know where to find them?"

The hard questions. Why did Santa come for some children and not others?

"He'll know where to find them," Alexandra said quietly, reassuringly.

The world seemed to go still around him as he took in the scene. He looked at Alexandra: her hair put up, the apron on, her cheeks rosy from taking the cookies from the oven. Her gaze met his, her dark brown eyes glowing with softness, light.

As long as there were people like her, pure love, there would always be someone showing Santa where to go, he realized.

His heart felt as if it would burst for loving her, for the glimpse he had been given into his own future.

This, then, was the ingredient he had missed for each Christmas where he had failed his daughter.

It wasn't about giving his daughter the perfect Christmas, but about showing her, one small step at a time, that Christmas wasn't about what you got, but about what you gave. Kindness, generosity, compassion. Even to strangers. Maybe especially to strangers.

Alexandra made him want to be a better man. A man worthy of her. He suddenly couldn't wait to bring her the joy she so willingly brought others.

He needed the perfect Christmas gift for her.

And he knew what it was going to be. A ring. But he

didn't think he was going to be able to wait until Christmas to give it to her.

"What's that little smile mean?" Alexandra said, tapping his lip with the tip of her wooden spoon.

"You'll see," he promised her. "You'll see."

It was the morning of December 14. Alexandra stood in the front foyer of Parker and Parker. It was snowing lightly outside which was absolutely perfect. She had just shown the bridal party up the stairs to their private suite. Though she dealt with brides all the time, she was not sure she had ever seen one as beautiful as Ivy, radiant with love and excitement.

Now the happy chatter of the bridal party and the crinkles of bags being opened—the oohs and ahhs of rediscovering the dresses—drifted down to Alexandra.

Normally, she would feel a little ache of longing, but today her attention was already moving past the charm that ran through the entire venue. It could not look more perfect. Everything was in place.

Hailey's flowers were, as she had known they would be, extraordinary. They lent to the sense of enchantment that had been created at the beautiful mansion that sat on the edge of Central Park.

Her staff would take it from here: they would be in the background of the entire wedding, making sure that no detail was overlooked, no last-minute problems were left unsolved. Tomorrow morning they would take things down, erase it all as if it was Cinderella's glass slipper and it all disappeared at midnight.

She, herself, never attended the wedding or the reception. She never helped with the takedown. It was too difficult for her to see something she had worked on for months and months disappear in the blink of an eye, like a sand-castle dissolved by waves.

As for not attending ceremonies and receptions, at first it had been too painful for her. She had known vows ex-changed, perfect days, would remind her of her own failure and trigger a deep longing in her, start a fire of yearning she would not be able to put out.

But as the years had gone by, she was not so sure if it was about that anymore. It was just that her routine had hardened into a suspicion. As if her *not* being there was part of what guaranteed great results.

Usually, on this morning, the day of the wedding, as she checked final details, as she breathed in the beauty of what had been created, she felt a sense of loss.

All weddings, but this one in particular, were all con-suming. They filled her. She lived it and breathed it.

Usually, saying goodbye to it all left a yawning sense of emptiness, of what next. Usually, she was already piv-oting her attention to the following wedding, to bigger and better, to yet another event that would fill any holes in her life.

But now, at the top of those stairs, the door marked Pri-vate swished open, and Drew came out. He came down the stairs, two at a time, grinning.

When had his smile become so beloved to her?

When had it become the thing that filled all those holes in her life?

He came to a stop in front of her and looked at her as if she was the only magic in this place.

"Here," he said, and he passed her a beautiful, creamy square of an envelope that reminded her of a wedding in-vitation.

With him watching with obvious enjoyment, she slid it open.

The pleasure of your company is required
on the evening of December 15
at Seventh Avenue and Fifty-Ninth Street
7 p.m. at the horse-drawn carriages
Please bring swimming attire
RSVP

"Swimming attire for a carriage ride?" Alexandra asked.

"Ah," Drew said, "be prepared to be surprised. Dress warmly."

She cocked her head at him. "Dress warmly? And bring a swimsuit?"

"That's me. I like to keep my lady on her toes."

My lady.

Even standing there in all that grandeur, Ivy and Sebastian's wedding was wiped from her mind with the ease of a note erased from a chalkboard.

She needed to find swimming attire. Nothing she had would do. She knew that. It was New York. But still, a gorgeous, sexy bathing suit in December? Was it possible?

"I have to go," she said.

"You forgot to RSVP," he called after her, evidently pleased that he had rattled her.

Well, they would just see which of them would be rattled tomorrow night!

"Yes," she called over her shoulder. "I'll be there."

Yesterday's light snow had deepened today. Alexandra arrived just before seven, a small bag over her shoulder. The new swimsuit was in the bag, and she was wearing a new, sleek black winter coat. She had on a matching set of white cashmere accessories: beret, gloves, scarf. Her staff had debriefed her about the wedding earlier in the day. It had gone perfectly. Scenes from Twitter feeds were being picked up by all the entertainment programs and media.

Still, all day, she'd had an edgy feeling. As if something was wrong, as if she was missing something. Something important.

That feeling finally eased and then disappeared as Drew came toward her. It was as if, in the pre-Christmas crowds, she alone existed for him. He came to her, took both her hands, looked at her deeply, kissed her lightly on the mouth.

In that kiss, with huge snowflakes drifting down on them, was a white-hot promise of things to come.

He led her to a white horse-drawn carriage, delightfully decorated for Christmas. The horse blew great clouds of steam out his nostrils into the nippy air. He gave his head a shake, snow flew, and bells jingled. The carriage seat was warm under a blanket. Drew settled beside her, pulled the blanket over them, took her hand.

"Congratulations," he said. "The wedding is trending on social media. It's being compared to royal weddings."

But the truth was, it was Alexandra who felt like royalty, sitting in the carriage with her prince, the steady snow-muffled clop of the horse's hooves and the jangling of his bells like music in her ears. They were taken on the regular tour: Central Park was under a beautiful blanket of white. It was the perfect backdrop to the swirls of color and activity as they toured its most well-known sites: Wollman Rink, the carousel, the Chess and Checkers House, the Literary Walk, the boat pond and boathouse, Bethesda Fountain, the lake, Cherry Hill, and more.

And then the carriage pulled up at the walkway that was closest to Parker and Parker. In the distance it was lit up, a castle on a Christmas card.

The driver tipped his hat, and the sound of the horse

clopping off and the bells faded as they took the path to Parker and Parker.

"I don't understand," she said.

"You will."

"You don't have a hot tub."

"It's New York City. Anything is possible."

The words between Alexandra and Drew had faded. All that was left was energy. Awareness. Anticipation.

They entered his private quarters, and silence greeted them.

"Where's Genevieve tonight?"

"I gave Lila some tickets to *The Nutcracker* because of her interest in theater. I told her to take anyone she wanted, but she chose to take Genevieve. They're staying at her house after. A pajama party, I understand."

Alexandra understood, too.

She and Drew were going to be alone. Uninterrupted. Tonight was the night they had been building toward since the day they had met two and a half months ago. It was as inevitable and as timeless as the changing of the seasons, as the stars coming out at night, as the tide coming in.

His hand around hers, he led her through his darkened house to his bedroom. Her heart felt like a wild bird, captured inside her chest.

He nodded. "Through there. Put on your bathing suit."

She went through to his master en suite bathroom. It was a gorgeous room. The bathtub was certainly large enough for two people.

She put on her bathing suit. She had chosen a two-piece, the first one she had ever owned. It was skimpy, red and very, very sexy. Alexandra stood staring at herself in the mirror. It seemed a different woman than who she had been two and a half months ago looked back at her.

A confident, mature woman who radiated a certainty in herself.

That's what love did.

She loved him. And she felt loved in return. And the result of that was this radiant woman who looked back at her in the mirror: sensual, sure of herself.

She stepped out of the bathroom and into the master bedroom. Two wide doors had been thrown open, and the room was already cold from the breeze coming through. She felt the freezing air and snowflakes on her bare skin.

As if in a dream, she went to those doors and stepped out. And as she did so, there was a sense of stepping into a brand-new life.

CHAPTER NINETEEN

THE MARBLE OF the deck was cold on Alexandra's feet. Such was her state of mind that it felt delectable rather than uncomfortable. The brand-new life that she had stepped into had a dreamlike quality.

On the deck outside Drew's bedroom door was a hot tub, its water softly lit, sparkling turquoise, the steam rising off it in wispy clouds.

The entire deck was illuminated with the flickering light of what looked to be a thousand candles. They sputtered in the snow but didn't go out. Beyond the marble balusters that enclosed the patio area were the Christmas-lit trees of the glade that surrounded Parker and Parker. In the distance, even with the snowfall, the skyline of New York was visible, soaring and illuminated. The haunting notes of a reed flute added to the sensation of having entered a mystical space. A sacred one.

All that—save for the sense of the sacred—faded.

Even the impossibility of a hot tub suddenly appearing on his deck faded.

Drew was sitting on the edge of the hot tub, his feet dangling in the water. He looked as though he had been carved by Michelangelo—male perfection as snow melted on his broad chest, taut belly, sleek muscle, his flawless skin pebbled with cold.

He got up from the edge when he saw she had appeared, and stood. He was wearing a pair of slim-fitting black shorts that molded the large muscle of his thigh. He padded across the deck, leaving wet footprints, stopped and looked down at her.

She felt as if she could drown in the green depths of his beautiful eyes. She noticed the fringe of sooty lashes around them, the beginnings of whisker shadow on his cheek and chin. She felt the cold only as part of the backdrop of sensation.

Drew took his time looking, as oblivious to the cold against his naked skin as she was. He reached out his hand and swept her hair back from her face, tucked it behind her ear, then slid his thumb over and scraped it across her lips.

In the look in Drew's eyes, resting on her, Alexandra recognized that all things were possible. His hand found hers.

And he led her to the edge.

It didn't feel as if she was jumping off a cliff at all as she followed his lead and stepped into the water and felt its silky warmth close over her chilled skin.

Her sense of the sacred—of being part of the ancient dance, of one man and one woman finding each other against all odds in that endless sea of time and space—intensified.

There had been, already, so many words between them.

So much laughter.

So much shared experience.

They did not need to speak. The time for those things was not done, but it was not now. This was the time to acknowledge the other thing that had been a silent partner to their getting to know one another, shivering constantly in the background of everything else.

It was time to not just acknowledge but celebrate the

anticipation that had been building between them and that was about to reach fruition.

His lips found hers. Hers found his.

They had kissed before. Light kisses. Exploratory. Rich with a sense of discovery.

But this was different. This time, unspoken, they both gave it permission to go where it wanted to go. The barriers were down.

Completely.

His mouth sighed against hers, homecoming. And then the sigh deepened. He tasted, sipped, nipped, not just her lips, but her ears, her eyelids, the hollow of her throat.

She stilled him with a fingertip and then bowed her head toward his. And she tasted, sipped, nipped, not just his lips but his ears, his eyelids, the hollow of his throat.

The exploration that began as tender and lively deepened; it took on a hunger and an urgency. They touched each other. Delighted. Discovered. Explored. Nothing taboo. Nothing forbidden. Nothing off-limits.

Bathing suits were peeled away, discarded. They surrendered to owning each other.

When both of them could barely breathe from it, Drew stood, scooped her in his arms, lifted her from the water and stepped from the tub. She watched the water slide down the beautiful planes of his face, gilded in the gold of the candlelight.

He set her down and toweled her off, following the path of the towel with his lips. She took the towel from him and toweled him off, following the path of the towel with her lips. And then he scooped her up again. Alexandra gazed into this eyes.

Drew was not a warrior claiming his prize.

He was a man, reverent, who could not believe the gift he had been given.

He took her to his bed and tenderly, fiercely, possessively, he took her to places she had not known a human being could go. He took her to the stars and to the burning center of the earth; he took her to mossy green rocks beside bubbling brooks. He took her to exotic lands of heat and spice.

And then he rode with her to the very universal explosion where the earth began.

He stole her breath. Her heart. Her soul.

She had never felt so utterly complete. So utterly exhausted. So utterly exhilarated. It felt like the most natural and beautiful thing in the world to fall asleep with Drew whispering her name into her ear, and his arms wrapped protectively around her.

When Alexandra woke up, she was disoriented. How long had she slept? Ten minutes? An hour? Drew slept beside her, on his stomach, his arm thrown over her midriff.

But even that could not stop the anxiety from gnawing at her.

That feeling was back. More pressing than ever. That she had forgotten something. That something urgently needed her attention.

The feeling had deepened, almost as if danger lurked in a dark place just outside where her mind could touch, waiting.

She slid out from under his arm and padded quietly to the bathroom. She frowned. A phone was buzzing, and she realized it was coming from her purse.

Who would call her in the middle of the night?

And then, her heart falling like a stone, she knew. She knew what she had forgotten. Shame filled her.

And a kind of terror.

This was where passion led: to unbearable loss. To pain that seemed beyond a human's capacity to bear it.

She answered her phone.

Weeping, she quietly said hello to Brian and heard his sorrow for the baby they had buried together.

She remembered the perfect, tiny features, that one shock of golden hair like a halo. She remembered the stab of love—and loss—so sharp it had felt as if she was being cleaved in two.

And she knew a truth she had been running from since the day she met Drew. She saw the truth she had been trying to suppress as her life had opened up more and more to both him and Genevieve.

She was not strong enough to do it all again.

Not even maybe.

Drew woke up with a sense of well-being. Alexandra's scent was delicious in the air. Last night could not have gone any better. Today, his life was going to change forever. He was going to propose to the woman he loved.

He had a selection of croissants and jams. He'd make coffee, bring her a tray in bed, and on the tray he'd place the ring he had picked, a solitaire diamond. He'd known as soon as he'd seen it, it was the one. Simple, but perfect.

He turned his head to look at her, a smile of anticipation tickling his lips. Drew felt a ripple of shock and disbelief to see the place beside him was empty.

After just one night of sharing his bed with her, it felt wrong without her in it.

He listened. She must be close. Making coffee? Showering? But as he listened for those sounds, what came back to him was the hollow emptiness of no one else in the house.

He bolted from the bed, threw on pajama pants and stumbled through the house, frantic. She had to be here. Finally, back in his own bathroom, he stared at himself in the mirror.

And then he saw it.

A note, scrawled in whatever she could lay her hand to. It was lipstick, obviously, but to him it looked like blood.

I can't.

Disbelief filled him. She couldn't? After last night? He felt the exact opposite of *I can't.*

I can.

I can give my life to you.

My heart.

My soul.

My very breath.

How could two people possibly experience the same event so differently? A sense of failure rose in him bitterly.

He thought he had done everything right. He thought back over their time together and he could not see one misstep, one moment of dissension between them.

Egotistically, he had been giving himself an A-plus in the romance department. He had thought he had aced it.

He itched to call Alexandra, to ask her what had gone wrong. Where *he* had gone wrong. But he quelled the impulse.

He might end up begging her, and no matter how you cast that argument, you could not convince someone to feel the same way you did. He went back to the bed and opened the nightstand drawer beside it. He picked up the ring and stared at it.

He was not sure he had ever felt such yawning emptiness, such powerlessness, such an agony of emotion.

No, that was not true. He had. He had, and he had ignored that poignant reminder that love brought pain. Pain so terrible it felt as if a man could not bear it.

"Daddy?"

Genevieve came noisily through the front door. Now, as then, he had to keep going for his little girl. How was he going to do it?

The shock Drew was feeling morphed into something that felt ultimately safer, and certainly more powerful. It was how he was going to do it. He was going to feel anger instead of the breaking of his own heart.

How dare Alexandra lead him on when she wasn't ready or had issues to deal with? That was one thing. But his daughter trusted her. Loved her. And that was quite another.

"Up here, sweetheart."

"'Bye, Lila," Genevieve called.

He met Genevieve outside his room, picked her up and gave her a squeeze.

"What's up, pumpkin?"

"*The Nutcracker* was the best," Genevieve said. "There were some scary parts, but I wasn't scared. There were kids in it. Can I be in it? Next year?"

Next year?

He wondered how he was going to get through the next few days and weeks, never mind next year.

"I can't wait to tell Macy about it. And Alex. I wish they could have come. I wish you could have been there, Daddy."

For a while, it had been as if they were part of a family, as if they were being invited in to all that warmth and closeness.

And now they weren't, just like that.

How did he break that to Genevieve?

"How would you like to go to California?" he said, a man desperate to outrun pain.

The trip was, predictably, a disaster. Genevieve was querulous and given to tears. She wanted to be at home. She wanted to skate again. Sled. Build snowmen. Make cookies. She wanted Alexandra.

And he did, too. For a man trying to outrun pain, he wasn't sure why he had to carry that ring around in his pocket. Touching it, holding it, feeling the warmth of it. The ring reminded him how real it had all been. How could something so real dissolve like this?

Carrying the ring made Drew hang on to some faint hope that there had been a terrible mistake. That she would call him and explain it all to him.

Every time his phone alerted, he hoped for just that. His heart hammered in his throat until he realized it wasn't the distinctive church bell tone he had assigned to her.

The bright, warm days in California blended together, and the merriment of the amusement parks and the playfulness of the beach, rather than soothing, seemed like sacrilege to him.

There was no phone call. And yet, he could not bring himself to call her. How did you argue with *I can't*? Did you insist she could? Did you insist you knew her better than she knew herself? Did you beg? Did you tell her you felt as if your world had turned to ash and cinder? What did it matter what his world was doing in the face of *I can't*?

Didn't love ask you to put the needs of another person ahead of your own? And after all that, all the time they had spent together, all the joy they had shared, she had made her decision.

And there it was.

Stark. In the note he could not bring himself to throw away, any more than he could put the ring away. The note he studied every night after Genevieve was in bed, as if some secret, some sort of answer, would reveal itself to him.

He gave up on California after just a couple days. Genevieve was not charmed by it, or distracted from her fury that Alexandra had disappeared, without explanation, from her world.

Back in New York, he made himself go through the motions of Christmas. He took her to see Santa at a department store.

"What did you ask Santa for?" he asked carefully, trying hard to hit just the right casual note to pry her secret from her.

His daughter glared at him. "I asked him for a mommy."

"Uh—"

"And I want it to be Alexandra."

And then she was weeping. He had not officially told her Alexandra would not be around anymore, trying to shield her from the pain with platitudes and distractions. But obviously she was drawing her own conclusions. The absence was weighing heavily on her. Was his lack of explanation making it better or worse?

"Let's go do our Christmas shopping," he said, trying to cajole her out of it, distract her. "You have to choose something for Lila."

The tears dried up a little bit. She perked up. "And for you. And for Macy," she said. "And for Alex."

He had warded off the tears. He wasn't going to object to any of that if it meant he didn't have to deal with a four-year-old throwing a tantrum in the middle of Macy's department store.

But as it turned out, Drew's reprieve was short. A week later, on Christmas Eve, he was exhausted from crying and tantrums. He thought it was probably exactly the wrong time to show up unannounced but hoped he could be forgiven. He was a failure at all things Christmas, after all.

With snow falling in giant flakes around him, he found

himself standing in front of Shaun and Shelley's house. Genevieve was dancing excitedly beside him, the handle of a bag of wrapped gifts clutched in her fist.

When the door squeaked open, she screamed, "Merry Christmas!"

Drew wondered if he was the only one who could hear how desperate she was for exactly that.

CHAPTER TWENTY

I<small>T WAS</small> S<small>HAUN</small> who opened the door.

"Genevieve wanted to drop off these gifts for you."

Shaun took the bag that Genevieve proffered with her most angelic smile. As soon as he looked at the bag, she darted by him into the house. "Macy!"

"Sorry," Drew said.

"Not at all. Happy to have you both. To be honest, I was wondering why you haven't been around. Macy's missing Genny like crazy."

Drew scanned Shaun's face to see how much he knew, to see if he could offer a clue as to Alexandra's pulling the plug on the relationship.

He was aware Shaun was looking at him with grave sympathy.

"Man," he said, after a moment. "You look like you've been run over by a truck."

"Thanks," Drew said wryly, and thought to himself, *A truck named Alexandra.* "Genevieve picked out something for Macy, Ashley, Colin and Michael. If you could look after getting things to Heather's girls, Adelle and Catherine, as well."

He thought of how he knew their names. Of how he had sat through each of their Christmas concerts. Of how he had begun to think of Shaun and Shelley as family. Of how he had looked forward to getting to know Heather better. He felt bereft when he thought of his life—and Genevieve's—moving on without them.

"Are you coming in?" Shaun asked.

Behind Shaun, Drew could hear the noise, Genevieve's laughter rising above it. The lights of a Christmas tree blinked on and off.

He wanted to step into that house so badly. He wanted Alexandra to be there waiting for him.

People can love too much, his aunt had warned him. He hated that. He had wanted so desperately for her to be wrong that he had overcome every survival instinct that screamed within him, and he had tried again.

"No, we'll be on our way. Genevieve picked something for your sister. If you could make sure she gets it."

"Ah, so you're not seeing her. That explains why she's even more in hiding than normal."

Drew cocked his head at Shaun. "What?" In hiding? Alexandra?

"It's unlikely I'll see her, mate."

Drew's head flew up. Somehow, he had pictured her sliding seamlessly back into the loving fold of this family. In the million reasons he'd come up with for that note— *I can't*—that had been one of them. That he was poorly equipped to give her what she wanted.

Family.

Hadn't he shared each of his failures with Genevieve? Hadn't he shown he didn't have a clue what the big family events were, never mind knowing how to celebrate them? Hadn't he fallen asleep during her nephew's Christmas concert?

"What do you mean? She'll be with you for Christmas, won't she?"

"No, she won't come. Hasn't for years."

Drew felt stunned.

"It's a bad time for her," Shaun said quietly. "We keep thinking she'll get over it, but she's got the softest heart of anyone I have ever known."

That's what Drew had thought, too. Until he'd received a note with two words on it. *I can't.*

"I think if you break her heart, it's broken for good."

Did he say this with a meaningful look aimed at Drew?

Drew wanted to explain there was little chance of him breaking Alexandra's heart, since she had beaten him to the punch.

But his mind was sluggishly turning over the fact Alexandra—expert on all things Christmas—had not celebrated with her family for years.

"The baby," Drew said, suddenly, slowly, out loud.

"You know about the baby, then," Shaun said, with a new look of appraisal. "She trusted you with that."

"What time of year did she lose the baby?" Drew's heart was thudding so loud in his ears, he thought Drew might hear it.

"This time of year," Shaun said sadly. "December 16. I can't forget it, because it's our Colin's birthday, too. A few years later. A cruel coincidence."

It felt as if the world darkened around Drew.

He had been licking his wounds. He had been making it all about him. He had been indulging his bitterness and anger.

She trusted him.

And suddenly it didn't matter to him if Alexandra loved him back. He could not bear for her to be alone with her pain. His aunt was wrong, after all. People could not love too much.

He could not love too much.

"Can you keep Genevieve for a bit?" he asked.

Shaun had the slightest smile on his face. It was approving. "You got it. Wait a sec. Take the gift from Genevieve. It might get you in the door."

Drew fished through the bag for the package with Alexandra's name on it and took off down the steps, running.

Christmas Eve, Alexandra told the stuffed green toad on her lap. *It's just another day.* Warty looked unconvinced.

She stared glumly at *Hatchets for Halloween*. She told herself she had chosen it only because it was the most un-Christmassy movie she could find.

She had told herself maybe it would provide a distraction from the pictures on her phone. She was afraid she was getting a permanent swipe mark on her screen from looking at them so often. Silly selfies from the hockey game. Beautiful vistas from the balloon ride.

But again and again, she went to those pictures of the perfect first day of snow in Central Park, her and Drew kissing either side of a snowman's cheek, joy shimmering in the air around them.

The movie, rather than being a distraction, reminded her of watching it with him. She loved rubbing salt in the open wound of the choice she had made to walk away. She pulled the Rangers cap down lower over her eyes, tightened the scarf she had retrieved from the snowman around her neck and cuddled Warty closer.

A choice to live without pain. For a person who had made that choice, it seemed to her she was in the most terrible pain she could have ever imagined possible.

And, worse, what if she had caused him pain? And Genevieve. It was Christmas Eve. What were they doing? Did he have a clue how to be Santa Claus? Did he know you had to put out milk and cookies? How would he know that? He had probably never done it. It was one of those things his horrible aunt would have relegated to the *nonsense* pile.

Her hand inched toward her phone, as it had done a thousand—or maybe a million—times since she had walked away. *Call him.*

The knock came on the door, loud.

Christmas Eve, she told herself bitterly. *It must be Santa Claus.* She got up, tugged back the curtain and peered out. She flipped it back down, her heart beating so hard.

"I saw you," he called. "I need to speak to you. It's urgent."

She flattened herself against the wall, trying to stop from breathing too loudly. She couldn't open that door. He would know. She was dressed in her pajamas. Her hair wasn't combed. She had on his scarf and the hat he had given her.

What a coward she was.

"It's about Genevieve."

Her self-protective mechanism abandoned her. She shoved Warty behind a flowerpot, went and threw open the door. "Drew? Is Genevieve all right?"

"No," he said, stepping into her foyer. "She's not."

This was the kind of person she was. Even worried sick about Genevieve, his scent filled her and she felt that treacherous stir of longing. "What's happened?"

"She sent this gift for you."

Alexandra's ragged breathing evened a bit. No medical emergency, then. No other child lost at this time of year when it seemed inconceivable people suffered losses. And yet they did, nursing their brokenness alone as the world celebrated around them.

"Even though you've broken her heart, still she sent a gift."

"I didn't mean to break her heart," she whispered.

"Mine, too."

"Oh, Drew, don't you see, it's better now than later?"

"I wish you would have told me," he said quietly.

She went very still.

"I wish you would have told me that December 16 was the worst day of your entire life."

"See?" she said harshly. "You think I'm someone I'm not. You want to hear the awful truth, Drew? I forgot. I was so swept away by you I forgot."

She had begun to shake. He dropped the parcel he had been holding in front of him and closed the small space between them.

He gathered her in his arms, and she wept. "I forgot," she sobbed.

"It's okay," he said over and over, his hand stroking her hair as if she was a child. "It's okay."

"It's not," she said, finally, but her voice lacked conviction and she remained with her head pressed against the solidness of her chest.

"Maybe," he said, after a long time, "this is what love is meant to do. Make us forget. Allow us to move on. It's not time, after all, that heals all wounds, Alexandra. It's love."

"I'm scared," she admitted. "Drew, I'm so scared."

"I know."

"Not just scared. Terrified. That I will lose again. That something will happen to you. Or to Genevieve."

"It's too late," he told her softly.

"What do you mean?"

"You already love us. If something happens now, it won't matter if you're part of our lives or not. The pain will be the same. If you heard, ten years from now, I had been run over by a reindeer—"

"A reindeer?" She laughed in spite of herself, and then sighed against him.

"In honor of the season. But I digress. If you heard, ten years from now, that I had died, I think your pain would be as great as if you had spent every day of it with me."

"Is it that obvious how much I love you?" she asked.

"It is now. I'm stupid that way. I should have gotten it right away. F in the art of love. I'm willing to work to improve my grade, though. If you'll have me."

"If you'll have me, more like," she said. She tried one last time. "What if I lose another baby? I want to have babies with you. I'm so scared."

"I want to have babies with you, too."

"You do?"

"Oh, yeah. And I'm scared, too. That life has surprises for us. Not all of them pleasant. That things will not always go according to plan. That we will suffer tragedies and sorrows. But I think love gets you ready for those things. It makes you stronger every time you share a laugh, a look, a touch. It's like we'll put love in the bank to withdraw, to get us through our tough times. And life will have tough times, regardless. But we will be stronger together than we could ever be alone."

His voice was so soft she could barely hear it.

"Alexandra?"

"Yes?"

"I don't want to be alone anymore."

She was crying. She was crying because she had caused him pain, and he had come anyway. She was crying because she was afraid, but not as afraid as she had been before he was part of her life.

She was crying because life—capricious, scary, unpredictable—was, in the end, beautiful.

Mysterious.

In the end, love was everything.

"Alexandra, marry me."

"Yes," she said, and even though she said it quietly, it felt strong and loud and true. It felt like she was shouting an affirmation to life from the mountaintops. "Yes," she said again.

EPILOGUE

THEY MARRIED A year later, on December 16, to honor not the tragedy of love, but how the power of it remained in you, and carried you, through hardship. Through sorrow. Through the unexpected. Through the detours and the bumps in the road. Love was the flickering light, deep within you, that led you through darkness.

Drew and Alexandra's marriage proved his aunt wrong every single day. You could not love too much.

Nor could you use it up.

This was what Drew had learned so far. The more you loved, the more it strengthened your own light.

Once, he had hoped Genevieve would know all the things about family that he had never known.

But he did now, and so did Genevieve. Family was somebody who had your back. Family was somebody who would risk anything to bring you happiness in your darkest moment.

Though Parker and Parker was now the wedding venue of choice for all of New York City, they had not married there.

In fact, Alexandra had not wanted a traditional wedding at all. She had wrinkled her nose when Drew suggested it and said she didn't want their perfect day to feel like another day at the office for her.

She had also said no to the gown.

They had gotten married in Shaun and Shelley's snow-filled backyard, in puffy snowsuits and hats and mittens, with an honor guard of snowmen lining the "aisle."

There was no way to have a wedding party without hurt feelings if they chose Macy and Genevieve as flower girls, and so they had all of them, Genevieve and Alexandra's six nieces and nephews, as their wedding party.

And after they had said their vows, they had a snowball fight and made snow angels and drank hot chocolate and ate Christmas cookies and laughed until their stomachs hurt.

Now, as their second anniversary approached, Alexandra was pregnant. Terrified. Radiant.

Hopeful.

Above all else, the hope shone through.

It was that same hope that humanity had carried since time began: that hard times would not last forever. That tragedy would be balanced with joy. That darkness would eventually give way to light.

And that when it seemed as if it all had to fall apart, as if the whole world was disintegrating, love would be the thread that bound it all together.

* * * * *

THE
BILLIONAIRE'S
ISLAND REUNION

SUSAN MEIER

MILLS & BOON

To my Facebook friends,
who let me be silly and funny every morning.

CHAPTER ONE

THE HOUSE, A five-bedroom Colonial in Oilville, Ohio, with six bathrooms and an elaborate backyard made for entertaining, was a symbol of everything wrong with Cade Smith's childhood. His parents had made him a pawn in their protracted divorce as they battled over a bunch of two-by-fours and furniture. Neither had really wanted the old-fashioned monstrosity. They just hadn't wanted the other to have it.

At eighteen, he'd prayed for a Solomon-like judge who would cut it in two and ruin it for both of them, then realized they'd already done that to him. With the way they'd ranted about each other to him and torn him up over the choice of who to spend every holiday with, they'd split his life right down the middle, making him live in two different worlds.

He shoved open the door of his rented SUV, stepping out in the chilly April morning air, shaking his head, as he strode to the front entry. He was over all that. Thirty years old and a billionaire with his partners, Trace Jackson and Wyatt White, he'd gotten beyond his mom throwing dishes and his dad buying a gun. He was even over the heartbreak he was sure they caused him with his first love.

He snorted. Did anybody really want to be dating the kid whose parents fought on Main Street, made the

preacher cry and put hidden cameras in each other's bedrooms looking for dirt they could use in court?

Reese Farrell hadn't wanted to. That's for sure. When
she'd dumped him, she'd shattered his heart so thoroughly,
there were days he didn't think he'd survive.

But he had. And he had a great life in Manhattan. So
why was the pain of his past roaring through him like the
winds of a category five hurricane?

He paused at the door to draw a long, life-sustaining
breath, deciding that returning to his small town after
twelve years away had to be bringing back all these memories. He hadn't even *thought about* Reese in at least ten
of those years. His dad and the gun? As long as Martin
Smith still owned it, that was something Cade would have
to monitor. No forgetting that.

He pushed open the door of the Colonial. Blaring hip-
hop music greeted him, along with a totally remodeled
downstairs. The open floor plan allowed him to see the
whole way into the white kitchen that sat beside a family
room decorated with a mishmash of furniture. Very Bo-
hemian. Of course, his dad's most recent ex-wife had been
about twenty-two—

He rolled his eyes. He had to stop being snarky. His dad
had had a stroke. His current trophy girlfriend had run
like a rat deserting a sinking ship. His mother didn't give
a damn. As always, Cade had to stand in the gap.

"Dad?"

The music swallowed his call. With a sigh, he headed
to the den, where the controls for the sound system used to
be. Finding another remodeled space, this one an odd shade
of green with beanbag chairs his father would never be
able to sit in, he scanned the buttons and ended the music.

He walked to the high-ceilinged foyer again. "Dad?"

Muffled voices came from a closed-off room to the

right—where the dining room had been when Cade had moved out to attend Harvard. He started toward it, but the door popped open. A woman wearing black yoga pants and a tank top barreled out. Her red hair had been pulled into a short, bouncy ponytail and her green eyes spit fire.

Recognition poured through him like a bucket of ice water. "Reese?"

She halted as if she'd walked into a brick wall. "Cade?"

His heart stopped, along with his breathing. Surely to God she wasn't dating his dad!

She pushed past him. "Did you turn off my music?"

He pivoted to the right, his gaze following her as she marched to the den. Taller now, with full breasts and a perfect butt, she found the controls and in seconds the house filled with hip-hop again.

She stormed out, breezing by him on the way back to the former dining room.

His stomach couldn't take it anymore. He had to ask. "What are you doing here? Are you dating *my dad*?"

Her eyes widened as her mouth fell open. "No! I am not dating your dad! I'm his nurse. His physical therapist gets here in ten minutes. He has to be stretched by then."

The picture that formed in Cade's brain almost made him gag. "You're stretching him?"

"Most of last week I also helped him into the shower. Wanna yell about that too?"

"I wouldn't have to yell, if the music wasn't so loud."

"It's his motivation. Like torture. I don't turn it off until he's done the work."

Relief and humor hit at the same time. He snickered, then chuckled, then out and out belly laughed. "Now, that's worth four plane rides and a forty-minute drive from the airport."

"Yeah. I can see you really raced to get here. He had his stroke over a week ago."

"The doctors said he was fine."

"Your concern is touching."

He could have told her that there'd been an accident in one of his company's warehouses and he'd been in Idaho, answering to OSHA. It wasn't possible to get away, especially not when one of their employees had died. Plus, his dad's doctor had told him the stroke had been minor. Now that the plant manager would be taking over the rest of the details in Idaho, he'd been able to leave. But he didn't feel like sharing that information with a woman he no longer knew. Even if it would exonerate him of not rushing home, it was none of her business. From the day she dumped him like a hot potato, like someone who didn't deserve an explanation, everything in his life became none of her business.

His dad stepped out of the former dining room, which was now God only knew what if it had been set up so he could stretch and do therapy.

"Cade."

The hushed reverence in his dad's voice almost made Cade feel bad. Almost. His gun-toting, rabble-rousing father had been cleared by his doctors and he looked fine. Sure, his head was bald, and the tank top he wore over sweatpants displayed a pot belly. But, as the doctors had said, the stroke was minor. Two days in the hospital proved there were no signs of aftereffects. He appeared good enough that he shouldn't need a nurse. Though, perhaps whoever ordered the nurse recognized his dad needed a keeper.

Shouting to be heard over the music, his dad said, "Come on! Give your old man a hug."

He stepped forward as his dad did. What began as an

awkward squeeze filled with emotion. Damn it. He did love the old coot. If he hadn't been in Idaho dealing with an accident and grieving coworkers, he'd have been here the day the doctors called him, no matter how minor they'd said the stroke had been. His parents might be nuts, but he loved them. Which was the real paradox of being a child. Parents could be bat-smack crazy, and you'd still care for them, protect them, love them.

Unfortunately, his particular parents couldn't be in the same room without fighting. Which was why he never came home—and why he hadn't thought about Reese in over a decade. He'd been more than occupied at Harvard. Then the risky partnership with Wyatt and Trace, that made all three of them billionaires, had taken every ounce of his concentration. Now, the new business needed all their energy.

Cade and his father pulled apart. His dad wiped away tears. Cade blinked his back. He was so relieved to see with his own eyes that his dad was fine that he could barely squelch the emotion.

"You still have five reps of the last stretch to do."

He peered at Reese, strange feelings rumbling through him. He didn't remember her as being so bossy. She'd been happy, the highlight of his senior year in high school.

Funny how he'd never thought of her. He tilted his head. *That wasn't entirely true.*

He'd thought of her on his wedding day, right before he'd stepped out to the altar where the preacher stood. And the thought had been only a weird, fleeting *something*. Not a fully formed memory or wish. More like his dating past flashing before his eyes.

His dad made one final pass over his cheeks to dry them before he looked at Reese. "Aw, come on! My boy is here."

Reese caught his arm and led him toward the open door.

"I don't care. You might be okay with getting yelled at by Yolanda, but she scares me. Get back on the mat."

Cade leaned in and saw the room that had once hosted his birthday dinners was now a home gym.

As his father lowered himself to the mat, Cade said, "You two finish up. I'll go make myself a cup of coffee."

Reese grabbed his father's leg and stretched it over his shoulder. "Whatever."

Cade closed the door and ambled to the kitchen. The weirdness of seeing his first love shuffled through him. If he closed his eyes, he could picture her at sixteen, feel the tingles that always whooshed through him when she was around.

He groaned. Juxtaposed against his worry over his dad's stroke and the emotions rolling through him over losing an employee, thinking about how attracted he'd been to Reese was just plain wrong. He had bigger things to focus on, ponder, examine. A twelve-year-old breakup shouldn't be popping up on his radar. Even if the woman who had broken up with him was in his space for the first time since the quick conversation where she'd given him back his locket.

His brain filled with confusion, as his heart filled with pain. He'd been so stunned and hadn't really understood it was over until she'd refused to take his calls—

Oh, for heaven's sake!

Rehashing all that was foolish on so many levels that he took his coffee outside to the huge stone patio, pulled out his phone and called Wyatt to see how things were going in Idaho.

Reese Farrell relaxed her hold on Martin Smith's foot and slowly lowered his leg to the mat before she lifted it again for the second of five stretches that she would do on each leg. Though the work was easy, it required concentration, which prevented her from thinking about Cade. How good he looked as an adult with his pretty yellow hair and piercing blue eyes. How his golf shirt displayed the muscles of his shoulders and chest and showed absolutely no sign of fat around his middle.

Cade's dad grunted. "You know, it's hard for me to breathe when you press my leg over my shoulder like that."

She shoved the picture of Cade out of her head. After five days of coming to Martin's house every morning, cooking him a healthy breakfast and helping him with his exercises, they'd created a rapport that allowed him to be grouchy and her to be sassy about it because they genuinely liked each other. Five years ago, he'd been the investment counselor who'd advised her on the kind of loan to get to start her business. They'd talked on the phone once a week for about a year, until her company had hit the point where it supported itself. So when he needed a home nurse, he'd called her. Rather than send an employee, she'd kept the job herself. They were friends. Friends who teased each other, but still friends.

"*You* know, if you'd lose that lump of stomach, stretching wouldn't be a problem."

"Nurses and trainers. You're all alike. Always know what's best for everybody while your own life is in shambles."

She gaped at him. "My life is not in shambles. I run a successful home nursing agency."

"Yeah. Yeah. Whatever. You've got some cash. Don't we all?"

"No, Scrooge McDuck. Most people don't have a lot of cash. Myself included. You're the one who taught me to reinvest most of my profits back into the business until I hit the level of income I want."

"Is that why you wouldn't take ten minutes to talk with my son?"

She stole a quick breath to mask the shiver that rolled through her. She hadn't seen Cade in so long there were times she could almost forget he was part of her life. Which had actually been for the best. The night she'd needed him the most, he was at Harvard. Not answering her calls. Probably at a frat party.

The emptiness of how alone she'd been that night still stung. It had taken him four days to call her back. *Four days.* An eternity to a teenager who'd been raped and needed to talk to the man who supposedly loved her.

By the time he finally did return her call, she'd been tongue-tied and confused. She genuinely didn't know how to tell him that someone they knew had violated her in the worst possible way. She'd said nothing and he didn't press, as if he couldn't hear the pain in her voice and didn't realize something terrible had happened to her. The few calls they had after that were filled with talk of his studies, his new friends and, of course, his crazy parents.

When he returned for Thanksgiving vacation, she'd given back his locket—a better symbol of their love, he'd said, than a ring—and he hadn't argued. He'd shoved the necklace in his jeans pocket, walked away and simply never came home again. Not because of her, she was sure. Because of his gun-toting dad and crazy-like-a-fox mother.

And she'd been alone—facing therapy sessions that did help her recover—but still alone. When he'd promised— *promised*—he'd never leave her. He'd said that even away at school, he'd find a way to keep them close.

And the one time she really needed him, he hadn't answered his phone.

Was it any wonder she'd put all that in a box of memories and never opened it?

"When we're done, you're having coffee with him."

"I have other clients to get to."

"No, you don't. You told me that every Friday at noon, you're off the clock because I'm your last client."

She gritted her teeth, ignoring him.

"Come on," he cajoled, then grunted again when she stretched his leg over his shoulder. "One cup of coffee can't hurt."

She said nothing.

"I always felt bad that you and Cade broke up." He winced. "I might have been oblivious in the past, but even a small stroke makes a guy think. You dumped him because he never came home from university when my ex and I were throwing barbs at each other across Main Street."

"And sometimes plates." That wasn't how their breakup had happened, but there was no need to correct Martin. He didn't know the truth. Some fast action on her parents' part and the county district attorney had kept the situation quiet. Plus, Finn McCully wasn't sixteen. The court records had been sealed. Martin had no idea—no one in town had any idea—that Finn and his parents hadn't moved away for a new job. They'd relocated so they could hide that Finn was in a juvenile detention center.

Martin laughed. "Yeah, we were nuts through that divorce."

She gaped at him. "You cannot believe your behavior was funny."

He sobered. "Everything is funny once a few years have gone by."

Her stomach turned and she eased his leg to the floor, finishing the last of his stretches. Unwanted memories flitted through her brain—

Refusing alcohol from Finn, after he'd lured her under the bleachers at a Friday night football game.

The horrible realization that she was being followed as she walked home alone when her friend Janie veered off onto the driveway for her house.

The anger in Finn McCully's voice—"You think you're so special..."

She closed her eyes, pulled in a deep breath and dispelled the rest of the memory as it tried to form. She never let herself think about that night. She relegated it to a box as her therapist had told her and locked it tight, so it couldn't hurt her anymore—

But the image of the box, though powerful, worked only to a point. The trauma and damage of being raped rippled through her life, manifesting as a cautious streak so strong and so tight her rules for dating and sometimes simply living were ingrained to the point she didn't even have to think about them anymore. They subconsciously guided her life, her choices.

No one would ever hurt her again.

She took a breath, forced herself back to the present and Martin Smith. "Not everything becomes funny after a few years."

"Sure, it does!" Martin insisted as he did his three-part maneuver to get his roly-poly self off the floor: get on all fours, hoist butt into the air, pull torso upright.

He let out a "Whew," then said, "Cade never visiting probably *was* painful. But he was a kid trying to get control of his life. He couldn't do that here with me and his mom making a circus of our divorce. Plus, over a decade has gone by. I think you two need a fresh start."

"I don't."

Finn would have never come within ten feet of her had Cade been home to go with her to the football game. Even if Cade hadn't been home, if he'd returned her call that night, she could have opened up to him, sought his support about her rape. But no. He wasn't around Friday night or Saturday or Sunday. Her calls to him all went to voice mail.

When he finally returned her call, she'd frozen. Lost her nerve. Couldn't tell him any of it—

Damn it!

She'd worked with a therapist to forget all this and one five-minute encounter with Cade in Martin's foyer had it tumbling through her like an avalanche.

To get that memory out of her brain, she picked up the mat and rolled it, then remembered Martin's physical therapist would need it and spread it out on the floor again.

Luckily, the doorbell rang. "And there's Yolanda now."

Martin huffed out a sigh. "Send her in." He grinned. "Then go get that cup of coffee with Cade."

She left without answering and walked to the foyer, where she opened the door for Yolanda. They shared a few pleasantries, then she grabbed her jacket and sneaked out without a goodbye to Martin or another word to Cade.

They had nothing to say to each other and all he did was remind her of the worst night of her life. So, no. She wouldn't have coffee with him. If that meant not saying goodbye to Martin, so be it.

CHAPTER TWO

THAT AFTERNOON, WHEN Reese's phone rang and Martin's picture popped up on the screen, she regretted not staying long enough to say goodbye to him. She knew his heart was in the right place. Though his stroke had been minor, it scared him enough that he'd had a major change of personality. He'd told her that being reminded you won't live forever gives a person perspective, and for the past week he'd constantly looked for ways to be a nicer, more compassionate guy.

Despite their sarcastic banter, she'd been encouraging that. She couldn't ignore him now or he might lose the progress he'd made.

Sitting back on the desk chair of her cluttered home office, she punched the icon to answer her phone. "Okay. I'm sorry for not saying goodbye."

"No biggie. Actually, *I* want to apologize."

Her eyebrows rose. "Really?"

"Yeah. Yeah. You and I have been over this. I'm a changed man. I'm starting to see other people's needs. You didn't want to hear what I had to say this morning about you and Cade. And that's your right. I shouldn't have pushed. Which is why I'm going to add a gift to my apology."

Pleased that he really was changing, she smiled. "No need for that."

"I insist. I have a beach house in the Florida Keys. It's yours for as long as you want."

She blinked. "What?"

"A beach house. In the Keys. Yours for as long as you can take off work. I made your flight arrangements. I'll text you the ticket number so you can print the boarding passes. Return flight is open. You can stay a week. You can stay ten days. Hell, you can stay a month if you want."

Her breath caught. "Is this for real?"

"Yes."

She bit her lower lip. Not only did she have a business to run, but accepting his offer felt like taking advantage of a client. "I couldn't."

He laughed. "Why not? We've been in each other's lives and each other's business for five years. I'm not just a client. You were *my* client. And now we're *friends*." He sighed. "Come on, kid. We both know how much you did for me since the stroke, when there was no one else around to help me. But I'm good now. I've got a housekeeper for company during the day and Yolanda has agreed to do my stretches before my therapy." His voice softened. "The damned beach house sits empty most of the time. Look at it as a friend lending you his beach house."

When he put it that way, his offer made sense. She thought about her schedule and realized she had enough employees to cover her work. And after seeing Cade, awful memories of Finn's foul breath and fear kept clawing at her. A few days away might be just what she needed. Not only to clear her head but also to ensure she wouldn't accidentally run into Cade while he visited his dad.

"You're sure?"

"Yes. You're a good person. The kind of person I want to be someday. So consider the trip my thanks for showing me the way."

"I'll have to move some patients…"

"You have enough staff to handle it," he said as if he'd read her mind a few minutes before. "Just go. Take the break. The house is on the beach, stocked with food. All you need is to get yourself to the airport. Your flight is tomorrow morning at eight. I've even arranged for someone to pick you up and get you to the house."

The thought of going to a tropical paradise filled her with a joy she couldn't remember ever feeling. Not just a way to snuff out those damned memories, but some time to herself. No work. No clients. Just sun and sand. She hadn't had a vacation in five years—

"You know what? I will take a week at your beach house. Thank you."

Martin said, "My pleasure," then hung up the phone.

She called her assistant and instructed her to check the schedule to see if her clients really could be covered, then raced upstairs, lugged her suitcase from under the bed and began filling it. Realizing it might be nice to have company, she called two friends, neither of whom could join her on such short notice, but she didn't care. Once her assistant told her that her personal clients had easily been reassigned, nothing but happiness filled her brain.

Seven days to herself would be the best gift any friend had ever given her.

When Cade entered his dad's brand-new silver, gray and white kitchen the next morning, an attractive middle-aged woman dressed in scrubs stood by the counter making coffee.

"Good morning."

She glanced over. "Good morning. You must be Martin's son. I'm only here to make sure your dad takes his morning pills. Then he's on his own."

He walked to the refrigerator, found bagels and headed for the toaster. "Are you sure that's a good idea?"

"Yeah. Your dad's fine. His doctor's being cautious, though, having home nurses regulate his meds for the first few weeks and Yolanda coming in to get him on the right path with physical activity. I think his doctor's using the physical therapy as a gateway into a regular exercise habit as part of a cardiac rehabilitation program."

The words weren't fully out of her mouth before his dad walked in. This morning, he looked more like his fifty-six years than he had the day before. He had color in his cheeks and wore jeans and a T-shirt, not scruffy workout clothes.

He pointed at the bagels. "Don't make yourself breakfast. I have a housekeeper for that."

Cade stopped. "You do?"

"Yeah. She'll be here in ten minutes to make breakfast and tidy the house."

The pretty nurse winked at Cade. "And to make sure he eats right. Not just deli meat and slabs of cheese on white bread."

The nurse took a few pills from bottles that she'd pulled from the cabinet on the far right and handed them to his dad with a glass of water.

He threw them into his mouth, chugged the water and set the glass down with a satisfied clunk. "Happy now?"

The nurse laughed. "Yes."

Cade tilted his head, for the first time realizing his dad's nurse wasn't Reese. Emotion-filled memories spiraled through him. Things he'd forgotten suddenly poured through his brain. Reese had been the center of his world. He'd dated before he met her—mostly taking girls to movies or football games—but there had been something about Reese, a click, that had nearly rendered him speechless.

One day after study hall, he'd walked her to her next class, and that night they'd talked on the phone for hours. The following Saturday night they'd had their first date. They'd been inseparable for the year after that.

Then his parents had decided to divorce, the war over the Colonial had begun and he'd happily left for Harvard. But without warning, she'd become weird with him when he called. Then she'd stopped answering his calls. So, he'd come home for Thanksgiving and instead of the happy surprise he'd been expecting, she'd broken up with him with very little explanation. She just gave him back his locket and told him they were through.

The pain of that rose as if it were yesterday—

He shook his head to end it. He thought he'd stopped these silly memories the day before.

"So, you had your pills." The nurse's voice interrupted Cade's thoughts. "And your housekeeper is pulling into the driveway. That means I'm off."

"Off your rocker," Cade's dad replied, then ruined the joke by hugging the nurse. "Go. See you tomorrow. Same time."

Cade stared at his dad, as the nurse collected her purse and walked out the back door.

"She's a good girl."

His eyes narrowed. "You're not thinking about dating her, are you?"

"For a guy who has no one in his own life, you worry a lot about my dates."

"I'm home for a week or so, then I'm going to my beach house. I don't want to be blindsided."

"Then don't visit your mother. She's dating the preacher. Got religion, but I don't think it's going to last. If you had visited a week from now, you could have probably avoided that phase altogether."

He laughed.

His dad got a cup of the coffee the nurse had made and walked to the table. "This is decaf, you know."

Cade groaned.

"Sorry. Doctor's orders. At least until he's sure my blood pressure is under control." He sat and motioned to the pot. "Really, it's not so bad. Reese found this expensive stuff that's actually pretty good."

The mention of her name brought back memories again. Unexpectedly happy ones. First walk in the moonlight. First kiss.

His chest tightened at the same time that his brain tried to wrap his head around what was happening. He hadn't seen Reese in twelve years. He shouldn't care about a high school fling. Yet something about the way she'd broken up with him seemed off—

"It was weird that you had to run into her yesterday," his dad said as he added cream to his coffee. "Had I known you were coming I could have scheduled things differently. In fact, if you're staying for a week, maybe you could be out of the house while she's here."

He caught Cade's gaze and Cade's eyes narrowed. His dad had *that* look on his face. The one he got when he was lying. But how could asking him to leave the house be lying?

It couldn't. Once again, he was misreading things, making too much of things because his brain was on overwhelm from the accident at the warehouse. His mind was crammed with facts and figures and sorrow. Not to mention a sense of responsibility that just wouldn't quit.

"I gave her today off since you're here. But she's the nurse I want monitoring my meds. Though I don't really need her to stay full days, she usually insists. Wicked

Yahtzee player. But I beat her in Uno," his dad said, talking about two games they'd always played when he was a kid.

More memories drifted through him. The bad ones this time. How crushed he was that Reese had dumped him, but worse that she'd never satisfactorily explained why.

His nerve endings buzzed with indignation. Confusing thoughts rolled through his head about fate and responsibility and the simple, horrible truth of how much of life was out of a person's hands.

He stopped the thoughts, took a breath and told his brain to slow down. But he knew it wouldn't. Not because of a twelve-year-old breakup, but because he wasn't as nonchalant about the accident at the warehouse as he wanted everyone to believe. It was his job to make sure all companies followed OSHA regulations. His job to determine risk.

He took another breath. Though the logical part of his brain accepted that he had done everything he was supposed to do—so had the warehouse's general manager—and accidents happened, something inside him simply couldn't settle down.

Dealing with his dad and seeing Reese was just too much when added to the confusion and guilt he had over someone in one of their operations losing his life.

Dying. Someone had died on his watch.

He couldn't think about it without his chest hollowing out and his breathing going shallow.

"Of course, you could always fly to Manhattan and return in a few weeks, after the doctor clears me from needing a nurse to check my meds every day." His dad laughed. "Hey, by then, your mom will be over the preacher and you'll be able to visit her too."

"I only have the next two weeks off. Trace and Wyatt are running the business without me so they can each get time off around the holidays."

"Always hated that you stopped coming home for the holidays." Martin took a long drink of coffee. "Sure, you shuttle your mom and me to Manhattan for bits of your free time, but those visits are short too because you're always prepping to hop on a plane for that island of yours." He glanced at Cade. "How is that island?"

"Warm and sunny," Cade said wistfully. That was what he really needed. A week in the sun to sort things out.

"Okay. So, go there. Then pop in here on your way back to Manhattan so you can visit your mother."

"Since when do you care if I visit my mother?"

"Since I had a stroke and realized life is too short to be a horrible person." He motioned toward the door with his hands. "Shoo. I'm fine. I'll be here when you get back from your fishing paradise."

"I don't know…"

His dad sighed. "Cade, do I have to spell this out for you? That nurse that just left? She's cute. She's smart. She's unlike anybody I've ever dated. And I have a shot with her. I know it."

Cade frowned. Now, he understood his father's weird babbling. He wasn't lying. He was manipulating, trying to figure out a way to get rid of Cade so he could have alone time with the nurse.

Which wasn't such a bad thing. Not only was the nurse intelligent and pretty; she was also closer to his dad's age.

"Come on. You're harshing my buzz."

"If you mean that I'm in the way, harshing my buzz is not the phrase to use."

"Who cares? Get lost. Come back when your mother will be available. I know she misses you."

Leaning against the coffee counter, Cade considered that. He liked the new man his father was becoming. Especially dating a woman who really could be a partner for him. Plus, a trip to the island sounded good. He didn't want to see Reese anymore and relive a heartbreak he'd gotten over a decade ago. Especially not when he was dealing with the death of someone for whom he was responsible. He might not have been Roger's direct boss, but he owned the company that employed him. He had feelings rolling around in him that he didn't understand. He needed some time, and he was smart enough to know that.

His dad was fine, and his mother would be visitable in a week. It made more sense to go to the island now and spend time here later.

He pushed away from the counter. "You know what? I think I will have a cup of the decaf. Then head out for the island."

His dad smiled stupidly.

But why not? Nothing about his dad was normal. And memories of Reese wouldn't let him alone. Which—after twelve years—was just plain odd.

He needed to get away. What better place than his own island?

CHAPTER THREE

CADE CAST DENNIS AUDREY a weird look, as his pilot took the helicopter into the air to fly him from West Keys Airport to his island. Dennis wasn't one for small talk, but he also wasn't the kind of guy to grin without reason. Yet, his pilot grinned as he glided the helicopter into the sky.

Suddenly, the sound of Dennis's voice filled his earphones. "Storm." Dennis pointed as he said the one word.

Cade followed the direction of his finger and saw thunderheads forming.

Dennis's voice filled his earphones again. "You won't be coming back tonight."

Cade frowned. "I don't want to come back tonight."

"Good, because the approaching storm is going to be a doozy."

He knew about storms in this part of the world. They could be vicious. He hadn't checked the weather, but before taking off his pilot obviously had.

Still, it was unusual that Dennis made a point to tell him he wouldn't be coming back that night.

They touched down on the helipad on the far edge of the island, where a space to take off and land had been carved into the dense foliage. Dennis unloaded Cade's duffel from the helicopter, but Cade waved him off when he wanted to carry it to one of the bikes stored in the small shed to the right.

"I can carry one little duffel bag twenty feet. I'll call you when I'm ready to leave."

Dennis grinned again. "Sure thing." He saluted and climbed into the helicopter again.

It took off as Cade tossed his duffel to the basket behind the seat of his bike and slid on.

He closed his eyes and drew a breath, then another, then another, letting his body relax. This was why he'd bought this island. The peace and quiet that surrounded him was all his. He was far enough away from other landowners that he didn't get their ambient noise, but close enough that he could party with his neighbors if he wanted to.

Right now, a little peace and quiet sounded like just what he needed.

Pedaling the bike on the wide path to his retreat, he smiled as his muscles loosened. The big yellow house came into view. It was perfect for hosting a New Year's Eve week or weekend and yet not so enormous that he couldn't stay there by himself.

Climbing the few steps to the front door, he pulled in another long drink of tropical air and looked around. When he was a kid, he'd told himself that someday he'd have a place far, far away to go to when his parents made him a laughingstock. And though his parents' arguments didn't matter anymore, it was still fun that he'd achieved that goal.

He punched in the code for the front door, walked inside and frowned at the breeze blowing in from the ocean. He knew a storm was on the way, but it shouldn't be blowing inside his house—

Unless the back door was open?

He walked through the high-ceilinged foyer with the sunburst chandelier, passing the mostly white kitchen with bright orange designer floor tiles, and saw the back door had been folded to the left so that the living room and patio formed one big space.

Checking to be sure no one was in the infinity pool or the outdoor kitchen with a stone pizza oven and state-of-the-art grill, he dropped his duffel and raced to the door intending to close it. But he saw a woman sprawled face-down on a chaise lounge in the patio area. Lying on her tummy, she let one arm fall to her right and had her face buried in the soft cushion beneath her.

He'd heard of people paying housekeepers or grounds-keepers to get the codes for houses that were empty more than they were used, but he'd never actually found an un-invited guest in his house—

On his own private island—where there were no police. No one to call to get rid of her.

He stepped out onto the patio, then stealthily made his way over to the interloper. Temptation was strong to haul her cute little butt in the pink polka-dot bikini off the chaise. But he wasn't like that. Sure, he would investigate who let her in and fire that person, but he'd do it sensibly.

He reached down to shake her awake, but when he saw her top was unhooked so she wouldn't get a tan line on her back, touching her didn't feel right either.

He snatched his hand away.

"Get up," he said in his sternest *I'm a billionaire* voice. She didn't stir.

"Get up!" he said, louder and angrier than the first time.

When she still didn't move, he yelled, "What the hell are you doing in my house?"

Finally awake, she lifted her head, groggily turned it to the left and probably saw his denim-covered legs. She bounced from her stomach into a seated position in what seemed like one fluid movement.

Grasping her top in place over her breasts, she said, "Cade?"

Trying to keep his eyes on her face and away from any exposed flesh, he said, "Reese?"

She fumbled to reattach her bikini top and he pivoted away to give her privacy. But it was too late. His brain had taken a mental picture of her pale skin, full breasts and belly button ring. He was pretty sure the shiny red part was her birthstone.

"You can turn around now."

As he did, she grabbed a pink floral cover-up and shimmied into it. "What are you doing here?"

He gaped at her. "What are you doing here? This is my island!"

"No. It's your dad's beach house."

"My dad doesn't own a beach house. He uses *my island*."

A few seconds passed as that seemed to settle into her brain. "You own a whole island?"

Sun shimmered off her red hair that had dried in ringlets, probably after a dip in the pool or the ocean. Her green eyes held his gaze. And all he could think about was the summer they'd spent at the pool in the backyard of the Colonial, while both his parents were at work. Sometimes he'd invite friends to join them. Other times he didn't. Lots of times he just wanted her to himself.

He'd been so crazy in love with her. Not merely because she brought sanity to his otherwise chaotic life, but because she was fun to be around. A kid with a normal childhood, she knew how to make lemonade and no-bake chocolate oatmeal cookies from ingredients she found around the house. But she also loved playing video games on his advanced gaming system and lounging at the pool. Always dressed in a tiny bikini, she'd about driven his seventeen-year-old self crazy with lust.

When they'd finally given in to their feelings, their romance had gone from fun and exuberant to passionate and important. He'd have done anything for her.

The memory filled his chest with longing for simpler times, simpler needs. He got rid of it with a deep breath that puffed his lungs before he blew it out, releasing the yearning for something that could never be. Something that might not have ever actually existed, if the way she'd broken up with him was anything to go by.

"Yes. I own an entire island." He waited a beat. "What are you doing here?"

"Your dad told me I could use *his* beach house." She snorted. "He told me he was changing, getting generous."

"Yeah. Generous with my house." Cade ran his hand along the back of his neck. "He kind of persuaded me to spend the next week here…something about my mom dating the preacher."

An unexpected, joyful laugh poured from her. "Yeah. That's a real hoot. They're like the odd couple. Been together almost a month."

"Dad doesn't think it will last more than another week."

"There's a betting pool at the diner. I took three more weeks."

"You're gonna lose your money."

She grinned. "Only if your dad is right."

He chuckled, then drew in another breath. It might be odd to talk normally with her after twelve years of not seeing each other. But somehow they'd tumbled from awkward to normal in about three seconds. It felt good. *He* felt good. Almost himself.

"Looks like he set us up."

She straightened her cover-up. "Yeah. He wanted me to talk to you yesterday, but I needed to get on with my work."

He saw it then. A wisp of something that came to her

green eyes. It could have been sorrow or sadness, but when he gave it a few seconds of thought, he decided it looked more like exhaustion. She banked it quickly, as if she were accustomed to doing that, and something warm and protective filled him. Probably from the memories of how he'd felt about her all those years ago, how he would have done anything for her.

The weirdness of the situation returned. He combed his fingers through his short hair. "This is odd."

She tightened her hold on the cover-up. "Tell me about it."

"One of us should leave—"

"I will."

He didn't want to go, but her leaving didn't feel right. He sighed. "Not tonight." As if on cue, thunder rumbled. "Storm."

Her chin lifted. "Then I'll leave in the morning."

She said it as if she were angry at him, as if she had a reason to be angry with him, and that attitude went through him like a knife. That was how she'd been the day she broke up with him. Distant. Angry. As if he'd done something god awful. And he hadn't. He'd been too busy with the start of the school year at an Ivy League university. He might have been the smartest kid at his high school, but at Harvard he was average. If she hadn't been able to respect or understand how difficult his first year had been, then she wasn't the girl he'd thought.

He turned to walk into the house. "Sure. Leave in the morning. That's fine."

He wanted the memories of his past to stop, so he could clear his head. Her leaving was the way to assure that. If she was still angry about something he didn't even know he'd done, she could leave.

No problem.

* * *

With rain pounding on the roof, sounding like kettledrums, Reese went to the room where she'd stowed her luggage and toiletries case.

It wasn't so much a "room" as a suite with a sitting room in front, a huge yellow, tan and black bedroom with a king-size bed and a private bath that looked like a spa.

Staring at the two-person black-tiled shower with rain heads and total-body massaging jets, beside a freestanding black tub on black and white octagonal tiles, she suddenly gasped.

What if she'd taken the master bedroom?

Wouldn't it be embarrassing to have Cade mindlessly climb the steps that night and crawl into bed with her?

Her heart didn't know whether to swoon or beat out of her chest. She didn't date much. Rarely slept with anyone. Therapy had gotten her beyond her fear of sex. It was a normal, healthy sign of affection and when she found someone she genuinely cared for, she could be all in.

But she was particular, and technically she didn't know Cade anymore. Even though he'd become an absolutely gorgeous man, the whoosh of desire that washed through her was foreign.

And wrong.

He'd deserted her when she'd needed him most. He'd proved himself to be untrustworthy—

Still—

A private island, a luscious man—

Stop.

No one was crawling into bed with anyone. It was against Rule Number Two. *Must know your partner.* She hadn't seen Cade in so long that he was a stranger now.

It would also be against Rule Number Three. *No one-night stands.*

She shook her head. She hadn't had to refer to her rules in a long time. After over a decade, most of them, like Rule Number One, *Never put yourself in a sketchy situation*, were ingrained behaviors. The fact that she was remembering the rules her sixteen-year-old self had created in therapy told her something was "off" here. The thought that risky behavior even tiptoed into her brain floored her. Cade might be a stranger, but deep down she knew he was a nice guy.

Wasn't he?

He seemed to be.

But she also couldn't drop her rules without as much as an eye bat. She had to ascertain the best plan of action with him, especially how to behave around him tonight.

The storm made their situation worse. Without the driving rain, one of them could be on the beach, the other in the house. With the rain, there was nowhere to go.

Lightning streaked across the black sky.

Yep. They were stuck inside together. Would they end up eating together? Or watching TV together? Plus, if she'd taken his room, she had to give it back. So, would there be an odd dance in the hall as she carried her repacked bags to another room, and he carried his big duffel into this one?

And if this wasn't his room, where *was* he sleeping?

They had to have a chat. The sooner the better. Then she could watch TV in whatever room she ended up bunking, repack and maybe even be gone before he woke the next morning.

She quickly slid into yoga pants and a pink T-shirt and headed downstairs. She found Cade in the white kitchen with the stunning orange-and-white Moroccan design floor tiles with a complementary orange backsplash. Bread, deli meat, cheese and a jar of mustard were scattered on the big center island. Answering at least one question. Would she have to eat dinner with him?

No. She could make herself a sandwich while he had everything out on the counter and then take it to another room.

Relief smoothed her ruffled nerve endings.

Plus, while she made the sandwich that she would take to her room to eat, she could get answers to her other questions, calm herself and be able to sleep before going home the next morning.

He glanced up and saw her in front of the island. "Sandwich?"

"You read my mind." She got a plate from a cupboard and began layering bread, meat and cheese.

"There's beer in the fridge."

Her hand stopped halfway to the mustard. "Beer?"

"Or soft drinks. There's a wine room behind the den," he said casually as if every house in the world had a wine room. "And an actual bar in the family room in case you like cocktails or whisky on the rocks."

Rule Number Six, *Be careful around alcohol*, popped into her head. She hadn't been drinking but Finn had.

She took a breath. Hating that the most horrible night of her life kept running through her brain, she brought out the mental box again and shoved those thoughts inside. Then she locked it and tossed the key.

"I think I'll just have a soft drink. Is there anything without caffeine?"

He snorted. "What? Did you become a Mormon after we stopped dating?"

Her answer was quick and every bit as sarcastic as his. "Did you become snarky after we stopped dating?"

He rolled his eyes and she pulled back her sarcasm. She had information to get.

"The pilot, Dennis, took my things to the bedroom at the top of the stairs. If that's the master, I'll happily move."

"That's not the master." He put a slice of bread on top of what looked to be a work-of-art sandwich and headed for the fridge. Pulling out a bottle of beer, he said, "Master is on the third floor." He grinned. "Better view. I own it. I get it."

"I heard the rumors that you'd gotten rich."

He shrugged. "I found two partners who love to work. Wyatt is the brains of the operation. The guy with the big ideas. Trace is our memory and fact-checker. He's our detail guy."

"And you?"

"I like to think of myself as daily operations."

The normal conversation went a long way to nudge her rules out of her head as she began remembering what an average guy he was for a kid who'd been so smart. "Daily operations?"

"Trace hires and fires employees, but I handle benefits and salaries. I'm the actuarial science guy. I assess risk. Get insurance when needed or tell Trace and Wyatt to pull back from projects or investments where the risk outweighs the reward."

He took a sudden breath, and an odd expression came to his face as if something he'd said about risk brought him up short.

She almost asked him about it. Instead, labeling her curiosity as inappropriate given that she was leaving, she said, "Still a geek."

"Maybe. But look how it's paid off."

He said it easily, but his face contorted again. Did he really believe it had paid off?

It struck her that he was alone for his vacation. There was no ring on his finger. There were no kids clamoring to come with Daddy to the family's private island. His friends were his partners. Business associates.

He truly might be wondering if it was worth it—

That was none of her business.

Rummaging through the fridge, she found a soft drink without caffeine and picked up her plate with her sandwich. "So, I don't have to change rooms?"

He frowned. "No."

"Okay. Good night, then."

"You're going to bed?"

"No. I'll watch some TV upstairs."

He nodded. "Okay."

"I'll also call Dennis before I settle in and be gone in the morning."

"Don't call now. Wait until an hour before you're ready to go. Give him the night off with his family."

"Okay." She smiled slightly, not wanting to look like an ungrateful guest, but also impressed that he protected his employee's time off. She'd heard most rich guys were selfish. It was good to see he hadn't changed much from the nice boy she'd dated...the first guy she'd made love with.

"I'll call tomorrow."

"Okay."

With a nod, she turned and walked through the foyer to the main steps and up to the room she was using.

Rain pounded the sliding glass door that led to a small balcony with a view of the ocean that had stolen her breath when she arrived.

She sat on the sofa in the sitting room, ate her sandwich and watched an outdated sitcom she found on the TV that had to be connected to a satellite with supergood reception.

Then she changed into her pajamas and climbed into a bed with sheets so soft she sighed with contentment.

She supposed she'd always known Cade would make

something of himself. He'd been at the top of their class. Plus, his parents were both hard workers.

And crazy. She couldn't forget that working so hard had made them nuts when it came time to divide their assets.

Thoughts of her year with Cade flitted through her and she relaxed into the pillow to the soothing sound of rain that had finally slowed to a pitter patter. She remembered meeting his parents. Remembered the day she realized just how smart he was. Remembered their first kiss.

In the moonlight.

Her heart had about drummed out of her chest. God, she'd loved him.

First love, she supposed, was the strongest. First real kiss. First time of trusting someone with your heart. First true connection. Which was why their first time of making love had been so special.

She closed her eyes. It had been so, so special. And every time after that had been remarkable. They grew to the point where they could make lovemaking fun, like playing, or intense like giving their hearts all over again.

Which was why it was so hard to believe he'd hadn't taken her calls that weekend. Hadn't been there for her—

In her brain, she found a new box. Opened it. Put in the memory of Cade not taking her calls, leaving her alone to face the aftershocks of being raped. Then mentally locked it and tossed it into the beautiful blue ocean just beyond this house.

She fell asleep forcing herself to think about soft waves and fish.

She didn't want to like him. Not because he was a terrible person, but because when push came to shove, he hadn't been there for her.

But maybe that was lucky.

Besides the rape, there was something else he didn't

know about her. If they had stayed together, she would have had to tell him.

And just like her ex, Tony, he probably would have dumped her too.

CHAPTER FOUR

CADE AMBLED INTO the kitchen the next morning and frowned when he glanced through the sliding glass door and saw the mess on the patio. The wind had been sufficient to shake leaves from the trees and even a few branches.

He could call somebody to clean up. He had two groundskeepers under contract. Either would arrive at a moment's notice. But a little physical activity would go a long way to clearing his head.

He opened the fridge and almost drank milk straight from the carton, but remembered Reese was there.

The carton stopped midway to his mouth. *Reese.* He'd thought about her all night. When he finally did fall asleep, he dreamed about her. About happy times. About laughter and intensity. About feelings he hadn't felt before or since.

Not even with Brenda, his ex-wife, which he supposed should have been a red flag. And might have been why memories of Reese had popped into his head right before he'd walked out to the altar to get married. At the time, he'd given himself some jibber jabber about Reese being his first love. That's why he'd thought of her. But what if his brain had really been trying to tell him what he felt for Reese had been real love and what he felt for Brenda wasn't?

He shook off the notion. Particularly since he did not

believe what he and Reese felt had been real love. Otherwise, she wouldn't have unceremoniously ditched him.

After finding a glass, he poured himself some milk, made a bagel and headed outside. He took two bites of the bagel, then set it on the small patio table beside the first chaise lounge. Fresh morning air filled his lungs. The sun warmed the space, promising a hot day. The ocean lay before him like a blue goddess. The whole world was silent.

On a normal visit, once he cleaned the pool, he'd shuck his shorts and skinny-dip. With Reese there he couldn't do that. Though they had. All those summers ago, when they were young and life was easy, they'd made love in the pool. They would lay naked in the sun for hours talking about everything. And then one day it was over. Gone.

It had never added up, if only because Reese was the kind of girl who should have understood his first few weeks at Harvard were an adjustment. He'd told her what he was dealing with. She'd seemed to understand. Yet, when he'd finally come home for Thanksgiving, she hadn't been happy to see him. She'd dumped him.

He'd assumed it was because she'd found somebody else, and that caused so much pain he'd thrown himself into his schoolwork as a way to forget.

And he had.

Especially since he'd never come home again after that.

He returned to his bagel, took another bite and walked to the small cedar cabana to get the skimmer. Eventually everything would be drawn toward the waterfall of the infinity pool and be filtered in the catch, but he wanted to swim *now*. Thinking about Reese might be pushing aside thoughts of Roger Burkey's death but thinking about Reese wasn't good for him either.

So many unanswered questions that seemed to somehow knit into his bad marriage. Otherwise, why would he have remembered Reese before walking to the altar to marry Brenda? If he'd known why Reese had dumped him, would he have been smarter about the woman he'd chosen to marry?

He frowned. That didn't seem right. It didn't really connect or make sense.

But there was no denying his marriage had been a huge mistake. Not only had Brenda been a horrible choice for a partner—who'd made his life miserable with demands and public arguments—but also when they'd divorced, she'd wanted half his share of the corporation he owned with Wyatt and Trace.

Reese hadn't even kept a silly locket. She'd returned the one and only gift he'd given her.

Brenda had been so different from Reese that if he really took this to the logical conclusion, he might think he'd chosen Brenda for just that reason.

After all, Reese had hurt him.

Still, he couldn't shake the feeling that he'd done something wrong that caused her to break up with him. Given that she was the one who'd dumped him, she shouldn't be angry with him right now.

Yet, she clearly was.

The first panel of the sliding glass door opened. It folded into the second, which folded into the third, which folded into the fourth, opening his living space to the patio.

Wincing, Reese walked out. Wearing yoga pants and a T-shirt, she looked like she'd just woken up.

"Sorry. Every time I try to open only the first panel, the whole thing opens."

Her shy smile sent warmth through him, a longing that wanted to connect the past to the present. To figure all this out.

Which was stupid. Pointless...

Wasn't it?

He angled the skimmer over the pool. "If you only need to open the first panel, you have to be careful not to hit the button on the side of the handle."

"Oh."

He dragged the skimmer through the water, then pulled it out and dumped the leaves, branches and fronds in a small area off to the right, away from the patio. "Where's your breakfast?"

"I usually don't eat breakfast."

"There are coffee pods and a one-cup brewer if you're interested."

"Thanks. I am. I might not eat breakfast but I love my morning coffee." She turned to return to the house, then paused and faced him again. "And I wanted to say I'm sorry."

He froze. He hadn't exactly waited twelve years to hear her say that, but his eighteen-year-old self had been insulted, wounded, *hurt* that she'd discarded him without explanation. Hearing her apologize now wasn't merely surprising; it was unexpectedly welcome.

His chest loosened, but he couldn't quite figure out what to do with her apology. It didn't explain why she'd broken up with him, and something inside him desperately wanted to know what he'd done. And if he'd been the one to do something wrong, why was she apologizing?

"What exactly are you sorry for?"

"I didn't know your dad was setting us up. But I really should have thought this through and realized he probably didn't own a beach house. Somebody in town would have mentioned it. If nothing else, your mother would have griped about it. I should have seen through his offer."

Disappointment rattled through him. Then he called himself an idiot. Just because he'd thought about her and their past the night before didn't mean she had. And twelve years had gone by. He was an older, wiser version of the eighteen-year-old who'd been hurt by her. Why did he keep going over this in his head?

So he wouldn't think about Roger Burkey?

Maybe. But every time he and Reese talked, he got a nudge of a hint that he'd done something to make her dump him. And that really bothered him. He had absolutely no idea what he could have done, except that he was so busy at Harvard that he hadn't even had much time to talk on the phone. Still… She'd seemed to understand that. Or so he'd thought.

Their breakup was the one unsettled thing in his life. Even his bad marriage and subsequent divorce had sorted itself. His relationship with Reese was like a big question mark. And maybe this was fate's way of forcing him to put a period at the end of their sentence. He hadn't seen her in twelve years. Probably wouldn't ever see her again. This might be his one shot at closing that book.

He glanced over at her, saw her draw a long, deep breath as if enjoying the island's morning air, cleaned by last night's storm, as she took in the white sand and ocean before her. Tall and beautiful, with red hair that sparkled in the sun, she looked at his paradise with the kind of yearning that couldn't be hidden. She wanted to stay, and maybe she needed this time away as much as he did.

His curiosity spiked again. He had absolutely no clue what had happened to her in twelve years. As much as he wanted to close the book with her, he also just plain wanted to know how she'd been.

"Have you called Dennis yet?"

"No. I thought I'd have coffee and pack first. That way I would be ready when he got here."

Her logical voice reminded him of the Reese he'd known

before she'd split them up, and he said, "Sounds like the Reese I know. Organized. Thorough."

She faced him with a smile and all he saw was *his* Reese. The girl who'd loved life, *loved him*.

"Funny you didn't say that I was happy."

"You were always happy." But the shadows had returned to her green eyes again, and he suddenly didn't want closure as much as he wanted to make things right. Clearly, he'd done something for her to break up with him, and even if she decided not to tell him what it was, maybe doing a good deed for her could appease the weird feelings inside him.

"Don't call."

She faced him, her green eyes confused. "What?"

"Don't call Dennis. Stay."

"I don't want you to have to leave your own house."

"I'm not going. We'll stay here together. The island is almost twenty acres. There's a beach, a pool, a big house... and bigger islands where you might want to go sightseeing. Plus, I take the boat out and fish most of the time. Some days I stay until dark. There's a good chance we won't even bump into each other at mealtimes."

Her face softened, though cautiously. "How do I get to the other islands to sightsee?"

Ah. He *was* tempting her. "I usually take one of my boats over, and most days I could drop you off before I go fishing, but if you want to go at odd times or want to come back early, I'll give you the number of my guy."

"You have a guy?"

"Yeah, he runs a boat service. Kind of like a car service with a boat. And the islands are great. You can visit a different one every day if you want. I have a couple of bikes. Take one and you can get around more easily."

Her eyes softened. "Wow." The sadness he sometimes heard in her voice dissolved into awe.

He motioned at the quiet, empty world around them. "It's a different way of living down here."

"I see that."

He laughed. "Trust me. You're going to love it. Plus, most of the vendors know me. So, I have accounts. If you need something like a tour guide, drop my name and they'll bill me."

Her chin lifted. "I'm not poor."

And here came the anger, the defensiveness. There were so many pieces to this puzzle that he simply couldn't dismiss it.

"Never said you were poor. Just offering you a chance to have some downtime." He headed inside to dress to go out on his boat and leave her alone to make her decision. "Choice is yours."

She debated the merits of staying for the whole five minutes it took to make toast and coffee. When she carried her breakfast outside to eat at one of the three round patio tables, the decision almost made itself. The peace of the area surrounded her. Looking out over the ocean, she felt one with the universe. Her tired brain began to revive, to remember all the reasons she should leave, but her body wouldn't let her. It wanted to walk on the beach, swim or tour his little island on one of the bikes.

After only a few seconds, her brain got on board. It began imagining the breeze blowing her hair as she rode a bike and drank in the scents of the foliage all around her.

She ate her toast and opted to give it a few hours. She could take a walk on the beach, explore the island on a bike and come back and swim. If he had returned from his fishing trip and she found him lounging around the pool, that would mean they'd be in each other's way and she'd call Dennis and leave. But at least she'd have had one great, restful Sunday morning.

It made so much sense that she raced upstairs, slid into a bikini and put her list into action. When Cade hadn't returned after her swim, she took a nap.

It was past seven and she was upstairs in her suite when Cade finally entered the house. He didn't make a lot of noise, but he made enough that she knew he was downstairs. She heard the sound of a television but closed her suite door and silence reigned. She took a bottle of water out to the balcony off her room and watched the ocean for hours before she headed inside and fell asleep.

Monday morning, she woke feeling like a new woman. A day of exercise and sun must have been exactly what she needed. She slid into a swimsuit and a cover up and headed for the kitchen.

Unfortunately, when she reached the door, she saw Cade at the counter and stopped dead in her tracks. He wore a blue T-shirt over printed aqua shorts, bringing out the color of his eyes. One day of fishing on the water had turned his skin reddish brown. His yellow hair had begun to lighten.

"Good morning."

With his slight tan and disheveled hair, he looked like he belonged here. On the beach. In the luxurious kitchen. Given that this was his house, she told herself that only made sense. She also told herself to be civil. Maybe even nice. He didn't have to let her stay. And she clearly needed the rest. Civility might get her another few days.

"Good morning."

He smiled briefly. "Given any thought to going into town sightseeing?"

She popped a pod into the coffee maker. Testing the waters to make sure he was still okay with this arrangement, she said, "Maybe tomorrow."

"Sounds good." He picked up his muffin and headed for the patio.

Relieved that he was so easygoing, she drank her coffee at the kitchen counter, reading the news on her phone. When she was finished, she cleared her dishes and headed outside to get a bike.

When she returned from her ride, he was on the beach. From the patio vantage point, she could see him edging his way into the water and eventually, when it got deep enough, diving in. She watched his muscular back work as he swam out into the waves and her heart skipped a beat, as memories poured through her.

Because spying on him, remembering their past, wasn't part of the deal, she shrugged out of her cover-up, took a short swim in the pool and found a comfortable chaise. But even though she intended to read a book on her phone, her gaze kept rising to watch him swim. How casual he was. How comfortable. And the oddest thought hit her.

Was this what it was like to be a billionaire?

She almost asked him when he ambled up to the patio about an hour later. But she didn't want to talk to him. She most certainly didn't want to be curious about him.

He didn't say anything as he walked past her, into the house, but all her nerve endings tingled. Which—she told herself—was simply the weird feeling of living in a house with someone and not talking to them.

They didn't really know each other anymore. They both wanted a rest. The house was big enough for them both.

That was sort of their deal.

But when he came out at about three that afternoon and walked over to the big grill, he said, "I'm making steaks for dinner. Want one?"

She peered up at him over her sunglasses. Shirtless, still in his swim trunks, he casually dropped two steaks to the grill.

"Dinner? Now?"

"We don't eat on the clock here in paradise. We eat when we're hungry."

"But won't we get hungry again at night?"

He shrugged. The gorgeous muscles of his shoulders lifted. "Then we'll have a sandwich."

With the pool between them, she stared at his perfect back, the way his butt looked in the pale blue swimming trunks, then his long legs.

"You've gotten taller." The words spilled out even before she realized she was thinking them, and she could have bitten off her tongue. Their deal was no contact. But he started it when he brought out the steaks.

He looked over his shoulder at her. "You did too."

Relief rippled through her. Glad he didn't make a big deal out of her slip, she leaned back on the chaise.

"So rare, medium or well done?"

She sat up again. "Rare is good." Setting her phone on the small table by her chaise, she said, "Is there anything I can do?"

"Like?"

"Make a side dish? A salad?"

He shrugged again. "There's usually potato salad in the fridge."

He casually turned away and she stared at him. All those questions she'd had about him while watching him swim came tumbling back. He took for granted that everything he wanted would be at his fingertips.

"How do you know it's not old and spoiled?"

"The potato salad? I look at the use-by date. But, honestly, I call a service before I come down here. Things like steak are in the freezer, but the service comes in, inventories what's in the cabinets and refrigerator and updates everything."

"Wow."

He faced her with a frown. "Wow what?"

She glanced around. "I just… I don't know. It's all so perfect."

He snorted. "My life?"

She considered her answer for a second, trying to be neutral, but curiosity overwhelmed her and she said, "Yeah."

"It's not."

She rose from the chaise. "Now, don't be snooty. I didn't mean to insult you. But I've never even thought about what it would be like to have so much money I didn't have to work."

"I work!"

"Again, not trying to insult you. But I work, too, and I don't make nearly enough money to own an island."

"You could."

She laughed. She hadn't eaten lunch and the scent of the sizzling steaks lured her to the grill. Standing beside him, she said, "Not hardly. I have lots of customers in a three- or four-town area. But I'll never make a billion dollars."

"What if you franchised? What if you turned your idea into a business model that you could sell, then took the company public and cashed out?"

"Now you're just talking crazy."

"Not really. People make money three ways. From producing a good, providing a service or selling an idea. You could continue to provide the service, branch out, hire more people, go into more towns and earn a decent amount of money. But if you want to get rich, you have to provide all the stuff it takes for someone else to use your idea, then take a percentage of their proceeds."

"I know how franchising works. It's just not what I do. I'm a nurse with a business degree who likes her job just as it is."

"Then keep doing it."

"Seriously? After all those suggestions, you're telling me not to do anything?"

"Sometimes happiness and enjoying what you do is undervalued in our society. When I die, all the money I've accrued doesn't come with me. It actually becomes meaningless to me. Like I worked my life away for something that doesn't matter."

She gaped at him. "You hate your job?"

"No! I love my job." He took a breath. She saw a debate raging in his eyes before he said, "Mostly. There are some things that aren't easy—" He stopped again, drew another breath. "I'm just saying money's not the only measure of success. I think being happy is the greater measure."

He waited a beat, then said, "Are you happy?"

She didn't hesitate. She knew the wrong answer would cause him to probe. And she'd rather die than have him probe, digging around until he bumped into her secrets. "Yeah."

"Good. I'm glad."

Something about the way he said it warmed her heart. She'd felt uncomfortable about him for so long that it was nice to have positive feelings for him.

He chuckled. "I'll even give you the island once a year for a vacation."

"I told you. I'm not a charity case."

"When a friend lets a friend use his island, it's not about charity. It's about sharing. Don't you share?"

"Sure. I just never thought of billionaires as being people who share."

"Why wouldn't we? We're the ones with the best toys."

She laughed. Again. And for the first time since she'd broken up with him, she missed him. Her heart filled with a yearning so profound her breathing stopped. As much as the feeling nudged her to recognize staying might not be a good idea, it also made her long for time with him. Her common sense warned her that might be the worst decision of her life, but she just wanted to spend a couple of days in the pure, innocent happiness they'd shared as kids—even though she knew it wasn't possible. She was different now. Damaged. Plus, they couldn't have what they'd talked about as two teenagers planning a future.

She could never forget that.

But her yearning wasn't about the future. It was about now. What they could have now. Maybe if she didn't push too hard, didn't want too much, these next few days would satisfy the little ache in her chest that popped up every time she looked at him. Wouldn't it be fun to get to know him again? To laugh? To be silly?

She considered again that that might not be smart, but she silenced her usually wise brain.

Just for once, she didn't want to think about tomorrow, about consequences, about any damned thing except having some fun.

CHAPTER FIVE

THEY ATE THEIR steaks with the potato salad Reese found in the refrigerator, just as Cade had told her she would. When their meal ended, they went their separate ways. He actually took a short nap and woke when she returned from a walk on the beach and plopped on the chaise beside his, surprising him.

With the lazy, late afternoon sun shining down on them, it felt so damned right for her to be next to him that it seemed as if no time had passed between that summer twelve years ago and this minute. Different pool. Same people.

Happiness stuttered through him and he sat up. "Hey, you know what we need?"

She peered at him over her sunglasses. "What?"

"No-bakes."

"The cookies?"

He nodded.

She laughed. "Seriously, you're hungry?"

"No. I just want a treat."

She lifted herself off her chaise. "If you have the right things in the kitchen, I can make them. But I think I want to shower first. I'm all sweaty from my walk."

He sat up. "Write down what you need, and I'll check the cupboards while you're showering."

She headed inside. "Sounds like a plan."

When she reached the kitchen, she grabbed the notepad and pencil attached to the refrigerator by a magnet. "Let's see… Sugar, butter, vanilla, milk…"

He ambled up to the center island. "I know we have those."

"That leaves oatmeal and cocoa powder."

"Cocoa powder?"

"Yeah. It's how cooks make things chocolate. Until you add the cocoa, brownies are blondies." She frowned. "You might not have it."

"You'd be surprised what the shopping service stocks."

She pulled away from the center island. "Okay. See you in about half an hour."

"Make it forty-five minutes."

Almost out of the kitchen, she turned and frowned at him. "What?"

"Just… Nothing." He laughed. "Go shower."

She left the room, and he didn't even bother looking in the cupboards. He wasn't a fan of oatmeal, so he was sure his service didn't stock it. Cocoa powder? He sincerely doubted they provided that either.

But he wanted the no-bake cookies. He liked the feeling of him and Reese behaving normally. Their inconsequential chitchat while grilling their steaks had taken away his brain's need to go over Roger's accident again and again and again. And having her plop down beside him was just…nice.

He would be careful. He would be honest. But he wouldn't argue with something that was working.

He picked up his phone and called Dennis. He told him to bring a box of oatmeal and cocoa powder.

Dennis laughed and said, "I'll ask my wife."

Cade agreed that was a good idea. "Don't take too long. Reese is showering. I need the stuff to be here when she's out."

Dennis said, "Got it!"

Cade disconnected the call, then he pulled the rest of the items Reese said she needed, set them on the big center island and walked out to the pool. In forty minutes, he heard the sound of the helicopter. In another ten, he heard the noise of Dennis riding one of the bikes up to the house. He got out of the pool, dried off and entered the kitchen the same time Dennis did.

He set a bag on the table. "My wife says these are what you want."

"What who wants?"

Seeing Reese in the doorway, Cade winced. "We didn't have the cocoa powder."

She peeked in the bag. "Or the oatmeal."

"And now we do," Cade said happily, trying to make light of the fact that he'd just spent a thousand dollars to get some cookies. He didn't give a damn. Dennis loved it when he did this kind of thing because the money was good. But he had a sneaking feeling Reese would not understand.

She surprised him by saying a pleasant goodbye to Dennis when he left and immediately started to stir ingredients into a heavy pan.

She took a quick breath and glanced up at him. "What would you have done if we didn't have the right pan?"

He peered at her. "The right pan?"

"It takes a thick, sturdy pan to cook the sugar and butter together. If it's too thin, the paste burns. So, what would you have done if we hadn't had this pan?"

He shrugged. "I don't know."

"Would you have sent Dennis to a big-box store, looking for pans?"

"Because we have the pan, it's irrelevant."

"Not really. It's all tied up in you being a billionaire." She shook her head. "Holy crap, your life is different."

He couldn't tell if she liked that. Still, if something about him had made her ditch him when he was eighteen, being different should be a good thing.

But he didn't want to risk it. He didn't want to risk whatever this feeling was that kept rolling through the air, capturing his heart, taking him back to the happiest time of his life. Not when he desperately needed something else to think about other than the worry that he'd made a mistake, that the safety protocols he'd approved hadn't been enough, and it was his fault that a man had died.

Was it so wrong that his poor brain wanted a rest?

If stopping conversations that might make her mad kept her here, then that's what he'd do. He grabbed a beer from the fridge and walked toward the open doorway that connected the living room to the outside. "I'm going to take a swim."

Focused on making sure the sugar and butter didn't burn as they reached the right temperature and consistency, Reese barely noticed he was gone. But when she measured the cocoa to stir it in, she paused.

God only knew how much money it had cost him to get the cocoa.

The truth of his wealth, his life, rippled through her. He was the same, but different. He'd always been a cut above the rest of the kids in their group. Strong enough to deal with his parents, he'd had substance that high school kids normally didn't have.

Her heart squeezed, then swelled with longing for all the things they'd lost. All the things they seemed to be finding again—

Gut-wrenching sorrow filled her so quickly, her brain wasn't fast enough to compartmentalize it. They couldn't "find" anything again. The dreams they had as teenagers weren't possible. Not only had a rape changed her, but she couldn't have kids.

She took a breath. *This* was exactly why she shouldn't be around Cade. She'd had her life under control for years and now suddenly everything wrong was closing in on her.

Because seeing him had her focusing on the past.

She frowned at the thought that had crept into her brain. Part of moving on had been learning to let go of the past. To use her thoughts to plan the future. To actually be present with people. If she didn't want to remember everything wrong in her life—and given that she and Cade didn't have a future—the trick to enjoying this week would be focusing on the present.

Maybe that was why her brain had kept making her curious? It knew the way to stop thinking about the past was to direct all conversations to the present, to who he was now. Or maybe to how he'd become who he was now?

After adding oatmeal to the hot batter, she found parchment paper, scooped out spoonfuls of fudgy batter and dropped them onto the paper to cool. She'd always thought Cade would stay in town to take care of his crazy parents. Instead, he'd opted for a university too far away to commute and never came home. Not even for holidays. She supposed work necessitated he settle in Manhattan with his friends. Which was lucky because he'd ended up wealthy.

But how had he met the two friends?

And how had they known forming a team would work?

There was a story there and for the first time in over a decade she had the chance to hear it. She'd loved him with every fiber of her being. How could she not want to hear how he'd reached his dreams?

She poured two glasses of milk and carried them out to the patio. "Now you've done it. I'm curious."

He rose from the chaise, took the glasses from her hands and set them on one of the round tables. "About?"

"You. For Pete's sake. We were two normal small-town kids. We went to the same school. Rooted for the local football team. Got ice cream at the Windmill. Honestly, if you'd asked me when we were dating, I would have guessed I'd be the one to leave and you'd be the one to stay."

"To take care of my crazy parents?"

"Yes!"

"Did they need me?"

She pondered that. "No. Once you were gone, they sorted everything out. After their divorce, they never talked to each other, but it didn't matter. Everything had been settled. Divided. There was no reason for them to talk. No reason to fight."

"I rest my case."

She gaped at him. "You left to force them to settle things on their own?"

"No. I wanted a good education. Having them finally settle their divorce was an unexpected perk. Like leaving them had killed two birds with one stone."

"Huh." She let all that rumble through her mind.

"What about you? Why didn't *you* leave?"

Safety and protection. Routine and family.

None of which she could tell him. Once she began opening those doors, it would be only a few steps before she told him her secrets.

And then what?

And then nothing!

He couldn't change facts any more than she could. Plus, she wanted this week to be relaxing. Not a rehash of her pain.

"Cookies will be cool enough to eat in about ten minutes."

He laughed. "Come on. I'm not asking for nuclear launch

codes. You can tell me why you didn't leave. I won't judge. I swear. No judgment here."

She sighed, scrambling for a way to satisfy him without even brushing up against her secrets. "It was me being sappy. You know?" She shrugged. "I didn't leave because I wanted to be around my family."

"Why didn't you just say that? You always loved your family." He rolled his eyes. "You certainly loved them more than I loved mine. In a way, your normal family gave me hope that there were regular people in the world while my parents spewed hatred and threw things." He shook his head. "Wow. That was a weird year."

He didn't know the half of it, and she suddenly felt a tiny nudge of guilt for not being totally honest with him, but that was for the best. They had a few days together. There was no place for deep, dark secrets. No time for anything serious.

Her voice soft, she said, "Yes. It was a weird year."

"Don't feel bad that you didn't leave town to find fame and fortune."

Her teenage dreams poured into her head. She'd wanted to move to Washington, DC, to work for a congressman and do important things. Another thing Finn had stolen from her.

"I never wanted fame and fortune. I wanted to help people."

"You *do* help people. Being a nurse is the very definition of helping people."

She said, "Yeah, I guess."

"No guessing about it. You've gotten my dad to do a billion things he'd never have done on his own."

She glanced down at the stone floor of the patio. "Stretching your dad is *not* how I saw myself helping people."

He sobered. "No. Probably not." He was quiet for a few seconds, then he grinned. "Wanna stop talking and go back to pretending we're kids again?"

She caught his gaze. Connection wove through her. He might be older, but he was still Cade. Fun-loving, easygoing Cade. The guy she'd loved. And maybe that was why she wanted this time with him? Because he could be silly. He could be carefree. Fun.

"Was that what we were doing?"

"Sort of. Remember how I'd grill something we'd eat for lunch, then beg you to make no-bakes?"

The recollection of those afternoons was inconsequential. Simple. Because they'd been two normal teens with working parents entertaining themselves. "Yes."

"Except we never sat around and waited for the cookies to cool."

She laughed and swatted his arm. "We never ate them hot!"

"No." He angled his thumb at the blue water behind him. "We'd wait in the pool."

She pointed at her yellow T-shirt. "I'm not wearing a swimsuit."

"Since when did that stop us?"

More memories flooded her. Swimming in street clothes. Swimming in their underwear. Swimming without any clothes at all.

He took a step closer. "You could swim in that T-shirt and those shorts, but there were times we swam without clothes. Remember?"

She did. Heat and need roared through her. Back then, he would have easily grabbed the hem of her T-shirt and yanked it over her head, and she would have giggled with delight before they both jumped into the cool blue water.

The memory, so sweet and so pure, filled her with such

yearning that she had to swallow before she could say, "I'm not that girl anymore."

He stepped back, away from her. "Well, I'm still that guy. Plus, I'm wearing my trunks. So, I will swim while the cookies cool."

He leaped into the water and did the butterfly stroke, bobbing up and down as his body cut through the waves his dive had made.

Her head tilted as she watched him, but the strangest realization took her attention. *He hadn't tried to change her mind.* Younger Cade wouldn't have let her stand by the pool while he swam. He would have found a way to get her into the water.

She could think he really had changed, but realized he'd simply grown up. He wasn't the hyper, happy guy she'd fallen for, the kid with the off-the-wall parents who felt he had to control everything. He was—

Better?

Himself...but better?

Another unexpected thought hit her. She liked grown-up Cade a hundred times more than eighteen-year-old Cade. Not that eighteen-year-old Cade wasn't fun. He was. He was silly and playful and there were days she simply could not get enough of him. But eighteen-year-old Cade had needed all kinds of assurances. With his parents doing embarrassing things and his being called to referee, he'd needed to know his parents' antics didn't bother her. He'd always needed to know she didn't think him crazy by association.

This older, more confident version didn't have those needs:

He was fine.

She glanced at him swimming. He *was* fine. He was very, very fine.

And they had been having fun until she'd ended it by refusing to go into the pool.

Maybe she should stop being the stick-in-the-mud?

If he was willing to set aside their past and play for the few days they had together, maybe she should stop shutting things down when he made suggestions that surprised her?

After all, she was the one who didn't want to revisit the past.

And she did want to relax. Have some fun. Innocent fun.

Realizing just how much fun they could have, she laughed. But as she turned back to the kitchen, a memory of their first date flashed in her brain—

He'd taken her to the movies, then the Windmill, the ice-cream stand in the center of their small town, with picnic tables where friends frequently gathered. People from her group had mingled with people from his. They were noisy, silly kids having fun. The mood was light when he drove her home and walked her to her door.

But when they stopped under the glow of the porch light, the way he looked at her told her that for him this was so much more, and she realized it was for her too. When he bent his head and touched his lips to hers, her heart had stuttered and something deep inside her exploded. Young and foolish, she'd believed she'd found "the one."

The kiss deepened. Their tongues twined like they'd kissed a million times before. Need crackled through her. Emotions she'd only read about in books found meaning.

They finally broke apart and just stared at each other for a few seconds. Then he grinned.

"Good night."

Her voice shivered when she said, "Good night."

He all but skipped down the sidewalk to his car and her heart swelled to capacity with real love—

Her breath stuttered, bringing her back to reality. She had been the craziest combination of happy and scared. But she'd been smart enough to know what she wanted and let things happen between them.

Would it really be possible for *her* to let go of all her inhibitions—her *rules*—her past—and just have fun the way they used to?

In the bubble of this island? Where nothing they did mattered?

Yes. It would. She would love to let her guard down and sink into the feelings that wanted to overwhelm her. To enjoy herself. Enjoy *him*.

The question was how?

CHAPTER SIX

CADE'S OLD SIXTH sense about cooling cookies returned easily and he was out of the pool and drying off when Reese returned to the patio with them.

He pointed at a small table between two chaise lounges. "Put them here." He tossed his towel to a chair and picked up the glasses of milk she'd brought out a few minutes before. He set them beside the cookies, then he lowered himself to a chaise and she cautiously lowered herself to the one beside it.

They ate their cookies in total silence. Curiosity about her nagged at him—especially her cautious streak. But for as much as he wanted to know everything about her, he was afraid to ask. Questions were hard. Answers were sometimes harder. He didn't want to offend her and have her leave. He wanted this time with her.

Fudgy cookie number two disappeared into his mouth. He took a drink of milk. She took a sip of milk. He grabbed another cookie. She settled into the chaise.

Awkwardness filled the air. It didn't seem right not to talk. But he couldn't risk forcing things.

She ate her second cookie in silence, and he knew if he didn't think of something quickly, she'd retreat to her room again.

Suddenly, the perfect idea came to him. "Hey! Let's take the boat out."

She peeked at him. "You're going to fish?"

"No. But you'll want to go to the other islands sometime. Let's head out now and I'll show you how easy it is to get there."

She thought about that, then sat up. "Can we get back before dark?"

"It's spring, remember? Lots of daylight left."

"Okay, then let's go."

Relief slithered through him. "Okay. Let's go."

He ducked into the T-shirt he had tossed to one of the patio chairs and slipped into his sandals while she found her tennis shoes. Then he led her down the path cut out of the thick foliage to his dock. His fishing boat bobbed on one side of the row of wooden planks that kept the vehicles loosely moored. The other side held his cabin cruiser. Not so big as to be braggy, but big enough to take a pretty girl out onto the water, the white boat sparkled in the sun.

She ambled up to it. "Nice."

"Expensive." He waved around the island. "All of this comes at a price. But it's what gives me peace. A retreat."

"I remember you wanted a place to run away to when your parents did crazy things."

He laughed. "Yep. This is it."

"I like it."

"I do too." He also liked that the awkwardness between them had disappeared again.

He helped her aboard and pointed to the steering area. "That, of course, is how we navigate. There's a tiny kitchenette and sleeping space below deck. Over there is where people lay out in the sun."

"Very nice."

He shouldn't have needed her approval, and he supposed

he didn't, but it felt good. Solid. Right. Like another step in making things natural between them.

He lifted the lid on one of the storage compartments that served as a bench seat. "Want a life jacket?"

She looked out at all the water, then laughed. "Yes."

He pulled one out and tossed it to her. "Here you go."

She slid into the vest easily but fumbled with the catches. He reached over and snapped them like the pro that he was, but his fingers skimmed her arms, chest and stomach sending nerves scurrying through him. They'd been as close as two people could be. When he touched her, a unique kind of energy filled him, and now they were supposed to be friends?

They had to be. He wanted to know why she'd dumped him. He wanted closure. But he'd give that up if they could be friends. Real friends, the way they had been. They'd been so close that he simply could not believe they were meant to dislike each other. They'd always had something special, and though they might not be lovers again, they could at least be friends.

He pulled away from her and headed to the helm, but her confused voice stopped him. "You're not wearing a life vest?"

"I don't need one. I swim like a fish."

"What if you get knocked unconscious?"

He turned to her with a chuckle. "Are you going to knock me unconscious?"

"No, but you could fall out of the boat and hit your head."

He frowned.

"Think this through. You get knocked out and sink like a stone. I can swim, but I'm not sure I can lug your body back to the boat."

"When did you get to be such a chicken?"

* * *

He asked the question as a joke, but Rule Number Seven, *Control the things you can control*, popped into her head. She wasn't exactly obsessive-compulsive about it, but she looked ahead to trouble and, if there was a way, stopped it.

Still, she wanted to drop her vigilance with him and have fun. He was letting his guard down. She could see that in everything he said, the way he kept trying to smooth things over. She could do it too. One step at a time.

She sucked in a breath. "I'm not a chicken. Just careful."

"Seriously, you used to have a daring streak that made me proud."

"Things change."

He looked ready to question her again, or maybe argue about the protective gear, but he sighed and wrestled himself into the life jacket. "Satisfied?"

The happiness she felt around more mature Cade filled her. She didn't exactly want him to be a different person. She'd loved eighteen-year-old Cade with passion and innocence. But the maturity he kept showing relaxed her, pushed her rules to the back of her brain, made her believe that eventually she would let go and have real fun with him. Not to risk her heart. Not to fall in love. Just to have a happy time together.

"Actually, yes. I am satisfied."

He grunted and headed to the other side of the boat. Walking past the steering wheel and what she assumed to be navigational equipment, he lifted the padded seat and revealed a cooler of beer. "Want one?"

She hadn't quite been able to bring herself to drink beer, but things were working out so well that having a drink together was just another step. "I don't suppose you have any wine."

"I do." He pulled out a beer for himself, set it on the padded seat and disappeared below deck. When he reappeared, he surprised her with a container of wine that looked like a juice box.

She took it. "Handy."

"This *is* a boat. Though I have glasses in the kitchenette, boxes are easier."

He motioned for her to follow him to what she considered the front of the vehicle. He explained the navigational tools, especially the safety protocols, relaxing her even more. Then he started the engine with the press of a button and took them out on the blue water.

She leaned back on the bench seat and closed her eyes, enjoying the rush of the wind as the boat plowed out into open sea. "This is great."

"I know," he called as he navigated the boat farther and farther out until, when she opened her eyes, she saw nothing but water.

"Wow."

He turned off the engine and sat beside her on the bench. Leaning back, he angled his feet on a convenient storage space.

"Do you see why I like relaxing on this?"

"Yeah. Though I'm not sure why a billionaire needs to relax."

He snorted. "You don't think responsibility for tons of money is stressful?"

"I think having tons of money looks like fun."

"How about having responsibility for ten thousand employees?"

She winced. "That's a lot of people."

"I am aware."

"And it would be stressful."

He looked down, studying his beer can. "We lost some-one the day before my dad had his stroke."

She blinked. With the way their conversations had all been so light and easy, that was the last thing she'd ex-pected him to say. "Lost someone?"

"At a warehouse. Guy was driving a forklift. He drove into a concrete wall."

Her heart skipped a beat as the eighteen-year-old Cade she remembered meshed with the mature adult, and she knew how hard that had to be for him.

She stared at the angles and planes of his handsome face, though he stared down at the hands holding his beer can and wouldn't look at her.

"I'm so sorry."

"Everyone thinks being in charge of insurance is bor-ing. But that also puts me in charge of safety protocols."

"You blame yourself?"

He peered up at her. "No. But, yes."

She knew that feeling, that odd, unfair guilt after being raped. When she wondered what she should have done. What she could have done. What she hadn't seen. What she should have recognized.

She took a breath, thinking of eighteen-year-old Cade again. Wondering what she would have said to him. Sim-ple understanding won. "I get that."

"You do?"

"Yeah." She really did. The connection she had felt with him trembled through her. Scary at first, then suddenly as natural as breathing. They'd always been on the same page. Always clicked. Though she didn't have guts enough to tell him about her rape, she did comprehend his anguish. "In nursing, we're responsible for patients in a way doc-tors aren't. We recognize that day-to-day little stuff counts. Even if no one sees it, I go the extra mile. Look for things other people don't. When something goes wrong, I take it apart like a jigsaw puzzle until I figure out why."

"My partners were understanding to a point. But they're not the ones responsible for making sure everyone is safe."

"True, but your case is different. Sometimes in life accidents just happen. There are some things no one can control." That had been the stumbling block in her recovery from Finn's attack. It wasn't an accident. There had been lots of blame to go around. Finn for getting drunk. His parents for not being responsible with the refrigerator of beer in their garage. Her for not thinking ahead, not recognizing the potential danger. But in therapy she'd realized that as long as you were placing blame, you couldn't heal.

"The thing is," she began slowly, not sure what she was going to say, but knowing the reasoning she wanted to get across. "You need some time to read the accident reports, figure out if there were things that could have been done to prevent it. Then implement those things. And do better."

Cade examined her face for a few seconds, not sure why the need to talk had pushed him, except she'd been the person he'd turned to in the last pivotal place in his life, his parents' divorce. And here she was again.

As crazy as it sounded, their connection was still there. She was as street smart, as full of common sense, as she'd been all those years ago. Talking about this with her fit the mood, the moment, the problem he was having.

And maybe even explained why he hadn't wanted her to leave. Deep down in his subconscious he'd known they'd come to this.

"They're doing an autopsy. The guy was older. The way it looked, he drove into the wall full force. Coroner said he might have had a heart attack or an episode of some sort. Maybe a seizure." He took a breath. "The forklift is also being examined. There could have been a mechanical failure." He shrugged. "It wouldn't change the company's responsibility to his family, but it would explain things."

"And make you feel better?"

"No. It would be another piece of the picture. I don't think there's a way for me to feel better. Having an accident that resulted in a death was a shock. But as you said, I can do better." He took a breath. "One thing I've learned over the years is every job you have trains you for the next one."

She nodded. "True. But I'm still sorry this happened."

He drew another breath, this one longer, needing a second to compose himself. Emotion over the accident flooded him, but so did an overwhelming surge of gratitude at having her here, listening, sharing his grief.

"Yeah. So am I."

They leaned back on the bench seat again, resting against the boat. He'd said his piece. She'd listened and offered some wisdom that helped his brain settle down. Now it was time to move on.

He glanced sideways at her. "Wanna swim?"

"God, no! Not with fish!"

"You are such a coward! Where's the girl I loved—"

His heart thumped. He hadn't meant to say that, to remind her that he'd loved her, but it slipped out. And he suddenly realized he stood by it. He had loved her, and he'd loved her because of what had happened between them just now. He could talk to her. Easily. Naturally.

Their gazes caught and held. Her eyes softened and filled with a million longings, but she quickly looked away. "We should probably get back."

And there she was again. Strong Reese. The girl he'd confided in—except stronger somehow. She didn't merely know what to say. She knew when to pull back, move on.

"You might have turned into a coward—"

She snorted.

"—but you're awfully smart. I can hear it in almost every word that comes out of your mouth. What happened that made you so smart?"

She leaned forward, pretending to adjust the shoestring of her tennis shoe. "Why do you think something happened? Maybe I just paid attention in school."

He shook his head. "The best learning comes by experience."

"Well, look at you, getting all philosophical."

"And look at you, evading my question. *Again.*"

She shrugged. "Because I think my story is a story for another time."

He leaned down to peer into her face. "So, there is a story?"

She held his gaze for a few moments and finally said, "Yes."

"And you'll talk about it eventually?"

She shrugged. "If we talk about everything that happened in the past twelve years, we're going to need more than a week on your island."

The way she so casually said she'd be staying the week stopped his heart. He might have needed her to hang around for a diversion and a chance to get an explanation on why she'd dumped him, but now they were having fun. Being friends. The way they had been when they were younger. He simply did not want that to end.

He'd already realized when he pushed too hard, she clammed up. Having her say she'd stay the whole week had to be enough for now.

They sat for a few minutes while he finished his beer, then he rose, walked back to the helm and started the boat again. He took them toward the islands, and as they breezed past the chain that made up the Florida Keys, he pointed out the bigger ones, the ones not privately owned, where shops and homes created colorful streets and boat docks frequently became block parties.

He watched the wind ruffle her hair but was more taken by the smile on her face. Even Trace, who loved boats as much as Cade did, was never as happy as she was with the wind in her hair and the setting sun winking at them.

Corresponding happiness cascaded through him, as the phone in the pocket of his swimming trunks buzzed. He casually slid it out, saw the call was from his father and clicked Refuse Call. He wasn't quite ready to talk to the old coot yet—

How could he be angry with his dad for setting them up this way?

Not only had they quickly gotten past the initial, confusing anger and awkwardness, but she'd been exactly the person to talk to about the accident at the warehouse.

He glanced back at Reese and she grinned at him. His heart filled and he returned her smile, unable to stop the suspicion that his new and improved dad might know something he didn't know.

Maybe Reese had said something to Martin when she'd been playing Yahtzee and Uno with him the past week?

Pleasure filled him. Just the thought that she'd told his dad that she'd loved the year she'd spent with Cade, or maybe that she missed him or maybe even that she was sorry she'd broken up with him, sent his brain in a million different directions.

But mostly, it changed his feelings about this trip, about what it might mean.

As he helped her onto the dock at his island, he told himself not to let his thoughts go too far. She was happy. He was happy. He shouldn't make a big deal out of it and want more.

They started up the darkening path to his house, but her steps wobbled and he caught her hand. Electricity sizzled through him. "There are lights that will turn on soon. Just let me hang on to you until they do."

"Okay."

Her soft, breathless voice intensified the electricity.

"I didn't pave this path because I sort of like the natural feel of the island."

"Makes sense."

"Now I wish I had."

She laughed. "Don't be silly. As you said, the lights will come on in a minute."

They didn't. Cade held her hand the entire way from the dock to the infinity pool.

When he should have let go, awkwardness stopped him. Standing on the patio in the moonlight, holding the hand of the first woman he'd loved, he almost groaned.

He should have just dropped her hand when it would have been a natural, easy thing to do! Now he was caught in a weird place between the past and the present and it was as confusing as it was filled with promise.

She glanced up at him with a soft smile. "I could use my hand back."

He sniffed. "Yeah. Sorry."

But he still held on to her hand, as that warm, wonderful sense of potential rippled through him. If she'd told his dad she was sorry she'd broken up with him, if she'd missed him—

Everything he believed about their past would be different.

Of course, if she'd said something while he was still at Harvard, he wouldn't have married a woman who'd caused him to decide marriage was for chumps and to vow that he'd never fall into that trap again. He would have stayed in their small town and joined his dad's investment firm. He would have been...happy.

That wasn't quite right. He was happy now. How could he not be?

He frowned. He might be happy, but he was also stand-offish and suspicious.

If he and Reese had stayed together, he might not have billions of dollars but he would still be wealthy. And he'd also have her. Have her laughter and homespun wisdom to mix with his intelligence. Together they would have been unstoppable—

He needed to know. If she'd said something to his dad, regretted breaking up with him, missed him even a little bit, he needed to know. And there might be a simple way to find out.

With an easy nudge on her hand to bring her closer, he lowered his head and pressed his lips to hers. Tentatively. Almost like asking a question.

She stiffened at first and he thought she'd pull back, but as quickly as she'd stiffened, she softened, then stepped closer.

It was all the invitation he needed. He wrapped both arms around her and she slid her hands to his shoulders.

Their lips met in a joyful reunion of souls, pressing and nibbling at first, then opening to pure bliss. Happiness exploded, along with caution.

No matter what might have been, she had hurt him.

Twelve years had passed.

They were both different.

They could never re-create what might have been.

He felt that in their kiss. The ease, the simplicity, where there had once been teenage passion.

And he was old enough, smart enough to think this through before he did something he'd regret.

He pulled back, took a breath and smiled at her. "Good night."

Their gazes locked, she said, "Good night," before heading into the house.

He watched her, the full moon glistening off the water in his pool, the sounds of the ocean rhythmically lapping at the shore.

That hadn't been the kiss of two former lovers. It was something new. Something different.

Which could be for the best.

Or not.

He might have been telling her bits and pieces about what had happened in the twelve years that had passed since they'd seen each other, but she didn't know the big things, the personal things. Like a divorce that had ravaged his soul and made him cautious about relationships—forget another marriage. She didn't know about the connection he'd made with Wyatt and Trace, two men who felt more like brothers than business partners.

And he didn't know a damned thing about what had happened to her.

When he asked, she evaded. Always.

Which could mean she was hiding something important. Something she didn't want him to know.

He had billions of dollars. Assets he had to protect. A heart that had been shattered and a soul that was only beginning to recover. He might like her, but pretty soon she was going to have to spill the secret she so clearly was hiding.

Or he'd have to step back and return to the strangers-sharing-the-same-house suggestion he'd made when he'd first asked her to stay.

CHAPTER SEVEN

REESE NEVER SLEPT as well as she did that night. It might
have been the fresh sea air, but something cleared her
head and tired her body enough that sleep had come easily
and lasted until rays of sunlight drifted into her bedroom,
waking her—

She jerked up in bed.

He'd kissed her.

Not like eighteen-year-old Cade. Like the mature adult
she knew he was.

Joy flooded her. Yearnings morphed into possibilities.

She squeezed her eyes shut. Common sense told her to
stop the hope before it turned into something that couldn't
happen. It was one thing to have fun and do things together
and enjoy their time on the island, quite another to start
something. Like a relationship—

Oh, Lord. They could not have a relationship.

She had to talk with Cade and tell him she wasn't interested, but her happy heart and her bewitched soul did not
listen. She and Cade had connected when they'd talked.
But, even better, he hadn't pushed her. Waiting for the
cookies to cool, she'd refused to swim with him. He'd
swum on his own. She'd refused to tell him her story. He'd
accepted it. The more he accepted, the less he pushed, the
more she trusted him.

And just because he kissed her, it did not mean he was leading them to something serious. He could want what she did.

Some fun. To enjoy the few days they had left on the island.

Maybe the kiss hadn't been a surprise? Maybe it had been a logical next step? Not to something permanent. But a step to expressing what they were feeling in the moment. If she didn't try to define it, it could lead to something wonderful. A deeper, more fun few days than time spent swimming or on a boat.

Satisfied with that conclusion, she slipped out of bed.

So now what?

Needing coffee before she could think this through, she quickly dressed in yoga pants and a T-shirt and headed for the kitchen. Cade sat at the center island, staring at his phone.

She could be a coward, turn and go back to her room to wait until he was gone. Or she could be the mature woman she was, go into the kitchen and see what happened.

Stepping into the room, she said, "Good morning."

Instead of saying good morning, Cade lifted his phone. "Here she is now."

The faces of two men took up the entire screen. One said, "Hey." The other said, "So you're Reese."

Confused, she continued her walk to the coffeemaker, quietly saying, "Yes, I'm Reese. Good morning."

She heard one of the guys say, "Shy?"

"No. I think she's one of those people who need coffee before she wakes up." Cade glanced over at her. "Do you want to drink your coffee outside or in here."

"Outside?"

"Okay. I'll stay inside. You go outside." He turned his phone to her again. "The guy with the glasses is Trace. Guy with the beard and the baby is Wyatt. My business partners."

She waved uncomfortably and said, "Nice to meet you," but his consideration both with giving her the choice of outside or in, and introducing her to his partners, increased the feeling that she could trust him.

She made her coffee listening to him talk to his friends about their business, then took the big mug outside, lowered herself to a chaise and stared at the beautiful blue sea.

Twenty minutes later when her coffee was gone and she was about to plan her day in her head, Cade came out of the kitchen and plopped down on the chaise beside hers.

"They think you're beautiful."

The silly, bubbly sensation she had when she woke returned. The way she felt about him had changed so fast it should scare her. She should be packing her bags and calling Dennis. But they had what was left of a week. Not the rest of her life. They'd always had fun together. Now he was proving she could trust him.

There was no need to run. Not when she so desperately needed some fun in her life.

He frowned. "You don't know that you're beautiful?"

She smiled at him. "I'm normal. Average-looking at best."

He shook his head. "No. You're beautiful. You have that whole red hair, green eyes spitfire thing going on."

Pleasure rippled through her and she knew she wanted to stay for more than a little fun. She'd missed him. Missed their connection. It didn't matter that anything that happened between them would be only a vacation fling. She didn't want forever. He probably wasn't thinking about forever either.

Still, the best way to make sure things didn't get out of hand would be to manage the amount of time they spent together.

She said, "You're crazy," and rose from her chair. "I think I'll take a bike ride."

He smiled and lay back on the chaise. "Okay."

Relief filled her. Once again, he hadn't pushed. She walked into the house, ran up the steps to her bedroom, slipped into a bathing suit, then put on a big T-shirt over her suit and headed off. She took a ride around the island, and the feeling of control intensified.

He was an adult. So was she. They were friends. Had been lovers. They finally had a chance to see each other again. It was not wrong to want to enjoy that. He wasn't pushing. If something happened, it would happen naturally—

And she wanted it.

She rode the bike up to the front of the house, then rolled it into the garage before entering the quiet foyer. Realizing Cade was probably fishing, she ambled through the main room to the open doors for the patio, stripping off her T-shirt so she could jump into the pool.

But as she lifted her foot to step outside, a woman said, "He left you a note."

Her heart about jumped out of her chest. She pressed her hand to it as she turned to see a tall blond woman standing by the big center island in the kitchen.

"You scared the crap out of me." She took a breath, calming herself, knowing an intruder wouldn't tell her Cade had left her a note. Would she?

"Who are you?"

"Nina, the maid. I'm here Tuesdays. Cade forgot. I surprised him too." She waited a beat, then repeated, "He left you a note."

"Okay." She turned toward the kitchen.

"Never seen him leave anybody a note."

Not sure what to say, Reese only smiled. She got the implication. It was unusual for Cade to leave a note, so Nina the housekeeper was wondering about their relationship. She was in good company because Reese had no idea herself.

She glanced down at the note.

Gone fishing.
Hope you're having fun without me.

Her heart stuttered and all the emotions of being a teenager desperately in love poured through her. That was what he used to say when she took an afternoon to be with her friends. The memory of the intensity of his feelings back then automatically brought joy to her soul, but little warning bells tinkled in her brain.

Since her arrival on the island, she'd had moments when it felt like they'd gone back in time and were picking up where they left off, but she hadn't taken them seriously. What if Cade had?

Worry tightened her chest. Back then, they'd been two naive kids, planning a future together with careers, marriage and kids.

Kids.

Her breath stuttered. Surely, he didn't see them picking up where they'd left off, resurrecting dreams…reviving that future?

He couldn't. It was unrealistic. And he was smart. Too smart to think something so wrong.

She told herself she'd made too much of a stupid note and headed over to the open doors again, slightly annoyed that Nina kept watching her. As she finished tidying up the kitchen and the living area, her gaze strayed to Reese as if she were some sort of anomaly.

When the maid was gone, Reese forced herself to forget the odd way Nina had watched her and the fact that

Cade leaving her a note had meant something. He liked her enough to tell her where he was so she wouldn't worry.

It was nice...sweet even. And a good sign that he had feelings for her beyond housemate.

All that was positive. She would not make more of it than that.

When he returned from fishing at five, she closed the book app on her phone and set it on the small table beside the chaise.

"Catch anything?"

She also wouldn't let herself feel nervous around him. They'd kissed. They'd built trust. They were back to being friends. She was on board with a vacation romance. The next move was his.

"I catch things. I just can't always use everything I hook so I give it away. Gave a tuna to the people two islands down."

"You gave away a tuna? I love tuna!"

He shrugged. "Thought we'd go out to dinner tonight."

Though he'd tried to be casual, she realized he was making "the" move. This was a date. He was asking her out.

Her heart thrummed. For once in her life, what she wanted, what she'd envisioned was actually happening.

Except—

"I didn't really bring the kind of clothes a person would wear to a restaurant."

He laughed. "This is Florida. If you have shorts, a decent shirt and flip-flops, you're golden."

Happiness filled her. She was going on a date! Not with the kid from her memories of being sixteen, but the guy he was right now. A golden-haired Adonis with a sharp mind and a sense of humor, who loved cookies.

"I'll need fifteen minutes to change."

"You've got more like an hour. Unless you'd like to spend some time touring the island before we eat."

"You made a reservation?"

"Guilty."

She shook her head. "Pretty sure of yourself."

He glanced around. "Competition's limited here on Cade Island. Thought the odds were on my side."

She groaned at his bad joke. "All right. I'll take the whole hour and make good use of it."

With the extra time, she fixed her hair and applied makeup. She might be wearing shorts and a tank top, but the need to look her best egged her on. When she finally came downstairs, she found him in the kitchen with a beer, reading his phone.

"Anything interesting happen while I was in the shower?"

"Nope. World's still spinning. Lucky for us." He finally peeked up at her. "Lucky for *me*. Geez, you look great."

She smiled and curtsied. "Thank you, sir."

He led her to the back door, and they walked through the patio on their way to the path to the dock.

He led her through the foliage to his boats. No longer a stranger, she stepped onto the small cabin cruiser and immediately went for the life vests. He sighed when she handed his to him.

"I'm not going to fall out and hit my head."

"Humor me."

He put on the life vest, then helped her with hers. The first time he'd secured it, she'd barely noticed the brush of his fingers. Knowing this was a date, every touch, every sweep of his hands against her arms, chest and tummy whispered through her, bringing back the best parts of their time together as teenagers.

When she was settled, he started the boat. In a few minutes, they were docking at a lively, noisy island. They walked down the pier toward the street. Reggae music poured from a tiki bar crowded with people spilling out onto the sidewalk, dressed in everything from ragged cut-off shorts to sparkling dresses and tuxes.

"Could be a wedding party."

They walked past, but she turned to look back, totally curious. "Really a wedding party?"

He shrugged. "Why not?"

"Who can afford this stuff?"

He chuckled. "It's not as expensive as you think." He pointed down the street, toward colorful houses, some with white fences. "A lot of those homes are rentals. It's not much more expensive than renting a house in Ocean City or Virginia Beach."

Her head tilted as she thought about that. "This is like a town of tourists?"

"Yes and no. Some of these houses were passed down from generations of people who were born here. Other houses are second homes. And some houses are second homes that people can afford because they rent them out half the year. So, we have tourists, part-time residents and residents."

"Should be an interesting bunch."

"Oh, they are."

He guided her to a restaurant a block away from the dock. They were led to a table outside and she eagerly looked at the menu. "I'm ordering tuna."

He groaned. "Really? You're trying to make me feel guilty?"

She lowered the menu so she could grin at him. "You've had it all over me the whole time we've been here. Feels good that you slipped up and I can tease you."

"I've had it all over you?" He snorted. "You with your sad eyes that let me know you needed a rest, so I let you stay?" He harrumphed. "And on your terms. *You've* been calling the shots."

One of her eyebrows rose. "Oh, so you haven't wanted to stay out all day fishing."

"Yes, I have wanted to stay out all day fishing."

"So, I didn't call any shots. Which means if anyone's on higher ground it's you."

He sighed dramatically. "Maybe."

"Maybe?"

"All right. I have a few more bucks than you and a few more toys."

She considered that. "I don't think I have *any* toys."

"Not even a sled?"

That made her laugh. "Nope. No sled."

"I refuse to feel guilty for having money."

A soft breeze blew to them. It smelled like the sea, sunblock and happiness. "I wouldn't. If I were you, I'd *live* here."

"There were days I considered it. Trace spends most of his time in Italy. He jets back and forth for important things. But he goes to a lot of meetings via the internet."

"Really?"

"Yeah. He owns a vineyard with his fiancée. Her dad just bought a second vineyard and they're part of the renovations on that one too. Beautiful places both of them."

"You've been there?"

"Yes. After my first visit I understood why Trace settled there. And not just because Marcia grew up there. There are some spots that call to people. Trace's was Italy." He glanced around. "The Keys are mine."

She looked around too. "I get that."

They were quiet for a minute as they studied the menu. When the waitress came over, they ordered wine. She scurried away to get a bottle, returning with a nice red and a basket of bread, ready to take their orders.

Reese really did choose the tuna. Cade rolled his eyes before ordering shrimp scampi.

"I love shrimp scampi."

He caught her gaze. "We can share."

"Don't think this is getting you part of my tuna."

He laughed, then grew quiet as he took a sip of wine. After a few seconds, he said, "Do you think my dad saw something that we didn't?"

She glanced across the warm bread at him. "Excuse me?"

"My dad. I mean, he clearly set us up. Do you think he saw something about us that we didn't see?"

Fear skittered through her. Not because she thought Martin might tell her secrets. He didn't know them. But even so, Cade was edging them toward a discussion about her. Her life.

Or God forbid, the future.

His note edged into her thoughts. The way he'd sounded like his teenage self. The guy who'd wanted to marry her, have a gaggle of kids and live happily ever after.

She held her voice steady as she said, "Something we didn't see... Like what?"

He shrugged. "I don't know. I'm wondering if he thinks we never got over our first love."

She snorted. "Don't even try to say you've never dated anyone else."

"Actually, I was married."

She didn't know why that surprised her. He was gorgeous and rich. Of course he'd found a woman who wanted to marry him.

Surprise unexpectedly morphed into sadness that he had replaced her when she'd never really replaced him. She'd fallen in love once. She'd actually loved Tony enough to marry him, but his proposal had ended in disaster, not merely heartbreak, a feeling of failure followed by complete worthlessness—

She took a breath to stop that train of thought. So she'd never gotten married? After the breakup with Tony, she hadn't *wanted* to get married. And Cade had. She could accept that in a person who was only a vacation fling.

"I'd say congratulations, but you said you *were* married. I'm guessing it ended."

He winced. "Nasty divorce."

"Like parents, like son?"

"No. We didn't buy guns and throw plates. It was more that after two years of torturing me, pouting over perceived slights, publicly embarrassing me, my ex wanted a share in the original corporation. She wanted half of my one-third when the business had been well established before she entered my life. She had no hand in helping us build it. And we had a prenup that gave her a generous settlement." He shook his head. "But she fought like a woman scorned when she was the one who cheated on me. I had to hire a bulldog for an attorney."

It sounded enough like his parents' divorce that she blinked. Luckily, it wasn't her place to point that out.

He shrugged. "It ended up being a good thing that the marriage failed. In our final outrageous argument that totally ended things, she told me that she didn't want kids." He sighed. "I know I was stressed out at the time, but everything about our marriage came into focus in her rant. I suddenly saw that I'd gotten married because I'd wanted a family. Hearing her say she didn't was like culture shock. But the next day at work I realized Trace and Wyatt were my family. I didn't need to build something I already had. So now, marriage is off the table for me."

She stared at him. In what he probably considered a straightforward statement of facts, he'd addressed at least two important subjects. First, he'd gotten married to have a family. *To have kids.* Second, he didn't want to get married again. His friends had replaced his desire to have a family.

Cautious, she said, "You're sure that reasoning wasn't just the emotion of a bad divorce?"

"I don't make decisions like that lightly."

He might not make decisions lightly, but this was the kind of thing she needed to be 100 percent certain about. "So, you've given up on having kids?"

"I don't think you understand how busy I am. How little time I would have for children." He snorted. "That was Brenda's number one complaint. I had no time for *her*. It cost me a pretty penny to get out of a marriage that had been a judgment error. I subconsciously went in looking for something specific and didn't realize I'd gotten the whole thing wrong until that day she blew up and I saw we'd never been on the same page. I took some time and really thought about what I wanted out of life... And realized I already have it."

Reese's head spun. If all that was true—and she had no reason to doubt it—he had just made their situation perfect. Even if their fling lasted beyond this vacation, there would be no talk of the future, marriage, kids. No horrible sense that they would eventually have an uncomfortable conversation. No waiting for the other shoe to drop when she'd be forced to put all her secrets out on the table.

Satisfied and knowing it was time to change the subject or at least lighten the mood, she glanced out at the blue water. "You think you lost out on your divorce, but you still have enough money to own an island."

He grinned. "Yes."

"So, stop whining."

He laughed, but it wasn't the easy laugh of a guy who was happy. He was nervous, as if there was something else he wanted to tell her. Maybe another warning before he allowed their relationship to get too personal?

Before he could say anything, the waitress arrived with their food.

As she walked away, Cade picked up his spoon and knife. "I didn't bring up my dad or my divorce to make either of us uncomfortable. My dad throwing us together could have just as easily turned out badly. I should call him and tell him to butt out."

As if Martin would listen. "You could."

Cade sighed. "I shouldn't have to. He knows I'll never get married again. I have the example of his and my mother's glorious marriage, then my own dismal failure." He rolled his eyes. "I'd have to be crazy not to have learned that lesson."

She cautiously said, "Crazy does run in your family." But another thought struck her. He didn't have something else to tell her. He'd brought the discussion back to marriage because she hadn't yet acknowledged or accepted that he didn't want one.

He was a billionaire with money and his sanity to protect. And so far, she'd evaded all his questions and had given him vague replies when he'd talked about himself, about what he wanted and didn't want in his life.

He needed to hear her say she accepted his terms.

"Cade, you didn't have to explain why you'll never get married. I get it. I'll never marry, either."

He frowned when he looked at her. "Bad divorce?"

"No. I never married." She shrugged. *Her* heartbreak over Tony had taught her the same lesson he'd learned. Marriage wasn't for everyone. "I think I'm not the marrying kind."

He gaped at her. "Really? *You're* not the marrying kind?"

"Don't sound so surprised. I own a business. I want to be successful—"

"You should do the franchise thing I was telling you about."

She blew her breath out on a sigh. "No. Whatever I do, I want to do it my way. And marriage doesn't factor into any of that for me."

"So, we're on the same page?"

She couldn't tell if he intended for that question to sound like they were negotiating an agreement, but her chest and stomach didn't know if they should fall or fill with tingles. Whether he'd intended it or not, he'd opened the door for them to—

Well, do just about anything they wanted. No strings attached. No commitment.

The strangest feeling enveloped her. Part fear, part awe, it rolled through her as anticipation.

Without being bossy or intrusive, he'd proved they really could have a fling and walk away because neither one of them had any illusions about what they were getting into. Just as a smart businessman didn't go into a deal without all the facts, he'd gotten their expectations out on the table.

Her heart jolted. Her breath stuttered.

They were about to go back to his very private island where there was no one to stop them and no one to see if things turned romantic.

CHAPTER EIGHT

AFTER DINNER, THEY strolled around the island, getting ice cream, even though both were still full. She talked about her business. He talked about his friends, about Wyatt being handed a baby he didn't even know he had when an old girlfriend popped into his penthouse announcing she was going to United Arab Emirates for her job and he'd have to care for their child.

The more Cade talked, the more she understood his stance on marriage. Only his friend Trace was happily engaged, but he'd had to make huge concessions in how he worked. Part of the reason the Three Musketeers—that's what Reese had decided to call them—were so successful was the fluidity of their lives.

She understood that because her virtually nonexistent personal life was part of why she was able to create and manage her own business. She filled in for workers who called off. She could do her billing and banking in the middle of the night. She could sit on her sofa, watching television, and create schedules, read résumés, study situation reports.

All her time was hers.

Just as all of Cade's time belonged to him.

They returned late enough that the lights on the path blinked on, and they strolled up the walkway to the patio holding hands. Clearly happy from their date, he smiled down at her.

"I'm going to take a midnight swim. Wanna join me?"

Anticipation stole through her again. She knew exactly what he was asking. But as limited as their remaining time was, she decided to take the night and let everything about them settle in. Not merely in her brain, but in his too.

Plus, the evening had been perfect and if she'd misinterpreted his intentions when he'd explained that he'd never remarry, she did not want to ruin it. She wanted to take home the wonderful memory of good food and wine, and conversations that spoke of connection and easy happiness.

She rose to her tiptoes and brushed her lips across his mouth. "Thanks, but I'm actually very tired. I think I'll go to my room."

He caught her elbows as she pulled away and brought her back to him for a proper kiss. His lips swiped over hers, then nipped until she opened her mouth and allowed their tongues to twine.

Arousal built. Soft and sweet at first, then hot and greedy. But she stood by her decision to give them one more day to make sure this was really what they both wanted.

She pulled back and pressed her palm to his cheek. If she were being honest, she had to admit there were times when this felt like a dream. Too good to be true. And maybe that's why she sought the confirmation of another day.

"Good night."

He held her gaze, his blue eyes gleaming, his breathing shallow. "Good night."

She turned and walked into the house, remembering their first kiss all those years ago, the way he'd grinned as he ambled down the sidewalk of her parents' home, and she let her lips lift into a goofy smile. She totally understood why he'd grinned. There was nothing like the feeling that you'd found someone who understood you and someone you understood. And she wanted to hug that to herself for another few hours.

Just in case the bubble burst.

She could have thought herself a pessimist. But life had not been kind to her. The rape had been bad enough. Six years later, the discovery that she couldn't have kids had cost her a man she'd loved.

But with Cade not wanting a commitment or a family, there'd be no talk of marriage. No reason to discuss the issue that had caused Tony to look at her with pity and walk away. No reason to even believe their relationship would be longer than their stay here.

It really was perfect.

For something designed to be temporary.

Cade woke early the next morning and raced downstairs. He made scrambled eggs, toast and bacon. By the time the scent woke Reese and brought her to him, sniffing the air as she entered the kitchen, he was pouring champagne into orange juice in fancy flutes.

"What's all this?"

In her tiny tank top and pajama pants, with her pink cheeks and disheveled hair, she looked warm and sleepy. He imagined if he touched her now, she'd melt into him and he could kiss her senseless in about ten seconds.

"There's no point in having money if you don't enjoy it."

She chuckled. "I'm not much of a breakfast eater."

He gestured to the food on the center island. "You're going to turn all this down?"

She picked up a piece of bacon and nibbled. "Oh, Lord, that's good."

"Haven't had bacon in a while, have you?"

She took another bite of the bacon, closing her eyes in ecstasy, making him laugh.

"Grab the mimosas. I'll put everything else on a tray and follow you out to the patio."

She happily agreed. When she opened the door and saw the table, set with good china and a centerpiece of fresh flowers, she stopped. "What time did you get up this morning?"

He headed for the table. "Six." He winced. "Maybe five thirty."

Her head tilted as she examined the display. Then she took a breath, gazing out at the blue water, before she turned to him. "This is perfect. Thank you."

Her appreciation of simple things had always moved him. When it came to material goods, he had everything he wanted. Her blue-collar family provided necessities and only a few extras. She'd never complained—was always happy with what she had. But when he'd done anything nice for her, she'd blossomed. And his heart had bubbled with joy.

As it did right now.

He had to swallow before he could say, "You're welcome."

He set the tray of food on the table, then pulled out her chair for her.

She ate more than he did because he found himself watching her instead of eating. He couldn't remember ever being so happy, so content. Realizing they had only today, Thursday and Friday, he vowed to make every one of those days the best he could for them both. He worked hard. She worked hard. Their private lives were scant at best. Fate had given them some time together and he intended to take advantage of that.

Even if it didn't result in them sleeping together.

She'd run away from the perfect opportunity the night before. Probably because she'd wanted to make sure it was the right thing for them. If that was the case, he'd keep them going in that direction.

If she'd run because she didn't want what he did, then he'd be a gentleman. A good host. Because he liked her.

Not entirely sure which way she was thinking, he kept all his options open.

"I thought we'd fish this morning."

She peered over at him. "We?"

"Aren't you curious?"

She set down her bacon, tucked her hair behind her ear and asked, "About what?"

"If nothing else, you should wonder how someone could spend eight hours alone on a boat."

"Yeah, that does sort of make me ponder your sanity."

He laughed. "We leave in ten minutes. I'll text Nina to come and put all this away and we can head out to the boat."

She frowned, clearly not totally on board with the idea. "What should I wear?"

"I liked that little pink bikini you had on when I got here."

Her frown deepened, wrinkling her brow. "I don't need special fishing clothes?"

"You can wear a life vest if it makes it more official for you."

She rose from the table. "The life vest is essential equipment." She turned toward the house, then faced him again. "You're wearing one too, bucko."

She pivoted toward the house and he laughed so easily and so naturally, his thoughts jumbled. He'd never felt this way with any other woman and for a flash he wondered if that didn't mean something. He couldn't imagine growing tired of her. He couldn't imagine her getting demanding. He could see them having discussions, making decisions together—

Then his phone vibrated, and he saw the caller was his dad and those thoughts evaporated into stardust, along with unicorns and other things that didn't actually exist.

With memories of his dad's stroke still fluttering through him, he didn't bother with hello, just said, "Everything okay?"

"Yeah. Yeah. It's all good here."

"Go out with your nurse?"

His father had the good graces to laugh. "Funny thing about that. I only told you I was interested in her to get you to go to the island with Reese, but weird things started happening. She really is as wonderful as I'd said. And she's pretty. And nice."

"Well, well, well… Maybe you are changing."

"So, I'm guessing your good mood means you aren't mad at me?"

Cade blew his breath out on a long sigh. "The first time in twelve years that I come home and you meddle?"

"But you're happy."

"We're getting along."

"You're more than getting along. Your voice is light and springy…"

"Where do you come up with stuff like *light and springy*? I don't even know what a springy voice is."

His dad laughed. "I'm just saying that maybe if you'd come home sooner, I could have gotten you and Reese back together sooner."

His blood turned to ice water. The thought of "being together" with anyone brought up all his defenses. Worse, his dad *had* expected something permanent to happen. Something neither he nor Reese wanted. He knew that because of their conversation the night before, but he didn't know much else. He'd given her at least three good ins to tell him about her life, and she'd rejected them all.

Could be a warning sign that something in her life could screw up their simple tryst. Or it could be that Ohio was as boring as he remembered. A couple of hours on the boat would probably have her warming up to him enough that she'd start talking and hopefully she'd confirm why she'd raced away the night before.

That was the plan, and he wasn't deviating from it because his dad had called and messed with his thinking.

"We're not back together. We're getting along because we both needed a rest. And this could have blown up in your face if Reese and I weren't mature adults."

"Actually, that's my point, Cade. You are mature adults now. Things could be totally different this time… Oh, I gotta go. Yolanda's here."

With that he disconnected the call and Cade sat staring at the phone. He hadn't had the chance to say his piece about meddling, and, worse, he'd given his dad the wrong idea. Then his dad had hung up before Cade could change it. Whether he'd been forced to disconnect the call or not, it was clear his dad was playing matchmaker for two people who didn't want to be matched. He'd tried finding a mate and failed miserably. And Reese had said she wasn't the marrying kind. She wasn't looking for a commitment—though she'd never satisfactorily explained why—

The horrible sense that she was hiding something filled him again, but he shook his head to clear it. It was probably nothing but the aftereffects of feeling manipulated after talking to his dad.

Reese came out of the house in a filmy white cover-up that showed peeks of pink gingham.

She'd worn the bikini he liked.

He could jump the gun and think that was proof that she liked him and hadn't left him alone on the patio the night before because she didn't want anything to happen between them. But they had a whole morning on the boat to figure this out and he needed to get it right. Not make assumptions.

"Are you going fishing in your shorts?"

"I could. But I want to change." He displayed his phone. "My dad called."

She winced. "Did you yell at him?"

"I'm not secure enough in his recovery that I'd yell at a guy who just had a stroke."

She snorted a laugh and walked to the table, where she chugged the rest of her mimosa. "Go get dressed. The sooner we get out on the water, the sooner we get home."

He said, "Okay," and headed into the house. But he stopped in the kitchen as the strangest thought hit him. What if she wanted to get back from fishing because she had...plans for them?

His heart stuttered at the thought that she might try to seduce him, and he snickered at his foolishness. He needed to get a hold of his wayward imagination and let anything between them unfold one step at a time. With clear understanding at every step.

His libido protested that that was assuming a lot, and he should make a move. He told his libido to settle down and be patient. She'd told him she still found him attractive in their kiss the night before. The other stuff might take a little longer to sort through. He could not get this wrong, the way he had with Brenda.

They drove the fishing boat out onto the clear blue water. He reached into the cooler for a beer and offered her one.

She sniffed. "After a mimosa, a beer would be an insult to my palate."

He laughed. He'd stopped the boat in a spot so far out that the shore was like a thin line on the horizon. He showed her the rods, the bait.

"So, you have special bait that's designed to lure the fish in?"

"Thus, the word *lure*. It's a fishing *lure*."

She frowned. "That hardly seems fair."

"Why are you taking the side of the fish when we're attempting to catch dinner?"

"I just think it should be an even match."

He shrugged. "They have advantages. We have advantages. Trust me, it's a fair fight."

"We'll see."

He stood on the stern, wearing a life vest, not having a second beer, wondering about the fairness of his lure for the first time ever—because she was bossy. But it felt right, like a check-and-balance system that made him laugh and gave him the sense that she wasn't just a visitor. She was a part of this fishing trip.

He grabbed his favorite rod, remembering how he and Reese had clicked all those years ago. When they'd talked about marriage and kids it had seemed right. Like an inevitability. They'd automatically assumed a good life, a stable, happy life, meant getting married and having kids—

Probably because her family was so normal and the one thing he'd always wanted was to be normal.

Now he knew he didn't need those things. He already was normal. A normal businessman. He didn't need anything else.

Too bad he hadn't figured all that out before he'd married Brenda.

He faced Reese again. "Okay. So now that we have the bait—"

"Lure—your unfair advantage—"

He sighed. "Now that the *lure* is on the hook, I'm going to cast off. Like this." He pulled the rod back over his shoulder and swung it around. The reel spun, sending yards and yards of line into the air until it landed far away from the boat.

"Wow. How are you going to know when you have a fish?"

"The line will jerk and go taut."

"Ah."

He held the rod as she stared at the line. A minute turned into two, which became three and then somehow seven.

"Is it supposed to take this long?"

"There's no time limit on how long it takes for fish to see the bait." He reeled the line in and cast it out again, keeping the lure moving. "If there are no fish here, we'll move to another spot, hoping to find them."

She smiled out at the sea. "Makes sense."

Her serene face made him glad he'd brought her with him that morning. She loved being out on the water. He did too. He loved to fish but he also knew part of the allure was being far away from everyone and everything, on water that caught sunlight and reflected it so well that the whole world seemed to sparkle.

She removed her cover-up and stretched out.

Everything male inside him awakened at the sight of all the supple flesh exposed by her skimpy bikini. In the years that had passed, her breasts had grown while it seemed her waist had tightened. He'd bet he could span it with his hands—

Realizing he needed a cold shower or at the very least a splash in the face, he said, "You know, if you want, we could stop fishing and swim."

She opened one eye. "No need. I think I might catch a nap."

He reeled his line in and cast it out again. "And you also refuse to swim with fish."

"There is that."

He laughed. "You're funny. Different. But the same."

Without opening her eyes, she said, "You already pointed out that I turned into a coward. I say *mature adult*. But, hey, you have a right to your opinion."

His rod tensed and he looked out over the water, staring at his line. Nothing more happened so he relaxed but by that time he glanced at her again, he saw she was asleep. He could have stood and stared at her all day but forced himself back to casting his line.

As odd as it sounded, realizing he had created a normal life for himself began to erase the worry that Reese might have a secret. His very good, very normal life was in Manhattan. Even if she had a secret, anything that happened between them would be confined to this trip. Plus, she'd said the important things. That she wasn't interested in a permanent relationship. Whatever they had probably wouldn't last beyond this week.

He could stop wondering. In the end, any secret she had didn't matter. They weren't trying to re-create the idyllic life they'd imagined as teens. They were two ships passing in the night.

Eventually, he caught two tuna and drank another beer. Warm air and silence enveloped them in their own little world. He loved being in the stillness of the ocean, but he loved even more that he and Reese were reconciling their past. Not by creating a future. But by behaving like adults.

He caught a third fish, then put away his rod and prepared to head home.

"Hey, sleepyhead. You have to get up. You're going to have a suntan in the shape of a life vest."

She yawned and stretched, and he didn't stay around to watch the way her muscles would pull beneath soft, sun-warmed skin. He didn't want to see her hair shining or her green eyes twinkle with happiness. He already wanted to make love to her so badly he couldn't focus on anything else. No sense making things worse until he knew she wanted what he did. He needed to be certain she hadn't bolted the night before because she didn't want to become lovers. That she'd stopped them only to be sure that was what they both wanted.

The trip on the boat was supposed to get her talking or at least help him see if she agreed that their fun together should go further—

Actually, it might have. A woman who didn't get the concept of fishing, who didn't want to swim with fish, who didn't drink beer…had spent three hours on a boat with him.

If he asked himself why, the only answer could be that she liked spending time with him. Or maybe just plain liked *him*.

Enough to want to make love?

He guessed he was about to find out.

CHAPTER NINE

WHEN THEY RETURNED to the house, Cade was different. The second they arrived on the patio, he tossed his shirt and jumped into the infinity pool. As a person who lived in Ohio, the heat got to Reese too, and she shucked her cover up and joined him.

Doing a slow backstroke, she floated on top of the water.

From beside her, Cade said, "This is nice."

She opened one eye. "Yeah." The perfection of it overwhelmed her and she pushed herself upright to tread water. "Seriously, thank you for letting me stay."

He laughed. "It's been fun having you here."

She smiled.

He smiled.

For a few seconds they simply started at each other. Maybe remembering the past. Maybe enjoying the moment. Maybe realizing their intense connection was as natural as the rhythm of each heartbeat.

Maybe deciding that was okay.

Everything was okay here on the island.

A force that felt a lot like gravity pulled them together. Their lips met slowly, easily as they floated in the warm, soothing water. He slid one hand around her neck and the other to her lower back to steady her, but she eased her legs up, hooking them around his waist. He took advantage and moved his second hand to her back so he could tilt her and deepen the kiss.

The feeling of déjà vu enveloped her. All fear flitted away and was replaced by a sense of security so strong it was as if someone pressed a button and tossed her back in time.

This was how she'd felt making love before she was raped. The sensations that slid through her were like coming home. Like being herself again.

Finally.

The word echoed through her and a desire to weep nearly overtook her, so she reached around to unsnap the top of her bikini and then threw it to a convenient chaise. Her breasts met his chest, her nipples hardening on contact. Her soul filled with contentment that knitted to reality. This was how it was supposed to be. Not frantic to stay one step ahead of the memory of fear. Not simple and regimented, as it had been with Tony. But fun and joyful. Natural like breathing. But passionate. So intense that thought wasn't necessary.

And that's what she needed. The reminder that every time a man touched her, she didn't need to explain to herself why this feeling was allowed, why it was different from Finn.

She could simply enjoy.

The kiss went on and on. His hands roamed her back. Contentment rippled through her like the warm water bumping her legs and butt. Arousal awoke in her belly.

He broke the kiss to nuzzle her neck. "You're so beautiful."

She laughed. "So you've said."

"Because it's true."

She skimmed her hands down his back, enjoying the solid muscles before she ran her tongue along her shoulders to his chest. "You're salty."

"The curse of being a fisherman."

She laughed again and he brought her back to him for another long, lingering kiss. This time his hands moved from her back to her breasts and belly. She answered his movements but took them one step further, allowing her fingers to slide beneath the elastic of his swimming trunks. She pushed them down enough that eventually he kicked out of them. Then he slipped his hands into her bikini bottoms and had them off and tossed to the chaise in what seemed like two seconds.

Naked, aroused, they slid against each other in the warm water. Her heart filled with happiness and her skin prickled with goose bumps when he lowered his head and took a straining nipple into his mouth. Her hands cruised his torso, sliding farther and farther down, eventually stalling on the muscles of his butt.

His lips roved her chest. Her muscles trembled with a longing so fierce it demanded to be satisfied. Without giving him any indication of what she was about to do, she shifted in the smooth water and joined them.

His head fell back, and he groaned. She buried her face in his neck. Their connection had always been electric. This was beyond compare.

It took only a few seconds before they found a simple, easy rhythm that built into a frenzy of need. Every cell in her body came alive. He kissed each inch of her skin that he could reach. Her bones dissolved into molten lava. Need and greed bubbled through her, a desire to take, not wait. It seemed she'd waited forever.

But as an orgasm stole her breath and everything inside her melted with joy, he sucked in a long drink of air and said, "Refresh my memory... Why'd we break up again?"

She laughed because she knew that's what he expected of her. But the question in his voice sounded real, sounded like it was coming from a guy who'd never reconciled their ending.

And in a way she hadn't either. It had been too abrupt. Other things had consumed her energy—while school consumed his. They'd made mistakes and been drawn away from each other by circumstances. And both still had a bit of a hole in their hearts.

Maybe that was why fate had brought them together for this week?

They needed to talk about that night.

They drifted on the water for a few seconds before he leaned down and nibbled her neck. Sated, happy, it took a minute before he could bring himself back to reality.

"No one's ever pushed me to the point that I've had unprotected sex."

Laughing, she ran her hands down his back. "Not to worry. I never have unprotected sex. We're safe."

"What about pregnancy?"

She stiffened. "No worry about that."

He lifted his head to catch her gaze. "Are you sure?"

"Yeah."

Something in her voice wasn't quite right. "Are you okay?"

"Seriously? I just had some of the best sex of my life. Of course I'm not okay. I'm…sort of wonderful."

He anchored himself against the pool wall, then reached out, caught her hand and tugged her beside him. "I'm sort of wonderful too."

A weak, confusing laugh escaped her. He peered down at her again. "You seem to be losing your wonderful."

She winced. "I think there are some things we need to talk about."

The secret.

The thing he'd sensed she'd been hiding.

He wasn't sure he wanted to hear that now. He'd sorted his past and their nonexistent future. There was no need.

He tilted his head as he studied her. "All week I tried to get you to tell me about your life and you pick now? I was going to wait twelve to fifteen minutes and show you how crazy I am about you again."

She trailed her fingers up his chest. "I was hoping you'd say that." She peeked up at him. "But if I don't tell you some of this now, I'll never tell you."

Fear stuttered through him. He'd let her stay in the hope that eventually she'd explain why she'd broken up with him. What if that was the thing she'd been keeping from him? Her secret.

"When you first left for Harvard, I went to a football game with my friend Janie."

He held her gaze, not sure he wanted to hear this now—not when they were so happy. Not when he wanted to keep everything simple between them. So many years had passed. They seemed to have forgiven each other. Fear that she'd ruin the few days they had left stiffened his muscles, made his chest ache.

She hesitated, her tongue darting out to moisten her lips. "Right before the game ended, when everybody was whipped into a frenzy because the score was tied, Finn McCully kind of half dragged, half begged me to come under the bleachers with him."

"Finn McCully?" The name jarred him out of his depressing thoughts. "I haven't heard his name in forever."

"There's a reason for that." She sucked in a breath. "He offered me beer and I refused. He gave me a hard time, insisting that he knew I drank—which I didn't—and I was being a snob not partying with him."

Not at all expecting that, Cade gaped at her. "What the hell was he talking about?"

"I don't know. It was so out of character that I just got myself away from him. Janie and I walked home and after she veered off onto her driveway, I got the horrible feeling I was being followed."

"I do not like where this is going."

"Well, you're going to hate the rest because he pulled me down an alley between two houses into the garage Dusty Buchanan used to do off-the-books bodywork on cars."

Cade's heart stopped. The air he drew in felt like wet cement. Finn McCully had been a big guy. Not fat. Tall and muscled. Cade couldn't see little sixteen-year-old Reese being any match for him.

His chest tightened with an emotion that somehow combined sympathy and fury.

"He told me that I thought I was so special. A princess. Because I was dating you. Then he raped me."

Cade's breath hissed out. "Son of a bitch."

"I don't even think he realized that what he was doing was wrong. He was drunk and so smug and proud of himself as if he should win an award. Then he let me go without argument. I raced home. My parents called the police and took me to the hospital. There was a rape kit, and he was arrested."

A weird sense of total disbelief rippled through him. She wasn't a liar, but his parents lived in that small town. It was farfetched at best that he wouldn't have heard this story.

"How do I not know any of this?"

"Because there was a plea deal. My parents worried about me, about gossip, and backlash, and the DA offered Finn a reasonable punishment, so we agreed. The thing of it was Finn wasn't sixteen. He was still a minor. He got some jail time and probation and had to register as a sex offender."

"That's it?"

"His parents also moved out of town."

He remembered that. Vaguely. Which was why Cade barely remembered him, why he hadn't even heard Finn's name in forever.

"They promised to get him help and keep him away from me. Which was what my parents believed I needed. Finn's dad also said they wanted to be closer to the detention facility where he would be serving his sentence. Finn had to agree to therapy and Alcoholics Anonymous... Because believe it or not, he didn't remember any of it. Said he blacked out." She pulled in a breath. "But DNA doesn't lie."

Cade gasped. "He didn't use a condom?"

She hesitated. "No."

He shifted away from the pool wall so he could stand in front of her, look at her face as she spoke. Sorrow for her hit him like a punch in the gut, along with a red-hot anger that knew no bounds. "I could kill him."

She looked up at him. "Really? I'm not quite at the let-bygones-be-bygones stage, but I won't let him steal the rest of my life. He took a million things from me, Cade. Like our relationship. And other things. Little things. Big things. Things I can't even define or describe. I won't let him have anything else."

That made so much sense, his anger lessened. He rubbed his hand along the back of his neck. "Why didn't you tell me?" Upset for her, he looked at the sky, then back at her again. "You should have told me. All these years I thought you dumped me because you'd found somebody else."

"I did try to tell you." She took a breath. "I called and called that night after I got back from the hospital."

He frowned at her.

"I left messages, but you didn't return my call for four days." She closed her eyes. "By then I'd lost my nerve."

"You should have found a way to tell me—"

"After it took you four days to return six calls? There was *nothing* you could have done. My parents made sure he was brought to justice. I went to therapy. Dealt with it all." She caught his gaze. "I'm okay."

Confusion and sympathy coiled through him. His voice soft, he asked, "Are you? Really?"

She shook her head and swam to the pool ladder. "You know what? I think I'll go back inside for a while."

She was out of the water and swiping her bathing suit and cover-up off the chaise lounge before he even realized what was happening.

Disappointed with himself for being so clumsy, for undoubtedly saying all the wrong things, for not giving her comfort and unconditional support, he sprang out of the water to follow her.

But he stopped by his swimming trunks, putting them on to give himself a few minutes to think.

Part of him wanted to follow her to her room. The other part knew he was out of his depth. His parents throwing plates at each other was nothing compared to a sixteen-year-old girl being violated by a smug drunk. He wanted to hold her, to somehow make everything okay, to protect her from anything ever happening to her again... But when he had turned sympathetic, she'd run.

She hadn't run when he'd asked questions. She hadn't backed down when his voice might have sounded skeptical.

She'd run when he'd wanted to hold her. To sympathize. To be angry on her behalf.

He rubbed his hand across his mouth. *Oh, Lord, was he out of his element.*

But he did understand one thing. She didn't want him to feel sorry for her. His Reese had never wanted pity or sympathy or for anyone to underestimate her.

Which meant she wanted to be treated normally.

After twelve years that made perfect sense. Undoubtedly, she *had* dealt with it. She'd made a good life for herself. She might not be exactly the person she'd told him she wanted to be when she grew up, but she was close.

The truth of that settled into him slowly. After he'd told her about Roger Burkey, he'd appreciated that she hadn't pushed him for more information or smothered him. Telling her the truth of what was bothering him had bonded them enough that when he'd caught her hand to lead her to the patio, he hadn't wanted to let go. He'd kissed her.

Sharing his story had brought them closer. That's why they'd been so easygoing with each other on the boat, in the pool. And why she'd told him about Finn McCully. He'd trusted her with his troubles. Then she'd trusted him with a secret.

It was another step.

And he had blown it.

Sitting on the balcony off her suite, Reese saw Cade walk up from the dock. He had three fish on a string—fish he'd obviously forgotten when they'd left the boat. He took them around to the side of the house, where she couldn't see him.

She leaned back in her chair and would have fallen asleep but she couldn't tolerate just sitting around, upset that he'd ruined her confession before she could finish, before she could assure him that she was fine. Adjusted. Normal in all the ways that mattered.

His sympathy dragged her right back to those weeks, when her whole life had changed, and she was barely old enough to deal with it. She wanted to shake him silly because she wasn't that girl anymore.

But wasn't that the point?

She wasn't that girl anymore and neither was she the girl Cade had fallen in love with.

Not about to sit around and brood about something she'd long ago survived, she bounced up in her seat, slipped into shoes and retrieved a bike from the garage.

She rode around the island, letting her anxiety and borderline anger with Cade dissolve into nothing in the fresh island air. By the time she returned, the scent of grilling fish filled the area. Stowing her bike in the garage, she decided to pretend nothing had happened and walked through the house, directly to the patio.

"Hey! What smells good?"

"Dinner."

She glanced at the table that had been set for two. Wine in an ice bucket. Pretty glasses. Dishes she would call good china.

"What's all this?"

"I didn't want to put tuna and veggies grilled to perfection on paper plates."

She laughed, but inside she died a little. He'd made a gorgeous dinner, set the table and would probably treat her with kid gloves for the rest of the trip. No more fun. No more laughing. Just him fawning over her as if she were a fragile doll. Not a woman who'd struggled and persevered.

She couldn't imagine what he'd do if she told him she couldn't have kids and thanked her lucky stars that he'd turned that into a nonissue.

Swallowing her disappointment, she said, "Is there anything I can do to help?"

"Yeah. Check the fridge to see if there's potato salad."

She shook her head. "You're a creature of habit."

"Which probably makes it very easy for my shopper to keep the place stocked and me happy."

Turning to the open patio doors, she said, "Probably."

She found the potato salad and would have brought it straight out, except he'd gone to such trouble to make the table pretty that she thought she might as well join in on the fake happiness. Disappointment returned in a wave. His reaction proved they'd never really get back to the place they'd been when they were kids. Despite everything she'd felt while they were making love, they'd never hit that level of trust where they could tell each other everything and accept each other for who they were.

And that was her real dream. The thing she wanted more than anything else. That she could be honest with someone, be herself with someone, and they'd still love her.

When she reached the outdoor table and set the glass bowl in the center, he glanced at it, then at her.

"What's that?"

"A nice dish to match the other things."

He frowned. "Really?"

"Yes."

"I only brought out the good dishes because of the tuna." She looked at him.

He lifted one of the tuna steaks. "Tell me that isn't beautiful."

She laughed uneasily. From watching him fish, she knew he thought of being out on his boat as only one step below religion. Maybe he really did think the fish was worth good plates? "It's beautiful."

"Okay, then."

She took a breath. He sort of *was* behaving like himself. She could stew about his reaction to her confession and ruin their last days together or she could face it outright.

Since she was an outright sort of girl, she knew they had to have the conversation.

"All right. Thank you. I do love the tuna. But I just want to make sure you don't feel sorry for me. That you treat me normally."

He put the tuna back on the grill and walked over to her. "I can't treat you normally."

Sadness permeated her soul. "At least you're honest."

"I can't treat you normally because I believe you deserve to be treated special. When a guy really likes a girl, he wants to treat her special. Not because of her life circumstances but because it's what guys do. I'm guessing it dates back to the cavemen, when a guy would go out and kill a bear so his woman would have fur to keep her warm at night."

She stared at him as her face scrunched with confusion. "What?"

"Caveman. Deep down I think all men have a little caveman in them and if they don't, maybe they should."

Now she really wasn't following him.

He put his hands on her shoulders. "I like you. I like you so much that sometimes I can't breathe for the happiness that bubbles up when I realize you really are here with me. I want to do nice things for you. That's all. No deeper meaning than that. We have a couple of days. I want to enjoy them. I didn't mean to insult you. It was all a shock for me. But I'm over that. And I vote we take advantage of the rest of our time."

In total agreement, she rose to her tiptoes and brushed a kiss across his lips. "Okay."

He smiled. "Okay."

She truly hoped he meant that.

CHAPTER TEN

THEIR DINNER WAS FABULOUS. Reese told him it was the best food she'd eaten in forever. He would have thought she was overcompensating, working to make him believe her trauma was no big deal. But he remembered what he'd concluded about how he had to trust that she really was fine and treat her the way he had been.

So they teased and laughed, cuddling together on a chaise to watch a movie on a big-screen TV that rose from the stone counter a few feet down from the grill.

She gaped at him. "You have everything."

He looked down at her. "I do now."

She huffed out a dramatic sigh. "Don't say things like that. You don't want anything permanent. I don't want anything permanent. We're just supposed to be silly."

Worry seeped into his soul.

They hadn't only been silly. Surely it meant something that they'd told each other some of the worst events of their lives?

He immediately convinced himself their confidences might have been nothing more than catching each other up on the years that had passed. He'd already decided this was a moment snatched out of time for reconnecting and fun. It was Wednesday night. Only Thursday and Friday left. Then this was over. She'd be gone. He'd return to

Manhattan. His real life. The little piece of normalcy he'd carved for himself.

Their being together was a fluke. A respite. He wouldn't ruin it.

He didn't let himself think any further than that as they watched the movie. When it ended and another movie began, he slid lower on the chaise, pulling her with him. He nuzzled closer. She did too. Her hands drifted to his shoulders as his found her waist. Peace and contentment were overshadowed by common sense.

"We can't do what I want to do on a chaise lounge."

"We used to."

"We were younger and more agile." He nuzzled her neck. "Besides, I'd like to have you in my bed."

She cuddled closer. "So romantic."

He laughed, rose from the chaise and caught her hand to help her stand. Without a word, he led her through the kitchen up two flights of stairs and to the master bedroom. When he opened the door on the room with sharp red-and-black geometric designs and a white shag carpet between the bed and the door to the master bath, she gasped.

"Fancy."

He leaned against the doorjamb. "I like to think of it as sexy."

She walked over and slid her hands up his chest. "It is. All bright and bold."

He kissed her. When the kiss ended, she pulled back and smiled.

He studied her face, saw the courage mixed with femininity and remembered why he'd loved her so much. She really was the adult version of the sassy sixteen-year-old he'd loved.

He kissed her again. And again. Eventually they made their way to the bed, where they stripped away each other's clothes and made love like two people so happy to be to-gether there was only one way to express it.

He wondered for a second what would have happened if she hadn't broken up with him, but he couldn't see a happily-ever-after. Had he been told about her rape, he might have killed Finn and he, not Finn, would have been the one to go to jail.

In a roundabout way, his not returning her call might have saved them.

Even though it tore them apart.

But she didn't want to discuss that and neither did he. With no future for them, there was no point in digging too deeply into the past.

He woke the next morning with her exactly where he wanted her. Tucked beneath his arm, nestled against his chest. He took a long breath, running his hands from her shoulders to her butt and back up again with a satisfied, "Mmm..."

Before he could check to see if she was awake, the sen-sor on the wall alerted him that the front door had been opened. Confused about who might be entering, he slid away from Reese as carefully as he could, threw on a pair of shorts and a T-shirt, in case it was Nina who had let herself in—or God forbid his dad—and headed to the stairway.

At the bottom stood Wyatt, his baby girl Darcy strapped to his chest in the tactical baby carrier that made him look like a Navy SEAL who couldn't find a sitter. Though his beard had been trimmed, his dark hair poked out in all directions.

Cade scrambled down the stairs. "What are you doing here?"

Wyatt made a shh-ing noise, pointing to the baby who

was fast asleep. He whispered, "We needed a little away time."

"I have a friend here!"

Wyatt stopped, studied him. "I know. The woman you showed us in the video call."

"Yes! I told you, she's an old *girlfriend*."

Wyatt grinned. "Well. Well. Well. That's interesting. I'm guessing either you're hoping something will happen between you or something already has." Familiar with the house, he walked toward the kitchen. "I would say I'll leave but you're so secretive about your women that I'm curious."

Cade raced after him. "Leave anyway!"

Wyatt stopped beside the center island. "At least let me see what she looks like."

"You saw her in the phone."

Wyatt rolled his eyes. "Please. I saw a blurry image walking across your kitchen. Let me meet her for real, then I promise I'll call Dennis."

Reese walked into the kitchen. "Call Dennis about what?"

"Our host is having a hissy fit because I brought my baby here for two days of R&R." Wyatt shifted the discussion like a professional.

Reese walked over and peeked at Darcy, then smiled up at Wyatt. "She's adorable!"

"Her mother is gorgeous."

At the mention of Wyatt's ex, Reese glanced around.

"Don't look for her. She's in United Arab Emirates. Which is why I have custody of Darcy. And we wanted two days away. But I don't think Cade's going to let us stay."

"Don't be silly," Reese said easily. "I'll happily leave so you can have some time here."

Cade glared at Wyatt.

"No need for you to leave," Wyatt said smoothly. "In

fact, I was thinking exactly the opposite. Darcy and I will spend today and tomorrow, then leave and you guys can add two days onto your time here to make up for the fact that we barged in."

Reese's eyes widened. "I can't add two days—"

Cade crossed his arms, leaning against the kitchen counter, so angry with his meddling partner he could have spit fire.

"Why not? Do you have airline reservations?"

"Sort of. I have a return trip ticket but it's open-ended."

"Meaning, you can pick the time you leave?"

Finally seeing what Wyatt was doing, Cade pressed his lips together. Their "idea man" always had an angle.

"Yes."

"So, instead of going home on Saturday, go home on Monday. Or Tuesday morning. Whatever. Your choice."

Reese only looked at Wyatt.

Cade laughed and took pity on her. Pushing himself away from the counter, he said, "This isn't a fair debate. Reese hasn't had coffee yet."

"That's right," Wyatt agreed. "She's not awake until she has coffee. Saw that the other morning when Trace and I called."

Reese reached for a coffee pod and hit the start button on the coffee maker. While it warmed up, she retrieved a mug, put in the pod and set the works in motion.

"I don't have a problem with staying an extra two days," Cade interjected casually. "We could go into town again on Sunday. See if we can find a farmers' market."

It was, without a doubt, the stupidest idea he'd ever come up with, but he wasn't as skilled as Wyatt at rearranging the truth to get his own way.

Still, Reese's eyes narrowed as she considered it.

Wyatt didn't wait for a reply. "Thanks. We just want two

days. A little time to relax after striking out with nanny interviews all week. Which bedroom is free? I want to put Darcy in her swimsuit."

"I'm in the master. Reese is in the room at the top of the stairs."

As Reese turned to pour cream in her coffee, Wyatt's eyes widened, and he nudged his head in her direction as if totally perplexed by the sleeping arrangements.

Cade stifled a groan. Pushy, meddling Wyatt was going to say something wrong. He just knew it. "Go take care of Darcy. I'll make breakfast."

Wyatt's eyebrows rose. "Those eggs I like?"

"Yes."

"Okay. Cool. See you in ten."

When he was gone, Cade walked to Reese and slid his arms around her from behind. "I'm sorry. Wyatt and Trace are more than partners to me. They're like brothers. They have an open invitation to come here."

She turned in his arms. "That's okay. Baby's cute. He's the guy you were telling me about the other night."

Cade leaned down and kissed her. "He is."

"And he looks like he needs a break."

"He does. But I'd much rather if it was just you and me here."

"I'll check my schedule. If my staff can continue to work without me, I'll add Sunday and Monday."

He pulled back. "Really?"

"Sure." She winced. "I'm starting to feel like I never want to go home. Which should make me get my butt onto that plane before I abandon my common sense. But what's two more days?"

He placed a smacking kiss on her lips. "Two more days will be perfect." Especially since Darcy napped a lot and sleep-deprived daddy Wyatt usually napped on the bed beside her crib. Even with them here, he and Reese would have plenty of alone time… And if they didn't, they could always go out on the boat.

Technically, Wyatt had gotten him two more days with Reese. He should be thanking him.

Cade headed for the refrigerator. "Okay, I'll make the eggs and bacon. How about if you toast some bagels."

"Sure."

She put bagels into the toaster, then retrieved dishes from the cabinet. She set them in front of the chairs by the kitchen island. The toaster popped and she raced back to get the bagels. She did that three or four times while Cade fried bacon and scrambled eggs with green peppers and onions.

By the time Wyatt appeared with his little girl decked out in a bright red one-piece swimsuit, a sunhat and over-size white sunglasses, everything was waiting for him.

"This is nice." He walked to the closet and pulled out a high chair, which he dragged to the center island.

Cade leaned in to whisper to Reese. "He stores a lot of stuff here. There are cribs in two of the bedrooms."

"I have to ride a bike from the helicopter pad. If I didn't leave stuff here, I'd look like a circus clown peddling down your path with all her things on my back."

Reese said, "Makes sense," then dug into her breakfast, making Cade hide a laugh, remembering that just the day before she'd said she wasn't a breakfast person. "I'll have to call my staff this morning to make sure our schedule can handle me taking two more days off."

"What's the point in owning a business if you can't take time off?" Wyatt asked as he picked up his fork to begin eating. "We don't exactly come and go as we please, but Cade, Trace and I aren't slaves to the jobs. We like our fun."

Cade glanced at her. "It's true."

She shook her head, then laughed. "I know how hard you guys work. How dedicated you are."

"Which makes us all the more determined to have fun," Cade said.

She picked up her fork again. "You two are crazy, you know that?"

Cade said, "Yes," as Wyatt said, "Absolutely."

"I'll call my staff when we're done eating."

After breakfast Reese went to the den down the hall to call her administrative assistant and her assistant manager to get the scoop on her clients. Cleaning the kitchen, Cade laid down a few ground rules for Wyatt.

"Number one, give us our privacy."

Readjusting dark-haired, blue-eyed Darcy so he required only one hand to hold her on his lap as he fed her a bottle, Wyatt said, "Of course."

"Number two, don't interfere. I know that in our company we complement each other. That everybody has their own specialty, so we count on each other. But, seriously, when it comes to romance, I'm okay on my own."

"Whatever you say. You'll hardly know we're here." Wyatt handed him the baby. "Take her. I've got to set up her umbrella and her baby pool."

Accustomed to helping Wyatt with Darcy when he brought her to the office, Cade easily slid the little girl into his arms. "You have a baby pool?"

"Shows how much you pay attention. That and her beach umbrella are in the cabana."

He settled Darcy on his arm. "Okay."

Wyatt left and Cade looked down at the beautiful little girl. "How are you ever going to stay sane with that guy as your role model?"

Darcy giggled as if she'd understood him.

"I'm telling you. He's overprotective and bossy."

Reese entered the room on a laugh. "You could be describing yourself."

"No," Cade said. "I have caveman moments. He has a god complex."

She strolled over.

Cade continued, "Which is why he really does need breaks. He takes the baby places like this where he's got the peace and privacy to work and care for her without the stress of worrying that having a baby around is bothering other workers."

"He doesn't seem like the kind to care about something like that."

"He does. He seems all casual and nonchalant, but he had a weird upbringing. Rich dad. Mom who ran the society pages. He pretends to be cool and not give a damn what anyone thinks but he's always watching."

Reese said, "Hmm," reached for her mug from that morning and began making a second cup of coffee. "Doesn't he have a nanny?"

Cade rolled his eyes. "He's had nannies. I think the last count was seven. And he's fired them all. I don't know what he's looking for in a caregiver, but so far he hasn't found it."

She took Darcy from Cade's arms and nuzzled her. "Maybe he just likes being with her."

"They have sort of been joined at the hip since the night his ex dropped her off."

She nuzzled Darcy again. "Babies always smell so good."

"Since when do you go around sniffing babies?"

"Nurses care for people. My company's helped out a new mom or two."

He studied her as she gooed and cooed at the little girl,

who looked like she was trying to talk. He'd never seen anyone as sweet or angelic with a baby as Reese was.

He remembered when he got engaged to Brenda. Back then, he'd thought that he'd wanted kids. Those feelings rose up in him again, but he dismissed them with the logic he'd had the day before. He was very successful and very happy with the status quo.

"You should take the job as Wyatt's nanny."

She laughed, lifted the little girl and blew on her belly. "Not on your life. Live in Manhattan? Give up the dream of expanding my business—"

Wyatt walked into the kitchen. "Who's expanding a business?"

"Me. Maybe. Eventually."

"I told her to franchise," Cade said. "She doesn't want to be only a manager. She likes the nursing part."

Wyatt grunted as he washed his hands. "Too bad. Franchises done right can be gold mines."

Cade bent toward Reese and whispered, "He could do most of the business plan for you in a few hours of his spare time."

"I don't have any spare time," Wyatt said. "I have a baby."

He reached for Darcy, but Reese held her away. "Are you kidding? She's adorable and happy and we're going to play in the water, aren't we, sweetie?"

Wyatt said, "Are you sure?"

"Yes! Go... Hey, maybe you and Cade could take the boat out and fish?"

Wyatt slid a sideways glance at Cade, who gave him a cold, hard stare.

"Nah. No fishing today. But I wouldn't mind being able to have a beer or two."

Cade balked. "It's morning!"

Wyatt shrugged. "It's vacation. Seriously, I never get

to have a beer anymore. I have to be awake and alert because I'm the one caring for Darcy."

Reese laughed. "Have a beer. Have a few. When she's tired, I can put her down for a nap."

Wyatt smirked at Cade, who shook his head. But he knew his friend needed a break and he had to admit there was something about seeing Reese with Darcy that gave him a mushy feeling in the pit of his stomach.

He reminded himself of his first marriage, reminded himself that Reese had her own goals, and the feelings went away.

After Reese slathered Darcy with sunblock and Wyatt found her sunhat on the kitchen floor where it had fallen during breakfast, she and the baby played in the pool. She marveled at the little girl's resilience. She'd essentially been abandoned by her mom and given to a dad who was only learning to care for a baby. Yet she happily splashed in the water and babbled about nothing as Reese played with her.

Her heart unexpectedly swelled with longing to be a mom, to have a family. She could see herself bringing her own little brood to a beach house, teaching them to swim, teaching them about the ocean, about waves that moved in and tickled their toes and then raced out again.

She quickly squelched the vision along with the need that tightened her chest and sent a keen yearning singing through her veins. Tony's reaction to her not being able to have kids had been humiliating. There was no way on God's green earth she'd risk telling another man she couldn't have kids. No way she wanted to see that look of disappointment and endure the sense that she wasn't good enough.

She shook off the memory. Her life might not be perfect,

but it was hers and it was the right life. There was meaning and purpose in helping people. Her employees were her friends. Her clients were her friends. She was a part of her community. Lots of people had far less. Jobs they disliked. No meaning or purpose in their work.

And she did get to play with babies. They popped up in her world all the time.

She had a lot to be thankful for.

She took Darcy out of the water and sat with her under the big blue, coral and lime green beach umbrella to play, making sure the baby didn't get too much sun and simply enjoying the sweet little bundle of joy.

Wyatt swam, got a beer, then sat at a patio table with Cade, talking business, high-level stuff that perked up Reese's ears and filled her with curiosity, but mostly went over her head. Partly because she was only half listening. Partly because the amounts of money they so casually threw around were astronomical.

Darcy grew tired after a second time in the pool and Reese fed her a bottle, took her upstairs, put her into tiny pajamas and rocked her. She cradled the baby like the precious bundle that she was, watching her blue eyes drift closed.

As she laid her in the crib, the pull to linger and simply stare at her tiny face filled Reese. Though it was wrong, she let herself pretend—just for a second—that this was her baby, her child to mother and protect and love with all her heart. The yearning tripled and a sense of loss flooded her but she shook her head to get rid of it.

She'd long ago learned to appreciate what she *did* have and accept what she didn't. She'd built a happy life for herself. So why, suddenly, did her heart keep softening with longing?

Because of Cade?

She frowned as she thought about that. Sixteen-year-old

Reese and eighteen-year-old Cade *had* made plans—detailed plans—for the future. They'd wanted a big house, a brood of strawberry blonds, laughter and connection. *He'd* wanted a family. A real family. He'd wanted all the things she'd had with parents who behaved like real parents. He'd wanted to play games with his kids, go to their football games and cheer for them when they played soccer. He'd wanted to steer them to the right university. To counsel them about life. To have *that* connection.

And now he didn't?

In a way that didn't make sense.

At eighteen, he'd been consumed by the need to have his own family, to raise his kids with patience and love, and his just dropping that vision didn't seem right.

Of course, he'd endured a terrible divorce and he'd made a good life for himself too. Just as she had—

No, that wasn't entirely true. She hadn't *decided* to let go of the dream of getting pregnant, having kids. Fate had chosen for her. And it hadn't been easy to accept it. For a while, she'd considered a few options for creating a family. Adoption. In vitro. But Tony's reaction had been so bad that she'd known she'd never be able to get close enough to another man to risk telling him. To risk not merely another heartbreak but also the humiliation of being told he didn't love her enough to take an alternative path.

So she'd accepted her infertility and found another way to have a good life.

Cade's story was entirely different. Losing a marriage shouldn't have made him decide not to have kids—

She shook her head to clear those thoughts.

For all practical intents and purposes, she and Cade were having a vacation fling. She shouldn't be thinking too deeply about his life. About what he wanted and what he didn't want.

She took one final look at the baby, letting her teenage dreams with Cade drift off into nothing, then pulled away.

Finding a baby monitor on the dresser beside the crib, she brought it down to the pool and set it on an available table. "We'll hear her if she fusses."

Wyatt said, "Thanks."

"You're welcome."

"You wouldn't happen to want to be a really well-paid nanny, would you?"

"Already told Cade I don't want to live in Manhattan."

Cade said, "It's true."

She eased down to sit on the edge of the pool, dangling her feet in the cool water. Wanting to help Wyatt, she said, "But I wouldn't mind giving you a hand finding a new nanny."

Wyatt peered at her. "You could do that?"

"Sure. I interview nurses and caregivers all the time. I know more than qualifications count. I look for certain personality traits."

Wyatt beamed. "Exactly."

"Great. We can do video chat interviews. Send me some résumés of candidates you like, and I'll have my assistant set them up when we get back home."

"Or," Wyatt said, "how about if I call my assistant now and have her set up second interviews from the batch of people I talked to this week, then we can do the video calls this afternoon."

"You have some candidates?"

"Yes. Three or four seem great. But having been burned by seven, I'm a bit gun-shy."

Reese laughed and walked to a chaise to stretch out. "Have her organize the second interviews for this afternoon and I'll sit in. We'll make the decision together."

Wyatt reached for his phone. "I would appreciate that."

Reese said, "I'm happy to do it," then settled into the chaise, her normal self again. She enjoyed helping people. *That* was her thing. She didn't fret about what she didn't have or couldn't do. She didn't overexamine other people's motives and decisions, like Cade's. She focused on the positive.

As Wyatt walked into the house for quiet to call his assistant, Cade came over and plopped down on the chaise beside her.

"He found our stash of no-bakes."

"The cookies?" Reese laughed as she faced him. Their gazes connected and her heart thrummed. He was so handsome and so normal. No pretense. Just a very smart guy who was making the best of his life just as she had. There was no reason to dig any deeper.

"Putting them in the freezer wasn't exactly hiding them," Cade continued, shaking his head. "But he ate them frozen."

"Barbarian!"

Cade laughed. "He *is* a barbarian."

She laughed too, glad they had this happy, easy connection.

He rose from his chaise, held his hand out to her. "Let's go take a walk on the beach."

"That's a great idea." She took the hand he offered. "For as many days as we've been here, we haven't walked on the beach!" When she got her balance in front of him, she leaned in and kissed him. "I can't think of anything I'd rather do."

She smiled but the sense that something was wrong with this picture suddenly hummed along her nerve endings. For a second she wondered if they both weren't merely pretending to be happy, settling for less than what they'd always wanted together.

But she quieted those thoughts. Twelve years had gone by since they'd created those silly dreams. Circumstances were different now. Cade no longer wanted to get married, admitting he'd also dropped his desire to have a family. That's what she needed to focus on.

Especially since what they had might not last beyond this week.

For the next few days, she would simply make him happy and be happy herself, as she put their silly teenage dreams in a box and locked it.

CHAPTER ELEVEN

REESE AND WYATT spent the afternoon by the pool video-conferencing with nanny candidates. Cade entertained himself by swimming, walking down to the dock and being the one to retrieve Darcy when she woke.

At five, when the video interviews were still going strong, he pulled the high chair out to the patio, put the baby in and started grilling pork loin and veggies.

They ate at six, with Reese and Wyatt discussing the contenders for the job as Darcy's caregiver. At eight, Wyatt put the baby to bed, but he was back with the monitor to continue the nanny discussions.

Cade raised the TV from the stone counter and set it to watch a movie. Reese and Wyatt made second calls to two of the interviewees, needing to ask a few more questions for clarification. Wyatt was a billionaire. His child was a potential target for kidnappers. His penthouse was a treasure trove of art. They had to take all that into consideration when they chose his nanny.

Rolling his eyes, Cade shifted on his chaise lounge. He'd never seen Wyatt take this long to make a decision. The guy was a risk taker. But right now, all he was taking was Cade's girl. How could two simple clarification calls take *hours*?

The movie finished and, tired and bored, Cade announced that he was going to his room.

Reese chirped, "Good night!" But Wyatt only grunted.

A bit annoyed, he undressed and showered with all fourteen jets pulsing around him. His feeling of abandonment like raw sores, he spent longer under the spray than usual. He knew he was being childish, particularly since Wyatt would be leaving in another day. But memories of Reese refusing to talk to him after she broke up with him lingered. He now knew why. She'd suffered a terrible trauma—and hadn't been able to confide in him. When the chips were down, she'd leaned on her parents, which—given her age—was the right thing to do.

Unfortunately, even that good logic didn't stop the recollection of how alone he was those weeks when he went back to Harvard after that Thanksgiving. Losing her had resulted in him bonding with Trace and Wyatt. But in the back of his brain the loss had lingered. Even at eighteen, he'd known what they'd had was special. Important. Losing it so abruptly, with little explanation, had left him adrift and empty.

Of course, not knowing what had really happened, he'd also assumed she'd ditched him for someone else and had eventually concluded what they'd had hadn't been real. Just a bunch of hormones and entertainment.

But what if it hadn't been?

What if it had been real?

Brenda's image popped into his brain. He'd married her because she fit his life. At the time, he'd assumed the way she'd eased into his penthouse, his charity events, his bed meant he loved her. But he'd never had extraordinary feelings for her. He'd simply wanted to fill a spot, be married, start a family.

Because he'd always wanted a family. No matter how he tried to tell himself he'd satisfied that need by having friends who were like brothers, he couldn't deny his longing to be a dad.

The truth of that was like a splash of cold water. Was that why he'd had those feelings watching Reese with Darcy? Had seeing them together reminded him of everything he'd wanted as a kid?

Did he want those things again?

With Reese?

He stepped out of the shower and grabbed a towel, scolding himself. All this stuff rolling around in his brain was the result of having too much time on his hands because Wyatt had kept Reese busy.

He and Reese had both come to the island to have fun. Not to try to mend a relationship that had died twelve years ago. They also couldn't re-create the past. She'd suffered a trauma. He'd made foolish choices.

So, no.

No turning back. No thinking about the future.

When he finished drying and walked into the master bedroom again, he stopped.

Reese was in his bed. Asleep.

His heart turned over in his chest. Not only did she look exhausted from a morning of babysitting Darcy and an afternoon and evening of helping Wyatt find a nanny, but she'd come to his room. As naturally as if she belonged there.

He thought about foolish choices and long-ago dreams and shook his head, not letting himself go there again.

This is a vacation fling. Nothing more. She might belong in his bed for the next few days, but he wouldn't take his thoughts any further than that.

He slid beneath the covers as quietly as he could, so he wouldn't wake her. But her floral scent drifted to him. She'd showered too.

He closed his eyes and savored the sweet smells, disappointed that she hadn't come to his room to shower. If she had, she could have joined him.

Tomorrow, he'd tell her to bring her things to the master. Because she did belong here, and he wanted her here. It was part of the easy fun they were having.

Not a big deal.

He cuddled against her and fell into a deep, refreshing sleep, refusing to let his thoughts go any further than this day, this moment.

They woke at seven almost simultaneously and curled into each other for a long, thorough lovemaking session. They showered together and she slipped into the yoga pants and T-shirt she'd set on the chair in the corner of the room.

Downstairs, he made coffee. She made cinnamon toast, another simple but fun thing she knew how to make because of having a normal childhood.

Wyatt walked into the kitchen with Darcy strapped to his chest. "We're going to swim a bit, then pack up to leave."

Cade worked not to sound sarcastic when he said, "So soon?"

Wyatt laughed. "I'm back to being relaxed. Plus, I have a nanny coming tomorrow morning. I need to get home and prepare myself to orient nanny number eight."

Reese said, "Hey, she's great! And if she isn't, Peach Osgood was another good candidate."

Wyatt put Darcy in the high chair, fixed himself a cup of coffee and sat down at the island. Helping himself to some cinnamon toast, he said, "Seriously. Thank you so much for joining me on those interviews yesterday."

"Hiring a nanny is a lot like finding a good nurse. They have to have a heart for the job."

They drank their coffee and ate their cinnamon toast

chatting about nothing, then Wyatt took the baby to her splashing pool. After tidying the kitchen, Reese and Cade strolled out to the patio. Reese sat at a table scrolling through texts and emails from her staff, as Cade played with Darcy while Wyatt looked on.

After lunch, Wyatt dressed Darcy in tiny jeans and a T-shirt, then came back downstairs to say goodbye. He headed to the garage to get a bike, but Cade said, "Wait. I'll come with you."

"Really?"

"Yeah. I'll stick your duffel bag in the basket of my bike and make things easier for you."

"Since when do you want to make things easier for me?"

Cade motioned for him to go to the garage. "Since always."

Wyatt settled himself on the bike, Darcy securely strapped to his chest. They headed off through the foliage.

"You spent a lot of time with Darcy yesterday and today."

Cade gaped at him. "I spend a lot of time with her every day! You're on a call. I'm holding the baby. You need to read something. I'm the one taking her to the window to look at the tall buildings."

Wyatt harrumphed. "Guess I got a nanny just in time."

"I'm not complaining. I like her."

"That was kind of what I was hinting at. I think your feelings about what you want out of life are changing. Not just because you like Darcy but I saw how possessive you were with Reese."

Cade balked. "What?"

Before Wyatt could answer, the sound of Dennis approaching in the helicopter filled the air.

Wyatt got off his bike and Cade reached for it, shouting, "I'll put your bike away. You get the duffel off mine."

Wyatt nodded. Cade put Wyatt's bike in the outbuilding. The helicopter got closer and closer, the noise almost deafening.

Still, when Cade returned, Wyatt shouted, "Don't ignore what I said about what you want out of life. If Reese is changing you, make sure it's not just nostalgia."

Cade held back a sputter of indignation. He'd already figured out what Wyatt had said. He didn't need to be reminded that he didn't really want all those old dreams with Reese. Or to be told it was only nostalgia edging him in that direction. He wouldn't say or do anything foolish. He'd learned that lesson long ago.

Unfortunately, with the slowing helicopter blades still making noise, he couldn't get into this with Wyatt now. So he simply said, "She lives in Ohio. I live in Manhattan. Neither one of us would ever move to the other's city. We're both fulfilled in our careers. We know what we're doing."

The helicopter blades finally stopped. Wyatt slapped Cade's shoulder. "Okay. Great." Then he ran toward the waiting vehicle, Darcy on his chest, duffel bag over his shoulder.

Cade waved goodbye, watching them. Wyatt was gruff. His current living arrangement was busy. But there was a happiness, a contentment about him that would have made him tease Wyatt, except he was happy too.

At least until Monday afternoon. Or Tuesday morning. Whichever Reese decided was the end of their trip.

His heart dipped with disappointment that his time with Reese was running out, but he shook his head to clear it. Now that he had everything figured out, he wasn't ruining it by giving in to unwanted, unwarranted longings for things he'd long ago decided weren't right for him.

He did not want to think about the future. He and Reese

had both come to the island for rest and relaxation. Nothing more serious was happening.

The helicopter took off and Cade got back on his bike. In ten minutes, he was storing it in the garage and walking to the patio, where Reese lay stretched out on a chaise by the pool.

Her long limbs were an interesting shade of reddish brown. Not sunburned, but on their way to tan. "How come a redhead like you isn't all sunburned?"

She didn't even open her eyes. "Sunblock."

"You can get tan through sunblock?"

"Sure. Though it takes a few days."

And they'd been there for six days. Mostly outside. He glanced around. They were always on the patio because it was beautiful.

Paradise.

Usually when he had thoughts like these, he was on the beach. He turned to ask Reese if she wanted to go for a walk with him, but she looked comfortable and he was determined to stay away from confusing thinking so he only said, "I'm going for a walk on the beach."

He left the statement open, giving her a chance to decide if she wanted to go with him.

She said, "Okay," didn't ask or offer to come along and seemed content just as she was. Because they weren't two peas in a pod. They weren't joined at the hip. They weren't resurrecting a "once in a lifetime" thing. They were two friends, who had become lovers. Again. They'd done this before, and the last time had ended miserably. This time, they would be able to walk away with neither one of them getting hurt.

He left her alone, ambling down the path that led to the sandy beach. He walked a few minutes, picking up shells to see how far he could throw them from the shore. But after a few throws that got boring.

He glanced up at the patio, where Reese lay, soaking up sun, knowing the walk would have been so much more fun if she'd joined him.

An itchy, weird feeling slithered through him. For a second, he wondered if he would no longer be happy on this island if she wasn't with him, but it was so preposterous that he let it go and waded into the blue water until it was waist high, then he dived in.

After twenty minutes of swimming, he walked back to the patio, found a towel and rubbed it over his dripping hair.

She opened one eye. "We should play Yahtzee."

He laughed. "Yahtzee?"

"Yeah. I fell asleep twice and I'm starting to worry that I won't sleep tonight if I don't get up."

He sat sideways on the chaise beside hers. He didn't like the thoughts he'd been having on the beach. But instead of fighting the fear that the island wouldn't be as much fun without her, he'd come up with a workaround. He'd figured out a way to compartmentalize everything he was feeling, to have it make sense, so it fit.

"Did you ever stop to think you need the rest?"

She peeked over at him. "Maybe."

"Then you should take time off a couple times a year. It's why I have this place. Why Wyatt and Trace have an open invitation to come here. When you're in charge of as much money as we play with, there's stress. Not because we worry about going broke, but because we employ thousands of people. They count on us to provide wages, benefits."

She sat up. "That's it exactly. My job's not difficult. My employees are great. But I am responsible to make sure they get a paycheck. After five years of no time off, I think it got to me."

Satisfied that he was on the right track, he chuckled. "Probably. I'll add you to the invitation list. Give me your email and once a month when the code to open the house changes, you'll get the new one. You don't have to check in to see if anyone's here because there are five bedrooms. In fact, Trace, Wyatt and I have had some of our best times when we surprised each other, and all came here at the same time."

She glanced up at him with a smile. "So, I'm part of the in crowd."

He rose. "I think you earned that honor when you helped Wyatt find a nanny."

Her smile grew into a grin. "It's like I'm in a secret society."

Having officially categorized her as friend with the open invitation to the island, there was no more confusion in his mind about what was going on between them.

He bent and kissed her forehead. "Yeah. You're happy now but wait until it sinks in for Wyatt that you could franchise. He'll be at your door at two o'clock in the morning someday, with a fifty-page business plan."

She laughed.

"I'm serious. You helped him. He won't rest until he helps you." He took a long breath and glanced around. He thought about her request to play Yahtzee. When she'd gotten here, she'd seemed interested in touring the islands, but every time he'd been at the house, she'd been here. He didn't think she'd ever gone over on her own to sightsee. She'd certainly never requested he drive her there.

She always had been shy about asking for things, about getting her own way, which was probably the result of being one of three kids, not an only child, as he was.

This was another thing he could fix.

"Do you really want to play Yahtzee, or would you rather tour the islands?"

She straightened a little more on the chaise. "Actually, a tour of the islands sounds fabulous."

He headed for the door. "Go get dressed. Shorts. T-shirt. Flip-flops. Don't embarrass me by looking like a tourist."

She laughed, but he turned suddenly, another thought striking him. She'd spent their last two days like a vagabond. Changing in her room and sleeping in his. He'd already decided he would ask her to bring her things to his room. This seemed like the perfect time.

"Why don't you bring your suitcase to my room?"

"Right now?"

"Yeah. Thanks to Wyatt, we have two more days. It just seems inconvenient for you to dress in one room and sleep in another."

She frowned, as if she couldn't understand what he was asking.

He groaned. "Come on. Don't tease. We're having fun. Bring your things to the master. Make both of our lives easier."

She gathered her clothes and cosmetics and carried them to the master suite. By the time she got there, the room was empty. The shower was still warm from Cade getting ready for their tour of the islands, but he was nowhere around.

She set her things on the marble countertop of the double sinks, an odd sensation moving through her.

Sleeping in his room was one thing. Having her toiletries beside his felt so permanent—so weirdly like a step she didn't want to take. Almost as if she had given him the wrong impression—

She liked the idea that he thought of her as one of his

friends. Like Wyatt and Trace. Someone with whom he would share his island. It was a way of being in his life without being in his life. But she hoped he wasn't thinking anything more was going on. If he believed things were happening between them that shouldn't—that *couldn't*—then they'd have to have that awkward conversation. The one she didn't want to have with *anyone* ever again.

She showered telling herself not to go overboard. So he was giving her access to his island? She might think it was a big deal. But he didn't. As he'd said, billionaires had better toys. They were the ones who *should* share.

She showered and dressed, then returned downstairs to find Cade on the patio talking with Trace on the phone. When he flashed the phone to her, gathering her image for Trace, she smiled and waved. "Hey, Trace."

"I told him you now have access to the house anytime you want."

She stopped halfway to a chaise lounge.

She'd teased him that granting her access was like bringing her into a secret club, but hearing him announce it to Trace felt weird—

Significant—

That's what had been bothering her. *Significance.* It was significant to be sharing his suite. Now, he had told his friend she had an open invitation to come to his island. Add those two together and it felt like they were becoming a couple.

She stopped that thought, reminding herself that his world was abundantly different from hers, the way he thought about things was different. He considered this house much more than the vacation home she saw. To him it was a sanctuary. Not merely for himself. For his friends too. He clearly considered her a friend.

Plus, at no time had he ever mentioned that he would be at the beach house when she was.

She was reading into things only because being with Darcy had reminded her of their old dreams. But those dreams couldn't come true. And they had a mere two more days on the island. She needed to get back into relaxation mode and stop thinking!

He disconnected his call and took her hand. They walked down the path to the dock, he helped her into the boat and—without as much as a nudge from her—he slid into his life vest. She forced herself not to make a big deal of that. He was being a smart boater. Nothing more.

They traveled a bit north, edging in close to the islands so she could see the highway that connected them, then they headed south again.

"I thought we'd spend time on Key West."

"Okay."

"I want you to see Mallory Square." He peeked back at her. "There's shopping and restaurants, plus street performers and a gorgeous view of the sunset. Not to mention chickens who roam the streets."

"Chickens?"

"Yep. Real chickens. Gives a whole new meaning to *free range*."

She laughed, her apprehensions easing. "Sounds nice."

"*Nice?* It's amazing. And that's why I like the Keys." He pointed east. "I can be over there, on my own private retreat when I want peace and quiet. Or come over here—" he pointed at Key West, which grew increasingly larger as they approached it "—when I want to have fun. Mingle. Get a beer with overenthusiastic tourists."

"Okay. That sounds…" Not like a guy who wanted commitments. But a guy who liked his freedom. Which relaxed her even more. "…like tons of fun."

"It is!"

Their easy conversation went a long way to remind her that he was a happy-go-lucky person. Plus, they'd only just found each other after twelve long years. They'd spent a week together. *A week.* He wasn't asking her to be his girl-friend. They weren't in a relationship. He'd asked her to move into his room because they were sleeping together, having fun. As he'd said, it was simple convenience.

They docked at the island and she removed her vest. He took her hand again and led her into a thickening crowd.

"This is their sunset festival."

She looked around. Sea air and heat enveloped everything. "Festival?"

"Every day about two hours before sunset, there's a little informal celebration." He pointed to where a crowd was gathering. "Most times that I've been here there's been juggling, a one-man band, a magician…and a guy who has house cats who do tricks."

She giggled. "House cats who do tricks? I can't even get my cat to lift her head when I get home from work."

"His cats are great. It's actually pretty funny."

"Can't wait to see it." She really couldn't. He'd taken their situation from strained to natural with a simple boat ride and a walk around the crowded island.

He let her watch the performances to her heart's delight, then got them seated in the best place to see the sunset from one of the outdoor restaurants.

They ate shrimp talking about everything from the wonder of Mallory Square to Wyatt's misspent childhood.

"I think he's making up for that now."

"To his parents?"

"Yes. He impresses his dad with his ability to make money and his mother by staying out of the society pages."

"If she's a true society lady, I would think she'd want him *in* the society pages."

"The only times he's ever made it was for bad behavior. Drunk at gallery openings and fundraisers."

Reese winced. "Yikes." She thought for a second, then said, "He doesn't drink much now."

"Nope. He wasn't ever an alcoholic. He was more like lost. Once we found our niche, he found purpose."

"He isn't just making money to impress his dad?"

"Started out that way. Now he loves it."

He paid for their dinners using a bank card but put down cash for a healthy tip. "This way the waitress gets the money immediately."

"Funny that you should know that."

"My ex had been a waitress."

Mellowed by the once-again easy conversation between them, she slid her arm beneath his and nestled against him as they made the slow return walk to his boat. "Really? Why did I think you'd married a stockbroker or banker?"

He snorted. "From the way she tried to get part of my company?"

"Maybe."

Perfection floated on the air with the scents of coconut sunblock and the sea. It followed them home on the boat ride and up the path from the dock to the patio.

He opened the house with a few taps on the security pad by the kitchen door and they walked inside, through the kitchen and up the stairs to the master.

As soon as they entered, he took her in his arms. "I love having you here."

She couldn't tell if he was talking about having her with him on the island or in the master. But she didn't let herself overthink it. She loved being here. Both on the island with him and in his most private domain. She desperately wanted the rest of the time they had left to be happy. She didn't want to think about things that didn't matter in a vacation fling.

She shoved them out of her mind and stepped nearer. "I love being here."

He gave her lips a chaste brush, then the innocent kiss deepened. Contentment spread through her. Tingles warmed her spine. With a nudge of his palm against the small of her back, he pressed her closer. Then his hands roamed up her back, and down again, so he could slide them under the hem of her tank top. His nimble fingers found her bra closure and released it, before gliding to her breasts.

She groaned and stepped back, allowing him to strip away the tank top and bra. Before bringing her close again, he removed his shirt.

Her hands slid to the muscles of his shoulders. For a few seconds, the sheer joy of getting to touch him again, kiss him again, nearly overwhelmed her. She basked in that sensation as they kissed and touched some more before their shorts began to feel like an unwanted barrier and had to go.

Then they tumbled to the bed. His bed. Big and luxurious, it was a sort of symbol of his wealth, his privilege. But she knew that no matter how smart he was, how hard-nosed he was about business, he was still a guy who liked to have fun.

With a quick shove to his shoulder, she toppled him to his side of the bed and straddled him.

"What's this?"

"You said you liked me better bold and adventurous."

He chuckled. "Just how bold do you plan to get?"

She pretended to ponder that. "Why don't we wait and see?"

With that she bent and ran her tongue along his collarbone to his chest. He slid his hands up her back. There was something about the combination of *them*. Something that made every touch, every caress, sizzle. They teased and tempted each other to a breaking point, then he shifted their positions, flipping her to her back, and entered her.

Electricity crackled through her and she moaned at the sensation. So did he. Outside the wind picked up. The first signs of a storm. But safe and happy, they ignored it.

He fell asleep before she did, and she turned in his arms to simply look at him. His face was perfect. Angles and planes arranged to create high cheekbones and a strong jaw.

Sated, content, she had the sense that this was the way it was supposed to have been. That they weren't supposed to have lost each other. That they *were* supposed to click like two puzzle pieces. That Finn McCully's sin somehow threw a monkey wrench in fate's plans and ruined the life they were supposed to have.

Except—

If Cade hadn't left his parents to go to school, would he have met the two friends who became his brothers? Would he have become rich? Would he be the mature, logical, strong guy she was falling in love with?

She drifted closer to him. Would she love being with the Cade who would have resulted if they'd stayed together?

Or would they have grown apart? After all, without that night, she would have studied political science and headed for the office of a congressman or senator in Washington, DC.

If he'd stayed in Ohio, he would still be refereeing his parents' fights.

Would she and Cade have become two entirely different people?

Worse, would they have drifted apart when she'd been told she couldn't have kids? When his dream of having a family changed?

She shuddered to think about it. How much harder would it have been to have lost him the way she'd lost Tony? Tony had adored her but he couldn't stay with her because she couldn't give him the family he wanted, the way he wanted. If she thought she'd suffered from feelings of being incomplete—not good enough—just plain not *enough*, when Tony dumped her, how much worse would it have been to have lost Cade that way?

She shook off the feeling. But she couldn't get rid of her concern that their relationship wouldn't stop at the end of their stay. There was a good chance they'd visit the island at the same time. And then what? The more time they spent together, the more they could tiptoe toward really falling in love. And if not love, toward growing close enough to drift into deep discussions. She didn't want to be drawn into conversations that would lead her to tell him she couldn't have kids. She didn't want to disappoint him.

Still, part of her wished he would be with her every time she came to the island. That part wished they'd swim and eat no-bakes. Make love in the pool. Laugh a lot. Never be serious. Play Yahtzee and go for boat rides, but never want more.

The hollowness of that wish rolled over her. Was this really what she wanted? A permanent hookup?

She slid away from Cade, thrashing a bit to find a position that was comfortable, and failing. What seemed like the perfect arrangement—what *was* the perfect arrangement—was empty.

But what was the alternative?

A real relationship?

Telling him her deepest secret? Watching his expression change when she admitted that she couldn't have kids? Hearing him say he didn't want her?

She didn't want to go there with Cade. Didn't want to see the pity in his eyes that she'd seen in Tony's. Didn't want to have to watch him struggle through a period of indecision until he eventually slid out of her life. Or stayed in it and compromised. Meeting her only at the beach house. Never taking them beyond playing in the pool together.

When she was working, running her company, living her life as a vital part of her small town, she was enough. She was *more* than enough. She had a place. A future. It had taken years of work to get there. She wouldn't risk her hard-won self-respect and dignity.

Especially since he'd said he didn't want anything more.

He didn't want anything more.

She didn't want anything more.

As long as she didn't overthink this, they would be fine. The only problem was… She couldn't stop thinking.

CHAPTER TWELVE

CADE WOKE SATURDAY morning to find Reese gone. He jumped out of bed and into shorts and a T-shirt and raced downstairs, worried that she'd packed up, intending to leave. After all, she was supposed to stay only a week and yesterday had marked seven whole days they'd been on the island.

Wyatt had extended their stay, but Cade had felt the difference in her the night before. He hadn't been able to come up with the words to ask why she'd rolled away from him and kept tossing and turning. Maybe because it seemed foolish to say, "Hey, why are you restless?"

It also seemed intrusive. Particularly when the urge to ask her kept getting stronger. He liked her. He didn't want to see her unhappy. And he'd sensed there was something really bothering her.

Still, they'd been together only a week and the desperate need he had to take care of her was wrong. As Wyatt said, it was nostalgia. Plus, it took them to emotional places neither one of them wanted to go.

So, no. He hadn't asked her why she'd been tossing and turning. Thanks to Wyatt they had two more days on the island. Only two days. Surely, he could keep his feelings from going too far for two days.

Of course he could. As Wyatt had said, part of what

he felt for her was an echo of what he'd felt in the past. Their being together had an air of picking up where they left off. But they weren't. They couldn't. They were two different people now.

Recognizing that, he would control himself. Not make something out of nothing.

Unfortunately, he still didn't know why she'd been restless the night before.

He found her in the kitchen, mixing batter. "What are you making?"

She grinned at him. "Muffins."

He cautiously eased to the center island. "Really?"

"There was a boxed mix in your cupboard." She held up an odd pan of some sort. "And see? Here's a muffin tin."

Radiating happiness, she did not look like a woman who hadn't been able to sleep because of something important the night before. So maybe she'd simply had trouble finding a comfortable position?

The first stirrings of relief tiptoed into his tight chest. "What kind of muffins am I getting?"

"Banana nut."

His stomach stilled. "I love those."

"Clearly someone knows that because the boxed mix was right there." She pointed at a cabinet.

He took a seat on one of the stools in front of the island. He was getting muffins and Reese was behaving normally. Whatever had made her restless the night before was gone.

But here came the real test. "Wanna fish with me this morning?"

"You mean, do I want to rest on the boat while *you* fish?"

"You could bring a book."

She laughed. "I have a ton I can read on my phone. In

fact—" She chewed her lower lip as if she were thinking. "Maybe I'll listen to an audiobook."

He reached to take a taste of the batter, but she swatted his fingers away.

"It's quiet enough out there that you could certainly listen to a book."

"Audiobook it is."

She smiled at him and his nerve endings calmed completely. She would be going home Tuesday morning or maybe even Monday night. He refused to mar their time together with worry or pointless speculation. From here on out, it was nothing but fun.

He got dressed to go out on the boat while the muffins baked, then ate two reading his phone on the patio while she dressed. He held her hand as they walked down to the dock and put on a life vest when she did. Except this time when he closed the catches on hers, he kissed her for every catch, teasing her, making her laugh.

She put her earbuds in and settled on the bench seat, closing her eyes as she listened to her book. For Cade, the whole world righted. As she listened and he fished, he thought about how nice it was to be with her, to have her in his life again, and was glad he'd decided to give her the codes to the house. To keep her in his life.

Because they were friends. Maybe not in a real relationship. But definitely friends. He would never even tiptoe toward making what they had a relationship. His marriage had been a disaster. Brenda wanted things he couldn't give. Not gifts or money. But time. It was as if she didn't understand the concept of work. Didn't understand he had goals and responsibilities—

Though Reese did. Mostly because she had those same issues, goals and responsibilities.

Still, they lived in different states. Different worlds.

Even dating wasn't an option. He could visit her in Ohio, but he hated Ohio. She could visit him in New York... But he'd much rather they both flew to the island when they wanted to see each other.

He'd already given her access to the beach house. He could easily tempt her to the island a few times a year. They could enjoy each other's company and not risk what they had with talks of making it into something neither of them wanted.

He caught a few fish but when he was done for the morning, he realized she was fast asleep.

Laughing at her, he nudged her butt with his foot. "Get up, sleepyhead."

She bounced up, saw where she was, looked at her phone and groaned. "Damn! I'm going to have to backtrack to try to figure out where I drifted off."

"Maybe the book was boring?"

She shook her head. "No. The book is great. I just feel like I can't get enough sleep."

"You work too hard." But thoughts of her tossing and turning the night before returned. He could ask why, but wasn't that going a step too far? Making more of what they were doing than they should?

He finished putting away his fishing gear. "Maybe you don't sleep enough at home? Most people who come down here spend the days fishing and the nights on the island partying. You've had the most low-key vacation of anyone I know."

Her head tilted and she smiled at him. "It didn't seem to bother you."

He leaned in and kissed her. "No. It did not."

They took a slow, scenic route back to his island. She stood beside him at the helm, asking a million questions about how to drive the boat and he happily answered them.

He liked watching her get familiar with the cruiser, his island. Her interest said she would come back. By herself sometimes. But also, he could have Dennis call him when she came for some R&R. He wouldn't join her every time, but enough times that eventually he could call her and ask her to come with him when he was coming down for a rest. No pressure on either one of them. Just the way he liked it.

Happy that things were working out, they held hands walking up the path from the dock. When they reached the patio, he stopped and looked around.

"What's different?"

Confused, Reese repeated his movements, her gaze inching around the pool area. Their fishing trip had been just like the first one—nothing different there. The storm the night before had knocked a few palm fronds to the ground but in a way that was normal here on the island.

"I don't see anything…"

He laughed, then leaned down and kissed her. "Maybe it's that you're here. I like having you here. I like *you*. It's so easy and comfortable."

She peeked at him, totally unsure why he thought he had to spell that out.

He dropped her hand and walked toward the grill. "I'm thinking we'll have hamburgers for lunch."

Reese said, "It's three."

Cade shrugged. "I made dinner reservations for eight thirty tonight. The sun will probably be setting as we take the boat over to the island. The view will be spectacular."

And romantic.

He'd timed it for her. He knew she loved the boat. He knew she loved the sunsets. The thought that he'd put into their dinner plans filled her heart, shot happiness through her—

Of course, he'd also said having her with him was easy and comfortable. Making dinner reservations was all part of keeping things organized, so they didn't get complicated.

"But that also means we won't be eating until around nine. So, I'll grill some burgers for lunch."

She shook her head to clear it of too much thinking, and said, "Good idea." But the hollow feeling about what they were doing returned. She might have forced herself out of her doldrums from the night before, convincing herself that what they had was not a threat to her secrets, but she wasn't sure she liked this odd, empty feeling.

It was almost as if deciding that what they felt would go no further than this had ruined it. Almost as if she couldn't enjoy it if there was no future. Part of the fun of their relationship had been planning their future and looking forward to being together forever.

The very idea brought her up short. She couldn't have it both ways. Either she told him she wanted more, which meant she'd also have to tell him *all* her secrets. Or she enjoyed what they had. Period.

Knowing there was only one answer to that, she walked into the house to get the potato salad and iced tea.

After they ate the burgers, Reese backtracked in her audiobook, searching for the last portion she remembered, then she got comfortable on a chaise and put in her earbuds, intending to spend a few hours listening to her book. But after about ten minutes, boredom overtook her. She found another book, this one a bestseller she'd been dying to read, but again, an antsy feeling skimmed her skin.

She watched Cade casually putter around, mostly tidying the patio area, getting rid of leaves and branches that had fallen in the storm the night before, and tears filled her eyes. Here she was, at the top of her game, with the man she'd always loved, on a tropical island. In most people's point of view, this was as good as it got.

So why did she want more?

Why couldn't she just enjoy this?

CHAPTER THIRTEEN

THAT EVENING, THEY took the boat to the island. Cade let Reese steer for a few minutes, and she threw herself into the role with gusto, as they watched the setting sun. He didn't hesitate to take her hand as they strolled to the restaurant, but he didn't linger over the street performers the way they had the night before. She seemed nervous again. Unhappy. So out of sorts that it physically hurt him not to ask her what was wrong.

But that wasn't their deal. They weren't supposed to get any closer than they already were. As it was, they'd confided some fairly big things. He didn't want this to tumble into something neither one of them intended.

Which meant their conversation while they ate was slow, meaningless. A few times Reese tried revving things up, but he could see her heart wasn't in it. So they took the boat back to the island.

As they walked up the path to the patio, his phone rang. Caller ID told him it was his father. He blew his breath out on a sigh, clicked to answer and said, "Hey, Dad."

Reese peered over at him with her first real laugh all night, and he rolled his eyes.

"What's up?"

"I thought you'd be home by now."

"Wyatt came down. Stole two of our days so we decided to add two days to our trip."

"Oh. Good."

"You don't sound like you think it's good."

"No. No. It's fine. It's just that your mom and the preacher called it quits."

He covered the phone's microphone, leaned toward Reese and whispered, "Mom and the preacher broke up."

"Damn. I lost ten bucks."

He laughed and put the phone to his ear again. "That's too bad."

"It is. She finally looked happy. I was hoping you'd be home to visit. You know. To cheer her up."

It still amazed him when his dad behaved kindly toward his mom, but he didn't want to jinx it by mentioning it. "We're leaving Monday night. Maybe Tuesday morning so, yeah, I'll pop in to see her."

His dad said, "Good. Good," but an odd tone wove through his voice.

"Everything okay with *you*?"

"Yeah. I'm great." He dropped his voice to a whisper. "Lila's here."

"Lila?"

Reese's eyebrows rose and his dad's voice lowered even more. "My nurse. We were on our way to the movie when the rumor about your mom hit."

Realizing why Reese's eyebrows had risen—Lila was her employee—he laughed. "Oh, so you're on your way to a movie with your nurse."

"Shh. Don't ruin things before they start."

Cade held back a chuckle. Though it was weird watching his dad behave like a normal middle-aged man, Cade liked seeing him happy. "All right. I'll call Mom and let her know I'm coming home."

He disconnected the call as they reached the patio. Facing Reese, he said, "Give me ten minutes to call my mom."

She leaned in and kissed him. "Sure. I'll run upstairs and put on a bathing suit."

He caught her hand and pulled her back to him for another kiss. "Or not. I'm not opposed to skinny-dipping."

She laughed and headed into the house.

Cade dropped to a chaise lounge. He hit the contact button for his mom and in a few seconds her face appeared on his screen. It was clear she had been crying.

"Cade? What's wrong?"

"I'm fine. I'm calling about you."

She batted a hand in dismissal. "Oh, I'm okay." She peered at the screen, as if trying to see over his shoulder. "Where *are* you?"

"I'm at the island with Reese—"

"Reese Farrell?"

"You know another Reese?"

"Oh, my goodness. No wonder you look so happy."

"I am happy. But don't go overboard. We just saw each other for the first time in twelve years."

"You know, all twelve of those years I felt bad because I was pretty sure our divorce battles had something to do with your breakup. It's good to see you get a second chance."

The words *second chance* sent anxiety scurrying through him. It was impressions like that—reactions like that—that could ruin everything for two people who weren't looking for a commitment.

"Mom—"

She shook her head again. "Sometimes I don't think you realize how lucky you are. You have everything. You're smart. You're handsome—"

"You're my *mother*. Of course you think that." Stopping that discussion before she blew things out of proportion, he said, "Dad just called to say you and the preacher weren't an item anymore."

Her face fell. "Your dad knows?" She took a quick breath, looked at the ceiling and said, "Stupid old goat probably told everyone from the pulpit at tonight's service."

Cade frowned. "I don't think it's wise to call a man of the cloth a stupid old goat."

"He *is* a stupid old goat. Do you know what he told me? That I wasn't marriage material, and that people were talking about us."

"Isn't being the center of attention your thing? You usually like hearing that people are talking about you."

"Not this time. Not this way! Cade, I changed completely for that man."

"Maybe you should be glad it's over? You can go back to being yourself."

"That's the point. I loved being the person I was with him. I loved that life." She paused, then shook her head. "I loved him."

He saw that in her face. Not the love. The loss of love. The genuine pain that hadn't been there when she and his dad divorced.

"I'm sorry."

"Yeah. Me too."

"Hey, maybe you should just pack up and come down to the island? We're leaving but maybe that's good. You'll have the whole place to yourself."

"Or I could bring some girlfriends and we could drown our sorrows in margaritas." She sighed. "I haven't had a drink the whole time I dated that man."

Cade blinked, realizing the level to which his mom had changed, but he also heard the sadness in her voice.

"Anyway, the island is yours. Bring your friends. Call

housekeeping and tell them to stock the place full of tequila and triple sec."

She laughed. "I guess that would be better than sitting around here feeling worthless."

He remembered that feeling very well. After Reese had dumped him, he'd felt like he had no meaning in his life. Luckily, he hadn't merely found it in his studies. Wyatt and Trace and their big ideas had brought him back to life.

"Call your friends."

"Right. Okay. I love you, kiddo."

"I love you too."

The sadness in her voice stayed with him after he hung up the phone. He rose from the chaise when Reese came to the patio wearing a little blue bikini. "Thought I said remove everything."

She laughed and dived into the pool. "You were also on a video call with your mom."

"Oh, right."

He stepped out of his shorts, then unbuttoned his shirt and tossed it and his shorts toward the kitchen entryway before he dived in with her.

He swam to her, reached behind her and had her bikini top off in what he knew was record time.

She swatted his hands. "Hey! Don't I get a little sweet talk?"

"No-bake cookies."

Her face scrunched. "What?"

"No-bake cookies. They're sweet."

She laughed and shook her head. "You're so weird."

She sounded so much like her sixteen-year-old self that his heart filled with memories that dissolved into present-day emotion. He'd never felt about anyone the way he'd felt about her. "No. You're wonderful."

She eased over to him, wrapping her arms around his neck. "That's better."

He kissed her. All the emotion he felt when she'd laughed over his no-bake cookie joke filled him with a crazy joy. It was everything he could do not to tell her he loved her.

But just like his desire to ask her what was wrong the night before when she was tossing and turning, he knew some things were off-limits. Some things would draw them too close. Some things could give her the wrong idea.

He let the kiss go on as he slid her bikini bottoms down her thighs until she could kick them off. They seemed to drift endlessly. With nowhere to go and no one trying to reach them, their world was peaceful and silent. So perfect it was as if time stood still.

Treading water, Reese walked her fingers up Cade's chest. "Getting dark. Looks like we'll be making love in the moonlight."

He caught her hand, not sure of the significance of that. "Oh, yeah?"

She met his gaze with warm green eyes. "Don't you remember us talking about that?"

As the memory materialized, he yanked her to him, pressing her against his chest. "Vaguely." They'd been kids, with very adult dreams, wishing for some very adult things. "We knew it would never happen, though... Privacy issues."

Her breathing became unsteady. "Yeah. Your parents were always home at night. But there's no one here now." She glanced around with a laugh. "*Really* no one here except you and me. How many people do you know who buy their own island just to make sure they call the shots?"

"Hey, Trace bought a vineyard in his favorite part of

the world. It's at least five times the size of this island. To me, it's no different."

She eased against him to nibble his neck. "Maybe."

He kissed her. Slowly at first, then the kiss deepened, as he realized what she'd said was true. He did a lot of things to control his life, control his world. Even the way he continually monitored his feelings for her, making sure they didn't go too far.

But that was working. It kept them from saying or doing something that would ruin their time together. Only an idiot screwed with something that was working.

They made love slowly with him thinking about perfection. All the years he'd had this house he'd believed it was utopia. With her here, it was perfection. The distinction was slight, but enough that he felt it, enjoyed it.

An hour later, in the master suite, they showered off the pool water, and the scent of her bodywash filled the room. He inhaled deeply, savoring it and her chatter about going home to a ton of paperwork.

As she combed out her wet hair, he listened and laughed with her, then suddenly all he could do was stare at her.

He was going to miss her.

Not in the sense that they'd had fun and he wished it could continue. He would go back to Manhattan knowing he'd left a piece of himself behind. His penthouse would be cold and empty. The city would be a cacophony of noise that had no meaning. Nothing would make him laugh.

Nothing would make him *feel*.

Pushing that out of his brain, he led her to bed and she fell asleep almost instantly. But he couldn't stop thoughts of how difficult it would be when he returned to Manhattan, where his life was work and more work.

He suddenly understood what had happened with Trace. Why he'd left Manhattan for Italy to purchase a vineyard in the place that called to his soul. Then he'd found the love of his life and changed everything about the way he lived.

More than that, Cade finally saw what his mom had been trying to articulate. She'd found love and lost it. And now her life was back to being cold, empty. Margaritas with friends where there had once been purpose and meaning. The warmth of companionship. The closeness of someone you wanted to be with and who wanted to be with you—

What he had with Reese—the connection, the click—wasn't something that came along every day. He wasn't engaged in life without her. He wasn't *happy* without her. He was okay. His life was good. But he wasn't really *happy*.

But with her? Everything was better. Brighter. Filled with promise.

And he was going to walk away? Be like his mom? Always on the cusp of something wonderful, but never living it.

The thought shocked him, but he realized that's what his crazy musings all week had been about. He'd been working to figure out what had been under his nose all along. He *did* want everything he and Reese had planned when they were kids. Not because he wanted a family or to become a dad, but because their pairing was unique and wonderful, and he didn't need six weeks or a year to figure that out. He'd seen it at eighteen.

And he had to act. Right now. Before she went home. Before either one of them had too much chance to think so much they ruined the truth of it.

He loved her. He had always loved her. And she loved him.

They belonged together.

She stirred beside him and he realized she was awake.

"I think you should marry me."

She laughed and nestled against him. The feeling of rightness, of permanence, suddenly filled the room, as if it had been hovering, waiting for him to see it.

He sat up, taking her with him. "Don't you feel it? We belong together. Granted, we might not want to get married tomorrow. But there's no reason we can't seal the deal today."

Reese blinked at him. She'd been jarred out of her light sleep, but she could swear he'd just said they should get married.

She blinked again.

His earnest eyes held hers. "I love you."

He said it slowly as if it surprised him, but also filled him with a sort of desperation, and her heart swelled with longing. She understood why he wanted them to make a commitment of sorts right now. The last time they'd felt this way, fate had screwed them royally. He didn't want to risk losing what they had again.

He also realized there was something else hiding in the shadows, waiting to ruin their lives again. He'd alluded to it. She'd avoided conversations. He didn't have to have insider knowledge or a keen sixth sense. She hadn't been subtle about the way she dodged his questions.

Of course he was desperate. He wanted to seal the deal before her secret ruined everything.

She had to swallow before she could say, "I love you too."

Gripping her shoulders, he pulled her to him and kissed her. Deeply, passionately, with the familiarity of someone who knew her. Someone who wanted her. Someone who loved her so much he ached with it.

He broke away, saying, "Seems to me there's a proposal on the table."

She blinked back tears and pulled away. Part of her begged her to take a chance, roll the dice, tell him the truth.

The other part didn't want to see the look of disappointment or feel the pain of rejection. She just wanted this week. Something she could hold in her heart and think about when she was lonely.

"Cade, you know I don't want to get married. We already talked about this, remember?"

He studied her for a few seconds before he said, "Do you think this is a fluke? That there isn't a reason we ended up here together?"

She pushed herself to be light, to shift his focus, so she could get herself out of this discussion before the conversation went too far. "There *was* a reason we're here together. Your dad."

"He might have gotten us here, but we picked up the rest. We've always belonged together. Our breakup might have separated us for a while, but we couldn't be in the same house for two days without gravitating together.

"You said you wouldn't let Finn steal any more of your life than he already had. Well, this is another piece. Another thing he stole. Had that night not happened, you and I would have stayed together, married, had kids. This is what should have happened. All those dreams we talked about while swimming at the Colonial? All those plans we made? I want them. I don't want Finn to steal anything else from me."

She stiffened, easing away from him. He'd told her he loved her, but the more he explained, the more it seemed he wanted them to go back in time, back to something that couldn't be.

"This isn't about Finn. Not anymore."

"Then what's it about?"

Her gaze drifted back to his. To his unbelievably handsome face. To those earnest eyes. He might have seen a difficult side of life with his parents, but he'd never really known trouble. To him life was simple. Find something you want, go after it.

While her life could be a study in compromise. Have dreams…realize they'll never materialize. Find something you want…lose it. Tell someone your truth…be humiliated.

Figure out what you can have—realistically—and settle for that.

That's what her life was. Settling.

He huffed a bit and fell back to his pillow. "I will wear you down."

Which was exactly what she was afraid of. She turned to look at him, naked, sprawled on his enormous bed, the symbol of his wealth. But also his intelligence and kindness and generosity.

The urge to throw herself into his arms and accept his proposal roared through her. Except she had a secret. In a way, having no one know she couldn't have children hid a big part of her. It protected her, sure. But she'd suffered alone in silence. This might be her chance to end that.

Or to end her relationship with him, when he couldn't accept her as she was. Especially after nothing more than a vacation fling.

She took a breath. She had a choice. Tell him or bail before she had to. There was no middle of the road here.

Sliding her phone off the bedside table, she got out of bed and headed into the bathroom. She flushed the toilet to keep Cade at bay but also to cover her phone call to Dennis, who told her he could be there in thirty minutes.

Thirty minutes.

She would pack and be gone in thirty minutes because she could not share the truth with him. Not yet. Maybe after a few trips here together, weeks or months of getting reacquainted, she would be able to confide in him. But not now.

Not until he was ready to hear it and she was ready to say it.

She turned toward the bathroom door. Cade stood leaning against the jamb. "Is this another one of those times you're not going to tell me what's wrong?"

"Yes." She took a breath and smiled, taking the sting out of what she had to say. "We need to spend a little more time together before we spill *all* our secrets."

He groaned. "Come on. We are older, smarter than we were when we were teenagers. You know it as well as I do. We blew our first chance. But we turned out okay and now we're back. There isn't anything you can't tell me."

Her heart lifted as the new, mature Cade surfaced. Maybe she could tell him?

She licked her lips. "Okay."

"So, spill."

She slid her T-shirt over her head to give herself a breath of time to think it through. Everything he'd said so far had been about belonging together. He'd said he loved her. And she believed that. But he had to say something that would make her feel that the love he had for her wasn't just lust mixed with happiness. That it was something that could survive hearing she couldn't have children.

"I want to."

"Then do it!"

She studied his face, working up the courage to tell him. But she remembered how Tony had worshipped the ground she walked on and after one sentence stepped back, away from her. They'd dated an entire year before they'd gotten to that point. She and Cade had spent a week together.

If what she and Tony had couldn't survive, how could the nostalgia of one week get her and Cade through this?

When she didn't answer, he ran his hand along the back of his neck. "I'm not sure what you want me to say."

That you love me for me?

That we could face anything together?

That nothing would ever break us apart again?

"I know what happened with Finn scarred you. I wouldn't for one second downplay that. But you told me that and we worked through it."

Except he'd gotten it all wrong at first. He'd sympathized instead of seeing her strength and courage. If he pitied her now, she'd melt into a ball of sorrow.

"We need time."

"We don't have time. I have this horrible sense that if I let you go now, you'll never come back."

"To this beautiful island? Of course I will!"

"Don't be flip! It's our breakup all over again. You having a secret and instead of facing it you run!"

She froze.

Dear God, he was right. Because of Tony's reaction, she'd never told another soul she couldn't have children. She'd run. Hidden.

Just as she had after being raped.

She thought back to those weeks after Finn had violated her. Thought back to how she'd desperately wanted to tell Cade, but he hadn't called and, in the end, she'd realized she'd always felt a little uncomfortable being the poor girl dating the rich kid. They'd come from two different worlds. Had two different sets of life experiences.

She hadn't kept her secret about being raped because she'd lost her nerve. She'd lost her nerve because she'd never felt secure in Cade's love.

Was that what was actually happening now? That deep down she was realizing that she couldn't tell him she couldn't have kids? Not just because she didn't want to disappoint him. But because she didn't want to face the fact that she didn't really belong with him.

Wasn't the right person for him.

Never had been.

"We are lucky to love each other the way we do. We cannot walk away from this. Not when we can have all the things we talked about twelve years ago, great jobs, a strong marriage and a family. Kids to love and cuddle and train to be great people."

He was like a happy yellow Lab. Filled with crazy enthusiasm, he saw nothing but perfection in their future. She remembered this side of him and knew that was really what had broken them up the first time. Being raped marred the perfection he saw. Perfection she always knew she didn't have. Rather than tell him, she broke up with him.

Now, she had a secret that would mar his view again.

Her voice a soft whisper, she said, "The future you think you see with me will never happen and maybe that was our problem all along. The only trouble you ever really saw was from two parents behaving badly. Any problem you had you could solve with money. But some problems are about more than throwing money at them and hoping they'll disappear. Real life can get ugly."

He blinked in surprise. "Well, that's not fair."

"Life's not fair."

He stepped closer. "This is why I knew we needed to have the big talk right now. To work some things out before you bolted. I realized yesterday that something was bothering you. If I'm honest, I'd seen it a time or two before that too. I gave you your privacy. I never asked. But I'm asking now."

She stared up at him. Saw those earnest eyes again. Took a breath. Knew it didn't matter how he reacted; they didn't belong together. "I can't have kids."

Cade only stared at her. His long pause made her so raw and so vulnerable, she trembled. But he looked gobsmacked—so shocked he couldn't speak.

He couldn't handle it.

And she couldn't handle him placating her.

She turned away, tossing toiletries into her suitcase. "I called Dennis. He said he'd be here in thirty minutes. That was ten minutes ago. I need the rest of the time to get ready to leave."

"Dennis can wait!"

"It's nighttime. He needs to get me to the airport and go home to his kids. And I want to get home. I've got work to do."

The way she talked about simple, ordinary things when something so important hovered in the air baffled him until he realized she was locking him out. She *had* locked him out.

"Don't do this."

She turned and smiled at him, though her smile was weak, her eyes were empty. "I'm just leaving as we said I would."

But he knew with the certainty of a man on death row that he would never see her again.

She rolled her suitcase to the door. Smiled again. "I'll catch you next time I'm here."

She walked down the steps and he bounded after her. "No! My God, Reese! How can you tell me something like that and just walk away?"

She pulled in a long breath. "I've known this for six years. You're just finding out now. I think you need a little time to process everything, and I need to get home. To get back to work. I stayed a day longer than I was supposed to. My staff's probably pulling out their hair without me."

He barely listened to the hollow excuse. "I know what you're doing. You're shutting me out. Just like you did twelve years ago."

She acted as if she didn't hear him. She was in the garage and had her suitcase in the back basket of a bike before he could stop her.

That was when he realized he hadn't dressed. He couldn't cycle to the helicopter pad naked. He raced upstairs and jumped into shorts and flip-flops before rushing to the garage for a bike.

Pedaling faster than she could, he nearly caught up to her. But Dennis was waiting. He grabbed her suitcase with a grin, asking about her trip.

"It was great," Reese said, as if she hadn't just had one of the most serious conversations of her life. As if everything in her life was fine when Cade knew it wasn't.

They ran to the helicopter and disappeared inside.

Cade watched her leave in the darkness, too shell-shocked to be sad…but also seeing things he'd never noticed before. She was the strongest, most stubborn person he'd ever met. If she wanted to power through this, she would. She could pretend for all the world that she was a happy businesswoman, taking care of other people.

Because that was how she hid. That was how she survived.

But it also hit him that every time she'd needed him, he hadn't been there for her. He'd tried tonight but he'd been stunned. And she was one step ahead of him. Always one step ahead of him. Maybe because he'd never been confronted by a real problem, so he didn't know how to respond, react, quickly enough to stop the damage?

Reese had said it.

He'd never had a real problem, never hit a roadblock to what he wanted, and tonight he'd come face-to-face with one he had absolutely no idea how to handle. What to say. How to stop her.

He thought back to their conversation. He recognized he must have gone off track, said something that shut her down. But he didn't know what—

Or why.

He reminded himself of his dad. Good at business. Bad with relationships. Really bad with sticking his foot in his mouth.

Which might make Reese correct. If he really was as clueless as his dad, maybe they weren't right for each other?

Maybe she deserved someone better?

CHAPTER FOURTEEN

REESE HAD TO wait until Sunday morning to get a flight. She arrived in Ohio Sunday afternoon, feeling like Cinderella the day after the ball. Except she hadn't left behind a glass slipper. Cade would not be searching the kingdom of Oilville, Ohio, looking for her. He now knew they weren't meant to be together. She wasn't who he thought she was. She could not give him a child. She was willing to try a workaround. Use a surrogate. Adopt. But with hours to think it through, he hadn't so much as phoned her to suggest it.

If she caved and called him, because she loved him, because she wanted him, she would never feel understood or loved. She would always feel she had to work to keep his love, rather than rest easy in the fact that she had it.

She unpacked and called her assistant, who filled her in on everything that had happened the days she was gone. Nothing unusual. Nothing pressing.

She disconnected the call and ran her hands down her face. Eight days ago, this job was her life. Taking care of people satisfied her. Now?

Now she was confused and empty. With a wound in her heart that she didn't know how to heal. She couldn't lock this away in a box. It wasn't a bad memory. It was a true loss. A gaping hole. A longing for things to be different when she above all people knew that sometimes things couldn't *be* different. You had to play the hand you were dealt.

Her phone rang and she reached for it, looked at Martin Smith's smiling face and groaned. Not ready to deal with him, she hit Dismiss Call and picked up a stack of bills her computer spit out based on the billable hours input into her system by her employees.

Her phone rang again.

Martin again.

She hit Dismiss Call.

Her phone rang again. She saw Martin's smiling face and groaned.

The man was like a bad cold.

She clicked to answer the call. "What!"

"Hey, I just wanted to see if you enjoyed your time at the island. Stayed more than a week!" he said excitedly. "Did you have fun?"

She put her elbow on her desk and her chin on her closed fist. She considered lying. She considered yelling at him. Instead, she took a cleansing breath and said, "You shouldn't have meddled."

"Meddled?"

"Does playing matchmaker ring any bells?"

"So, what you're saying is that it didn't work."

"No. Martin. I'm saying you shouldn't have set us up."

"Why? My boy do something?"

She sighed. "No. He was… We had fun."

"Reese," Martin said softly. "I'm hearing love in your voice."

She said nothing as tears swelled in her eyes.

"It's what I want for my boy. I've always known it was a mistake for the two of you to break up. And it was my fault. Mine and Marge's. I wanted to fix it."

"Yeah, well, maybe it wasn't a mistake for us to split. I can't be what he wants. What he needs. What he deserves."

"He deserves a woman who loves him and as a guy who's never had that I'm speaking from experience."

"Goodbye, Martin."

"Reese... Wait!"

"Goodbye."

Exhausted, she climbed the stairs, shed her clothes and took a long, hot shower in her simple shower/tub combo. She hadn't grown so accustomed to the luxury of Cade's island that she couldn't come back to the plain but adequate system. She'd never had delusions of grandeur. She could live in an RV and be happy. But she missed Cade. She missed that feeling of connection. She missed his friendship and his passion.

He'd made her feel loved, supported, sexy, then just like the last time, reality took it all away. He didn't understand, *couldn't* understand that she didn't want long discussions. She wanted him to love her unconditionally. She'd wanted him to hear she couldn't have kids and love her anyway.

When he hadn't, all those feelings of inadequacy from twelve years ago had returned.

And why not? She really wasn't who he thought she was.

Instead of picking up her normal routine on Monday morning, she sent a new nurse to Martin's house. She couldn't send Lila, not after a Saturday night movie date, but she also didn't feel like facing more of Martin's inquisition.

At exactly the time the nurse should have arrived, Martin called her. When she didn't answer, he called her again. She turned off her phone.

Cup of coffee in hand, still in her pajamas, she walked into her silent office and took a seat at the desk. That's when it settled in on her that she was alone. Really alone.

Not because she didn't have anybody, but because no one really knew her. As long as she kept secrets, she would always be one step removed from everyone in her life. Never be close to anyone. She'd tried telling her secret once and lost the only man since Cade who'd supposedly loved her. Cade might not have said she was worthless the way Tony had, but he'd also never told her she was okay. Perfect the way she was. The woman he wanted no matter the circumstances.

But how could he say it? She'd held back something important and when she'd told him, she was no longer the person he thought she was.

A vital twenty-eight-year-old woman who could give him a child.

Now she was a shadow of who he'd thought she was.

Hours later, when Reese was knee-deep in reviewing the billable hours report her computer had posted after spitting out bills and payroll checks, her doorbell rang.

Tired of looking at numbers, she rose, stretched and headed for the door.

The bell rang again.

"I'm coming! Keep your pants on!"

She opened the door. When she saw Cade, her heart lifted, then sank like a stone. She hated that she'd admitted her deepest, darkest secret to him. Hated that she'd shocked him to the point that he could barely respond. Hated that she wasn't the person he'd believed she was.

Hated even more that he looked fabulous. Not because he was good-looking, though he was, but because every fiber of her being yearned to see him, yearned to touch him, yearned for him to love her.

"I understand you being angry with me."

She shook her head. "Cade, seriously, I've had enough. I can't go over this one more time."

"Okay, then how about this? I love you."

Her heart ached. She loved him too. In some ways, she believed she'd been waiting for him to come back to her. But that didn't change the fact that she couldn't have kids. That she felt worthless. Empty. Less than. She knew those feelings were wrong. She knew that eventually she would have to overcome them, that maybe losing Cade was the key to figuring out how. He'd been shocked when she'd told him she couldn't give him kids. How could she expect him to say she was perfect the way she was? When she wasn't?

"Love doesn't solve everything."

"I think you're wrong."

His answer was so unexpected, she laughed.

"Look, Reese. Maybe I see this differently than you do, but I don't think I'm wrong. You're not broken. You're you. Perfect the way you are. Everything else is part of life."

She stared at him. She'd heard him say *perfect*. The simple word had stopped her heart. But it was what he'd said after that stalled her breath. "Part of life?"

"Sure. If you can't have what you want, you don't go through life longing for it. Other things pop up. That doesn't make them less than the first thing you wanted. In fact, sometimes the second thing you get is better than the first ever would have been." He sighed. "Is anything I'm saying making sense enough that you'll let me in your house? So we can take this off the porch?"

His answer wasn't flip or offhand. He'd done some deep thinking about this. Her heart lifted a little more.

She stepped back, allowing him entry. It was a risk to let him in, but her aching heart couldn't turn him away. Not when there was a chance that he really did understand.

He walked in but waited until the door had been closed before he said, "I realized that I'd proposed all wrong on Saturday night. My mom had said something about me not appreciating that I have everything and that night I saw that we belonged together. I proposed before I gave you a chance to get adjusted to us. But I know this is what I want. What I've always wanted. I lost you once because I got the whole situation wrong. I won't lose you again for the same reason."

Oh, he was such a dreamer.

"It's not the same. You might have misinterpreted the first time because I never told you about Finn. But not being able to have kids is the reality of my life."

"No. It's the reality of your body. But it's not the reality of your life. Everything about you suits me. You make me laugh. You talked me through a difficult time. You don't like to fish but you love being on the boat. And there are going to be things you like that I don't… But all that does is give us a chance to be ourselves so that when we do have time together, we'll love it all the more."

Her eyes began to fill. She tried blinking away the tears, but he held her gaze. His heart in his eyes.

"We fit. We always fit. And, honestly, though eighteen-year-old me was so preoccupied with school that he didn't see you were drowning, I'm not that kid anymore. I've grown up. I'd do anything for you. Fight anyone for you. But most of all I just want the chance to love you."

Her chin wobbled as sobs tried to overtake her. She said nothing. Only stared at him. Longing for everything they could have together tightened her chest. She wanted to jump into his arms and weep… But the memory of being let down held her back.

"Hey. If my dad can change, I sure as hell can change."

She laughed through her tears.

"Come here."

He held out his arms and she stepped into them. Warmth

suffused her as the longing to believe him pressed so hard her chest hurt.

"Not being able to have children doesn't make you less than. It simply means we look at other options. You are whole and perfect as you are."

The logjam of pain and tears building in her chest and eyes burst and she began to cry in earnest.

"You aren't just my rock. You hold my heart. And you are my soul. Part of me will never forgive myself for letting you down twelve years ago, but I think that just means I won't screw up this time."

That made her laugh and she leaned back to peer up at him. "The worst thing anyone can ever do is promise perfection. It's unattainable."

He loosened his hold on her so he could capture her gaze. "Okay. How about this. I promise to love you. Just as you are. Forever."

"That's a good promise."

"Right now, you could give me the reciprocal promise. I'm on as shaky ground as you are. You are everything I've ever wanted—"

She bounced to her tiptoes and pressed her lips to his. She tried to keep it simple but it shifted to intense within seconds. Tongues twining, their past, present and future merged.

"You are the most kind, loving person in the world. I'm so happy with you. Could we just enjoy that for a while?"

"Yes."

He kissed her again, then took a step back. "And I just want to clarify… This isn't a second chance. This is a new beginning. But I found this at the jeweler last night—"

He pulled a locket from his pocket. A heart similar to the one he'd given her when they were teenagers.

"Oh, my God."

"It's not the one I gave you originally. I didn't keep it. Bad feelings attached to it and all that." He laughed and looped the new locket around her neck. "I wish I had the first one. Because it's a touchstone. A reminder of what we knew in our guts all those years ago. That we belong together."

She laughed through her tears. "Agreed. This locket is enough to seal our relationship."

He shook his head. "Does that mean you don't want this?" He pulled out a box with a diamond engagement ring.

Her gaze leaped to his. "I thought we were taking this slowly?"

He shrugged. "We are. Sort of. But I want the commitment. I never want to let you go. But I also never want any doubt between us about who we are and that we belong together."

She threw her arms around him again. "I do love you and we do belong together. I want the commitment too."

He said, "Thank God," then he kissed her and everything in both of their worlds righted.

EPILOGUE

THE HOSPITAL'S LABOR and delivery room was nothing like Reese expected. She knew Cade had pulled strings to get a private room, but she didn't realize they'd be spending the entire adventure in one place. No operating room. No delivery room. Just a homey little space that looked like someone's bedroom.

Meredith Oliver groaned and rubbed her hands across her belly. "Here comes another contraction."

Reese lifted her shoulders and caught her gaze. "Breathe. Remember? Like this."

Meredith mimicked the quick, shallow breaths Reese demonstrated. She and Cade had chosen her to be the surrogate for their baby because she was older, closer to thirty-five than twenty-five, and settled. She and her husband had two children they adored. Grateful and happy, they wanted to give back. Going through the process with her had been like having a smart tour guide.

The contraction stopped and Meredith took a long cleansing breath before she squeezed Reese's hand. "I told you this was a piece of cake."

Cade's phone rang and he walked away as Reese squeezed Meredith's hand in return. She already knew how grateful they were that she'd agreed to be surrogate for their little boy. She and her family had become such a part of Reese's and Cade's lives that Reese knew their friendship would last forever.

Standing close to the door, Cade said, "Are you sure?"

Reese glanced over.

Meredith shook her head. "I hope he's not making some kind of big deal with Wyatt and Trace."

"He promised he wouldn't." She smiled at Meredith. "And he never breaks his promises."

"We're going to have to get him to teach Jim that," she said, referring to her husband.

Cade strolled over. "Teach Jim what?"

Reese slid her arm around his waist, including him in their birthing group. "How to keep all his promises."

"You have really got to stop telling people about that. You're ruining all my street cred in Man World."

Meredith laughed as Cade pulled Reese away from the bed. "We need to talk."

"We do?"

"Yes. That call was from an adoption agency. A woman has chosen us to be her baby's parents."

"I thought we took ourselves off the lists."

"Looks like we missed one."

Reese blinked and finally saw the gobsmacked look on Cade's face.

She laughed. "What? Are you panicking?"

"No. Yes…" He ran his hand along the back of his neck. "She's due in two weeks. We'll have two babies at the same time."

"We'll raise them like twins."

He gaped at her. "You're okay with this?"

"We were planning on having a few children. Having two only a few weeks apart will be fun." She nudged him. "It's not like we can't afford help."

He let that settle in for a few seconds, then he laughed

and pulled out his phone and redialed the adoption agency number. "When do you need us in New York?" He paused, slipped his hand around Reese's waist and winked at her. "We'll be there."

When he clicked off the call, he said, "I hope you're ready for this."

"I hope *we're* ready for this."

He laughed and they edged back to the bed, where Meredith was experiencing another contraction. The doctor came in, put on rubber gloves and examined Meredith.

"Okay. Looks like we're ready."

Reese looked at Cade.

Cade looked at Reese. "See? Even he knows we're ready."

* * * * *

COMING SOON!

We really hope you enjoyed reading this book.
If you're looking for more romance, be sure to
head to the shops when new books are
available on

Thursday 11th November

To see which titles are coming soon, please visit
millsandboon.co.uk/nextmonth

MILLS & BOON

MILLS & BOON

THE HEART OF ROMANCE

A ROMANCE FOR EVERY READER

MODERN

Prepare to be swept off your feet by sophisticated, sexy and seductive heroes, in some of the world's most glamourous and romanti locations, where power and passion collide.

HISTORICAL

Escape with historical heroes from time gone by. Whether your passion for wicked Regency Rakes, muscled Vikings or rugged Highlanders, aw the romance of the past.

MEDICAL

Set your pulse racing with dedicated, delectable doctors in the high-pre sure world of medicine, where emotions run high and passion, comfort love are the best medicine.

True Love

Celebrate true love with tender stories of heartfelt romance, from the rush of falling in love to the joy a new baby can bring, and a focus on emotional heart of a relationship.

Desire

Indulge in secrets and scandal, intense drama and plenty of sizzling ho action with powerful and passionate heroes who have it all: wealth, stat good looks…everything but the right woman.

HEROES

Experience all the excitement of a gripping thriller, with an intense ro mance at its heart. Resourceful, true-to-life women and strong, fearless face danger and desire - a killer combination!

To see which titles are coming soon, please visit

millsandboon.co.uk/nextmonth

MILLS & BOON

Coming next month

CHRISTMAS WITH HIS CINDERELLA
Jessica Gilmore

'At some point I will have to go back to real life, and I don't know how I'll survive the shock when I am the one offering tea, not accepting it. Plus, if I carry on like this, I am not sure I'll even fit in my clothes come January, which for someone who has one carefully selected travel wardrobe is a serious issue. And yet I can't stop.'

'Isn't indulging the point of Christmas?' he asked, and she shot a pointed look at his own barely touched tier of treats.

'For some.'

He laughed again as Elfie took a bite of the Yule log, closing her eyes as the intense chocolate hit flooded her taste buds, glad of the distraction. Sombre, work-focused, curt Lord Thornham she could handle, but her unexpected suite mate, the man she enjoyed making laugh, the one she was so aware of she could probably describe every millimetre of his wrists was another thing entirely.

No matter that she had her own bedroom and bathroom, sharing the hotel suite felt a lot more intimate than an anonymous bunkroom.

His laptop left on a coffee table, the book he was reading—he liked vintage crime, apparently—on a sofa arm, a bookmark denoting his spot. She saw him in his socks, in his post work version of casual, with his hair shower-wet and as he took his first coffee of the day. She saw the weariness descend at the end of another long, long day and noted how his schedule was all work and no play. Even his dog walks focused on work as she and her camera shadowed him, capturing as many moments as she could for posts, stories and the popular Walter blog on the hotel chain's website. She challenged herself to make him smile, and once or twice had found herself being gently teased in turn.

Then there were the charged moments... The times when silence descended and it was far from comfortable. The moments when she was achingly aware of every sinew on his forearms, his deceptively muscled thighs and the smooth planes of his stomach, the way his hair rebelled to fall over his forehead and the darkness of his eyes. The way he looked—or deliberately didn't look—at her. The heated caress of his eyes when he did.

Continue reading
CHRISTMAS WITH HIS CINDERELLA
Jessica Gilmore

Available next month
www.millsandboon.co.uk

MILLS & BOON
MEDICAL
Pulse-Racing Passion

Set your pulse racing with dedicated, delectable doctors in the high-pressure world of medicine, where emotions run high and passion, comfort and love are the best medicine.